Anne MacLeod lives _____ ck Isle, and works as a dermatologist. Sh _____ se work has taken her from Cape Breton to Salzbu _____ poetry collection *Standing by Thistles* (Scottish Cultural _____ s) was shortlisted for a Saltire Award. *Just the Caravaggio* was published by Poetry Salzburg in 1999.

THE DARK SHIP

www.11-9.co.uk

THE DARK SHIP

Anne MacLeod

DEDICATION

For Effie, and for May

First published by

303a The Pentagon Centre
36 Washington Street
GLASGOW
G3 8AZ
Tel: 0141-204-1109
Fax: 0141-221-5363
E-mail: info@nwp.sol.co.uk
www.nwp.co.uk

A catalogue record for this
book is available from the
British Library.

THE SCOTTISH ARTS COUNCIL
National Lottery Fund

11:9 is funded by the Scottish Arts
Council National Lottery Fund.

ISBN 1 903238 27 7

Typeset in Utopia
11:9 series designed by Mark Blackadder

ACKNOWLEDGEMENTS

It was Effie and Frank MacIntyre on a
wet Sunday afternoon six or seven years
ago who first introduced me to the *Iolaire*:
I am grateful to them. I would also like to thank the
Scottish Arts Council for the Writer's Bursary which
bought me time to write this book:
my colleagues Trish Gordon and James Vestey
for their support: May Marshall, Effie MacIntyre and
Joanne MacLeod for their early reading
of the manuscript: Donnie *Barra* Macleod
and John Mackay for their help with the language:
Ian Stephen for the story of the doomed lovers Alan
and Anna, and for
answering so many questions about boats:
Bruce Pearson and QOH Museum at
Fort George: the endlessly helpful staff at Dingwall
Library: Alasdair Fraser for
Return to Kintail: George Coppard for
A Machine Gun to Cambrai (Iain's poem
The Warning was inspired by an incident
in this book): Marion Sinclair and
all at 11:9: Sam Boyce my agent:
my family for their patience:
Jim for being there:
you for reading.

Printed by WS Bookwell, Finland

CONTENTS

Urlar (Ground) 1

Di-h-aoine (Friday) 15

Di-sathuirne (Saturday) 46

Di-domhnaich (Sunday) 93

First variation 117

Second variation 165

Third variation 201

Fourth variation 230

Ceol mor (The great music) 248

Iolaire (Eagle) 321

Gaelic glossary 375

A Private View 377

To be an islander is to
inhabit real space on a real earth.

IAIN CRICHTON SMITH

*

Dark waters into crystalline brilliance break
About the keel as, through the moonless night,
The dark ship moves in its own moving lake.

WILFRID GIBSON
The Dark Ship

URLAR
(Ground)

1939
*

The night is starless, overcast, wind from the west promising rain. It whistles through Stornoway's empty streets: narrow streets, blacked-out buildings huddled below scudding cloud. There is a sense of fearful anticipation, a community holding its breath – with nothing moving but the wind, and that so strong, so sharp with salt, it would have the bones off you.

Nowhere in this small town will you escape the sea. Streets end in sea, face sea or harbour. Low white cottages are crowded between waves; spindrift. Only in the very heart of the town do buildings rise above two storeys. Sraid Crombhail has terraces that soar three floors up, all windows dark, foreboding.

The churches in the town centre have more space round them than the houses. They stand taller, prouder. They too show no light but snatches of muttered prayer, Gaelic psalm or sermon seep from blacked-out windows. Inside, the pews are packed with servicemen solemn in their military outfits, mainly naval (Royal Naval Reserve for the most part – this is Lewis after all, the map less land, more water). Some young servicemen have as yet no uniform, but are easily identified by their pallor. Their taut-faced families sit closely round them, striving for a semblance of confidence, normality. Kit bags edge the aisles, are stacked in neat mountains behind fonts, behind church doors.

At the dock in the centre of town, a dark ship waits, barely perceptible against the water. The captain stands on the dimly-lit bridge, consults his watch, his charts. In the boiler room, the engineer checks dials, monitors steam pressure. The cook in the galley is stacking eggs, bread, corned beef. His assistant drops a tray of cutlery.

1

'Shite!'

'Not again,' says the cook. 'It's back in the wash with them, a' bhalach. We can't be giving the boys food poisoning before they reach the mainland.'

The young lad picks the knives up, but fails to notice a sharper knife hidden in the bundle he has grasped. He cuts his finger nearly to the bone. The cook sighs, binds it for him, stoops to lift the cutlery himself, dropping it in the metal sink. Several of the fork-handles stick up through the foamy water, for all the world like ships' masts, sinking, blood-flecked. The cook thinks it's an ill omen, shakes his head.

'You'll need to keep that finger dry. I'll put the kettle on, boy. You'd be better with some tea inside you.'

The boy knows the tea will be laced with rum, sticky with sugar. He takes the tin mug in both hands, cradling it, grateful for the spreading warmth, though his finger aches the more. He nods to the cook. They sit together, sip the brew as heavy footsteps ring out on the metal gangway far above them. Mail bags for the mainland are carried on board, stowed neatly in the hold.

The cook pulls out his watch.

'Murdo's late the night.'

'Aye. He'll have been at the communion, maybe.'

'The blackout doesn't help.'

'We're lagging too. Better get back to it, eh?'

The boy carries the empty mugs over to the sink, then finds a rubber stall to sheath his finger. Every movement hurts, will go on hurting. He plunges his hand in the scalding water, gets the first shock over.

Opposite the pier lies a row of low neat cottages, built edge to edge, their white walls shining even in this moonless dark. The side gate of the end cottage is banging, banging. If you look, you'll see the catch is broken. It always was, but sometimes in the winter the gate swells up with brine and rain and the goitred wood sticks firmly on the path, will not budge. It is not winter yet; the gate swings free, leads us to a small bare yard, paved.

It's hard in this blackout to see the wash-house with its green beyond. In any case, the green is tiny, no flowers grow there, even grass seems loath to flourish, but wind swirls and the Monday washing generally dries when it is carried from the wash-house and pegged out on the line – sheets and pillow-slips, underpants and shirt-tails, dancing. Now the wash-house swims in darkness but the back door to the cottage is slightly open, casting the only ghost of light we've seen so far, a flicker of candles.

In the kitchen, Mairi's hunched by the fire, working the old black rocking chair, back and forward, forward and back. Her fingers grip the wooden arm-rests tightly – so tightly that even in the dimness you can see how white they are, how strained. Mairi's thirty-nine years old now, old as the century, with hardly a grey streak in the fine thick head of curls she's tried to catch and tame with hairpins. Iain, her son, keeps moving to the door, looking out, returning with impatience to his own seat by the blacked-out window.

'Where can he have got to?'

'He'll be here, don't worry. He won't be late tonight, Iain. He promised. You heard him.'

'But look at the time!'

'Iain! Sit down. Stop prowling. You're like a bitch in heat!'

'I don't think so!'

Iain laughs, and Mairi laughs with him, her anxiety softened temporarily.

Iain is ready, has been ready all the afternoon, nervous in his best work suit, his favourite tie. He checks his bag over and over, puts on his hat, takes it off again, glances in the mirror, combs his hair. Time and again he takes out his army papers, reads them, folds them, slips them carefully back into his inside pocket. Look, there's his name: Iain Calum MacDonald Morrison, written clearly on the envelope. It will be on the papers too, with his date of birth, January 1919. What a pair they are, Calum has often said it, herself a daughter of the century, and Iain a child of the bitter peace wrested from the Great War.

3

Mairi watches dry-eyed, seeing her son as clearly as you'd see the Harris hills before a storm – tall and confident, excited at the thought of this new war, the very picture of innocence and inexperience.

'Iain..' she begins and finds she cannot go on.

Iain looks up, 'What, Mam?'

'Nothing. I was just wondering..'

'Wondering what?'

'Is there anyone.. anyone special.. you'd want to be in touch with while..'

'Girls, you mean?' Iain blushes. 'No. No, Mam, there isn't.'

'Has your father spoken to you?'

Iain's blush deepens.

'About girls?' Mairi persists. 'It's a different world, Iain. War changes everything, makes everything more.. urgent. You have to know how to take precautions.'

'Mam. Do you think Dad'll be much longer? We should be off by now.'

'He'll be here. We've half an hour yet.'

Mairi goes back to her rocking, staring at the fire. She is not sure she has said enough. Perhaps she said too much. In the flickering light she looks perplexed, more like a girl of seventeen than thirty-nine. Iain comes over, takes her hand.

'I'm a grown man.'

'Yes,' she lies. 'I know. Look at the size of you! Twice the height your father was at your age.'

'Oh – the olden days,' Iain jibes, gently. 'When you were a girl, and all the streets of Stornoway paved with gold!'

Mairi shakes her head. 'It wasn't golden, Iain, how could it be? But life had its ups as well as downs, its moments.'

'Look out, she's off again!'

'You think I was always old!'

'I'm sure you weren't,' Iain smiles.

Mairi shakes her head again. 'I can read you like a book, Iain Morrison. You don't fool me.'

But Iain's set her off, sent the years cascading.

*　　　*　　　*

It's 1916, Mairi's working in her father's shop, the finest draper's and clothiers in the Western Isles. There are others, of course, but only at MacDonald's is quality uniformly good, and cut and style consistently the latest fashion. They've even sourced a khaki of such convincing depth of shade that tailors from Huntly to Perth apply to them for stocks of it.

This excellence is due in the main to the business acumen of Mairi's mother who, born in Dumbarton, met and married Aeneas MacDonald when he ventured south to try his luck in the Glasgow cloth trade. Maisie's parents had by then moved from Dumbarton to the terraced house in Partick where Aeneas first sought city lodging; there he found Maisie, the eldest of three beautiful daughters, wafting perfumes from the exclusive confines of Buchanan Street, where she worked in fashion, practised it with some success, her natural elegance and eye for detail charming many a jaundiced eye. Aeneas could not be immune to such pure style offensive, and Maisie was flattered by his obvious regard. The softly-spoken, serious islander had money and, moreover, good shoulders. She would rather have stayed in Glasgow, of course, but this was never an option and she set herself the task of re-outfitting Stornoway, Glasgow-style.

If there are some in town who feel Maisie puts on airs above the station of a mere draper's wife, none can deny her taste. Her advice to customers is, has always been, eminently tactful yet truthful.

'What do you think?'

'I'd go for the straw. The ribbon is exactly your shade.' Maisie would quietly remove less suitable distractions, giving her customer room to focus. Yes, if you can afford it, MacDonald's is the place to shop, particularly for Sunday hats. And there is no denying how hard they work, all three MacDonalds, husband, wife and daughter. There is only the one child, no son and heir. Maisie was ill throughout her single pregnancy.

At sixteen Mairi is as able as either of her parents, having gradually assumed almost equal responsibility in the day-to-day running of the business. She has twisted her chestnut curls into a thick plait that nestles at the nape of her neck, and adopted the unobtrusive dress-style of the efficient shop assistant. Her colouring is much less striking than her mother's auburn, and shop-suitable greys and browns do not suit her as well but she is beautiful for all that, a fresh-faced girl with eyes that are most definitely green if seen in good light.

She has clear opinions of her own. Mairi reads her father's newspapers as avidly as he does himself but is sensible enough to keep up with her mother's fashion interests. She doesn't find it difficult. An able scholar, Mairi is also a realist. Her parents would never think of sending her to university.

She keeps her head down, reads as well and widely as she can, and works hard in the business, selling khaki and mourning clothes and sensible but stylish wartime patterns. She keeps in touch with those school friends she meets through work, or church, but as her best childhood friends were mainly boys, her social circles are limited. Still, her mother does allow her to attend the monthly dances at the town hall with her cousin Effie's family and it is that evening's dance Mairi is thinking of as she closes the shop door one bright Friday evening.

What will she wear? Her white lace blouse is torn. She won't have time to mend it tonight, though she'll need it for Sunday. She's been looking, that afternoon, at the new stock in from Glasgow, the plainer lines; wants to take a green blouse home to try. Her mother will not let her.

'No, Mairi. You know *the beauty of the king's daughter comes from within.*' – the usual response to such requests for brand new stock.

Mairi is disappointed. The colour is perfect for her.

'You mean the draper's daughter must not steal the thunder of paying customers!'

'That's about right.'

There is business sense in this, Mairi has to agree, but.. it leaves her with the problem of what to wear that night. Her blue silk should be kept for very special occasions.

She closes the shop door, confronting the street's brightness. The teashop across the road is closing too, Seonaid, pulling the blinds down, sees Mairi, waves. Mairi smiles, waves back. Seonaid, nearer her mother's age than Mairi's, has been her lifelong ally. Seonaid would understand about the new blouse. Seonaid, if she'd been there, might have talked Maisie round. She sometimes did.

As a child Mairi used to spend long hours sitting in the back shop playing with her doll, or reading, or fingering the stock, inventing new uses for the garments, or making new, fantastic words for the textures and smells of different fabrics. Delicate white bloomers became white moth's wings; rolls of Harris tweed, the wool-fat as greasy and rich in it as on the sheep's uncrotalled back, was *scrapestink*. Not that she was supposed to touch any of these goods, far less handle them, sniff them.

The highlight of those dusty mornings, bored afternoons, was Seonaid arriving with cakes and tea for the afternoon or morning breaks and, on a good day, she would stay a little while, share the day's news with Maisie, even talk to Mairi and her doll. Seonaid is unmarried, remains so by choice. Her only suitors, she says, are either too tall or too thin, or too serious; or they live too far from town. Seonaid does not fancy living on a croft; or so she says, time after time. She likes her freedom.

'Will Seonaid ever get married?'

'What a question, Mairi!'

'I think she likes the shop too much.'

'Maybe.'

Mairi waves to the round figure disappearing behind the last firmly-pulled-down blind. Ah well, time for home.

The lock is set rather low, ornate and intricate, and Mairi lays her basket of groceries on the pavement as she bends to slip the heavy key through the shining brass keyhole. The stained glass panels, red and green and blue, attract her eye. She can see her own reflection in the central glass, mirror-like, the shop in darkness. What does she see? A ghost of herself, a single smiling ghost, intangible, insubstantial as the latest Glasgow fashions mounted on the tailor's dummy just beyond the counter. The dummy, the Glasgow silk, even the bolt of khaki on the counter beside it seem part of the reflected image, integral; passing carts and glancing sunlight change it too. It's odd. It sometimes frightens her, this moving, shadowy reflection, but today she barely notices, gets on with the business of locking up. That's sometimes difficult, the lock temperamental; but now the mechanism clicks easily enough. The key rotates and slides out smoothly.

Mairi steps back and, standing up, is astonished to find herself bowled over and thrown hard against the lower panels of the door, her basket upturned, all the contents splayed across the pavement. Her right hand lands in the bag of eggs her mother charged her to carry carefully home, and the four ripe peaches Colonel Johnson brought them from his forcing-houses roll limply in the gutter. Worst of all, she finds her skirt flailing above her knees, and her legs firmly entangled with a pair of rough tweed trousers filled out by the tall young man who has landed on top of her, his full weight threatening to endanger her breathing.

'Good God, Iain Murray!' she gasps. 'Will you ever look where you're going?'

'I'm sorry, Mairi.'

Iain doesn't sound sorry, not a bit.

'You don't sound sorry to me.'

Mairi tries to untangle her legs, smooth her skirts over her knees. This is not a simple matter, and Iain makes no effort to help the process, rather seems to hamper it. Mairi stares at him, pointedly.

He, in turn, is staring at her legs, seems more than a little dazed.

'Iain! Wake up! Did you bang your head? What's wrong with you?'

He does not answer, goes on staring distractedly.

Mairi blushes. 'They're legs, Iain. Have you never seen a pair of legs before?' She tries again to free herself, reinstate

8

decorum. She pulls her skirt down so it covers her knees again, Iain's too.

'Not yours,' says Iain. 'Not since you were nine or ten.'

'Stop blathering and help me up!'

Mairi holds out her right hand, which is dripping egg yolk.

'Mairi!' Iain protests. 'Look at you! This is my best suit.'

'It was you that broke the eggs!' Mairi begins indignantly, but lapses into a fit of giggling at Iain's outraged expression.

'If you'd thought to look where you were going!'

'Me?' says Mairi. 'I was merely straightening up. Who was the one charging along the road like a herd of elephants? Me? I don't think so!'

Iain sighs, fishes his white handkerchief from his top pocket, wraps it round his hand before he takes her sticky yellow one. Their legs are still entangled. It proves impossible for them to stand up simultaneously.

'Iain!' says Mairi, 'Move your legs. Move backwards. Get out of my way. Now!'

'*You* move.'

'How can *I* move? I'm squashed against the door. You're the free radicle here.'

Iain frowns. 'Radical? Where do politics come into this?'

'I said rad*icle*, not rad*ical*. Shut up and get up!'

Iain moves backwards on all fours, freeing Mairi's legs at last. She rubs her left ankle ruefully, hides it in her skirts.

'What do you mean, radicle?' Iain persists.

'Nothing. It's just chemistry.'

'Hardly a young lady's subject!'

'Och, Iain, you sound just like my aunt. Don't be stuffy!'

Mairi's making free use of Iain's white handkerchief, wiping her hand clean of yolk and egg-white, splinters of shell. He sits back against the shop door now, beside her, wishing he could still see those neatly turned ankles. It's odd how girls change; odd, he thinks. Here's Mairi, for instance, he used to play football with her, get up to all the nonsense of the day, for all that she was more his brother's age – and now she's got ankles. Ankles a fellow would want to look at, even in woollen stockings, even when she's spouting chemistry. Chemistry, of all things! Definitely odd.

'Who were you running away from?'

Mairi hands him back his handkerchief, too wet and sticky now to go back in his pocket. Iain takes it gingerly, holds it by the driest corner, frowning. He stretches toward the upturned basket, tosses the handkerchief into it. 'Iain, that's *my* basket.'

'Och, keep the handkerchief! Have it as a present.'

'Getting fastidious in your old age, eh?'

Iain shrugs.

'You haven't answered my question,' Mairi persists. 'What was all the hurry? What are you up to, Iain? Did you rob the bank, or what?'

He smiles, stands up and finally helps Mairi to her feet. 'I was only going home.'

'At that speed?'

Mairi stoops for the bag of broken eggs. Yolk and albumen slide everywhere.

'Let me give you this in return. I know you've always been fond of eggs.'

Iain jumps back, shakes his head.

'We have our own hens.'

Mairi laughs, drops the eggs back on the pavement. 'You haven't answered my question. Maybe you just felt like a burst of speed? Maybe it's a new rule that town hall clerks must be athletes so they can race round the town faster, delivering council mail?'

'I was going home,' says Iain. 'To tell my mother..'

'How is your mother?' Mairi is not concentrating now, gathering up dusters and peaches and biscuits, and stacking them untidily in the basket.

'Not too bad,' says Iain, bending to help. He notices the last peach which has rolled into the doorway, retrieves it. 'I'm going to France, Mairi. Enlisted today – joined the Seaforths.'

Mairi holds her hand out for the peach. It's bruised. The early flush lingers, too soft, on her fingers. She feels Iain fingers, warm and strong. Iain's fingers. Mairi looks away. Iain, going to

France. In uniform.

'I've never been to France,' she says. 'Not even to Glasgow. I've never been out of the island.'

They stand, hand-locked, in silence. Iain wants to speak, can think of nothing but Mairi's skin brushing his. She breaks away first.

'Are you all right?' he asks. 'Did I.. you.. hurt yourself?'

'No,' she smiles. 'I'll survive until the dance, I think.'

Iain beams. 'You're going to the dance? Great. I'll see you there. I must go now.. have to get back to tell them the news at home before they hear from someone else.'

'They'll be very proud.'

Iain stretches out his hand, strokes Mairi's arm lightly. 'Don't forget. I'll see you early. I have to run!'

'Watch where you're going this time!'

Iain sprints along the street, but rounds the corner safely. Mairi sighs, picks up her basket, then remembers the eggs which next door's dog is now demolishing.

'Oh, Dileas,' she sobs. 'Dileas.'

The collie eats the bag, licks the pavement clean.

LONDON 1996

*

A huge antique stove in the centre of the hall, the only source of heat, was not coping well with December's damp, for all its tiled distraction. Zoe thought it odd to see bagged anthracite vying for space in the converted church with over-filled shelves of second-hand and antiquarian books. They stretched from floor to ceiling in newly constructed bays between former aisles and low stained glass windows. In the upper galleries fine wrought-ironwork had been enthusiastically painted fresh spring green, clashing with most of the paintings displayed there; some of these, confusingly abstract close-to, showed to better advantage from the old communion table that acted as service point for Heaney's Books. There was no till, the assistant mentally totting up each bill as she packed purchased books in recycled polythene (some of the bags very crushed indeed). And there was no cash box other than the drawer in the table's ornate side; no sign of Visa or Switch outlet. Zoe was glad she'd brought her cheque book. She did not always carry it.

Not that there seemed much risk of being served. The assistant was engrossed in a cardboard box of heavy gold-chased books. She fished them out, one after another, set them on the counter without taking any notice of Zoe. She did not stop, did not look up, until she had retrieved the very last book from the box, a slender volume covered in faded leather.

'Medical books? Do you specialise in them?'

The assistant shook her head. 'They came with this.' She waved the small brown book at Zoe. 'It was all or nothing. I don't think we'll ever sell this lot, but it's difficult to find the Murray, and we hardly ever get it in this condition.' She turned the book so Zoe could see and read the title *A Private View*. She didn't recognise it.

'What is it?'

'Poetry. First World War,' the assistant held the book with reverence, 'by Iain Alexander Murray. Don't you know the name? Have you never seen *The Dark Ship*?'

'The boy in the film? I didn't know he wrote. May I?'

'Of course. Shall I wrap those?' The assistant laid the book on top of the medical tomes, stretching her hands for Zoe's purchases. 'Actually,' she smiled, 'it would go rather well with these. It's a good bit more expensive, though.'

Zoe handed over *Wine, Women and War* and *With a Machine-gun to Cambrai* and picked up Iain Murray's poems. For the most part they were short, printed in Gaelic and English on creamy, thick paper. Though the book had obviously been read, and often, the pages remained clean, the spine intact. Zoe turned back to the frontispiece, to the photograph of Iain Murray. She gazed at him for a long moment, glanced back through the poems.

'How much did you say?'

Later, jolting in the tube uncomfortably close to five Japanese schoolgirls, their armoury of video cameras jingling as the train rattled round the Victoria line, Zoe found herself fumbling for Iain Murray's book. It had gravitated to the very bottom of the crushed green carrier bag Heaneys supplied. But the leather was *so* soft and the book fitted her hand perfectly, so perfectly it might have been made for her. Just to hold it brought such comfort, Zoe didn't know why.

She carved herself a little elbow room, found the page with Iain's photograph. And there he was, smiling confidently through the century, his blond hair shorn to stiff precision, indubitably highland.. and yet.. there was something of the young Picasso there.. you could almost taste it. Danger. Duende.

Zoe stared at Iain so long she forgot to change at Green Park, had to double back from Oxford Circus. The Japanese girls seemed to have made the same mistake; or she might have found a different, indistinguishable group on the second train. Either way, their cameras and umbrellas left Zoe with bruised ribs, as their unfamiliar voices danced round her. For once, she did not notice, did not complain.

She lingered in Piccadily, tasted the poems over lunch, reading them again as she savoured the café latte. By the time she finally arrived at the office, the weekly meeting had drawn to a close. Jane, her producer, was unimpressed.

'I thought you were going to Heaney's to pick up two books.'

'I was.' Zoe handed over *A Private View*. 'And I found this as well. Do you remember *The Dark Ship*? A forties film, I think. They used to show it on the BBC every Christmas, that and *Trouble in the Glen*.'

'The one about the shipwreck? Is that a script?'

'No. Poems. War poems. Iain Murray's poems.'

'The young blond guy?'

'Yes. See what you think..'

Jane gazed at the photograph of Iain Murray. 'When was this taken?'

'1917.'

'And is he still alive? Have you traced him?'

'Jane,' said Zoe. 'You've seen the film. You know what happened.'

DI-H-AOINE

(Friday)

STORNOWAY 1916

*

Mairi loves dancing, has always loved it. There's nothing in the world like gliding round a good wide floor, skirts swirling, cheeks aching with unending smiling – and touch, the touch of one hand, one arm against another in the measure of the dance, in the laughter in the music – Mairi loves dancing, has always loved it. What girl of sixteen doesn't?

She is dancing the Schottische with Iain Murray whose feet float easily six feet above ground. The boy's so happy to be going to France, as if he's joining a huge party, as if he's won a prize. You can see it in his eyes. He thinks the world is at his feet, anything possible. Mairi understands. She knows how little Iain enjoys his job; he would have preferred work on the open land. She knows he's never been able to sit for more than five or ten minutes at a desk, and is happiest tramping moors, shooting geese, fishing the small brown hill-loch trout – he even prefers cutting peat to the constraint of office work, strangled by shirt and tie. The weekend on his father's croft never made up for the prison term of weekdays; he's always said that to anyone who'll listen, including his boss, who shakes his head and laughs. No one takes Iain seriously, he's always been too charming to be taken seriously – until now. It's a serious business, France.

War has had its effect on the island. So many men away, more in uniform. There aren't many here tonight out of uniform – there's the usual naval crowd, from the Depot; a few soldiers sporting the kilt and khaki of the Highland regiments; only the young boys and old men stand out in civilian clothes. One or two, like Iain, are glowing, radiant as bridegrooms, the toast of the evening.

And it's such a lovely evening. Mairi has danced every dance, never quite out of breath, though her cheeks are rosy now and her eyes unusually bright, their delicate green heightened in some odd way by the pale blue ribbon knotted in her hair and at her throat. She's glad she wore the blue silk blouse with its frilled caped sleeves and swirling skirt. She'd had these for her cousin Chrissie's wedding. They're not what she would normally have worn, but Iain's news has turned a simple dance into an occasion. This is the second set she's had with him, and her aunt will be watching every move.

Having married off one daughter, and seen Effie comfortably engaged to the youngest son of Colonel and Mrs Johnson, Aunt Anna has it in mind to see Mairi's future similarly settled. Mairi is not that keen to be shackled at sixteen, or seventeen, or twenty-six, for that matter. Luckily her parents are of the same opinion.

'Anna!' her mother had exclaimed last Sunday when Anna broached the subject. 'What are you thinking of? Mairi's just a child.'

'No more a child than my Effie!'

'Exactly. You know I've always said sixteen's too young for an engagement.'

Aeneas, fond of his sister, and less suspicious of her intentions, tried to smooth the situation over.

'It's good of you to think of the girl, Anna, but..'

Anna would not take the hint. Her voice grew louder, almost shrill. 'Your Mairi is a strong-willed girl, always has been. A girl like that, with ideas of her own.. well it's dangerous, that's all. If you take my advice you'll see she's married good and young before her own inclinations and all that reading have a chance to lead her into troubled waters.'

'Anna, what exactly are you trying to say?' Maisie allowed anger to creep into her voice. 'Does our Mairi show the least sign of impropriety when she's out and about with you?'

'No, but..'

'Is she rude, impolite? Does she.. fraternise.. unduly?'

'No..'

'There you are then. The subject's closed.'

Mairi, hovering outside the parlour door, balancing a tea tray, knocked and entered now, putting a firm end to the conversation. She had heard everthing, but gave no sign of this, calmly laid the tray on the table in the bay window, withdrawing to the kitchen and the library book she was currently engrossed in.

'What are you reading now, girl?' said her father later that same afternoon. It was not at all like him to breach the silence of the kitchen.

'A library book,' Mairi looked up, startled.

'Obviously. What's it called?'

He'd never questioned her choice of books. Mairi kept her voice as neutral as possible as she replied, '*Dubliners*.' She held her breath.

Her father nodded cheerfully. 'I'm partial to travel books myself. Always was.'

Mairi, closing the book, smiled. Her father hovered on the threshold. 'Still..' He seemed to have more to say, to be having trouble finding words. Mairi raised her eyebrows, waited. 'Lass,' he said, 'your mother and I wouldn't want you..' What now? He must have seen this book reviewed, as Mairi had. It was controversial, certainly.

He shook his head. 'I mean,' he said, 'we wouldn't want you to be getting itchy feet, thoughts of distant travel. We'd miss you in the shop. And at home. And think what geography did for me! Blew me all the way to Glasgow. That's a long way from the island, longer than you know.'

'You came back.'

'I did,' Aeneas frowned. 'At least I tried to. But the island has never been quite the same, Mairi, for all that.'

This time the door swung closed behind him, and Mairi stared, perplexed, at the solid rectangle of painted pine. She heard him reassure her mother, out in the hall.

'Anna's got it all wrong. The girl is up to her eyes in travel-books. I was myself at that age.'

'Where?' Maisie asked.

'At home, I suppose.' Aeneas shook his head. 'I never had time for reading in the shop.'

'No. Where.. what place.. was she was reading about?'

'Cardiff,' said Aeneas. 'Odd choice, but what harm will it do? It's better than chemistry.'

And there's Anna, in all her finery, squinting now, waving at Mairi as she pivots round and up and down the hall with Iain. Anna had been delighted with Iain's enlistment.

'Your family must be so proud of you, young man. We all are.'

Iain beamed. 'I was afraid it would be over before I was old enough, that I'd miss all the fun.'

'Not a bit of it,' Anna said. 'You young folks have all the fun in life in front of you. Remember that!'

Knowing her aunt's mind, Mairi turned away, blushing. Iain, noting the blush, smiled even more broadly. Anna patted both their shoulders. 'It's a wonderful night,' she crooned. 'A magical night.'

'What is she like?' Mairi sighed as Iain whisked her round the floor.

'Queen Victoria, I think,' said Iain with conviction. 'Except that Queen Victoria smiled more!'

Mairi giggled. 'Iain! Anna's a lot younger than Victoria was. And thinner. And her hair isn't white, not yet. And she has the second sight, and the power of the evil eye.'

Iain looked suitably cowed. 'Of course,' he said. 'Just like Victoria.'

Mairi smirked, 'I'll pass on your compliment. She'll be charmed.'

Now, as they spin to the dance's dizzy close, Iain registers Anna's look of wrapt approval. 'See, she likes me. She must have heard.'

Mairi chokes, 'I'll make sure she does! That'll sort you out, you big-headed lump.'

Iain chooses to ignore this. 'Mairi,' he says. 'Would you like some lemonade? Run along and and speak to Calum while I, a true Sir Galahad, fight my way through the vicious throng.' He bows low, kissing her hand ostentatiously, though dancers round about them stare, amused. Mairi shakes her head. When Iain's in a mood like this there's no distracting him.

'Iain, stop showing off. And where is Calum? You're sure he's here tonight?'

'Am I sure? I was talking to him earlier..' Iain peers through the dancers. 'Though I can't.. ah. Follow me, fair lady. Sir Gawain is indeed here within the hall, but verily the knave doth seem a little.. under the weather.'

'Iain, please!'

'I'm only aspiring to be the perfect knight. Correct me if you will, but when you were seven or nine summers (I can't remember which) you spent weeks and months instructing us in the ways of the Round Table.'

'Iain, I'm warning you! If there's any more nonsense..'

Iain bows low. 'Oh well,' he says. 'I didn't mean it. I was only pretending you were fair.'

'Iain!'

'All right, not pretending, hoping. Don't nip so hard! And don't throw any more eggs! You should see my suit. By the way,' he grins, 'how are your legs? Mine are still aching, after that little jousting session.' He stares at Mairi's legs so hard she's almost persuaded he can see them through the layers of silk and petticoat. She cannot for the life of her think of a suitable retort. He laughs. 'There.. straight ahead, look.. there's the man you're looking for.'

Still laughing, he steers her to the far end of the hall where Calum Morrison lounges on a chair below a gilt-framed mirror which shines above him, halo-like.

'Calum. A drink?'

Calum shakes his head, pats the half-bottle in his pocket. Mairi thinks it's as well Anna cannot see him. Iain waves. 'Look after Mairi, Calum. I warn you, she's excitable tonight. And fey.

Keeps thinking she's the Lady of the Lake, or something like that.'

'Waterhorse?' says Calum. 'Selkie?'

'I'll come back and rescue you, I promise.'

Iain's blond head disappears in the crowd.

'Well,' says Mairi. 'It's good to see you, Calum. Where have you been hiding all these weeks? You haven't been in the shop. We've missed you.'

Calum makes no answer. He takes out his half-bottle, unscrews the top, slowly. Even this quick draft is enough to release more whisky fumes than Mairi likes. Calum stares ahead, ignoring her. Mairi is distracted by the sight of her hair in the mirror: her blue bows have come loose with dancing. She fixes them with practised fingers, moving to the place where the mirror's curve dips low, affording her a better view. Not five feet tall, she's always regretted her lack of inches. She's right in front of Calum now, her silk blouse floating directly before him; rippling, perfumed. The faintest hint of sweat escapes from lace-caped sleeves, as she interweaves straying curls and looping ribbon.

Calum finds himself uncomfortably aware of Mairi's rounded body, the tiny waist, the small firm breasts: his eyes, drawn to those soft curves, will not leave them. He shuts his eyes, imagining that landscape free of linen, free of lace. The room is spinning slightly. He tightens his grip on the screw-top bottle.

'Do wake up, Calum.'

Mairi sits down beside him. Calum keeps his eyes closed, sighs.

'What's up with you? What's wrong? Speak to me, Calum!'

Calum will not answer, steals another sip from the screw-top bottle, twisting the cap with reverence, as if it were holy, the one thing he'd been brought into existence for, focusing on the screw-top, on the bottle, on the certainty of hand-warmed glass. He doesn't know what else to do.

Mairi's worried. This is not the Calum she's used to. There is something seriously wrong. He will not speak, will not even look at her. He doesn't seem drunk, exactly, but still.. she stands up, tries to peer through the sea of faces for Iain. There's no sign of him. She waits now, does not know what else to do.

And Calum studies Mairi's back, the sloping shoulders draped in lace, the smooth line of the blue silk of her skirt. When she moves, she rustles gently, a soft breeze in the dawn's first wave, like the new slow waltz that's echoed in his head all day.

He had not realised the tune was meant for Mairi.

He swings his gaze around the hall. Everywhere he looks there are men and boys in uniform, and girls laughing, flirting with them. Not one of those boys or men is without a partner, though all the boys out of uniform lack female company. Calum shakes his head, stares hopelessly after Mairi. He has no chance with her now. He thinks his heart is breaking.

There's still no sign of Iain. Mairi's not surprised. So many folk, and they'll all know the news, all want their say. It's an important night. Come Monday, Iain will be off with all the other new recruits to the Seaforth Depot on the mainland.

She catches sight of him at last, talking to Calum's father, who's standing with an arm on the young fellow's shoulder, looking as proud and pleased as if Iain were his own son. Iain obviously hasn't reached the refreshment table yet, or if he has he's lost the lemonade. Mairi sighs. As she turns, she feels Calum's eyes dart away from her. She feels his sadness.

'Calum,' she murmurs. 'What on earth is wrong with you?'

She comes to sit once more beside him, close, so close her right arm brushes gently on his jacket. Calum can't believe, or cope with, his body's reaction. His heart seems to explode. Mairi doesn't notice. 'Why aren't you playing? Won't you be playing at all tonight?' she asks. 'And why are you in such a state? You look as if you've lost a pound and found a penny, or worse, a farthing!'

Calum does not feel like that at all. Not at all. He's in turmoil, cannot answer. Mairi tries again, 'What's eating you?'

His face falls. He remembers. Mairi leans even closer to him. 'Did you hear Iain's news?' He flinches. So that's the way of it,' she thinks. 'Calum,' she whispers. 'We've been friends for as long as I remember, you and me and Iain. Can't you tell me what the problem is?'

Calum sighs, stares rigidly ahead. Opens his mouth as if to speak. At last he says, 'Mairi.. I went there with Iain. Today. Tried to enlist. They turned me down.' His voice is so low she has to bend to catch the words.

'Oh, Calum.'

He speaks louder now, bitter. 'And Iain.. Iain didn't even wait for me afterwards.'

Mairi has never heard Calum angry with Iain, never. That he should mention any of this! And as for Iain.. even from Iain Mairi would not have expected such thoughtlessness.

'Calum. I'm heart-sorry.' Mairi takes his hand. She strokes it, glancing involuntarily at his withered leg. Calum has his eyes closed. She thinks he did not notice. She hopes he did not notice. She musters her briskest tone. 'For it's their loss,' she says. 'Their failing, not yours. They should have put you in the band. Or intelligence. Strategic planning. You're by far the brightest of us.. always were.. top of the class each and every year.'

Calum swallows, fighting tears. 'Fat lot of good it did me.'

'Calum..'

He shakes the tears away. 'When my children ask me *What did you do in the war, Daddy?* I'll tell them I typeset the *Stornoway Oran*. That'll impress them, eh?'

'You do more than typeset. You write the whole thing!'

'What's the difference, Mairi? None. You know. *You know*. Don't patronise me!'

Calum pushes Mairi's hand away, has another swig from the whisky bottle. It's now half-empty. Mairi shrugs, makes no attempt to take his hand again. She sits there, silent, waiting, trying to find some inspiration, trying to think of anything that might help Calum through this. From time to time she steals a look at him. He will not meet her eye.

The dance flows on around them. Mairi likes to watch almost as much as she loves to dance; even in her anxiety for Calum, she manages to keep her eye on the crowd, see who's wearing what, who's courting who.

Effie skips by in her smart green blouse and skirt, with Alec Stenhouse, the new boy from the bank. Alec comes from the mainland, the north-east coast. He's sixteen, and speaks no Gaelic, a considerable disadvantage in Stornoway financial circles. Mairi has little Gaelic herself: her mother having come from Glasgow, Gaelic is not spoken in their house, though it was her father's cradle tongue. At school she and all the children were taught, by law, in English. Only in the playground did she hear the island's natural language. She has some words, can understand more than people realise; certainly enough to be useful in the shop when customers from the villages have no English. She finds Gaelic a lot easier than Alec's Doric, not that he lapses into it all that often.

He's a nice boy, Alec; pale-haired, reddish-skinned. He blushes easily. He certainly seems taken with Effie. Mairi raises her eyebrows at her cousin. Effie laughs. Effie's always been vivacious, and Mairi is inclined to think, like her mother, that sixteen was too young for Effie to have been engaged. She's carefree, a scatterbrain. Mairi really loves her, thinks of her as the sister she's never had. Sometimes, in fact, they have been taken for sisters, by visitors to the island. Not that there are many of those. (The locals are not fooled, of course: islanders know every family's history better than that family itself, and sometimes they know it even before it's made.)

Mairi tries to force herself to concentrate for a few minutes, see who's wearing what, how it looks. If it came from the shop.

When she goes home, that's what her mother will want to know.

But gradually, Mairi finds she's studying Calum rather than the crowd; and, to her surprise, he's handsome, even beautiful. Not that she hasn't known that face since childhood – all her life – somehow she's never actually looked, never realised its full potential – the fine straight nose, the tanned skin, the neat brows arching over brown, large eyes. He's not twinkling at her now, not playing the fool – perhaps that's it – perhaps that's why she never *saw* him. In his grief, Calum's let the barriers fall. Mairi turns away, confused.

'What is it, Mairi?'

'Calum?'

His voice – why has she never *heard* his voice?

'Stop shaking your head. You've been doing it for five minutes now. Folk will think I'm being rude to you.'

'You are. '

'Listen, Mairi. I don't need pity. I'll survive.'

'Yes,'

'And I'm all right.'

'You're much more than that. You know it.' Mairi aims for light-hearted, finds the tone too difficult. She's breathless, suddenly. Does Calum notice? He's breathless too; can hardly whisper.

'Too much of this,' he says. 'Too much.'

He lays the whisky bottle underneath his chair, turns to look at her again, his dark eyes widening. They sit and stare, and stare. It's a long moment. Mairi wants to sing. She wants to shout, Look, no hands! No hands!

Their arms are barely touching.

'Mairi! Calum!' Iain bursts into their silence. 'I've been an age. Couldn't help it. Better late than never. Lemonade, for my lady.' He bows to Mairi, before handing her a half-full glass. She wonders how much he's spilled, who he's spilled it over. She turns to Calum, laughs.

'You can't get staff these days, can you?'

Iain frowns. 'I didn't bring you any, Calum. Thought you had your own supplies.'

'I have. Would you like a strùbag?'

'Would I?'

Calum stretches for the whisky, passing it to Iain who adds it to his glass of lemonade. Mairi watches, hides her face behind her glass, twinkling at the pair of them, these two fine boys, no, men. For they are men, there's no denying it: Iain, a Viking horde, all by himself (she must remember to tell him that some day) and Calum, smaller, finer – Armada stock.

Mairi wants to be touching Calum once more, brushing against him, but she senses shyness in him now that Iain's here, a holding back. She wishes Iain would take the hint she offers silently, and go away. She wants to be with Calum, to walk with Calum, hold his arm, feeling beneath his jacket, the skin, the very bones of him.

'Iain, are you sure you want to do that?'

Mairi looks up, sees Iain drain the rest of Calum's half-bottle.

'Iain!'

'Och, we've done more, many a time!'

'Not at a dance,' says Calum. 'Not when you need to stand up sober!'

'It doesn't hamper your fiddling, not that I've ever noticed! I'll be fine. Mairi! Another dance? We'll show him. Come on, on your feet!'

Mairi smiles, shakes her head. 'I'd rather sit this out.'

Iain frowns, looks restlessly around. He can't stand still, wants to be on the move. 'Then you won't mind if I..?'

'Of course not. On you go.' Mairi looks at Calum, is pleased to see his face relax, the guarded expression of the last few minutes disappearing. 'Go on, Iain. Or you'll miss your chance!'

Iain moves off, smiling, slightly puzzled, as if there's something he doesn't understand, something he can't quite get the hang of.

'Do you think he'll make it?' Mairi whispers. 'It's a "Dashing White Sergeant".'

'Yes,' Calum nods. 'He'll be fine. The way he is tonight it would be hard for any amount of alcohol to have much effect on him. I've seen him in this state before.'

'Idiot,' says Mairi.

Calum shakes his head. 'I can't criticise. I had the other half of that half-bottle.'

'I meant you.'

'What?'

'Shh. Calum, aren't dances the best fun?'

Calum thinks about it. 'Don't know. I usually see them from

a different angle. Maybe if..'

He doesn't finish. Mairi puts her hand on his arm.

'Calum?'

'Yes?'

'I'm really glad you're not going to France.'

'Oh, Mairi.'

Calum's smile fades. For a moment, he'd forgotten.

Mairi's almost in tears, appalled at herself.

'Calum. I didn't mean to..'

Silence flares between them.

Calum stares into the milling crowd, thick with uniforms. It matters; it matters. One way or another, all the younger island men are going off to fight while he's left behind, a reject; the cripple they have always thought him, the useless cripple he always feared he might become.

Though Mairi doesn't think so: he glances down at her. She's staring at the dancers, dumbstruck. She didn't mean to hurt him. She has the best heart on the island, a heart as open as the windblown skies.

She's so young. She can't be more than sixteen, even with her hair up, even with that sky-blue skirt. He hasn't talked to her, not properly, for weeks, maybe months; and she's changed, he thinks she changed, become more confident, more herself, more like she was when he first saw her at the school – that day the teacher made him play for the inspector. He played 'Mairi's Wedding' and everybody sang, even Iain who never learned to sing in tune. They sang in Gaelic, even the inspector sang in Gaelic (for wasn't he a fiddler too?). Mairi, a child of barely four, sidled up to Calum after school.

'That was my tune you were playing. Will you tell me the Gaelic words?'

Calum sat in the playground there and then and sang the first verse for her till he saw Iain laughing, and said he saw her mother coming.

The new air rings again inside his head.

He should have known it was for Mairi.

She grabs his arm, suddenly.

'Look, Calum, look! Isn't that Ewan? Ewan MacLeod? Over there! Calum! Don't you see him? It is Ewan, isn't it? And he's *still* paddling!'

She's pointing to a soldier over on the far side of the room, an enormous fellow, broad-shouldered, red-haired. Calum hadn't recognised him. But it is Ewan; when he turns, there is no doubt, though he's grown a red moustache, and his face seems older, much more strained than Calum remembers. Ewan's waving his arms awkwardly as his partner swings away from him. Across the floor, it does look quite like paddling.

'The tricks you and Iain used to play on that poor boy! I'll never know how Ewan survived the pair of you. Remember the oars, Calum.. the racing oars? That was the best one!'

'How long ago was that?'

'It must be six years, Calum, six years anyway.'

'I suppose it must.'

It's interesting, thinks Calum, that Ewan didn't join the Reserve, that he's in the kilt and khaki of the Seaforths.

'Definitely paddling,' says Mairi.

Calum nods. 'Actually, it's something I'm not proud of. If you hadn't been there..'

Mairi looks up sharply, 'What do you mean?'

'Never mind. I'll tell you one day. What do you remember?'

Mairi smiles. 'Oh, the Battle of the Sea. You and me and Iain laughing! That kind of thing.. and the calculations. They were fun. I liked that bit.'

That's not how Calum thinks of it, though he'd learned a lot that summer. How did it start? He can't remember. Perhaps he'd been telling Ewan about the Oxford/Cambridge boat race. Or had the English teacher at their school not been to Cambridge in the long summer holiday and talked of punting, of students and schoolboys rowing, racing, making great speed on the quiet waters of the Cam? Ewan was easily impressed, that was the other thing, not the brightest boy in the village, not by any means, though he played football with great ability, with an understanding none of the rest of them could match.

Calum, of course, couldn't play football, because of his leg. He used to be the referee, shouting decisions from the halfway line that no one ever disputed. From a relatively early age, he had seen that the trick was to make himself the brains of the outfit – whatever the outfit happened to be. Perhaps that's why Ewan so often applied to him for help. The summer of the rowing races, it nearly backfired, nearly went badly wrong. How old were they that year? Eleven, twelve? He must have been at the big school, that was certain; he'd known all about streamlining, or enough to make it sound as if he did.

However it came about, Ewan had been fired with an uncanny enthusiasm for boat racing that summer. He went around challenging one and all to race him in the relatively calm bay by his father's croft; he beat them too, in his father's heavy sgoth, bending the heavy oars as if they weighed no more than matchsticks. He was older than the rest of them, far taller and stronger. And he had an axe to grind. He delighted in drubbing on the sea all those who'd sailed so swiftly past him on the page. Some of the other youngsters could hardly lift his father's oars; the form of the challenge was to row in Ewan's boat from the beach to the buoy and back again while Calum, the eternal referee, kept time.

Iain had risen to the challenge, and been beaten thoroughly which he didn't like at all. He and Calum and Mairi sat rueful on the sanded beach after his defeat, flinging stones and small shells at each other.

'Don't,' said Mairi. 'My mother will be cross if I go home with sand in my hair again. You should have seen my pillow this morning!'

'You should have brushed it last night,' said Iain, dredging her again with fine white sand.

'Shut up Iain,' said Calum. 'You're such a bad loser. Don't take it out on Mairi. It's not her fault you lost and she's much smaller than you.'

'I think I was best except for him. No one can beat him

anyway,' said Iain. 'No one.'

'Not in that boat,' said Calum thoughtful now. 'But if we had a boat that was more streamlined, a canoe, say, like the Eskimos use.. then you'd have a chance!'

'Fat chance of coming up with a canoe!' Iain scoffed. 'There's just no point in racing Ewan.'

'No there isn't. He should race himself,' said Mairi.

'How can you race yourself? Don't be stupid,' said Iain.

'No, she's right,' Calum said. 'Ewan could race himself! Time trials. He could go for the fastest possible time. Then, at least, your pride wouldn't be at risk. Stop it, Iain!' he yelled as showers of sand and pebbles rained down again on him and Mairi who was sitting close beside him. 'Don't be so childish. You'll really have to cure that temper! Cultivate a sense of humour!'

Iain stomped off on his own at that, and kept running away whenever Calum and Mairi looked as if they might be catching up.

Ewan was excited when Calum explained the notion of time trials to him. 'A race against myself? What a good idea!' He was the undisputed rowing champion of them all. He'd nothing left to prove against the younger boys, but he'd enjoyed the challenge, was pleased to find another.

Calum brought an exercise book next day, and every day thereafter. They kept careful note of Ewan's progress; the time, the time of day, the wind's direction and the tides, which could make such a difference to the actual figure. But once they'd worked out what they thought a reasonable system for equalising all these different factors, it became obvious that Ewan's best performances could not be bettered, not with his father's boat.

It was getting boring anyway. Calum was fed-up of sitting on the shore on wet and windy days, soaked to the skin with spray while Ewan struggled with the elements. He was fed-up of Ewan's mute disappointment when the converted figure for equivalent time proved no different for that day than the day before, or the week before, or even the week before that. It was difficult to raise the big lad's spirits. Calum had to make an end of this game, somehow.

One day, as they sat despondent, Calum said, 'What about streamlining then?'

'I don't know what you mean.'

'The only way we'll make things faster is by reducing friction.'

'How?'

'If we changed the shape of boat – say we could find a Red Indian canoe..'

The light in Ewan's eye died. 'There's no way we can get one. We haven't even any logs big enough to hollow out.'

'No. We can't change the boat..' Calum, looking out to sea, saw Neil Angus, their classmate, checking nets with his father. The great oars dipped and rose above the water, like elongated gulls' wings, now fat, now thin. 'Ewan! I've got it! We can't streamline the boat, but we can change the oars, make them thinner, lighter, less inclined to hold you back with water-friction!'

Calum held his breath while Ewan picked up one of his father's huge, thick oars. 'That's not a bad idea, little man.'

For days afterwards, Calum was warm and dry, though the summer turned wet and wild, and showed no sign of improving. He kept watch, standing at the door of Ewan's byre in case his father should come by and see how Ewan was slaving, planing the heavy oars to ridiculous thinness. A mountain of wood-tendrils, lovingly shaved, was slipped into the pigs' food each day. They didn't seem to come to any harm.

The first trial of the new oars fell on the last Saturday before they all went back to school. The weather was stormy, but there was no way they could run the trial on the Sabbath, this was the only possible time. There was another complication too: Ewan's mother went off to visit a sick friend in Breasclete and made Ewan promise, on peril of his living soul, not to let his younger brother, John-Angus, out of his sight for a single moment. John-Angus, a gentle boy with less nous than Ewan and none of his abilities, was actually Calum's age; they got on well enough. But he was a liability, accident-prone. Ewan didn't want to let him wander the beach in rough weather when Calum's eyes would necessarily be on the clock.

'Simple,' said Calum. 'Take him with you, as crew. He's not that heavy, not compared to the tonnage of the boat. It's our last chance, man.'

Ewan saw the sense in that. John-Angus was harder to convince. Eventually, though, they had him sitting in the prow, relatively calm. Ewan hopped into the boat, and signalled to Calum to start the timing. He raised the prototype oars. It was such a moment as Ewan never knew before, or after. He was so proud of his work, so certain of his coming success as he wrenched the oars through heaving water. Calum, on the beach, limped back and fore shouting advice through the megaphone they'd found in the village hall and requisitioned. It was for the greater honour of the village after all.

'Good work,' Calum called. 'Excellent!'

But even Ewan, after twenty minutes, knew he'd never gain the buoy, the wind and tide so strong. He was forty feet from shore, not far, but far enough for him to panic when the thinned oars, pitted against the largest wave they'd hit so far, bent alarmingly. The right oar snapped clean through, throwing Ewan off balance. He let go of the second, which the wave snatched quickly out of reach. John-Angus, who had through it all sat helpless in the prow started screaming now, his words indistinguishable, but his tone shrill enough to travel for miles above the wind.

Behind the ruined black house at the end of the machair, Iain, Mairi and three other boys, all victims of Ewan's prowess in the Battle of the Sea, rolled helpless with laughter. Calum heard them, signalled them to stop. They didn't.

Calum was really worried. How could he rescue the boys? They'd capsize and drown if they didn't make the shore. Ewan was in no state to think, besides, he couldn't swim. None of them could.

'Calum, what about the last oar?'

'Go away, Mairi.' Calum was impatient. 'I need time to

think. Don't bother me now. I'll give you the figures later. No.. wait.. what did you say?'

'Ewan's father has a spare oar in that boat. It's always there, unless you took it out, for weight?'

'No, I didn't. Well done, Mairi! Ewan, use the third oar!' Calum yelled. 'The third oar Ewan! Paddle! That's right. You can do it. Good!'

Calum was hoarse, exhausted, by the time the heavy boat slumped in shallows. He limped towards it. Ewan pulled John-Angus out and threw him on shore, in one vast, superhuman arc of movement. Then he turned into the tide, and vomited. Calum thought he could see flecks of blood dancing on the bile-laced foam.

Calum was thinking quickly now. He was fond of Ewan – if Ewan and John-Angus had come to harm, he knew the main responsibility was none but his; he was conscious too of the schoolboys still giggling behind the tumbled dyke. He dashed up to Ewan, smiling broadly.

'Ewan, man, you did it, smashed the record! I know we didn't finish, but you were doing so well – such equivalent speed. I've factorised the figures, man. You knocked a good ten minutes off all your other times!'

Ewan stood, astounded, while Calum rambled on.

'I don't know what we'll say about the oars.. to your father.. but wasn't it worth all the effort? Next summer, when we try again, we'll need to modify the planing technique. That was the trouble here, I'm sure. Next time, Ewan, man, we'll try a circular motion. What do you think?'

Ewan, unused to being asked for scientific detail, looked first confused, then, gradually, convinced; then proud.

The boys behind the stone wall all stopped giggling.

Calum didn't ask Mairi to check his figures for that trial, though he usually did. It was her main role in the proceedings. Next week, when she asked to see them, Calum found the book had unaccountably been lost. Probably, in the storm, it had been washed right out to sea. Calum assured her airily that the record was, however, indisputable. Mairi agreed, standing up for Calum against Iain who dared to question, this time, the referee's opinion.

Ewan told his father the oars were lost at sea while he was trying to teach John-Angus to manage the boat. For months, he scoured the shore each morning, in fear of washed-up evidence. He became known as the boy who knew the most about the sea; invincible.

John-Angus kept his mouth shut. Ewan had him well-threatened.

*   *   *

'Why so glum, you two?' Iain's set has reached the bottom of the hall, and in the measure he comes face to face with Calum and Mairi. He misses a step in talking to them.

'Iain Murray!' his partners yell. 'Concentrate, will you?'

'Sorry. Sorry!' Iain telegraphs apologies and turns his full attention to the set. He's dancing with Effie and Angus, her fiancé. The other three dancers include Ewan MacLeod and his brother John-Angus, bemused and blond as ever. They're squiring a young woman Mairi does not recognise.

'Who's that, Calum?'

'John-Angus. You've seen him before!'

'No, the woman. The girl he's dancing with.'

'I don't know. But then I didn't recognise Ewan. He's changed, hasn't he?'

'It's the scar,' says Mairi. 'And the moustache.'

'No,' Calum stares again at Ewan. 'Not entirely. I can't put my finger on it.'

'He looks a bit sad,' offers Mairi.

'He's smiling!'

'Yes, but he's heart-tired, you can see.'

'Whatever do you mean by that?'

She shakes her head.

Later, Effie tells them the girl is Ewan's new wife, a VAD

from Edinburgh. (This explains her smart dress, the almost Japanese simplicity of the bodice, Mairi and Effie agree.)

Ewan was in hospital for months, and no one knew; his parents somehow managed to keep the news completely to themselves, didn't even tell John-Angus. Ewan married his nurse, Myra, the minute he was convalescent.

'And why not?' says Mairi. 'Why wait?' She's staring at John-Angus, a wistful, clumsy angel trailing chaos round the room; uncoordinated, still baby-faced. 'It's as well,' she says, 'that boy will be staying at home.'

'Not for long,' Calum says indignantly. 'The Seaforths accepted *him* today. And *he* doesn't want to go!'

Mairi frowns. 'Calum! He's not old enough. He's six months younger than you, six months at the least. He must have volunteered.'

'More like his mother volunteered him! Och, Mairi, you know I wouldn't go round saying these things,' Calum groans. 'Not to anyone else. But how will John-Angus ever cope in the army? Who could teach him to march, even?'

Mairi shakes her head. 'Marching's a lot simpler than "The Dashing White Sergeant"!'

'Don't you believe it. The quickness of the foot deceives the eye!'

'You mean the hand.'

'I mean the belly. An army marches on its belly.'

'Only Napoleon's.'

'There's John-Angus, practising already.'

The lad slides halfway down the hall, gets up, blushing. Alec Stenhouse helps him to his feet, brushes him down.

Calum shrugs. 'Let's hope there's an Alec Stenhouse at the Depot, or that poor sod will never make it to the Channel.'

'Calum! Alec's a nice boy, kind. I've never seen him anything but helpful.'

'Isn't that exactly what I'm saying?'

Iain's set has now finessed down the hall. Iain heoochs, waves across the room to Mairi, who follows – can't ignore – his flamboyant progress. Calum, seeing her gaze, grows angry, cold.

'It's easy for some,' he says. 'Always has been.'

Mairi can't believe what she's hearing. 'Don't be jealous, Calum. You've never been jealous of Iain.'

Calum shakes his head. 'Who's jealous?'

'What's that anger, then, if it isn't jealousy?'

Calum blushes. Mairi sees an angry flush spread from his neck to his temples, his cheeks remaining oddly pale. He stares at his hands, unseeing, plucks feverishly at the hard skin edging his fingernails. He's always done this when he's embarrassed, all his life, not that it's good for the skin; encourages ragnails. He has elegant hands for a boy, long fingers, smooth flat nails, ink stained. He shouldn't pick the skin like that, Mairi's always telling him.

'It's *not* jealousy,' he insists, at last. 'It isn't, Mairi; it's.. it's.. frustration at being thrown on the scrap-heap! It's having a weakness shoved in your face, cancelling everything you may or may not be! It leaves you a nothing, a nobody.'

'You mustn't think like that.'

'I do, though. So does everyone else.'

'I don't.'

'You're different, Mairi. You and I were children together.'

'Yes,' she says. 'Remember that. Children are honest.'

She settles back in her chair, folds her arms, trying to think of some way, some bland form of words, to help. No words come. There is no way. There's no going past it. And when you come to think about it, Calum must have known in his heart that the army wouldn't take him. He's not stupid. He was rattling the cage doors.

She changes the subject. 'What are you reading just now?' It's not a subtle gambit, she knows. Calum may feel patronised, flounce off in rage. But he responds with surprise and what to Mairi sounds much like relief.

'HG Wells, actually. Why?'

'Which one?'

'At the moment, *The Island of Dr Moreau*. Before that *The War of the Worlds*.'

'Cheery,' Mairi nods.

35

'What about yourself? What are you reading, Mairi?'

She hesitates, '*Dubliners*. It's written by a fellow called James Joyce.'

'It's you that has it! I might have known. They told me at the library it was on loan. How are you finding it?'

'Cheery,' says Mairi .

'Don't be cynical. It doesn't suit you. How are you finding it'

Mairi smiles. 'Interesting,' she says, slowly. 'It's such a different atmosphere. And it's told so simply. I keep going back to one story, the very last story in the book. Can't get away from it.'

'Oh?'

'And it's all about a dance, actually.'

'*The Dead..*'

Mairi doesn't hear this, goes on, 'It's a great story Calum. It's really made me think, you know – even more than the war – about who we are, what we are; how the past and present fuse in our ideas, in us, in all the things we take for granted.'

Her face shines as she struggles to put her feelings into words, and fails. She has not come close, nowhere near. She cannot even really be sure what moves her in the story, though she's been deeply touched by the characters, their sadnesses, the snow. Especially the snow.

They don't get all that much snow on the island, not for any length of time, and it fascinates Mairi, always has: crystalline water, so cold it burns – so beautiful and transient, its transience not the least part of its urgent beauty.

Like love, Mairi thinks. Snow transforms the land in a quiet, breathless way, changing perspectives, making it impossible to remember or imagine what lies beneath the whiteness.

Alec Stenhouse is not sure whether he likes island life. He's not sure either if he likes Stornoway. He finds the climate damp and cold, the worst kind of cold to one brought up in Cullen, on the dry north-east coast where the Three Kings dominate a coastline lashed by North Sea waves. He misses the granite houses, the tidy squares and streets. He misses the green land beyond the town. He misses the good Doric tongue, not that

Aberdonians would classify his speech as Doric. He's a canny lad, though, and does not let even his mother know in letters home how bleak he finds this low brown island, scarred by peat bogs. He works hard, tries hard to understand the English he is offered; tries hard to make his own attempts at English (his second language after all) acceptable to these good and serious folk. For good and serious they are, and hard-working.

The best thing about the island (the one good thing, he says, when he's depressed, when his ledgers will not tally, or another Gaelic-speaking customer has disconcerted him by asking how he is *all over*), the best thing about Stornoway is definitely the girls, the bonny, dark-haired, dark-eyed girls. The fair-haired ones are beautiful enough, he just prefers dark hair. Always has. Effie now. If she was not engaged, he'd be camping at her gate. Metaphorically. Literally. Though it probably would not do any good, that gorgon of a mother would just ask him if he'd lost his way, and fail to understand his answer. He dreams about Effie nearly every night. Effie and her cousin Mairi, who's almost as beautiful.

He's been trying to dance with both of them all night, unsuccessfully. He doesn't count the country dances as dancing, more a social call. And Angus, Effie's fiancé, turned up halfway through the evening, foiling any hopes in that direction. Mairi's still here though, sitting with Calum, the reporter from the *Oran*, the young chap with the limp who usually plays fiddle in the band. He's supposed to be the best fiddler they've had on the island for half a century, so they say. He's a fine composer too. Alec is fond of music, can play a little himself; not like Calum, no, but he can make a fair attempt at some of the Scot Skinner melodies, enough to please himself, anyway. Unfortunately his landlady does not allow musical instruments. When Alec arrived, she saw the fiddle-case and informed him starchily that she did not allow violins to be played in her establishment. So that was that. He can hardly play it in the bank!

Word is, Calum's out of sorts tonight, heart-broken. The army wouldn't take him. More fool him for being upset, Alec thinks. Alec has a brother fighting at the Somme. Bob was called up at the very start, he'd been a Territorial, thought he'd get cheap holidays that way.

Some holiday. He's been in France for two years. Alec knows his letters home, cheerful and bright and positive, are lies designed to reassure their mother. Bob told him when he was home on leave what it was really like.

'Nane o' you kens,' said Bob, 'fit your lives here are restin' on, hoo much we swallow every day oot there – death an' mud. We a' live in hope o' getting fit we cry a cushy ane – an injury, large enough, but no' fatal – that'll send ye hame tae Blighty.'

'Funny word, Blighty,' said Alec. 'I dinna ken hoo they manage tae mak Blighty fae Britain.'

'It's Indian for hame. D'ye nae ken that?' Bob lit up a cigarette. His hands were shaking. 'This skelf in the airm wisnae bad enough, they want me back. But tak my advice, Alec – if ye've ever valued it – dinna be daft. Dinna enlist. Stay hame. Work like ye've nivver worked before. Dae sae weel at the bank they winna let you go. An' look efter Mither. We've done quite enough for the war in this family as it is. Aye, an' dinna worry about me. The ither men say I've a charmed life. We're superstitious there, ken. Nae surprising, eh? There's nae sense in any o' it.'

Maybe, one day soon, thinks Alec, I'll speak tae Calum, gie him Bob's advice. Maybe no'. These folk can be sae proud. And it probably wouldnae mak a blind bit of difference tae him. But I'll try, just the same. Meantime, I'll dae my best to dance wi' Mairi.

He starts to move across the room, slowly, imperceptibly. As the dance ends, he is standing next to Calum, in perfect position for a takeover bid. Calum and Mairi are sitting together in silence, an intimate silence. Alec knows, he's sensitive to such things. He hadn't realised.. Calum glances up at him. Alec smiles. Calum nods. Alec stays. When Calum looks up again, Alec's still there, smiling. Calum is forced to speak.

'Hello, Alec. Are you wanting something?'

'Nae frae you,' grins Alec, slightly nervous now. He leans in front of Calum. 'Mairi, can I hae the next dance wi ye?'

Mairi looks at Calum. What's happening here? Alec wonders.

'Go on,' says Calum. 'Dance. I have to play. I promised my father I'd play when Hamish left. I'll see you before you go.'

Alec's standing between them, eyebrows raised. Mairi nods, stands up. 'I'd be delighted to dance with you, Alec.' Together they move towards the middle of the floor. Mairi, well mannered, does not look back. Alec wonders if he's misread the situation between her and Calum. It's possible.

Murdo, Calum's father, comes to the front of the stage. His face is shining almost as much with sweat as with the good humour he is famous for. He wipes his forehead with a large red handkerchief, smiling at the crowd. 'Ladies and Gentlemen. Take your partners now for the last waltz of the evening. We've a special treat in store. Calum's going to lead us in two new tunes. We haven't heard them, so he'll have to hurry up getting that violin sorted out. We can't make up the introductions for him as we usually do!'

There's general applause, laughter too. Calum is well-known to be a stickler for perfection, tuning his fiddle as carefully and long as many a piobaireachd player tunes his bagpipes. But he's climbing up on stage when Iain dashes up, grabs his arm. 'Where's Mairi?'

Calum points to the back of the hall. 'On the floor. Look. With Alec Stenhouse.'

'But it's the last waltz, Calum!'

'That's right. I can't talk. I have to play now.' Calum nods, 'Right, Dad. I'm ready.' He turns back to Iain, who's still standing by the stage, rebellious, thwarted; the expression on his face reminding Calum of the younger Iain vanquished in the Battle of the Sea. Some things never change.

'Iain Murray,' Calum smiles, 'sit you down. Listen.'

Calum leaves Iain standing, moves centre stage. A spotlight flares, blinding him, drenching the hall in darkness. 'Can we have that off?' asks Calum, squinting, shading his eyes as best he can with his one free hand. 'I prefer to see you all. You're not that ugly!'

The dancers all laugh gently.

39

'See? You're beautiful,' says Calum as the spotlight fades, 'what did I tell you? All of you.' He checks his fiddle, does a little more fine-tuning as he speaks.

'Get on with it, boy!' his father shouts.

Calum sighs. 'You know how shy I am! You know how hard it is for me to stand up here. You know the fiddle never sings, short of a string.'

'Hmmph!' Calum's father shrugs. 'I'm only wondering if the fiddler's worth the tune.'

The crowd are used to this pantomime which Murdo and Calum take delight in re-enacting at some time during each of their performances. The hall rocks gently as Murdo mimes his frustration. Calum pretends not to see, maintains a perfectly solemn expression, fitting his fiddle comfortably beneath his chin, as if about to finally address the tune. But he stops, his bow in mid-air, turns back to the crowd.

'Actually,' he says, 'I should say I owe you all, even my father, an apology. I was supposed to be playing here all night tonight. I couldn't. I didn't have the heart for it.'

What's coming now? Mairi wonders. She holds her breath as Calum says quietly, almost whispers, 'I've been drowning my sorrows. They won't have me for France.' The hall is now so still you could cut the silence, mould it. Calum shrugs, 'I couldn't quite take it in.'

The sea of faces before him, folk from town, from the Depot, old school friends, their families, other people from the villages – all the faces look up, hanging on his every word.

'I wanted to go,' Calum's quiet voice reaches every listening ear, as if directed just for that one soul. 'I really wanted to go,' he repeats, 'to do my bit, like my old friend Iain Murray, and Angus Johnson, and John-Angus MacLeod, and all the other boys who enlisted today..'

Calum points them out, one by one. There's a huge outbreak of cheering now, deafening applause. Someone starts '*For they are jolly good fellows!*' at the back of the hall. Angus and Iain and John-Angus are pushed to the front, hugged, congratulated. John-Angus blushes, redder than a beetroot. Iain bows. Angus remains calm, sliding back to Effie who takes his arm, hiding her face on his shoulder.

'And we must not forget,' says Calum, 'those of you already in the field, like Dan Macrae of Back, and Ewan MacLeod from Sandwick.'

More clapping. Calum waits till it dies down.

'Nor must we forget all of you at home, who live and pray and wait for news; and work, day in, day out, conscious of the spaces in the fabric of your lives, thinking of your brave lads, confident of their endeavour on the field, or on the wave. All of which brings me to the first waltz. It was written for my good friend Iain Murray, who as I've said, is off to France in a few days – that's if he sobers up!'

The crowd cheers loudly once again. It takes several minutes for the laughter to settle.

'Off to France, or rather, off to Fort George on the mailboat, an act of conspicuous gallantry when you remember, as none of us will ever forget – how could we? – his talent for sea-sickness. What about the Battle of the Seas? When Iain got sea-sick just by rowing across the bay on the calmest day in summer?'

'Slander!' shouts Iain. 'Dan! You're my witness against this hooligan!'

'Iain,' screams Dan, 'how can I defend you? I was a witness of the Battle of the Seas, remember?'

Calum has to wait an age for the laughter to stop this time, partly because of Iain's feigned outrage.

'So you'll not be surprised at the working title of the first new waltz – Iain's waltz – *The Dark Ship*.'

Iain shakes his fist at Calum, muttering, 'Just wait, just you wait, my boy!'

'The second tune,' says Calum, 'is dedicated to a certain beautiful young lady. That's all I'm going to say. I know who it's intended for. I give you leave to dedicate it, all of you, to the one you love. The boys haven't heard it yet – haven't heard these tunes at all. They're playing blind – or do I mean deaf?' Calum ducks as his father, the pianist, and the other fiddler pelt him with anything that comes to hand, sheet music, fiddle bows, sweets, flowers. 'Will they ever grow up?' Calum grins, brushing petals from his jacket. 'Anyway, if their aged fingers make the odd mistake, you'll forgive them! Just this once!'

Murdo cuffs Calum on the ear. There are tears in both their eyes.

Alec Stenhouse turns to Mairi. Her eyes are shining. Goodness, thinks Alec, she's as beautiful as Effie, better. Maybe..

'Isn't he wonderful?'

'Calum? Yes, he's good with an audience,' says Alec, invariably truthful, though a little depressed. So his earlier notion had been right, Calum and Mairi do have an understanding.

'He's more than that,' says Mairi.

Alec considers this. Mairi is right, but he is too. Calum managed the audience well. That's a definite, separate talent. His performance, even before he plays, has been nothing short of masterly. No one on the island will dare call him a coward after tonight. The genius of it, Alec thinks, the sincerity, the spontaneity. He must get to know Calum better. Calum could be a friend worth having. He has an intellect, an open mind. And he plays. Maybe they could swap tunes. Maybe they could play together.

Calum raises his bow, and the first tune flows, ineffably sad. Alec can hear and feel the sea in it, he's on that boat, rocking on those tireless waves, unpredictable, edged with danger. It's a romantic passage, resonant with loss, with the inevitability of life and death, the clash of steel on water. And Mairi's in his arms, floating. Alec's as near happiness as he's ever been. They sail the crowded floor, caught in the flow, the tune.

Calum raises his bow and Iain, till that moment immobile, springs to life. He must have this dance with Mairi. What right has Alec Stenhouse to usurp his position, deny his opportunity, perhaps his last chance for months, to waltz with her?

He turns his head, looks quickly round the hall, assessing the few remaining unpartnered girls. There's Peggy MacLean, sitting wistful by the door. Peggy has a skin that's never yet grown out of freckles, never will, though she spends a fortune trying to bleach them. Her hair's too red, her nose too thin. She's too thin altogether. Too tall. Not beautiful. But she'll have to do. Iain smiles, catching her eye.

Peggy is astounded when Iain marches up to her, coerces her on to the floor. She accepts, intrigued. But he isn't good at dancing. He stands on her toes twice when his rhythm falters. Manfully, she takes the blame.

'Sorry, Iain..'

'It was nothing, nothing at all. Don't worry. You'll get better at it.'

Peggy tries to start a conversation. 'Have you enjoyed the dance? Hasn't it been a lovely evening? When are you off to France?'

Iain doesn't answer. He's preoccupied, staring wildly round the hall, trying to locate Mairi – ah! There she is. Abruptly, he changes direction, swinging Peggy round so roughly that she stumbles, stands on his toes, grinding them with her heel.

Her eyes narrow, almost to slits. What is Iain up to? She finds out soon enough. Having pushed her round the hall in such confusion that they barely hear the tune – the tune Calum specially dedicated to him – Iain abandons Peggy and marches up to Alec.

Calum raises his bow. Mairi turns to Alec Stenhouse, this steady red-haired boy she does not really know.

She's glad Alec seems preoccupied as they waft round the hall. She finds the music unbearably beautiful. She couldn't speak. It's sad, so sad. 'The Dark Ship' has the darkness of the psalms in it, the restless waves, and slanted sunlight, sparkling on the foam. Alec's a good dancer, surprisingly good. Mairi doesn't have to steer him, can follow his unobtrusive lead, drifting with the moment.

Calum nods to his father. The band fades gently into silence as the second waltz, Mairi's waltz, begins. Calum plays with all his soul, his heart, his disappointment, all his frustrated youth, and sensuality; he plays the tune for Mairi, with love.

As the band fades gently into silence, Iain abandons Peggy, taps Alec on the shoulder.

'My dance, I think.'

Alec, unprepared for this assault, stands meekly to one side as Iain waltzes off with Mairi. He sees the blue silk skirt flutter, shimmer in the crowd. He has the briefest view of Mairi's radiant expression as she stares towards the stage, to Calum. Turning, he meets Peggy's amusement. Alec shrugs, bows. 'Would you care to dance?' he asks.

Peggy smiles.

Calum nods to his father. The tune has changed into a happier yearning; Calum's second tune, and what a tune it is, going straight to the heart of you. Mairi is not sure what's happening. Alec, somehow, has disappeared. She couldn't say who her new partner is, has eyes for none but Calum. She can see him scanning the dancers, looking for her; Mairi knows he's looking for her. When their eyes meet she smiles, slowly. She knows the tune's secret name. She knows Calum's heart song.

Iain swings her round, sweeps her smartly round the floor, round the hall to the music of Calum's love. Everyone is smiling.

'Isn't Calum wonderful?'

'What did you say?'

Mairi looks up, noticing Iain for the first time. How strange, but everything is strange. She shakes her head. 'I said, isn't this a wonderful tune?'

Iain nods, 'Not bad.'

'Och, Iain, you're a Philistine. How did you like your tune?'

'I didn't hear it,' says Iain. 'Don't tell Calum. His tunes all sound the same to me. Hear one, you've heard them all.'

He's lying. Mairi frowns. 'Iain, why should you be jealous? You've never been jealous of Calum.'

Iain laughs, 'Don't you believe it!'

Calum can relax now, as the band take on the tune and play with it. His father's melodeon makes it sound different, almost French. The whole town is circling below him, a kaleidoscope of colour and uniform and love.

There's Mairi and Iain, of course, he keeps his eye on them almost without realising it. They're a well-matched couple, physically, Mairi's brown hair contrasting well with Iain's tow.

Alec Stenhouse, having been outflanked by Iain, looks perfectly animated with his new partner, deep in conversation till he looks in Peggy's eyes and stops mid-phrase. Calum nearly laughs out loud. He's seen this happen time and time again. He knows Peggy's eyes – quite the most unusual mix, one blue, one greenish, laced with rust. Alec stares deep into them, as if he'll never stop.

And Ewan MacLeod is dancing with his new wife, holding her so tight it looks as if he fears she'll slip away, be lost for ever. Mairi was right. There's something wrong with Ewan. He's lost his youth somehow, seems tired, ancient, as if the age of the whole world had settled just on him. John-Angus, on the other hand, steered across the floor now by his mother, appears truly happy for the first time that night, while she, sweeping the town hall floor in navy silk, radiates love and joy.

Calum keeps coming back to Mairi, Mairi and Iain. Mairi, whom he loves; Iain his friend, his best friend in the world. Calum is suddenly aware of just how much he loves them, loves them all, the swirling mass of dancers, his whole small world.

He sighs, closes his eyes, plays on.

DI-SATHUIRNE
(Saturday)

*

FRIDAY 2nd JUNE
(or is it Saturday morning?)

When is a waltz not a waltz? When it's a love song. I hope you're lying awake, thinking of me, as I'm thinking about you. It's so bright tonight, it won't get dark; it's nearly the longest day. The longest day, the shortest night – the shortest night.

I skipped home from the dance. Aunt Anna thought it very odd, kept telling me a young lady does not behave like that, but Effie and I were both so happy! We said it was the moon. Was there a moon? I don't remember. It was too bright to see. I'm not going to write any more, except, Effie told me Ewan's new wife Myra is going to stay in Edinburgh – imagine that – with her family, when Ewan goes back overseas. It won't be like being married at all! And after the war, it means Ewan will likely go to the city to live, won't come back to the island. It will break his mother's heart. It's just as well she's got John-Angus. He was always her favourite. Ewan knows that. He always seemed glad about it.

Effie was not best pleased when Alec Stenhouse danced with Peggy, seemed to get on with her very well. But that's not fair. I told Effie she can't be possessive about all the young men, only the one she's promised to marry. Effie sighed. Peggy's very taking, she said. It was not a compliment.

I told her I thought Alec was a sensible boy, and a lovely dancer too, much better than Iain, who pulls you round the floor like a sack of potatoes. A boy who looks as good as that should be more gentle surely? I said that to Effie. She shook her head, said Iain always got his own way far too easily, and some of his methods were reprehensible. That's the word she used. She obviously enjoyed saying it, rolling the syllables around.

'Mairi! You should have been up ages ago. What are you doing?'

'Coming!'

Mairi stuffs the journal in the middle drawer, under all the socks and vests tossed in there for darning. She checks her reflection in the dressing-table mirror, leans right up to it, pursing her lips. They won't stop smiling, twitch up into a smile again the minute she stops. Does she look as different as she feels? It seems to her she's glowing; even where the mirror's tarnished, there's a kind of light, a hushed excitement her work dress cannot cover. She secures the coiled plait at her neck with a couple of extra hairpins. That's better. Her hair at least looks serious. Trying to look suitably morning-solemn, she turns away, hurries down the stair.

These summer days, the light can be as bright at seven in the morning as at midday the rest of the year. That's when it strikes the pink stained glass at the top of the stair window, splashing into the hall, filling it with rosy brightness. Mairi plunges through, sails into the dining-room where her mother sits waiting.

'Not before time, my girl. If you can't get up more quickly, we'll have to stop these dances. Life is not all play.'

'Good morning, Mother,' Mairi takes her place at the table. 'Is father away already?'

'Not up yet. He and Alec Murray had a dram last night. I don't think we'll see your father at the shop before midday.'

'That's not like him.'

Mairi can't remember when her father ever missed an hour's work, except for funerals.

'That wild boy of Alec's has joined up,' Maisie sniffs. 'They went to wet the baby's head! Their expression, not mine!'

'What a daft way to put it,' Mairi smiles. 'Odd.'

'My view precisely,' Maisie sniffs again. 'Say the grace, Mairi. Then I'll ring for porridge.' Mairi clasps her hands on her lap, lowers her eyes.

'For what we are about to receive, may the Lord make us

truly thankful. For Christ's sake, Amen.' She shivers. It's never struck her what that prayer could mean. It's about food, yes, but suddenly it seems she could be praying to be grateful for everything, anything, even crumbs, even hunger. It would almost make you feel guilty to be happy. She shivers again. Maisie sniffs, rings the bell.

'Are you cold, Mairi? I think we should still have the fire on these mornings,' she nods. 'It's your father's idea that we shouldn't have it, not mine.'

The door from the kitchen opens now and Kirsty comes in backwards, bent under a tray of porridge and eggs and toast that is almost as big as herself. She swings round slowly.

'Good morning, Madam. Good morning, Miss,' she recites, as Maisie's taught her. 'It's a lovely morning.'

'Good morning, Kirsty,' Maisie nods. 'Just pop the things over on the sideboard. Mairi will get us what we need while you bring in the tea.'

'Good morning, Kirsty,' Mairi raises her eyebrows. 'Did you sleep well last night? Are you feeling better? Over the migraine?'

'Thank you, Miss,' Kirsty nods. 'The headache's gone. I still feel that bit sick, though.'

'I'm sure it will settle soon,' says Mairi. 'These things take a day or two. I'll come and get the tea if you're not feeling up to it.'

'Thank you, Miss.'

Kirsty bobs a curtsy, slips out of the room. Mairi stands up and makes for the sideboard.

'Porridge?' she asks.

'No,' Maisie sighs. 'Just a poached egg and some toast, please, dear.'

Mairi hands her a plate. 'I'll go and get that tea.'

The kitchen's in a state of unusual disorder and Kirsty's nowhere to be seen. The kettle's boiling briskly on the stove and the teapot stands warming on the hotplate. Mairi fetches a stool and stretches up to the high mantelpiece at the ingle for the black japanned caddy they've kept their tea in ever since she can remember. The convoluted shapes of the gold-traced trees and bushes still fascinate; and the fleeing lovers running before the mandarin's whip. When she was a child she couldn't understand the story, wondered why anyone ever thought it suitable for plate or tea caddy. The transformation of the star-crossed lovers into doves still did not seem to her a happy ending.

She measures out three spoons of tea, and one more for the pot, lifts the wide stove-kettle, fills the pot with spitting water, but cannot find the teapot lid. She's casting around the kitchen for it, scanning all the likely corners, when Kirsty trails in miserably, ill and pale. The teapot lid is in her left hand.

'Just what I was looking for!' smiles Mairi. 'Kirsty, how clever of you.'

'Sorry, Miss. I felt sick again, and when I went outside for air I forgot to leave this on the table.'

'Don't worry.' Mairi looks at Kirsty carefully. 'You look awful. I think you should go back to bed.'

'Oh no, Miss.'

'Call me Mairi. You know we're the same age.'

'I can't do that, Miss. Your mother – Madam – wouldn't like it.'

'I know she seems strict, Kirsty, but she'll understand. Anybody can get ill. You just need time to get over it.'

'I'm not going to bed, Miss. This'll pass. It's just the morning sickness.'

'Morning sickness?'

'Yes, Miss.' Kirsty's eyes fill with tears. 'I'm that way. I'm going home today to tell my mother. My father will kill me.'

The bell rings peremptorily.

'That's my mother wanting tea. Sit down, Kirsty. Stay there. I'll be right back.'

Mairi carries the brown breakfast pot into the dining-room.

'Where have you been? What took you all this time?'

'The cat's had an accident. I'm clearing up.'

'Where's Kirsty? I don't know what's got into that girl lately. Be sure you wash your hands well, when you're finished. And come and have your breakfast!'

49

THE DARK SHIP ANNE MACLEOD

Maisie pushes her plate of egg and toast aside as the kitchen door swings shut. Mairi's obviously lying. But there's something wrong with Kirsty, that's been clear for weeks. Mairi may find it easier to gain her confidence.

When Mairi comes back into the kitchen, she finds Kirsty sitting in the old deal chair. She still seems very pale. She looks up at Mairi.

'Didn't Madam wonder..?'

'Don't worry about my mother,' Mairi smiles. 'She's never awake in the mornings. That's why she sounds so cross.' She reaches for the smaller teapot. 'Have you had your breakfast?'

'No,' Kirsty shakes her head. 'I can't bear to eat. It's more than enough cooking the kippers for your father – I hate it – leaves me sick all morning. I'd been hoping it would go away, was all imagination.'

'Do you think you could manage toast?'

By the time the girls have finished tea and toast and butter, there's a little more colour in Kirsty's face, Mairi leans towards her, over the table.

'So let me get this right, Kirsty. You've been sick and weak in the mornings. For weeks. And you think you're *that way*.'

'Yes, Miss.' The girl looks wretched.

Mairi smiles, kindly. 'I don't think you've anything to worry about, you know. That's not how consumption starts.'

'No, Miss, I know,' says Kirsty, bursting into tears. 'It's not consumption I'm worried about. I don't have consumption, I'm pregnant, don't you see? That's what's making me sick every blessed morning in life, and my breasts as hard as turnips. I'm expecting a baby.'

'No,' Mairi comes round the table now and puts her arm round the sobbing girl, who turns away from her, moves over to the window. 'You can't be! You're not married, Kirsty.'

Kirsty's bitterness cannot be hidden any longer. 'Amn't I the one that knows it! You're just a baby yourself, for all you say we're the same age. You don't have to be married to make babies.'

Mairi flushes, bites her lip, embarassed.

'It's where your body leads you,' Kirsty sighs. 'The flesh is weak.. oh, they'll tell you they'll be careful, that you won't get caught.. but it's all a game to them, and it's the woman's left holding the permanent end of the deal.. the baby! How I wish I'd never seen the lights of Stornoway!'

'Kirsty,' Mairi's struggling, out of her depth, 'what are you going to do? What about the father?'

'I'm going home to Harris, have to talk to my mother. As for the father, I don't suppose he'll want to know.'

'But surely,' Mairi stammers, 'he'll want to marry you?'

Kirsty blows her nose. 'I shouldn't think so, Miss. His parents wouldn't have it. They're too rich. Anyway, he's a soldier, going to France next week. And he's already,' she sobs hoarsely, 'engaged to be married.'

'Kirsty!' Mairi can't believe her ears. 'It's never Angus?'

'He wasn't engaged at the start, Miss! He says he loves me.'

Mairi stares into the summer garden, lost. Outside, it's a perfect day. The roses by the garden wall have just come into bloom, and the dew lies heavy on those bushes in the shade, drenching the spiders' webs. They look uncannily beautiful. And there are so many of them – yellow and pink and red-red roses for love. Her mother's proud of them. Poor Effie picked a big bunch of those very roses last week – the day of her engagement. What if Effie should find out? And really, Mairi thinks, she has to find out, has to know. Marriage is a serious business.

What was Angus thinking of? And Kirsty – where can Kirsty go? Before last night Mairi would not have known, would not have understood how such a thing could happen, how Kirsty could allow herself to let it. Now she stands perplexed, gazing beyond the roses, scarcely hearing the Harris girl's quiet sobbing. She shakes her head, all too conscious of the joy that has been bubbling in herself all night, all morning.

'What will I do?' groans Kirsty.

Mairi answers firmly. 'We'll have to tell my mother. She'll know what's best.'

'No, Miss, please don't.'

'Don't *what*?'

Both girls start at Maisie's low voice, close behind them. How long she's been standing there is hard to say.

By the time Mairi sets out, alone, to open the shop, Maisie has the problem well in hand. She's sent Kirsty to lie down with a cool, minted cloth across her swollen eyes. Aeneas is groaning in the dining-room facing a switched egg with Worcester sauce and goodness knows what other bitter horrors in it. He'd never reach the end, it seemed, of Maisie's talents. One note has been dispatched, by hand, to Angus, asking him to call on Aeneas at eleven; another to the doctor, asking for a home consultation, urgently.

'Why don't we leave talking to the young lad till the doctor's been, my love? There may be nothing in it.'

'Aeneas,' Maisie groans, 'let's hope poor Kirsty is mistaken. That would be wonderful, make the rest of her life much, much easier; but think! This has happened to a girl under our roof, in our protection, a girl as young as your own daughter. How would you be feeling if it was Mairi sobbing her heart out upstairs?'

'But it's nothing to do with us!'

'Aeneas, does your sister Anna have a living husband?'

'You know she doesn't.' Aeneas's head is going round in circles. Talk about morning sickness, he feels dizzy now, and sick.

'Drink,' says Maisie. 'I've no sympathy for you. None at all. You're not ill; you brought this on yourself.'

'It's the smell of those kippers.'

'They were cooked for you, and at your own request. As I was saying, does Anna have another brother?'

'You know she doesn't. What is this all about, Maisie?'

'This boy, this incontinent boy, may or may not have left poor Kirsty pregnant, but whether or not he has, there can be no doubt he's been making up to the poor girl at the very same time as he's been courting your fatherless niece!'

'What do you want me to do about it? Call him out?'

'Don't be flippant. You need to let him know that's no way to behave!'

Aeneas is more awake now. He pulls himself together, downs the unfortunate concoction and feels better for it.

'Eggs and bacon next,' says Maisie, producing them. 'You'll not feel right till teatime, I warn you.'

'Maisie, where did you learn all this?'

'I had uncles in service. I'd hate to think you might turn into even a shadow of the drunken fools they cared for!'

Aeneas pays attention to his breakfast. By the time he's finished, his head is almost clear. 'Many another person,' he says, 'would blame the girl.'

Maisie frowns. 'The Johnsons may. I'm not sure. But they'll have to support the child.'

'What if the boy denies it?'

'Then we'll send Kirsty to Edinburgh, to my sister Esther. She can have the child away from prying eyes and, if she wants, come home.. a war-widow.'

Aeneas nods. 'She wouldn't have a pension.'

'We'd have to help out, in that case. But a bonnie girl like Kirsty, working in Edinburgh..'

Aeneas nods again. Another thought strikes him. 'Maisie, where did they..?'

'In our shed. She'd leave the side gate open and he'd slip in when we were all off to bed.'

'Good God! And we didn't ever notice!'

*   *   *

Iain has walked out to the Big House. He and Angus are planning a last day's fishing, over towards Callanish. Angus is still at breakfast as Iain arrives, and is ushered in to the breakfast room, which faces south and east and is full of sunlight. This is the smallest public room in the Big House, but it's larger than the croft Iain's parents brought five children up in. The Johnsons know Iain well. Though Angus went away to school in Edinburgh, he spent his summer months in Lewis, striking up a friendship with Iain when both acted as beaters for his father one Glorious

Twelfth. For Angus, the day was a bit of fun; for Iain's family it represented necessary income.

'Will you join us?' asks Colonel Johnson.

'I don't mind if I do. My mother's been that busy round the croft this morning, she hasn't had time to boil a kettle!'

'Is your father ill?' Mrs Johnson enquires, kindly.

'Goodness, no!' laughs Iain, accepting a plate of bacon, eggs, black pudding. 'He's indisposed but not ill, no, not ill.. he and Aeneas MacDonald broached a bottle of whisky last night to celebrate my enlistment.'

'A civilised enough practice,' Colonel Johnson smiles.

'It would have been if they'd left it there! But they finished it at one sitting, and what do they do then but break open another! And finish that!'

'Aeneas is not a drinker, I think,' says Colonel Johnson.

'Not at all,' his wife assures him.

'Neither is my father,' says Iain, laughing till the tears begin to roll down his cheeks, 'but they definitely polished off the second bottle too. And what does my father say this morning when he wakes with a head like a tumbled fank?' They wait, as Iain gains enough control to finish. 'He says, we'd have been all right, you know, if we'd been drinking malt! Son, never drink any whisky if it's not the best! Let this be a warning to you!'

'I've heard that said before,' Mrs Johnson smiles at her husband, 'but I'm mentioning no names.'

'It's a universal truth. We can take it, Iain, that your army career has been energetically and correctly blessed!'

'I think, Sir, the blessing's still in progress!' Iain laughs. 'Hair of the dog!' and the Johnsons and their butler, who has now entered the dining-room, all join in discretely.

'Excuse me, Sir,' the butler bows to Angus, 'this has been delivered for you. Apparently an answer is expected.'

'Thank you, Bates,' Angus takes the note. 'What on earth?' He reads the signature and laughs. 'Talk of the devil! It's from Aeneas.'

'I expect he wants you to settle your account before you sail?' drawls his father.

Angus scans the note.

'I'm sorry, Iain. Our fishing trip will have to be delayed. Maybe this afternoon? I've business to settle in the town.'

Angus has become noticeably pale. His father and mother, busy with their copious mail, seem not to see. Iain looks away. When Angus stands, he stands up too.

'I'll walk you into town.'

*   *   *

Calum does not usually go in to the office on a Saturday, but yesterday he had been so upset he did no useful work, and next week's *Oran* must be fully typeset by Monday evening. He knows he'll waste hours on Monday too, seeing off the boat that will carry Iain and the boys over to the mainland. If he doesn't get things in hand today, he'll be lost. He has to do it somehow.

The day of emotion yesterday turned out to be! And today – nothing. He feels completely numb.

As Iain said last night when they sat on the pier and watched the summer lack of night merging into day, it's as well you have your male friends. Men can't be friends with women. It's physiologically impossible. 'But men,' continued Iain, putting his arm round Calum's shoulders, 'men can be trusted, utterly. That's why I want to show you something, Calum, old pal. Come with me.'

'I'm going home, Iain, and you should too,' said Calum, sleepy by that time. He wanted to get home, just to lie in bed, thinking about Mairi. 'S'alright. S'on the way,' said Iain. 'You don't have to go out of your way. But.. you have to stay very quiet!' He put his finger to his lips. 'Very quiet! Shh. Don't make any noise!'

'Iain, you're drunk. Let's get you home.'

Calum stands up, his fiddle under his arm. 'Come on, old fellow. Home!'

'Follow me!' Iain whispered, staggering along the quay.

Calum was worried Iain might fall. Quite worried. Maybe not as worried as he'd have been if he hadn't had that half-bottle of whisky, if he hadn't been sailing on a restless tide of unrequited love. Not that he thought at the time it was unrequited. No, at the time he thought Mairi was certainly his own – the way she'd smiled at him as he played – the way she came up to him at the end of the dance, and took his hand and told him how wonderful his tunes were. She was pulled away by her cousin Effie, but her eyes said all the things he wanted to know. It had seemed truly perfect.

But when Iain stopped outside the MacDonalds' garden and said, 'Listen!' and they'd pressed their ears to the painted wood of the large garden shed, and heard..

..heard breathlessness, and sea-sounds and low male laughter and female moaning, wordless but ecstatic.

..and later, Iain long gone, and Calum, in dense shadow, marking Angus's careful, sinister exit.

..and rage and disappointment and jealousy strumming Calum with a resonance he'd never imagined possible.. *Mairi*..

He slid away, broken, careless of the notebook he'd left behind, filled with scraps of musical notation – only the last of these had a title scrawled above it – 'Mairi's Waltz'.

Calum sat dry-eyed on the pier as the new day grew more beautiful, dawn's pink fingers winnowing the remnants of the night. He resented this. How could nature be so out of tune with his despair?

He thought about drowning himself then, wondered how a drowning death would feel, the wide seas flooding in, the light dissolving; the body floating where it must, marrying the tide, cast up, unidentifiable, on some rocky shore. He could almost feel the sand in his mouth, in his hair, his bloated hands stretching, yearning for oblivion.

She'd be sorry. She'd know then what love was all about. They'd all know, all of them, how deep it had run with him.

He thought about darkness, light; how light, like love, like anger, never dies, but ricochets into a final illusion of darkness, of peace.

He thought about his love for Mairi. Gone. All gone.

It had been a day of bitter understanding.

At six o'clock he limped home, weary.

There is a great deal to be said for the comfort of routine. As Calum aches around the office, checking text, setting type, his tired mind relaxes, just a little. He is surprised at how much he's done already, how relatively little remains for him to do. He stops around eleven, thinks about making tea, then remembers he has not as yet had breakfast. He's hungry now he's remembered the possibility. Perhaps he's not as lovesick as all that – how can you be starving with a broken heart? Calum sighs. Perhaps he's shallow after all. Perhaps he's frozen. He shuts the office, wanders across the road.

As he crosses into the shade, he sees, in the distance, two clearly recognisable figures; the one broad-shouldered, of medium build, tow-haired; the other tall and slight, diffident. Even their strides indicate their differing personalities: Iain's confident, brash; Angus's neat but somehow halting. And he does halt abruptly, nods to Iain, and knocks on the door they've now reached. Aeneas MacDonald, grave and courteous as always, answers the door himself, shows Angus in.

Calum is not anxious to meet Iain at this moment: he particularly does not want to know the private business that brings Angus to Aeneas's door at that unusual hour, when Aeneas should have been at work. Feeling faint, rather sick, and with his heart thumping so loud he can hear nothing else, Calum dodges quickly into the teashop. He does not, therefore, see Iain skulking round the side wall of the MacDonalds' house, trying to look casual. He does not see Iain jumping quickly over that same wall, creeping round the house to the side window of the parlour, where he crouches, craning to catch the sober conversation on-going within. He does not see Alec Stenhouse, standing across the road from Iain, watching his antics with distaste, but not amazement. Nor does Calum see Mairi sitting at the only table in the teashop with any vacant space until he's thrown himself, breathless, into the remaining seat.

'Calum!' Just the one word. Calum glows, reaches towards her, then stops, remembering.

'How can you speak to me?' he hisses. 'How can you do

that? What about Effie? What about your cousin, eh?'

'What about my cousin?' Mairi blushes. How can Calum know?

'You know well enough what I'm meaning. Bitch.' The venom in his tone is unmistakable. Calum struggles to his feet, storms out of the teashop, leaving Mairi in tears and Peggy MacLean (who is sitting at the same table) mystified. Mairi dashes out of the shop after him, grabs his arm.

'Calum.. what's wrong with you today? What's happened?'

'I know all about your cousin's fiancé!'

'That's nothing to do with you, Calum. Nothing to do with us.'

'There isn't an us,' shouts Calum, unable to believe she could be so disingenuous – the Mairi he's known all these years! Such an able liar.. to sound so innocent when he knew.. what he knew. 'What kind of woman are you?' He shouts so loud the whole street can hear. 'What kind of a family do you come from? Leave me alone, Mairi. Don't come any nearer – or I won't be responsible for my actions.'

Mairi shakes her head, unable to take it all in. Calum turns his back, limps painfully away. He does not look back, does not see her slump against the wall in anguish. Between tears and rage, he finds himself back at the office before he realises he's left his wallet on the table in the teashop.

Peggy MacLean, with a front-row view of all the fun, finds it most interesting, as she says to Alec when he comes, at last, into the shop. She's been there for an hour with one scone and the one cup of tea, waiting for him. She's seen him there often on a Saturday. Seonaid has been watching Peggy's genteel antics with that scone with increasing frustration. Saturday's her busy day. Seonaid sees Calum's wallet too, sees Peggy stretch across the table surreptitiously to lift it. She steps smartly in.

'Thank you, Peggy. I'll make sure he gets that!' She tucks the wallet in her apron pocket, smiling. 'What else would you like to order?'

'Another cup of tea,' says Peggy, innocent and sweet.

Seonaid, just as sweetly, take Peggy's cup away and leaves it on the counter while she fulfils all the other orders in the shop, muttering to the cook, 'If you can't beat them, make them wait. That's my motto.'

'You'll not beat that one. Them as pays the piper..'

'That would be alright if she'd pay! If she'd order! She's keeping out good business.'

'Right enough, June's a busy month.'

Peggy's perfectly aware of Seonaid's gambit; she would have done the same, and rather earlier in the day. With Alec's entrance, Peggy becomes much less languid. He's younger than her, she knows that, but after all, he's in the bank, will be a great man one day, or at least, comfortably off. And he won't have to coarsen his hands working at sea or on the croft.

Peggy's phobia about calloused skin goes back to an incident in a byre when she was thirteen, newly pubescent. Her mother's second husband had followed her one day into the musty darkness. Peggy had the milking stool in one hand, the milk pail in the other. She was small, but she could kick.

She left the village that day, coming up to the town, where she stayed with an aunt and went into service. She's had several posts, achieving excellent references in every one. Now she works in the hotel, in reception. You meet a lot of people in reception, hear everything that's going on. She's known who Alec was since his first day on the island.

'D'ye mind if I join ye?'

'Be my guest,' Peggy smiles. 'Lovely to see you again.'

Alec smiles. Seonaid bustles up, 'Same as usual, Alec? Anything more for you?' her tone is noticeably business-like when she addresses Peggy.

Peggy smiles. 'I'll just share Alec's pot of tea.'

'I'm no' having tea, sorry, Peggy.'

'Oh.. I'll have a fresh cup, then.'

'I'll pop it on your first bill,' says Seonaid, smoothly. Peggy waits, but Alec does not offer to pay.

When it comes, the tea is scalding. Alec is, however, pleased with his cocoa, inches thick with beaten cream.

'Just like my mother gies me,' he twinkles, 'tae feed me up.'

'You could do with feeding up!'

Peggy's cheeks are aching with her strenuous effort to continue the polite, interested smile; she thinks, not for the first time, that men have it too easy. And they're thick. Alec doesn't seem remotely interested when she tells him about Calum's outburst.

'Of course,' she adds, 'it's all round the town that there's been goings-on in the MacDonalds' shed.. Angus Johnson visiting after midnight..'

'Effie's fiancé?'

'The very one.'

'And Mairi?'

'No. Of course not. It's that maid of theirs, that Kirsty! Nice girl, but no head on her, no sense at all. She probably thinks he loves her.'

Alec struggles to conceal his interest.

Peggy's disappointed with his neutral response. He returns to his cocoa, doesn't even shrug. It leaves a creamy moustache on his upper lip. She knows, suddenly, he's just a boy, more stupid than she'd thought; but she can't bear not to share with him one final nugget.

'And,' she says, 'this morning the doctor paid an urgent call to the MacDonalds'; and Mr and Mrs MacDonald aren't in the shop.'

'They're ill? I'm sorry tae hear o' that.'

'No,' snaps Peggy. 'They're fine. It's the maid that's ill.'

'That's a shame,' says Alec, going back to his cocoa. He's enjoying this game.

'No,' says Peggy. 'Kirsty isn't ill; at least.. Stupid man! Can't you put two and two together? And they let you work in the bank! Seonaid! I'll need to go. I'll have that bill now.'

The shop seems very peaceful when she's gone. Alec sits another five minutes at the table, going round and round it all, working out the possible ramifications in a town as small as

Stornoway. If it's anything like home, no good will come of this, no matter how things fall out.

He remembers a wee red-haired lass from Portessie, put in the family way by the under-manager of the bank at Buckie. The man's wife went into a decline. The fellow enlisted, and was killed last year at Loos. And the quine? No one ever heard of her again, least of all her family, who'd forbidden her to ever darken their door. A fishing family. Religious.

Alec often thinks of her, though he can't remember her name. He wishes he could remember it; wishes her, somehow, well. Still, he brightens now, Effie may break off her engagement, if this news becomes official as it no doubt will; and, though it will be a blow for Effie, he'll be in Stornoway for months.

'It's an ill-wind, Alec, my loon,' he sighs, 'an ill-wind.'

'Alec.'

Seonaid's standing at the table now.

'Will you do me a favour and take this wallet round to Calum Morrison, this bag of sandwiches too? He didn't order them, but I know they're his favourite sort. He forgot the wallet.. he was a bit.. upset.'

'Aye,' says Alec. 'Where will I find him?'

'At the *Oran* office. He went off in that direction anyway.'

Alec's no sooner gone than she takes off her apron, nodding to the cook.

'Mind the tables while I'm gone.'

She crosses the road to the MacDonalds. Luckily, it's quiet.

'Where is she?' she asks young Colin who is standing behind the men's counter. Gormless, Seonaid thinks. He could be sorting out those shirts, pricing things, dusting. But no, he's standing with his arms folded.

'Through the back,' he nods. 'She's..'

'Yes, I know,' says Seonaid. 'I'm here to put the kettle on. Watch the shop now, lad. You'd best sort out those shirts. I saw Mr MacDonald in the street. He may be here at any moment.'

Seonaid has the satisfaction of seeing Colin leap into action.

*   *   *

May can be a lovely month in Lewis, and Myra MacLeod, arriving with her husband of two weeks, seemed to bring the sun with her. A city girl, she's used to rural life. She has relatives in Glenurquart and visited there often in childhood. It has always been one of her favourite places.

Walking up to Innis Teallach from the cart that dropped them in Bunloit was something she looked forward to, year after year. The track to her grandfather's cottage on the lower slopes of Meall Fuar-mhonaidh was nothing more than rutted earth, fenced by birch and mountain ash. In spring there would be bluebells, primroses in plenty; in summer foxgloves lanced the growing bracken, and harebells and speedwell nestled at the edges of the path. Wild garlic grew in one place, a secret place by the splashing burn, and in another corner, her mother showed her wild orchids. As a child, Myra thought that fairies must live in this delicate wood; the adult Myra knew it for an enchanted place, protected by benevolent spirits.

The cottage itself sat further up, where the wood gave way to hillside, a fine cottage, two up, two down, with a wooden scullery at the back, and a large, productive vegetable garden in the lee of the house, bounded by a drystone wall her grandfather had built himself. It was rather grand as cottages go, befitting the status of head-keeper.

There was even a small piano in the unused, polished parlour and two neat bedrooms upstairs in the eaves, with rosy wallpaper and samplers of religious text above the brass beds quilted in grandmother's fine patchwork.

'I'll never know,' Myra said to Ewan, 'how they got the piano up there – it was bad enough carting flour and sugar in the summer drought – those huge bags, and the road so soggy, even then.'

'Maybe they took it in winter when the ground was frozen hard?'

'I never thought of that,' said Myra. 'They'd have needed a

regiment of horses any other time. Mud's powerful stuff.'

Ewan thought of the struggles he'd had shifting guns in mud, remembered Hay, in that last work-party; a small man, rather thin, who sank into the mud in a communication trench – the mud came right up over his thighs – it had taken four men levering with rifles to get him out, and Hay lost his boots. He borrowed a pair from a German corpse, saying *Thank you, friend* respectfully.

'In winter,' said Ewan, 'it would be easy enough.'

He worried that Myra might find his home backward and uncivilised; his mother impossible. But Myra was charmed with the wide Lewis skies, the profusion of flowers on the machair: the brown moors were no starker than the mountain slopes she loved. And the croft with its earth-floor worn by use to a polished surface, its stove and home-made dresser, and particularly the box bed in the parlour that was theirs for the duration of their stay – the croft delighted her.

She proved more than able, too, in her dealings with her mother-in-law, even when they were packing for John-Angus.

'Do you think he needs anything else? What about a compass? You always need a compass in a tricky situation.'

'No, mother,' Ewan sighs.

'Buy one,' says Myra. 'You never know.'

'What about a camp kettle?'

'Too much to carry,' Myra shakes her head.

'A first aid kit?'

'That's in the pack.'

'You're a good girl, Myra,' Sine MacLeod takes her daughter-in-law's hand, squeezes it. 'You're a comfort, and no mistake. I was worried when I heard Ewan was married that you might be one of those hard city girls. But you might have come from Breasclete. You've got the eyes.'

Ewan smiles at Myra. 'There's no greater compliment, from another daughter of that township.'

'Don't be blathering the hind legs off a donkey, Ewan. You were always that talkative.'

'Mother, I never got a word in edgeways!'

Sine turns to Myra. 'You've been good for him and no mistake. He never used to answer back!'

Ewan blushes. Myra takes his hand and squeezes it. His gentleness, his monumental, silent, gentleness is the thing she most loves in him.

The first time she saw Ewan, he was lying in his bed at the end of the ward, watching the dressings trolley roll inexorably towards him, his own fear palpable and growing rapidly, when the young lad next to him started screaming, screaming. It was almost unbearable, terrifying for them all.

Before Ewan came, the poor lad would scream before and through the dressing process, and for ages afterward, till the morphia took hold, sent him to sleep. But Ewan reached across the short space between their beds and took the young lad's hand. It steadied him. The screaming gave way to a whimper. Ewan did that every day, twice a day, till the boy died, though he himself had suffered severe abdominal lacerations and the stretching caused great pain. Myra had never seen tenderness like it.

'The constitution of an ox!' the doctor said. 'That's why he's still alive.'

'The constitution and the brain,' laughed Dulcie, the other VAD on Myra's ward. Dulcie and Myra had been working together since their first day on the wards. They'd laughed together, wept together, often and often.

'Don't be slick,' said Myra now. 'How did he survive, then, if he'd no brain? How come he's got the Military Cross?'

'O-oh,' said Dulcie, 'sounds to me like somebody's on the verge of becoming a bull-worshipper! I wasn't denying his heart, Myra, or any other bull-like capabilities!'

'You and your mythology,' laughed Myra. 'You're appalling! You should have stayed at university, my girl. There's no room for mythology in these four walls, not between five am and midnight, anyway.'

'I'm not so sure. Do you never think,' Dulcie's tone grew

more serious, 'we're re-enacting Troy? An ancient battle waged over enclosing walls?'

'I think we'll change your name to Cassandra!'

'I'd quite fancy that. Cassandra..' Dulcie tried the name, experimented with it.

'You daft thing! This war's dug in trenches, Dulcie. And they don't use champions. And if we'd only their heels to worry about, wouldn't that be fine?'

'You don't think these men are champions?'

'They're heroic,' Myra nodded. 'But..'

'I've had enough of this,' said the doctor standing up. 'You'll be calling them Ulysses before I know it. I'll die of jealousy. I don't want to be Agamemnon or Priam, and Paris isn't the place it was. Come on, Dulcie, we'd best finish that ward-round now.'

Dulcie raised her eyebrows, handed Myra both teacups, and flounced away.

'They're heroic,' said Myra softly. 'Victims often are.'

*   *   *

Ewan's sleep is erratic. He keeps waking in the dugout, the three week bombardment nearly at an end. The waiting is difficult – waiting is bad enough at any time, worse when you're hunched in a trench, shells winging over and around you. But the hardest bit will come when the waiting ends, for all the talk of good shows, of dancing on Fosse Eight. Ewan knows instinctively the tactics are wrong. They've been wrong every time: he's been here before.

The stand-to call. Breakfast, bacon and egg.

The silence of the forty minute gas discharge – the panic of the RE gasmen when they find their spanners misfit.

Dead calm, what gas they managed to discharge drifting back towards the Allied line; the German parapets blazing oily cotton, a barrier to the so-called accessory.

Movement along Fountain Alley to Hohenzollern impeded by stretcher-bearers, the wounded and the dead; even prisoners.

Rum.

The steady march up the sandbag staircase.

The parapet. Bullets.

Kilted figures blossoming in mud.

Ewan keeps moving slowly. 'Spread out. Easy on the left,' he calls.

No one answers.

*   *   *

Myra dresses quickly, rubbing the sleep from her eyes. She didn't sleep well at all, has been dozing since three, when she became aware of Ewan's absence. She'd been too tired to register his restlessness after the dance, his slight increasing wheeze. She fell asleep early, dreaming of the operating theatre; of Dulcie and the surgeon working with rapt concentration.

In her dream the theatre was packed, but not with students; the seats full of elderly men in city suits and generals' uniforms. There were women too, young women for the most part, dropping white feathers from the highest seats. The theatre was slowly filling up with feathers. They stuck to the surgeon and Dulcie too, where blood had splashed their operating gowns. With their stooping posture and precise elbow movements, they began more and more to resemble large white birds. Bleeding birds.

They were using chloroform, Myra was relieved to see. The soldier-patients were not so happy. Marched into the theatre in uniform and laid out on the table, they shrank in horror from the mask, the dropped liquid.

Not gas!

Dulcie removed boots and socks from each successive patient, rolling the trouser legs up almost to the knee before she helped the doctor to position the legs for the operation.

'Such a good idea of yours,' the doctor laughed. 'Don't know why we didn't think of it before. Fritz won't have anything like this!'

Myra watched mystified as Dulcie and the surgeon cut

through skin and sinew and bone, removing both heels from every soldier in the hospital, leaving the opened wounds to gape and red blood to flow freely into the gutter below the table, and right across the room.

'Now they're invincible!' Dulcie smiled, satisfied, as one by one the dying men were carried on stretchers back outside the hospital, and left there in their thousands below a huge sign as high as the Scott Monument proclaiming FRONT in blood-red lettering.

*   *   *

At five, Myra hears her mother in law get up and set the fire in the stove but when she comes through, the kitchen is empty. Sine sits in the byre, milking the second cow, wearing a shabby jacket that must, from its size, have belonged to Ewan. She glances up at Myra, smiling,

'Ciamar a ha uth? Have you come to practise milking? The trick is to wear Ewan's jacket. He always did the milking, and these foolish animals think I'm him when I've got it on. They behave better. Go and make yourself a stròbag of tea. I'm nearly finished here.'

'Mother, have you seen Ewan?'

'No,' Sine pauses. 'Is he not still in bed then?'

'He was breathless,' says Myra. 'Gets a touch of asthma. Since the gas.'

'It was a sticky night, right enough. He'll probably be off up the hill, if I know Ewan. He'll likely be hungry when he gets back. I'll make extra porridge.'

Myra finds John-Angus is sitting at the back of the byre apparently lost in contemplation of the sea. He's so different from Ewan in colouring, but his posture and mannerisms are unnervingly similar.

'Tell me,' she asks, 'where might Ewan go, if he were needing air and exercise?'

John-Angus smiles, considers.

'To the shore, maybe. Or maybe to the hill.'
'Show me. Please.'
There's an edge of worry in her voice.
'We'll try the shore first.'

*   *   *

Ewan cowers in a shell-hole, wheezing as quietly as he can, ignoring circling seagulls, twittering larks. He can't afford to move. If he disturbs the birds, he'll draw attention, forfeit meagre cover.

If he can make that next deserted trench he'll be safe; all he has to do is lie here, still and quiet, till the sun goes down enough for him to risk crawling back.

For the moment he lies flat, to fool the snipers.

*   *   *

Such a beautiful day. Folk in town who are not working are out admiring the unclouded sky, sitting at their doors, or working at fences and gardens more often drenched than cultivated. Effie, drifting towards her aunt's house, admiring Maisie's garden rich with hebe and mahonia, starred with potentilla, cannot believe her eyes when she sees a pair of navy trousers sticking out from the fuschia below the parlour window. As she comes closer, she distinguishes a pair of boots and a shock of tow hair that can only belong to Iain Murray.

'What on earth are you doing, Iain? Are you mad? Don't answer that. There won't be anyone in you know, but Kirsty. They'll all be at the shop. You know that fine! And that's not the door. It's the parlour window.'

Effie walks across the grass towards Iain who does not seem to have heard her. 'Speak up, man! Is it drunk you are? Did you not get home last night? That's hardly a bed of roses you've found there!'

'I'm not asleep,' hisses Iain. 'Go away Effie.. God, no.. Effie!'

He blanches, tumbles over into the fuchsia, discovering the

68

spiky nature of last year's cut-back growth.

'Is it drunk you are?' Effie says again.

'Shh..' Iain raises his finger to his lips, falling back again in the process, back against the sharp fuchsia canes.

'Why should I be quiet? Tell me right now what you're up to! If this is one of your convoluted dramas, I'm having none of it! This is my aunt's garden!' Effie's voice, never quiet, echoes through the MacDonald house. Maisie, standing in the hall in case Kirsty is called for, opens the front door quietly, glides across to Effie. She betrays no surprise at finding Iain crouching by the wall.

'I wouldn't sit there if I were you,' she says. 'That's where the toms do what they have to. Can't you smell it?'

'He can't speak,' says Effie. 'He's been struck dumb!'

'Not before time. Some reprobates, like children, should be seen and not heard! What on earth are you doing there, Iain?'

'I.. um.. was spinning a coin,' stammers Iain, going on more smoothly, 'for luck you know.. but it slipped out of my hand. Landed in this bush, though I can't see it anywhere. Still, if you find a half-sovereign when you're weeding hereabouts you'll know it's mine.'

'Powerful spinning,' says Maisie.

'Sovereign, eh?' Effie says. 'Iain Murray, you were up to no good! Hanging round folk's gardens when they're out at work!'

'Half-sovereign,' says Iain, glowering at Effie. 'If you find it Mrs MacDonald, you'll pass it on to my mother, please.'

He gets up stiffly, flushed with anger, sidles from the garden without another word, aware that Angus must have heard the whole thing. Oh well. He'll have to stick to the story of the lost half-sovereign.

Maisie turns to Effie with as natural an expression as she can muster. 'Did you want me, lass?' she asks. 'Were you coming in?'

'No. I wasn't expecting to find you here. I only came by to drop in Mairi's cameo, the one I borrowed last night.' She hands it to her aunt, who seems, she thinks, a little distracted this morning.

Maisie takes the brooch, nodding, 'You're a good child, Effie. Run along, then.'

'Aunt Maisie!' Effie cries, 'I'm sixteen, look! I'm all grown up!' She can't suppress the shout of laughter.

Maisie sighs. 'I'm getting too old, Effie. Blind.'

Relieved to see Effie off the premises, she goes back into the hall. The voices from the parlour continue, solemn and quiet; it's impossible to make out what is being said. After a few moments, Maisie hears Aeneas's footsteps moving towards the door; Angus's too. She ducks into the dining-room, out of sight, though she herself still retains a clear view down the hall towards the door.

Aeneas is angry. Maisie can detect it in the tense lie of his shoulders, the set of his head. Angus, on the other hand, seems defiant, leaves the house without a word. The men do not shake hands.

So that's the way of it. Maisie sighs. How will Kirsty manage now? She is most definitely pregnant; the doctor left no doubt, was very clear about it.

'An unfortunate business. And the father?'

'We don't know yet if he'll acknowledge the child.'

'When the whole town knows Angus Johnson has been meeting the lass nightly in your outhouse, denial is not that strong a defence,' Dr Smith sighed.

'It's as rife as that?'

'I'm afraid so, Maisie. The rumours have been current for weeks.'

'I wish they'd reached me, then.' Maisie suddenly looked tired, felt her age.

'Ah,' said Dr Smith, 'but that's the way of rumours, isn't it?'

'Yes. Well, thank you for your help.'

'She's a strong girl. She'll be fine. Don't worry. Are you going to send her home?'

'That's what she wants. They're a good family, of course. I did offer to send her to my sister in Edinburgh, but Kirsty's keen to go back to her village, and I don't know that isn't all for the best. You need your family with you at a time like this.'

'She's from Harris, isn't she? She said she has brothers in the Navy.'

'Yes,' said Maisie.

'They'll be glad of that baby yet, you mark my words.'

'You're right, doctor. A baby brings its own love.'

Aeneas stands on the door step, watching Angus's insolently casual progress down the path and back along the road. Angus is striding directly into the sun, his pale eyes watering, his face working with anger. For a common tradesman to reproach him – him! A mere draper! If Aeneas weren't so old, he would have hit him. He's conscious now of the older man's eyes boring deep into the back of his skull. He holds his head up, swaggers slightly.

If Aeneas tells his father..

No, he won't do that. No proof. And anyway, he'll be away on Monday. They have no evidence. They can't touch him.

Maisie moves into the now-grey hall, waiting for Aeneas. She stands in shadow thinking she prefers the hall in morning light. When the sun has swung this high, the rose windows no longer blossom, and the fashionable wallpaper seems dark, too heavy, unalleviated. Maybe Mairi's right. Maybe they should paint the wall plain white, though that would show the dirt, and might feel cold in winter. Still, light and air, that's what they want.

'What did you say?'

Aeneas, passing, must have caught her thinking out loud.

'You'll like it,' she says. 'Re-decorating.'

'Not again. Is Mairi not coming home for her meal?'

'I was expecting her, but maybe she's gone out with Effie.'

'Do you think we should get a telephone? I've been thinking..'

'Oh, Aeneas, we'd get no peace at home. For the shop, perhaps.'

'We should think about it.'

'Not that you need a telephone on the island for news to get about.' Mairi sighs, 'Doctor Smith tells me the whole town knew of Kirsty's midnight assignations.'

'It would be more surprising if they didn't.'

Maisie stares at the cameo she's still holding in her fingers, a likeness of her Glaswegian grandmother. She's never liked it, never found it it lucky, but Mairi is very fond of it, calls it her family heirloom.

She looks up at Aeneas, shrugs, 'How are we going to break it to Anna?'

Anna storms into the kitchen some fifteen minutes later. Her normally resolute face is dark with rage. She stands at the door, breathless.

'Well! Maisie, Aeneas, have you thrown that scarlet hussy out on the street?'

'No,' says Maisie. She'd like to hug Anna, but this is not the moment; better to let the rage run its course. 'Aeneas,' she goes on, 'is, however, going to take her home this afternoon, if you sit quietly and don't give him indigestion. Will you have some tea, Anna?'

She turns to the dresser, stretching towards the Royal Albert china she knows Anna particularly likes.

'What are you thinking of?' Anna fairly screams. 'That low conniving creature has ruined my Effie's happiness, and you're *taking her home*? That's what family means to you?'

'It's more than it meant to Angus,' says Aeneas drily. 'Sit down, Anna. He's denied responsibility.'

Anna sits down, stunned. 'So he's not..'

'I didn't say that. I said he's denied responsibility.'

'Well, that'll be the truth then.' Anna's faith in Angus is totally restored. She has wanted the story refuted. Better that than..

'Frankly,' Aeneas frowns, 'I wouldn't trust that young man's word on anything.'

'How can you say that, Aeneas?' Anna is outraged at her brother's lack of loyalty. 'The boy's engaged to your niece!'

'That doesn't make him honest.'

'You've never said that before!'

'I've never before been in the position to know the truth on a subject he's been lying about.'

'How can you say these things?' Anna's temper is rising;

Maisie can see it in the set of her eyebrows.

'That young man,' Aeneas says, 'could lie the hind legs off a donkey with chilling plausibility.'

'Anna, here's your tea. Milk? Sugar?' Maisie passes the cup smoothly across the table, then leaves brother and sister together, slipping quietly upstairs.

She finds Kirsty leaning over the attic stair, listening. 'What on earth are you doing there? You're supposed to be resting.'

'Oh, Madam,' Kirsty sobs into her handkerchief, 'I feel terrible. I've made everyone so angry.'

'Don't worry,' says Maisie. 'It'll pass.'

Her tone is matter-of-fact. She might, thinks Kirsty, have been talking about the weather, or a childhood illness. This irritates her slightly. Maisie does not seem to notice, but rattles on, 'Now, can I help you with that box? I've looked out some of Mairi's old baby things for you. Doctor Smith says you'll be fine. He's a good doctor, wise. He knows.'

She slips several baby gowns in neat tissue wrapping, two shawls and a selection of knitted boots and caps and mitts into the box.

'There. I hope we'll be able to close it.' Maisie smiles at the girl, at the pinched, wan face, still blotched by the morning's tears, 'I'm glad you'll have your mother with you, Kirsty. That's the thing I missed most when I found myself pregnant on the island.'

'Did you, Madam?' Kirsty affects interest, thinking it's like an adult to assume their experience relevant to any situation. She braces herself for the details.

Maisie, her hands still on the tiny garments, can't believe she's talking about this: she's never said a word to anyone, not in all these years. She feels a measure of kinship with Kirsty. She knows in her heart she'll never really belong here on the island; it's not her landscape, though she's made the best of it, for Aeneas's sake.

'I had my husband, of course,' she says, 'but no one else I was close to. I felt so alone, a complete outsider. It's not easy to get beyond that.'

Kirsty says nothing, stops listening: all she can think of is

Angus, his rich, smooth skin, the weight of him that first time.. even last night..

'I wasn't actually alone; people were kind in their way. And I wasn't well either, couldn't work, missed the shop. And men don't really.. you can't talk to them the same, can you, about the things you're frightened of, the changes in your body you know will happen, but don't expect..' Maisie shakes her head. 'No, you've chosen well, Kirsty. Go home to your mother and face the future openly and try to forget all about Angus Johnson.'

'He was just a dream,' says Kirsty, looking at her hands, turning them over, the skin so dry and sore, the painful hacks that crease the finger joints. 'Can you imagine me in the big house with hands like these?'

Maisie tries to change the subject. 'Have you a young man in Harris?'

'Yes,' says Kirsty, brightening. 'Donnie. Well, he's in France. I haven't heard from him in six months.'

'Ah,' Maisie's tone is non-committal.

'He's not missing,' Kirsty says quickly. 'Nothing like that. He's not much of a writer. Sends the occasional postcard. But what a piper!' She breaks off now, suddenly distressed. 'Madam, do you think I'm all those things she said?'

'I beg your pardon?'

'A hussy. A scarlet hussy. A low conniving creature.'

'Of course not. That's nonsense,' Maisie frowns. 'Anna's hurt for Effie; more than that, she's angry that her own judgment of Angus proved so wrong. But a lot of folk will blame you, Kirsty, small places are like that. You'll just have to close your ears, let it all flow over you, like rain off a gull's wing. Don't get too upset, for the baby's sake.'

'I know the minister won't like it. Nor my father either. It's a pity Angus wouldn't..'

'Kirsty, try not to dwell on that. It's not a possibility. But you're a strong and healthy girl, and you're a mother now. Think of the child. That's the most important thing.'

Maisie hears the front door slamming. 'Sounds like the coast is clear. I'll go down and get Aeneas to lift your box down the stairs. You get your hat on, dear, and.. let me give you some advice. Keep your head down, Kirsty. Just get on with life. Try not to pay too much attention to what people say. Sticks and stones.. you know. The things folk say need not affect you. It'll all work out, believe me.'

'Oh, Madam. They'll all be that disappointed and angry!'

'Not for long, Kirsty. You're a good girl, a great wee worker. We'd have you back any time. You must keep in touch with us, you know. Now,' Maisie hands the girl a white cardboard box, 'this is for you. I ordered it for your Christmas present, but you must take it now.'

'Can I open it?'

'Go ahead.'

Kirsty lifts the tight-fitting lid to find a dressingtable set, hairbrush, comb, mirror. If she'd been marrying Angus, she thinks, living at the big house, she'd have had a set like this in silver. Or gold. She pretends delight.

'Even a clothes brush! Oh, Madam. I've never seen the like! Thank you. I'm so sorry, Madam.'

'Don't be sorry, Kirsty, just enjoy it.'

*   *   *

The shop is humming busily when Maisie gets there at half-past two that afternoon. Mairi is subdued and a little pale. Effie has not been in, nor Anna. Maisie does not discuss the morning's business, even in the back shop. Too many ears, and actually, they're far too busy. Maisie wonders cynically if the scandal has brought the whole town to the shop, looking for news. That's a shade on the defensive side, she knows, dismissing the thought. The shop is busy because it's suddenly summer and people suddenly need the summer things they never thought they'd use, so never bought.

In the brief opportunity they have for tea that afternoon, she can't resist teasing Mairi. 'What did you make of the Joyce then?'

Mairi colours up.

'Cardiff, indeed'

'I never said that! I never said travel book either!'

'You and that father of yours must think I'm daft. Or blind! But he's an interesting writer all the same, the Joyce fellow,' says Maisie. 'Not that I read the book thoroughly in the two free minutes I had in the kitchen this morning.'

'Did I leave it in the kitchen?' Mairi frowns.

'Someone did. In the omelette pan. Which was luckily clean. I found it when I was making your father's breakfast'.

'I thought it was in my bedroom.'

'You thought wrong. I don't know if the library like their books omeletted. Or smelling of kippers.'

Mairi changes the subject.

'How's his head?'

'Improving, I hope. Do you know,' Maisie laughs, 'what he said to me? He said it wouldn't have been so bad if he'd been drinking malt! What idiots men are!'

'Idiots,' echoes Mairi, falling back into the silence she's wrapped herself in most of the day.

She cannot understand the change in Calum. The business about Kirsty is upsetting, certainly, but it hardly explains his reaction. He's never seemed all that religious, or bound by convention. And even if he were, the matter doesn't affect them.

'By the way, Mairi,' Maisie says, 'that Iain Murray..'

'Iain? What about him?'

'I'll explain later,' Maisie nods, ending the conversation, sweeping out of the back shop as the doorbell rings and a customer comes in.

'Good afternoon, Alec. What can we do for you?' Maisie stands behind the glass-topped counter, sun slanting through the skylight, haloing her still-bright hair. She likes Alec, favours him with one of her rare smiles. He blushes, thinking that Mairi's mother looks like one of the stained glass angels in Inverness Cathedral. Ethereal. Too pale.

'I wanted Mairi, actually,' he blushes again. 'Wondered if she might be able to step across the road and tak a cup of tea wi' me?'

'We're short-handed this afternoon,' says Maisie. 'Colin had to get off early for a family funeral. Go and have a word with her though – she's through the back, sorting stock.'

'Thank you,' Alec nods.

'And maybe you could tot up the invoices while you're there,' says Maisie. 'Make yourself useful. Just joking!' she adds hastily, as Alec's eyebrows hit the sky.

He stops dead, a slow smile spreading across his face. 'Got me there,' he laughs. 'Nae many folk manage that!'

Telling Calum about it later, he is still incredulous. 'I never thocht Mrs MacDonald wid hae a sense o' humour..'

'Why on earth not?'

'Well, jist.. at that age.. ye ken..'

For now, he slips behind the counter and passes through the heavy curtain into the stockroom where Mairi is unpacking a huge box of shirts, checking numbers and prices, and ticking off received stock on the order list.

She looks up from the shirts she's checking. 'Hello, Alec. Fancy one of these? Just the thing for the bank.' The shirt she's holding up is blue with alternating narrow and broad white strips and a stiff little stand-up collar.

'Weel, I ken the boss would go for the stripes all richt,' nods Alec, 'an the tight wee collar. But I'm nae sure it's my shade, exactly.'

'It is,' Mairi assures him. 'But if you're not happy with the style there's no point.' She puts the pinned shirt back into its cardboard box. 'These are quite expensive, though they are hard-wearing. You've probably got plenty of shirts.'

'D'ye really think it would suit me?'

'No doubt about it. Look, I'll show you the trick. Not many people know this. Come over here, Alec.' She beckons him over to the window, handing him a large hand mirror. 'If you want to tell if a colour's right for you, all you have to do is look at it in a mirror in natural light.'

She gives him one of the blue shirts now. Alec holds the shirt in one hand, the mirror in the other and waves his arms wildly, trying to catch the shirt's reflection in the mirror, wondering what she's on about. It's clear as mud to him. Mairi's bent double, laughing at his efforts.

'No, don't look at *the shirt* in the mirror! You have to hold it against your skin, see? Hold it below your chin so it's the main colour reflected on your face and in your eyes. Look at them. If your eyes shine, it suits you. See? That colour's great. But if you wore a sharp white shirt like this,' she says, handing one to him, 'you'd look ill, a bit off-colour. See the difference?'

'Fancy that,' says Alec, intrigued. 'I'll tak ane o' these blue anes, Mairi.'

'We may not have your size.'

'Aye, you do. Look! There's ane.'

He stretches over, lifting a shirt from the pile Mairi has just checked.

'Well,' she says, 'I think you must be quite the ideal customer! Coming into the back shop and serving yourself.'

'There's ane or twa shops in America that work along those principles,' Alec nods. 'I dinna fancy it, mysel. Half the fun o' shopping is the craic.'

'It might catch on,' says Mairi. 'Dafter things have.'

'Name one!'

'Moving pictures.'

'Mairi, they're brilliant! Hae ye never been?'

'No. I'd like to, though. Charlie Chaplin.'

'Chaplin, eh? Off to America an' didnae come back tae join up! Ye ken fit they sing aboot him in the army?'

'No.'

'I winna sing it all – it goes..

The moon shines bright on Charlie Chaplin
His boots are cracking for want o' blackin
and his little baggy trousers they want mending
before we send him tae the Dardanelles..'

'You've a fine voice, Alec. Where did you hear that?'

'My brother Bob telt it me. Some o' the troops are really scathin' aboot the wee mannie. But I dinna really blame the loon for stayin' awa'. Think o' a' the good his films dae cheerin' folk up. Scots abroad, eh? Wha's like us? Whit we dinna get up to!'

Mairi sighs, puts the mirror back in the drawer.

'Aye, like kites and telephones.'

'Sorry, Mairi, I dinna understand.'

Mairi doesn't understand either, but she needs to keep Alec talking. Alec was there last night when she sat close to Calum, happy. Seonaid said it would all come right, if it was meant. If it was real. Mairi knew it was real. Had been. Her voice runs on.

'My father's cousin works for Alexander Graham Bell.. He's Scottish, you know, the fellow who invented the telephone.'

'Aye, I ken the name.'

She can see he's mystified. No wonder.

'And Bell spends every summer in Cape Breton. That's in Nova Scotia.'

'I ken whaur it is, aye.'

She's warming to the story now. 'Well, Hamish – he emigrated nearly twenty years ago – lives on Bell's estate near Baddeck. And the folk that live there thought Bell had lost it altogether.. this really rich man, famous scientist and all, spent all his time playing with kites.. for twenty years he played with kites, more and more complex, bigger and bigger; kites big enough to lift a man! Some of them were that big it took three or four men to hold them down! Just imagine,' says Mairi, her face lighting up at the thought of it, 'flocks of enormous red silk kites soaring over the Bras d'Or lakes! It was beautiful, but no one had the least notion of what on earth the man was actually doing. The estate workers had decided – in fact, Alec, they were perfectly sure – he had run mad till he built his first flying machine. Then they saw he'd been working towards that all along.'

'I remember now,' says Alec. 'He wisnae the first to fly. I've read aboot this. But he invented some *aileron* thing, a loose bittie o' wing that shoogles in the wind tae stabilise the whole clanjamfrie. Is that no' richt? An' abody uses it.. all thae planes in France an a'.'

'I don't know about that,' says Mairi, frowning at the

thought of France. 'I never heard of that. But Hamish has another story about Bell – how he really loves children.'

'Oh?'

'Whenever children come round to his house – it's called Beinn Bhreagh – beautiful mountain – and they go all the time, because Bell and his wife encourage them, he stops work and talks to them for ages, even the very youngest of them, listening to them and answering every one of their questions. And one of the scientists asked Bell one day why he bothered with the children when they were such an interruption to his important experiments.'

'And why did he, Mairi? I dinna understand that mysel'.'

'Bell shook his head and said the day he stopped listening to children and their questions about the world, and *in particular* any questions on the current project, he would lose all possibility of fresh new thought; because only children ask the unexpected questions. He said you always learn from children if you listen properly. Their minds are open. The rest of us all think the way we're told to. We're automatons. Like soldiers in a battle.'

'Gosh,' says Alec. 'Strange, eh? Aye weel, maybe the man's got something there.. D'ye no think, though, Mairi,' Alec pauses, gathering his thoughts, 'that thinkin' in straight lines is a protection? It's hard tae go against the flood. Folk that thinks for themselves hiv a difficult time overcomin' convention.'

'You and Leonardo both!' Mairi laughs. She's feeling better. It's the first time she's felt happy since..

Alec blushes. 'I'll be off then. I'll pay through by,' he says, absentmindedly. 'Och, michty me, Mairi, I near forgot. I'd forget my heid if it wisnae attached to my neck.'

He rummages in his pocket. 'I'm tae gie this tae ye.' He holds out an envelope, pushes it into Mairi's hands and fairly dashes out.

Mairi, laughing at his sudden shyness, wonders what the note can possibly say.

When Alec comes out of the back shop with a shirt, Maisie

laughs.

'It's an expensive business.'

'What is?' Alec's fumbling in his pocket for money.

'Kitting yourself out in the modern style.'

'Oh,' says Alec, 'aye. Thank you, Mrs MacDonald.'

Even his ears have gone bright red.

It seems to take forever for his shirt to be parcelled up appropriately; but he's pleased with it. And that's a good tip Mairi's given him. She's a right nice lass. If there'd been anything about Effie she wanted to say, she would have come straight out with it. Maybe there's no news. Maybe Mairi doesn't know.

He crosses the road, sauntering back into the teashop. Seonaid laughs. 'We're seeing a lot of you today.'

'Must be your birthday!'

'That's my present, is it?'

'No, a new shirt for the bank.'

'I didn't know banks wore shirts.'

'Very funny.'

Alec sits down at the table he vacated twenty minutes earlier.

'What did she say?' asks Calum. 'Did you give it to her?'

Alec looks at him and sighs.

'What a sight you are, Calum. Did ye nae comb your hair the day? Look at your tie! It's bloody catastrophic!'

'Never mind my hair. What did she say?'

'You'll hae to be patient, Calum. Man, ye're older than me, ye should ken a' this! Gie it *time*. And no, she didnae read the letter when I wis there. How would she?'

'Why would she not come over, then? Did you tell her I was here?'

'They were busy. That Colin's off this afternoon.'

'Right enough. I saw him leave.'

'And no, I didnae mention you. Not at all,' says Alec pouring a cup of tea. 'It wisnae appropriate.'

'Then what on earth were you doing all that time?'

'Buying a shirt. Talking. Aboot telephones. Aeroplanes.'

'That'll be right.'

'Calum, you're through-other. You need fresh air, an early nicht.'

'Are you middle-aged, or what?'

'We could start wi' a walk. After tea. Or maybe,' Alec blushes now, stops suddenly.

'Maybe what?'

'Maybe I could bring my fiddle over to yours and we could play a bittie?'

'I didn't know you played? Great! Come and eat with us.'

'I would, but Mrs Harper would kill me.'

'Eat you alive, more like.'

'Young man, you're talking about my aunt!' Seonaid frowns. 'She wouldn't do that to one of her lodgers! No,' Seonaid shakes her head, 'not her. She'd roast them first. She's an educated woman!'

'I never said she wasn't!'

'Come after your meal,' says Calum. 'We'll have a real ceilidh. I could fair be doing with it.'

Calum stares out of the window across the road to the MacDonalds' shop. His face is pale, his eyes dark-ringed. He never looks that well at the best of times, but unhappy as he is now he looks, thinks Alec, like a consumptive poet. Seonaid, at the counter, looking at both boys, thinks they could do with feeding up.

'It's a dreadful thing,' Alec says, 'the love.'

Seonaid and Calum sigh agreement, staring into nowhere, wistfully reviewing past incursions.

'Aye, there's nae logic in it.' Alec sips his tea. 'Hey, Seonaid, any mair sugar?'

*   *   *

'So what would you like?'

Mairi and Maisie are walking home, having tidied the shop and locked everything away for the Sabbath.

'Och,' says Maisie, 'I'm not hungry. Bread and cheese, cold

meat. Scones. Will that not do? Your father won't be back till late and I'm sure the minister will be round.'

'Why?'

'He'll have heard about Kirsty. He'll want to know what's happening.'

'What is happening?'

Mairi has been wondering about Kirsty all afternoon, all through the gathering heat, a sticky, heavy heat. They don't get much thunder on the island, but this feels like thunder, almost.

'She's gone home,' says Maisie. 'Your father took her back this afternoon in the car. She decided that would be better than Edinburgh. They'll not be so cross at her when they see her arrive like that.'

'How was she?'

'Oh, bearing up. It won't be easy for her, you know. The family is that devout. And it such a small village.'

'And Angus?'

'Denies everything. Flatly.' Maisie wrinkles her nose. 'When even the doctor knew he'd been visiting her in the shed every night. People will probably say,' she says, 'I make my maid sleep in the shed!'

'You'll just have to laugh it off!'

'They won't say it to my face. Don't be daft.'

'Poor Kirsty.'

Maisie yawns. 'I'm sorry, Mairi. Could you get the tea? I need a nap if I'm to cope with the minister.'

'Aye, he's heavy going.'

'Mairi! At least you can make the tea and slip away. He'd probably prefer that. He'd be embarrassed to say too much in front of you.'

'I'd better stay then,' Mairi laughs. 'There I go again!'

'What do you mean?'

'Volunteering for an hour or more of lugubrious nothing. How do you manage to make me do it?'

'Me?' says Maisie. 'Didn't open my mouth. But we need to have a talk, Mairi. Not necessarily tonight.'

'What about?'

'I think the correct term is Reproduction. Don't, whatever you do, tell Anna. If she's still talking to us,' Maisie says as they swing the front door open. 'She'll want you married off before the week is out, you and Effie both, wild rascals that you are.'

'I heard that bit already.'

'I know you did; the tray was chinking away as you danced up and down with rage in the hall!'

'I never did!'

'Ha!'

In the quiet of her own house, Maisie cannot any longer fight the exhaustion that's been dogging her all afternoon.

'I must sit down, Mairi, before I fall down. Go and put the kettle – no – wait a minute,' she stops, taking her daughter's arm. 'What do you think of this? That Murray boy, that precious Iain, was skulking outside the parlour window this morning when your father talked to Angus.'

'What?'

'He was crouched behind a shrub, trying to hide and listen in! Would you credit it? If Effie hadn't come by and seen him..'

'Effie? No!'

'She was outside, Mairi. I don't think she knew we had Angus in here. Angus could hear *her*, though, and Iain. Your father says Iain's voice gave him quite a start. I'm thinking they'll not be quite so close after today.'

'I can't believe it.'

'That young man is bad news, Mairi.'

'That's what Effie says. I don't understand. Angus is supposed to be his friend.'

Maisie yawns. 'Well, with friends like that.. I'm sorry, Mairi. I'm about done. I need to put my feet up. Wake me in fifteen minutes, will you?'

The hall is cool, pleasant, after the humid pressure of the street. Maisie flops into the leather chair beside the fireplace, asleep before her head touches the anti-macassar. Mairi bends to kiss her forehead, then slips outside. She has not yet read the letter in her pocket.

Late in the afternoon she'd taken out the envelope, and been shocked to find Calum's writing, not Alec's. She'd assumed the note was one for her to pass on to Effie, or something about Effie (Alec is smitten, anyone can tell); but Calum's clear handwriting has burned a hole in her pocket and her equanimity all the rest of that hot afternoon. What does he have to say? If it's more of the same..

She'd rather not open the letter, for how will it prove otherwise? How can he have changed again? She scans the envelope, holding it against the light for clues; the sky offers none, grown overcast, purpling. Mairi stuffs the letter back in her pocket and wanders through the steamy garden, dead-heading roses, tossing limp petals in an old lop-sided trug. He loves me, he loves me not. She counts the dead-heads on each bush. Sometimes he loves her; sometimes she has to steal a dead-head from another bush, count that. She knows it for foolishness, all the same.

The first drops of rain begin to fall as Mairi reaches the far end of the garden. The roses are all tidied now, but she hasn't had time to clear the pansies. She'll do those tomorrow. Pansies are like roses in this: if you pull the dead-heads off, they flower more and longer.

And the rain is getting heavier, great wet drops slashing her face, leaving the cotton of her white shirt shining pink, transparent. As she scuttles back to the house Mairi notices the side-gate swinging open, catches a flash of red across the lane, at the corner of the Mayhews' garden.

People shouldn't drop rubbish in the street, she thinks. But this doesn't look like rubbish, it's a book, an exercise book, somehow trapped within the neighbours' hedge. She wonders if one of the Mayhew children hasn't lost it. That's possible. They may be worrying about it. Mairi slips across the lane and works the book free from its trap of wire and thorn, which takes a little ingenuity. By the time she's rescued it and run back into the house, she's soaked to the skin. The book is frankly drookit.

The cover sits awkwardly on rumpled pages, some of its red

dye in the act of seeping through the white, giving every sheet a deckled, blood-stained look. There's no name on the outside. The pages are filled with scraps of musical notation, makeshift clefs, in pencil. The only words, scribbled on the last page, above a sketched-out tune, are 'Mairi's Waltz'.

How did this come to be here? Her fingers tremble slightly as they trace the pattern on the dripping page. 'Mairi's Waltz'. She cannot read the music, but she has some knowledge of the theory, a notion of the shape of it: moreover, she remembers, all too clearly, the tune that Calum played, the tune she thought she'd lost.

Mairi sets the book on the dresser to dry, spreading the pages as best she can. She must read Calum's note now. No point in putting it off. Delay won't make the message any better, or harder. She takes a deep breath, pulls the letter from her wringing pocket.

The envelope is sodden, the ink gone all awry; the single page is just as bad, a sea of blue inconsequence; she can barely decipher a single word. She squints, looks at it closely. Is that last word *sorry*?

*　　　*　　　*

Myra's out of her mind with worry. They've waited all day and there's no sign of Ewan. He's not on the hill, he's not on the shore. He isn't in any of the nearby houses. She's visited them one by one, a lengthy business as she didn't want to say why she was there, didn't want to raise undue alarm. Sine thinks she's acting oddly, and Myra lets her think it's just the way of a jealous, insecure young wife. Sine understands that, respects it. It makes her feel that Ewan is properly adored. It makes her able to say with the confidence of years, 'He's always been like this, off by himself for ten, twenty hours. He'll come back smiling, never worry.'

At the evening meal, with the rain a deluge, Sine changes her mind.

'He's maybe gone with the boys to the bothan on the moor.'

'What happens there?'

'Ah.'

'The moon shines,' John-Angus smiles.

'Will you take me there, John-Angus?'

'No,' says Sine. 'You can't go there.'

'Calum might go,' John-Angus says. 'If he's not already there.'

'The fiddler? The boy that was playing last night?'

Sine nods.

'Where will we find him?'

'In the town. John-Angus will show you. But look at the rain!'

'You've been out in it all evening.

'I had to see to the animals, look after them.'

'Sine,' says Myra, 'I love you dearly. And your son. I have to see to your son, look after *him*. And I'm used to the country, remember?'

It's three miles to the town, three miles of downpour. Myra and John-Angus are chilled to the bone by the time they reach Calum's door. There's the sound of fiddles playing, and laughter.

'Well, they're in,' says Myra. 'Shall we knock?'

'Knock? What for?' John-Angus opens the door, sails in.

'John-Angus, man, it's you. Are you for a dram? And Myra! Lass! You're wet to the skin! Come by the fire.'

Calum's mother fusses round about them, brings a towel for Myra to dry her face and hands, puts the kettle on for tea.

But Alec senses Myra's panic. The girl is tense, her eyes quite wild.

'Fit's wrong wi ye?' he asks. 'It's mair nor rain.'

Myra nods, clenches her fists, unclenches them.

'We can't find Ewan,' she says in a voice so low so perfectly controlled they all know just how much she's worried. 'He went out last night for air – he gets a bit of asthma, since he got that touch of gas at Loos – and we haven't seen him since. Sine thinks I'm fussing, and I don't want to make a fuss, don't want to cause undue gossip, but I'm very worried.. Ewan gets these nightmares..'

'Where do you think he might have gone?' says Alec.

'His mother suggested a bothy on the moor,' says Myra. 'She thinks there might be some sort of party there?'

'No.' Calum shakes his head. 'We had to move the bothan. Too many new uniforms, what with the Naval Depot. Where else could he be? Has he not just taken off for a bit of space? He was always one for doing that.'

'Calum, we've been married two weeks, for heaven's sake! We haven't had a fight, or anything like that. The dance unsettled him I think, and he woke up in a nightmare, shouting.'

'My brother Bob aye does that,' says Alec. 'Sleepwalks an a'. Ken, the last nicht o' his last leave, we found him in oor neighbour's byre, shouting at the cattle tae march in ordered file! I had tae tak him back tae bed. In the morning he ca'ed me a richt fool, telt me I'd made it a' up!'

Myra smiles at Alec, grateful, turns to Calum. 'You know him best, Calum, and I know he thinks the world of you. Where might he have gone?'

'When we were boys,' says Calum, 'he'd have gone to the boathouse. You've tried there?'

Myra nods.

'And all along the bay?'

'We've tried all the neighbours' houses,' says Myra, 'and the cemetery; he took it hard to miss his grandfather's funeral. He wasn't there. Wasn't anywhere.'

'Drink this cup, lass,' Flora Morrison hands Myra a cup of thick black tea. 'Have you tried the peat bank?'

'No, we never thought of that.'

'He used to spend a lot of time there helping his Grandad, when he was just a young boy. That's where I'd look first. You go, boys. Put your fiddles up for one night. This lass is staying right by me. Bring Ewan back here when you find him. We'll soon get him sorted out.'

It's the voice of authority. Not one of them thinks to question it.

Outside, the sky is almost navy with rain.

'This isnae Lewis weather!' Alec shouts.

'No, there's usually more wind!' Calum laughs.

'Your mother seems awfu' certain we'll get Ewan at the peat.'

Calum shrugs, 'She has a knack.'

'Yes,' John-Angus tells Alec. 'Flora's famous for it. And she's always right.'

*   *   *

Under cover of the growing dusk, Ewan has at last been able to creep out of the shell-hole, wriggling to the nearest trench through grainy, fibrous mud. There are no corpses in it, which is something.

He encounters no threatening fire, though star-shells split the sky, closely followed by the rumble of artillery. Not that close. He seems safe enough.

The trench is long-deserted. Deep enough, but not in good repair, the firestep crumbled. Ewan has no strength to wriggle further; builds it up with clods of earth cut and waiting there. He refaces the parapet too, constructs, if not a funk-hole, a shelter from the downpour. It helps a bit. He doesn't seem to be have been hurt, though all his limbs are aching from lying still so long; his neck is tender too, burned to a cinder by the sun. The rain has not so much cooled his burned skin as inflamed it. His thirst is desperate.

He's lost his emergency rations, but all he has to do is wait. Help will come soon, or perhaps the enemy. He's ready enough. It wouldn't be the first time he'd disarmed a Boche patrol bare-handed. It's a matter of timing.

He doesn't really like the small sound neck-bones make when breaking.

*   *   *

'Are we nae there yet?' A river's flooding Alec's shirt, a river in spate. He's never been so wet. 'It's like the sea an' sky have changed roon'!'

89

'We'll be there soon,' shouts Calum.

'I hope tae goodness he's there.'

'He'll be there.'

'How can you be so sure?'

'Enjoy the walk,' says Calum. 'Like we said, isn't this the perfect Lewis summer?' John-Angus laughs immoderately, tripping over a stone, or maybe his own feet. He does not rise immediately. His pale blue eyes are focused on the skyline. 'Look,' he says, staring at the moor. 'Look at that, eh?'

'What?'

'Over there! Above the bank. That's new. That's not how it used to look.'

'What are you talking about?'

'That funny bump with the hole in it!'

'John-Angus, you're the limit,' says Calum, squinting. 'You're havering. There's nothing there.'

'Na, na. Show me fit ye mean, John-Angus.' Alec gets down on his knees to view the landscape from the lad's perspective. 'Ah, I see fit ye're at,' Alec whistles softly. 'Get doon, Calum. Look. The lad's richt enough. Thon bank is built up – *like a trench*.. I think.. we need tae think aboot this a minutey. Noo, fit will Ewan be thinking? Pit yersel in his place.'

'He'll be looking for friends.. or enemies,' John-Angus says.

Calum shakes his head at this, but Alec nods. 'Ye're richt there, lad, an' nae doot he'll be ready for both as weel. Is there ony way we can get tae the end of that peat-fitever-ye-ca'-it and walk along it?'

'Yes, but it's much farther,' says Calum. 'And it's wet!'

'We need tae go that way. Ewan needs to ken we're friends. Think fit his reaction wid be if he thocht us Boche! Calum, follow John-Angus. Keep yer head weel doon!'

*   *   *

Ewan's more comfortable now he has his grandfather to talk to. The old man brings him whisky from a hollow in the trench. Ewan drinks it gladly.

'Pure peat-water,' he laughs. 'But tell me, how did you end up in a funk-hole, Grandad?'

The old man's smile, as warming as the whisky, spreads across a face less lined, more etched. 'Och, we all end up in one eventually. Except you dug your own and I had mine dug for me.' He sits on the crumbling firestep, knocks his own dram back. 'Are you managing out there, my boy?'

'No. Not really,' says Ewan. 'It's not a possibility. That's not what you're supposed to say, of course. I wouldn't say it to my mother. She thinks it's all red wine and bully beef.'

'Is that what you tell her?'

'What else should I tell her? I'm hungry. Do you think they'll be long relieving us?'

'Hard to say.'

Ewan looks round, disgusted. 'They've fairly let this trench go. What a state. Must have been one of those English regiments; or worse, the Welsh!'

His grandfather laughs. 'That's what they all say. Spread the blame.'

'Shh.. do you hear pipes, Grandad?' Ewan whispers. 'That's a pipe tune! Do you hear them coming down the line? Do you hear them?'

The tune gets nearer. It's voices they hear, Scottish voices, singing, talking, some in Gaelic, some Scots. The three young soldiers who stumble up to Ewan have lost their helmets and are covered in mud. They stand to attention, salute badly. They're a raw bunch, even by trench standards.

'Private Stenhouse reporting, sir. Work Patrol. We've come to tak ye hame.'

Ewan stares at the three boys, salutes slowly. 'March in an orderly fashion, boys. We'll follow.'

'We?'

'Myself and my grandfather here.'

'Begging you pardon, who, sir?'

'No, he's gone. He's gone..'

Ewan stares in disbelief up and down the trench, stands on

the firestep, checks the parapet.

All the way back to Calum's house, his tears merge with the rain. When he sees Flora Morrison, he breaks down completely.

'Come in, my boy, come in. I've something that will help, something you can take back with you.'

She gives him whisky laced with herbs, gives something to them all, though she won't or can't say what it is exactly. Myra lays her head on Ewan's shoulder, comforted by the amber liquid. Alec turns to Calum.

'We'll try the fiddle again next week, eh?'

John-Angus frowns. 'Next week I'll be away, out of the island.'

'In the army, lad,' says Flora. 'Aye, you will. I'll give you something though, for when the big push comes. Put it in your rum. Mind you use it. It'll help.'

John-Angus smiles.

'I'll remember, Flora.'

DI-DOMHNAICH

(Sunday)

Myra's voice is clear as morning light. She lies on her side, facing Ewan who is stretched across the pillows, relaxed. He looks, she thinks, like a figure from one of those Italian paintings from Greek mythology – wouldn't Dulcie laugh at her for thinking that? The white rumpled sheets seem almost as if they've been arranged, draped over well-tuned muscles; the good wide chest, the strong arms capable of anything, everything. She wishes she could draw. There's not a spare ounce of flesh, and yet the size of him.. she'd asked him once how he managed in the trenches, being so tall.

'Och,' he said, 'I just sink deeper in the mud than most.'

His face is in the shadow of the bed-curtain, but he is smiling, at rest. She leans over, kissing his cheek, his forehead, slips her hand across the skin, traversing chest and abdomen, working gently down across the rubric of new-healed scars.

Ewan catches her hand as it brushes the tightly coiled red hair, the tender skin below it.

'Later,' he laughs, 'we'll do that again later. Read the passage for me.'

'You're sure that's what you want?'

Myra's hand is wandering.

'Yes,' says Ewan, firmly. 'I love to hear you read, especially that.'

She kisses his shoulder, props the book against the pillows by his ear.

'No,' says Ewan, 'do it properly.'

She moves the book an inch or two away. Her body moulds itself to his, a perfect fit. They are both conscious of the warmth, the certainty between them. Ewan thinks his heart will overflow with happiness. She reaches over, kissing him again, on the lips, then starts to read.

'In the beginning God created the heaven and the earth,

And the earth was without form and void: and darkness *was* upon the face of the deep; and the Spirit of God moved upon the face of the waters.

And God said, Let there be light: and there was light.

And God saw the light, that *it was* good; and God divided the light from the darkness.'

'We are in the light,' thinks Myra. 'We are not of the darkness.'
'We are of the light,' thinks Ewan. 'We are not in the darkness.'

'And God called the light Day, and the darkness he called Night. And the evening and the morning were the first day.

And God said, Let there be a firmament in the midst of the waters, and let it divide the waters from the waters.

And God made the firmament, and divided the waters which *were* under the firmament from the waters which *were* above the firmament, and it was so.

And God called the firmament Heaven.'

'I've always thought it odd,' says Myra, 'that the sky, the heavens were called the firmament when they're not firm at all.'

'Stop blethering,' says Ewan. 'Read the verses.'

'And the evening and the morning were the second day.

And God said Let the waters under the heaven be gathered together into one place, and let the dry land appear: and it was so.

And God called the dry *land* Earth; and the gathering of the waters called he Seas: and God saw *it was* good.

And God said, Let the earth bring forth grass, the herb-yielding seed, *and* the fruit tree yielding fruit after after its kind, whose seed is in itself, upon the earth: and it was so.

And the earth brought forth grass, *and* herb-yielding seed after his kind, and the tree-yielding fruit whose seed *was* in itself, after his kind: and God saw that *it was* good.

And the evening and the morning were the third day.'

'Don't you wonder what happened to Lewis?' says Ewan. 'What happened to our share of the trees? Eh?'

'Don't interrupt,' Myra pulls the sheet up over her bare shoulder. 'You got more than your fair share of water.'

'Is that a criticism?'

'No. You don't have trees, but look at your skies, look how broad they are. The stars must be wonderful here when it's dark enough to see them. You miss that in the city.'

'I did.'

'Don't I know it! All that moaning about streetlights being so bright you couldn't see Orion.'

'At least they weren't Very lights, as you so helpfully told me!'

It had been their first and only quarrel. Both felt bad about it. Myra stating she could never leave her work, leave the city; Ewan demanding that she must, if she married him. Myra compromised.

'If there was a baby,' she said, 'obviously I'd leave work. And once the war's over, once you're home, then we'll go where you go. Anywhere you want to.'

Ewan, already ashamed of his insistence that she leave, capitulated.

'But they'll all fall in love with you,' he said. 'How could they not?'

'And would I fall in love with them? How could I, when my heart's already stolen by a raving islander who will not give it back to me?'

Ewan changes the subject.

'What about Canada? Would you fancy that?'

Myra turns more on her side, so she can see him as she reads, this man she loves, this man whose life has been overwhelmed by darkness but not quenched by it. That's the difference in him. She had been lost till she met Ewan, lost in the lust and grief of war; now she seems lost in joy.

'And God said Let there be lights in the firmament of the heaven, to divide the day from the night: and let them be for signs, and for seasons, and for days, and years:

And let them be for lights in the firmament of the heaven, to give light upon the earth: and it was so.

And God made two great lights: the greater light to rule the day and the lesser light to rule the night: *he made* the stars also.

And God set them in the firmament of the heaven to give light upon the earth,

And to rule over the day and over the night, and to divide the light from darkness: and God saw that *it was* good.

And the evening and the morning were the fourth day.

'Enough?'

'No.'

Myra nods her head, goes on reading.

'And God said, Let the waters bring forth abundantly the moving creature that hath life, and fowl that may fly above the earth in the open firmament of heaven.

And God created great whales, and every kind of creature that moveth, which the waters brought forth abundantly, after their kind, and every winged fowl, after his kind: and God saw that *it was* good.

And God blessed them, saying, Be fruitful, and multiply, and fill the waters in the seas, and let fowl multiply in the earth.

And the evening and the morning were the fifth day.'

She puts the Bible down. 'You never fancied the sea?'

'Not really.'

'But the fishing's in your blood. Your father's a fisherman.'

'He's a crofter too. John-Angus, you know, is frightened of the water, always has been. I'm not. It's not the sea, really, that I don't like. But I'm of the land, Myra. Even in France, even in mud and chaos, I feel somehow a part of the land – not like the sappers, no; I couldn't tunnel deep into the earth as they do, spend my life in darkness, listening. I don't know quite how else to say this, it's difficult. Just – I'm not afraid of the land, not even the scarred and squandered land of France. It doesn't spook me the way it does some of the boys. I'm at home in its rhythms in a way I could never be in the vastness of the sea.'

Myra clears her throat.

'And God said, Let the earth bring forth the living creature after his kind, cattle and creeping thing, and beast of the earth after his kind: and it was so.

And God made the beast of the earth after his kind, and the cattle after their kind, and everything that creepeth upon earth after his kind: and God saw that *it was* good.'

'I was in a farmyard once,' says Ewan, stroking her arm, 'that was newly in the line of fire. It still had three cows in it. And six shells landed in that farmyard, in quick succession.. they whine, shells.. it's uncanny..'

'I know,' says Myra.

'Well, they call them dumb animals you know, but those three cows hit the dirt *so* fast when they heard the first shell, and didn't move till the lull after the last had fallen. Then they darted off in different directions, all of them. Not so dumb, I tell you!'

'What happened to them after that?'

'Don't know. I expect they ended up on a regimental table.'

Myra laughs.

'And God said, Let us make man in our image, after our likeness; and let them have dominion over the fish of the sea, and over the fowl of the air, and over the cattle, and over all the earth, and over every creeping thing that creepeth upon earth.

So God created man in his *own* image: in the image of God created he him; male and female he created them

– don't tickle, Ewan –

And God blessed them: and God said unto them, Be fruitful, and multiply

Ewan! What are you doing with that hand?'

Myra's voice is softer, darker, but she goes on reading.

'and replenish the earth, and subdue it: and have dominion over the fish of the sea, and over the fowl of the air, and over every living thing that moveth upon the earth.

And God said, Behold I have given you every herb bearing seed which *is* upon the face of all the earth, and every tree, in the which *is* the fruit of a tree-yielding seed: to you it shall be for meat.

'Ewan.'

The voice is no more than a whisper.

'And to every beast of the earth, and to every fowl of the air, and to every thing that creepeth upon the earth, wherein *there is* life, I have given every green herb for meat: and it was so.

And God saw everything that he had made, and behold, *it was* very good. And the evening and the morning were the sixth day.'

Myra smiles, closes her eyes.

'No, finish it,' says Ewan.

'I'm a bit.. distracted.'

'Finish it. Please.'

'Thus the heavens and the earth were finished, and all the host of them.

And on the seventh day God ended his work which he had made: and he rested on the seventh day from all his work which he had made.

And God blessed the seventh day and sanctified it; because that in it he had rested from all his work which God created..

... and made.'

Myra lets the Bible fall, its tissue-thin leaves sighing as she and Ewan move together.

Afterwards, he kisses her as she curls against him, her head on his shoulder: and she cleaves to him as if this hour would last forever, was forever; and the perfume of her hair, and the sweetness of her morning warmth and softness lap around him, a tender sea.

'Why did you want to hear that bit from Genesis?' she whispers.

'Well,' says Ewan, 'the day the chaplain came you read it on the ward.'

'I always have to do that. Dulcie won't – says she's tired of Christian mythology.'

'And you came to do my dressing..'

'I did that every day.'

'I loved you,' says Ewan, kissing her again. 'That's when I knew.'

'Hold me,' says Myra. 'They'll be back from church before we know it.'

*   *   *

The Sabbath is not a day for high emotion, unless it's in the sermon you're giving. The Reverend Bethune excels himself today, if he says so himself; gives thanks for all the young men willing to do so much for their fellows. Is not war, after all, a test for those who would deny the very existence of their Lord? Is war not bringing man back to God by the shining selfless example of these brave untutored boys who in their unquestioning love and trust demand our respect, our prayers?

He stands in his high pulpit, beaming round his eager congregation. The church is full. This is very satisfactory. Not that his church isn't always full. Here on the island, people are devout, the churches thronged; they always were. He knew they would be when he got the call. The Reverend Bethune knows only too well the sorrow of the minister in a failing congregation. His last charge, in the city, in the middle of Dundee, had been a disappointment to him, a severe disappointment. The people were poor, yes, working long hours in the factories.. it's the same in many places, he believes. Empty hearts, empty seats. The war has brought them rolling back, all those families with sons, nephews, neighbours at the front. It has brought them back to God, like Jacob and Isaac. They all know how it feels.

Every week there are new recruits. Even before conscription the number of young men from this parish flocking to the defence of the realm, indeed, the defence of freedom, was encouraging. The Reverend Bethune wishes he were young enough to go himself. There are chaplains attached to every regiment; indeed, one of his sons is even now working in this way, has set up huts where soldiers are able to obtain snacks and spiritual sustenance on their way to and from the front. The other boy, who served as a medical officer in the Dardanelles, is in hospital in Edinburgh.

Neurasthenia.

They haven't told anyone in the wider family, or on the island; wouldn't like this unfortunate lapse to blight his future career. Whoever heard of a doctor with neurasthenia? His wife has been unable to bring herself to visit, and he cannot himself easily leave his charge. They find it hard to believe that any of their offspring should have proved so weak.

When Edward Bethune looks at himself in the mirror these days, he sees a heavily built man with greying hair, whose narrow mouth is set into the same expression of necessary firmness and absolute belief that has directed his whole life. God is on their side. God and Kitchener. How can they doubt the final outcome?

'God is on our side,' he says, thumping the pulpit, 'God and Kitchener. This is a righteous war, and the righteous shall be gloriously blessed with victory!'

John-Angus, dozing in the front row, jumps. Sine passes him a pandrop, dunts John-Iain, her husband, in the ribs. He's snoring too loudly. Sine has no notion of how much she has in common with the Reverend Bethune; when Ewan was wounded she couldn't bring herself to share the news with anyone but John-Iain, who shook his head and said nothing, his usual response.

How could Ewan, big, slow, sturdy, reliable Ewan be as near death as they said? It wasn't true, couldn't be.

When they said he was missing she didn't believe it. He'd turn up.

When they said he might die, she went on working round the croft, sent her man out fishing trout.

When they said the boy was back in Edinburgh but would never recover from his wounds, she laughed. Her Ewan? Indestructible.

The wedding shook her, right enough; but the lassie was as nice as you could hope for, considering she was not from the island.

And John-Angus going off to serve the King! Well, it was enough to swell any mother's heart, her last sweet boy going off just in time to dip his toe in the great adventure. If he was unlucky, he'd miss the next offensive, the last great battle, the one everybody knew was going to sort things out, as the Reverend Bethune promised them this and every Sunday.

The Murrays in the pew behind sit proud, look smilingly on Iain, whose fine broad chest swells under the weight of such responsibility. Iain is the eldest of their boys. The next is not yet sixteen, too young to volunteer. His turn will come. Iain, knowing how much Allan would give to be in his shoes, plays to the audience, preens himself, looks down on his younger brother. Allan may be taller, and brighter at the school (there's talk, indeed, of him taking the scholarship examination for the university in Aberdeen), but he is very much second fiddle in the Murray household. Iain holds sway. It is, after all, his due. When Bethune thumps the pulpit, vowing glory and victory, Iain nods to Angus Johnson, across the aisle.

Angus acknowledges the gesture, returning it coolly. He is not the easy touch Iain thinks him. Though his face looks blank enough, he is in a black fury. For that common shirker to have followed him, spied on him!

Iain can expect no further invitations to the Johnsons, no opportunities for subtle blackmail. Having served in the Officers Training Corps at school, Angus will travel to Wrexham, train as an officer in the Royal Welsh. Whatever Iain learned at the MacDonalds' window will bring him no benefit, none at all, quite the opposite. Angus has already gone so far as to hint to his father that he should not, as he'd planned, write to Iain's Lieutenant-Colonel, praising the boy.

'He wouldn't want it,' Angus said. 'Devilish proud, these islanders.'

Colonel Johnson, knowing this to be true, stays his hand. The letter remains on his desk, unsigned.

Angus has not gone the length of discussing yesterday's business with his parents; thinks it unlikely the mud will stick. The girl is safely back in Harris. What proof has she? None. He looks at his father's profile, wondering again what the old man would do when and if.. it's Angus's opinion that Kirsty would get short shrift there, but he is less confident how he himself would come through the matter in his father's eyes. Best to say nothing. It might never happen.

The Morrisons, sitting immediately behind the Johnsons, listen to the sermon unperplexed. Flora and Murdo have no son at the war, no son at home but Calum.

Murdo is not listening to the minister, but thinking of a better way to arrange Calum's new tunes, very taking tunes, both of them; Flora, her thick black hair braided tightly round her head beneath her old-fashioned bonnet, is wondering if she has enough St John's Wort to give John-Angus, to see him through his training and on to the trenches. The boy is going to need it.

For his part, Calum sighs. Life is suddenly unmanageable. He curses himself for a fool, and a weak fool too. The war would be no picnic, but at least, if he were going, he'd be able to look himself in the eye, hold his head up proudly. And as for other matters.. he's appalled at himself, the power of jealousy, the urgency, the lack of balance in a heart ruled by it. He's never felt like that before, never been swept along in its destructive tide. The aftermath is hard to contemplate.

His new friend Alec, lounging in the pew beside him, is thinking of his brother Bob: he smiles, one of those wry and crooked smiles Calum finds so hard to interpret.

'The glory o' war, eh, Bob?' Alec whispers. 'Fit tripe!'

'Sorry. Did you say something?'

Alec hadn't realised he was speaking aloud. He blushes to the top of his tight stiff collar, the collar on the new shirt Mairi told him yesterday would go so well with his eyes.

'Just dreaming,' he says. 'Sorry, Calum.'

His eyes keep wandering across the aisle. He cannot see Effie, though he knows she's there.

The MacDonalds all look tired, and no wonder. Aeneas is exhausted, anyone can read that in the uncharacteristic drooping of his shoulders, guess it from the several cuts he's inflicted on himself in this morning's too-close shave. He doesn't do a lot of driving and yesterday's round trip to Harris, four hours in all, has taken it out of him; not to mention the difficult business at the other end when the reason for Kirsty's homecoming must needs be explained. Like Maisie, Aeneas feels they have let Kirsty down, should have protected her, somehow, from herself and Angus. Kirsty's father took the same view, though acknowledging that they have been good employers, kind and fair. Still, the family seem inclined to press the matter further. Aeneas is afraid the Johnsons haven't heard the last of it; hopes Angus will have taken his father into his confidence.

Mairi fidgets beside Aeneas, also preoccupied, afraid her glance may drift across the aisle to Calum, or along the pew to Effie whose slightly puffy eyes betray a night of weeping; Effie has not taken her gloves off, but her mother and her new ring are both missing. The ring was large, noticeable.

Maisie, at the far end of the pew, looks thin and pale, frankly unwell. She's been permanently exhausted for some months now, over-tired; she's been trying to ignore the slight persistent cough, the nights she wakes up drenched in sweat. It's her age, an early change, that's all. And it was a long day yesterday. A long day and long night, burdened by the raft of alternating remonstration and condolence delivered in person and at some length by the very Reverend Bethune, despite Mairi's shielding presence. Maisie wishes she'd stayed in bed, wishes life were somehow simpler; wonders where she'll find a new maid at short notice, how they'll manage in the shop until they do. She wishes the sermon would come to an end, this rhetoric of war, this recruitment drive – it's enough to put the young men off!

A sudden sharper noise explodes beside her, startles her; the report echoing to the rafters. Maisie jumps. Dr Smith, in the side aisle, turning in silent rebuke to his youngest daughter, who has dropped her Bible and is scrabbling on the floor for it, beneath their pew, catches Maisie's eyes. He raises his eyebrows in apology. He notices her pallor, the hollow cheeks. She's lost a bit of weight. That dress is too big in the shoulders for her.

Outside it's still sultry, may thunder again.

*   *   *

Sunday 4th June
Alec says Iain knew all along it was Kirsty in the shed, but.. Alec doesn't know Iain, not like I do.

103

Iain wouldn't do a thing like that, not to me.

And we were both drunk, of course, I said that to Alec.

When I saw Iain after church I told him that he'd got it all wrong, and he said he knew the whole story; and he'd heard about me shouting at Mairi in the street. He was distracted, I think, kept looking into the crowd emerging from the church. He went off to speak to Angus Johnson. Effie had just left him. I saw Alec follow Effie with his eyes, all the way down the street. He made no move to talk to her. He's a funny one, that Alec.

– Why don't you go after her? I said.

– It's nae the time, said Alec. Come here wi' me.

And he walked across to Mairi, dragged me with him.

– Bonnie shirt, he said. D'ye no think?

– It came from a fine shop, said Mairi.

– Whit's up wi' Effie?

Mairi shook her head.

– I don't know.

She looked at Alec, not at me. She kept looking at him as if she was afraid to look at me.

– I don't think she has her ring on, Mairi said. And.. I saw.. she gave Angus a letter.

– Mairi, I interrupted, did you not get my letter?

– Yes, she said, I got it. She still wouldn't look at me. But I couldn't read it, Calum. It got soaked, and the ink all ran. I have to go, I'm sorry.

She scurried after her parents then, taking her mother's arm.

– Come on, said Alec. Ken, it'll be raining anither river soon.

I couldn't leave it like that.

– Alec, I said. Run after Mairi and give her – I'd nothing in my pocket but a handkerchief.

– I'll just run after her, he said. I'll see you in the afternoon. Ye cannae send the quine a handkerchief.

Two days ago I was happy. Now I'm wrung out, like a torn net. Useless. And it's three o'clock and Alec hasn't come. And it's raining.

Calum pauses in his writing, takes up his fiddle. 'The Dark Ship' fills the room, uneasy as the ebb and flow of his emotions.

'Calum! Put that fiddle down. It's the Sabbath.'

'Sorry, Mother.'

Flora slips down the narrow staircase, stands by her window, sighs. A wind has got up now, driving heavy rain against the glass. The raindrops cannot hold to the spotless surface; try as they may to cling, stay complete and round and beautiful, one by one they are swept in swirling tributaries from her sight.

'Calum!' she calls.

'Yes, Mother?'

'I see Iain coming.'

Thirty minutes later, Flora calls up the stair again.

'Boys! There's Alec on his way up!'

Calum scarcely hears. Iain is sitting with his back to the narrow window and his hands in his pockets, saying terrible things, things Calum cannot quite believe. Alec hears the end of the speech as he comes in.

'And all's fair in love and war, Calum. You know that. And I thought when you'd berated her so publicly you wouldn't care about me asking her if I could write. I've always had a fancy for Mairi. You know that fine.'

Alec looks from Iain's confidence to Calum's set expression.

'I'll write to you too, of course,' says Iain. 'And Ewan has asked me to keep an eye out for John-Angus. We'll be training together. They'll likely put us in the same squad. Now, I have to run. I've a lot of folk to see. Excuse me, Alec.'

Iain turns at the door.

'I'll see you at the boat tomorrow, eh?'

He doesn't wait for an answer, swings jovially down the stair, whistling.

Alec just looks at Calum, doesn't speak. Calum turns to the window.

'Tell me he's lying, Alec.'

Calum stares at the heavy clouds sweeping the island. They're so low he feels he could almost touch them.

'Tell me he's lying!'

'He's exaggerating,' Alec says. 'I was there. All he did wis race past Mairi in the street and call out Will you no' write to me in France? She didnae answer, and her mother fair glowered efter him..'

When there's no response from Calum, Alec repeats 'I wis there, I tell ye! She's upset about your letter, Calum. Ye ken, it really did get wet, sae wet that a' the ink ran. That wis God's own truth. She couldnae read a word o' it.'

'Knowing my luck, it would. It's my own fault,' Calum says. 'If I'd trusted her as she deserved.. and anyway, if you were Mairi, and had to choose between me and Iain..'

'Nae contest,' says Alec.

'I know,' says Calum softly. 'I know.'

'That's nae whit I'm sayin,' says Alec. Can you no' see through thon bugger? He's no' half the man you are.'

'Iain's been my friend a long time.'

'Friend! If I hid friends like that, I widnae be short o' enemies!'

'You don't know him, Alec. Iain has his good side too. And he's in love as well. You heard what he said. All's fair in love and war.'

'A load of shite!' says Alec. 'He said fancy, no' love. That's lust, not carin'. Wid that dae for Mairi? Hae some backbone, Calum! Listen tae me.. here's whit ye should dae..'

*   *   *

Sunday 4th June
I hate Sunday afternoon. I wish I could go out. I wish I could go and see Effie.

I would write to Calum, but..

Iain asked me to write to him in France. My mother looked daggers at him when he asked me in the street.

He's going to France, I said.

Over my dead body, she said, will you write to that scoundrel!

He's not trustworthy, Mairi. Worse than Angus. That young fellow is only out for what he can get.

She stopped then because Alec had come up beside us. I like Alec. It's easy to talk to Alec.

It used to be easy to talk to Calum.

'Mairi!'

'Yes?'

'Come downstairs. We've a visitor.'

Mairi slips the journal in her drawer, tidies her hair. She hasn't tied it back and it's lying soft and wavy on her shoulders, falling burnished to her waist; it makes her feel younger, safer. Less complicated.

Maybe the visitor is Effie. Mairi stares into the mirror, thinks how happy she was only yesterday, how she couldn't stop her lips from smiling, how she'd looked at herself in this very mirror, trying to look calm, to reign the feeling in. Poor Effie. How must she be feeling?

Mairi scrubs her cheeks, trying to rub some colour into them.

'Mairi! Are you coming down?'

'Just coming!'

Mairi touches, briefly, the red notebook, now dry and lying quietly beside her bed, its wrinkled pages legible, where the letter had not been.

'Mairi!'

'I said, I'm coming!'

'There's a visitor in the kitchen for you. Rather wet. I said you'd make some tea,' says Maisie. 'Will you bring us through a cup?'

Mairi nods, moves towards the kitchen automatically. When she opens the door, she sees only the grey jacket dripping on the chair, the bunch of lilies lying on the table. The back door's open to the wind and rain. She fills the kettle, slams it on the stove.

'Calum,' she calls from the shelter of the door. 'What are you doing?'

He turns from the rose-bush he's bent over. His Sunday shirt is now wet through, plastered pink against his skin.

'I'm so sorry, Mairi. What you must think..'

Mairi takes the red, tight, rose, sees his finger bleeding.

'Roses have thorns,' she says, and looks into his eyes, and stops.

'The waltz..'

'Come back inside. Let me fix your hand.'

In the kitchen, Mairi lays the rose aside, finds a clean cloth, offers it to him.

'You're dripping blood all over! Come here, Calum.'

She holds the cloth out, and their fingers touch. She sees it in his face, the shock that's running through him too. The sharpness of it.

*   *   *

The Sabbath is wearing on. Most folk have had their brief cold supper, and sit in talk, or at their Bibles, staring at the wet grey world the summer rain has left them. No one works. It is anathema to work at anything but necessary tasks, or works of charity, the sick, the animals. Catriona Murray sits at her empty wheel, sets it singing, spinning air.

Catriona loves her son, but has few illusions about him; having watched Iain operating on his brothers and sisters, she knows his methods, all of them. She knows the subtle slyness his charm conceals, the depth of vanity behind that cheerful baby-face. But she feels there is strength in him too, and honesty he's never cared to practise. She hopes there is. She thinks he'll need it.

She never says much, Catriona, just sits and spins or knits, but she knows what's going on in the world, same one. She listens carefully, watches, forms her own opinions. Unlike her husband Alec, Catriona does not think the war is going well. Has she not seen, with her own eyes, the telegrams arriving, message after message from the front, brought on foot by old Nessie? Catriona knows, and Nessie too, that the cailleach's mere appearance causes dread as she walks slowly, slowly, through the townships. No, this war will not be won without great cost. There are so many men and boys away, so many lost already.

She's glad Alec is too old for the conscription, glad the other boys are much too young. Iain will have to go, and no one could have stopped him, least of all herself. He's that keen. And he'll be a good soldier, right enough: has always had a talent for fighting. Didn't she know better than anybody how many times Iain came home with his knees scraped, and his eyes blacked? And she'd have to clean him up before his father came home and took the belt out? War is a different thing, perhaps, but Iain has a fighting heart; and usually came out on top.

He is her first-born. She loves him unreservedly, despite clear knowledge of his failings. Did she not nurse him at the breast where he gnawed her nipples ragged? Did she not croon him to sleep for hours, night after night, month after month, only to have him wake, screaming, when she needed rest herself? Catriona has invested life and energy in Iain – her youngest, freshest years, her fiercest love; so it's hard for her to talk tonight, with the lump that will keep rising in her throat, however hard she tries to swallow, to seem light and happy. Iain's last night. To hear his father talk, you'd think the boy was off on holiday.

'Once you get to France,' he's saying, 'avoid the brandy. It's fatal. And go easy on the wine at first. You won't be used to it. You'll need to watch those French girls too. The kilt drives them daft, you know. They all want to go out with a Highlander. Watch your money carefully.'

Catriona sighs, lifts the empty spinning wheel aside. It's the Sabbath after all. She wouldn't want to court ill-luck, though the rhythm clears her head, relieves the ache that's growing in her troubled heart.

'Would you like a dram, Alec? Unless, of course, your head.. you'll have finished the animals?'

Alec does not stir, except to stretch his hand out for the glass. It's the old way. All the boys have copied it.

Unusually, Iain comes over to the dresser now, carries the glasses over to the fire, where he hands one to his father then smiles back at his mother, raising his own glass.

'A toast,' says Alec. 'To France!'

'France!' Iain drinks. 'I've a toast myself,' he says. 'Home! May I bring it honour!'

'Home!' says Alec.

Catriona is forced to look away now, pretending business with the fire. The acrid smoke is some excuse for stinging eyes. She slips out the back for fresh peat, leans against the rough stone wall, hiding her face in the striped petticoat she still wears round the croft. This is the hardest night of her life, harder even than the night they laid her second, still-born child to rest, a poor deformed wee mite they wouldn't bury in the churchyard. The tiny body got cold so quick. She remembers how cold it was, how she could not keep warmth in it, though she hugged the wee scrap to her till the very last moment.

Every spring, Catriona covers the tiny cliff top grave with flowers. It was a blow, but she got over it. She'll get used to the anxiety, the worry of not knowing where her son is, what he's doing. So many mothers have. She is not alone.

Inside, Iain sips the whisky, smiling. He feels good, here with his own people, in the only home he's known. It's a fine old croft, he's proud of it, wouldn't change it for all the wood panelling in the Big House, though he'd like his mother and father to have an easier time of it, God knows he would.

Iain looks at the heavy dresser his father hand-crafted in the first years of the marriage; the china plates and jugs and cups gathered carefully through the years. They are his mother's pride, these and the glasses and the silver teaspoons she uses on special occasions only, communions, and funerals. No doubt they'll be used for weddings too. The dresser and its treasures have been the family pride all his life, have an importance, a grandeur they'd never achieve in richer surroundings.

From tomorrow the croft, these crowded rooms, will be a memory. Iain is confident he will do well. He'll come back and marry Mairi. It's a shame about Calum; but after all, he had set his mind on Mairi first. Calum interfered at the dance. He shouldn't have done that.

Maybe, on the boat tomorrow, he'll have time to work on Angus ; a cold fish, the Johnson boy, if ever there was one. Though maybe it would be better to leave the matter, say no more. Hint, not tell. He's already said to Angus he was hanging round the MacDonalds in the hope of seeing Mairi – the farewell at the pier, if he can arrange it, if he could kiss her, say – yes, that would be a good idea: if he could kiss her, it would add substance to his protestations. And it would be no hardship to kiss Mairi. He wanted to; now he'd thought of it, the prospect was even exciting. It would be one in the eye for Calum too. Serve him right!

'Another dram?'

Iain smiles up at his father.

'Don't mind if I do. Where's mother?'

'Outside at the peat.'

'She's been gone a while.'

'That's women for you.'

'I'll maybe go and find her.'

'She'll be back presently, you'll see.'

But Iain rises from the wooden chair and slips out into the still June night. It's dusk; it won't get darker, hardly at all. The heavy cloud has cleared, and the air is fresher. The ground is still wet underfoot. She isn't at the peat. He finds her standing on the cliff, staring at the sea, at the looming rocks. The midges are terrible.

'What are you doing here?'

'Oh, just getting some air,' Catriona sighs. 'It's a lovely night'

'It's fresher, certainly,' says Iain, 'now the rain has stopped.'

'The thunder isn't in it any more. It's as if the temper has been beaten out of the skies.'

'Not before time,' laughs Iain.

'Iain, son..'

'Yes?'

'You'll be careful.'

'What else would I be?'

'I know you, Iain. I know life too. It doesn't do the heart any good to work only for the self. There's no honesty in it.'

'You've told me all this time and time again..'

'You'll be near death, Iain. War is not a game. You'll be near your maker.'

'What are you trying to say?'

'Just – we love you, Iain. We want you to be the best you can be; not the bravest, not the fiercest, but the truest, the best.' She points out to sea, to the Beasts of Holm. 'Our life is what we're judged by. In the end our actions stand as bare and open as those rocks, for all to see.'

Catriona looks at her son, his gaze now firmly fixed away from her, on the sea, the rocks. She thinks she'd have done better to hold her tongue. Iain, for his part, is shaken. He forgets how much his quiet mother sees.

'I'd never let you down,' he says. 'You know that.'

Catriona looks into his eyes.

'I promise,' Iain says.

Catriona wishes she believed him, or even his intent.

'Let's go in,' she says. 'Your father will be wondering where we've got to.'

Alec Murray sleeps well that night, the sound sleep of the righteous who have imbibed a suitable number of drams. If he dreams, it's of triumphal processions, handsome soldiers and bonnie French girls kissing him as he liberates their fresh green fields and spotless aprons. The wine is sweet, fragrant as early brambles. Catriona, however, tosses and turns, spends the night in fitful prayer; to ask for her son's safety when so many are at risk seems a selfish option. She changes tack, prays the war will soon be over.

Iain sleeps eventually, wakes at six. His mother is moving in the kitchen, stirring porridge. He can smell the fresh bannocks she rose at four to bake. It is the last morning of this part of his life, and the familiar sounds seem strangely poignant. His brother Allan's snoring on the far side of the bed, slower and

NOT ON THE 11:9 MAILING LIST?

11|9

Return this freepost card and we'll send you exclusive information on all new and forthcoming 11:9 fiction titles – flyers, newsletters, samplers, author facts, special offers. You'll also receive priority information on events and signing sessions.
Each card returned enters a draw every second month to win two 11:9 titles.

Alternatively, go to www.11–9.co.uk

Name ....

Address ....

....

Postal code ....

E-mail address ....

Date of birth .... male/female ....

Freepost NWP

louder than wee Hamish piping in the middle with his quieter intake of breath; even this cocoon of sound, that might have irritated him another day, seems valuable this morning. He lies and listens. This is home. Though he's glad to be leaving the island, all the sounds, even the cuckoos' relentless notes, are woven with morning light and the sweet smell of the baking into a cloth of home that he will carry with him. He likes that notion. He was good at the writing too, for all that Allan is the one they're going to send to university. The maths let Iain down, that and his complete inability to sit still for more than twenty minutes at a time. Sometimes, when he's walking on the beach or the moor, unless there's a ploy on, or a problem to work out, he finds words dancing in his head. He doesn't need to write them down. Since he left the school he's done little reading. Well, time enough for reading after the war, or when he's an old man.

Iain sits up slowly, swings his legs to the floor, slips on his trousers, stands and stretches. The last night in the cramped bed of his youth is over. Where will he be tomorrow? Fort George, certainly. And after? There's an odd gap in him, as if none of this was happening, no excitement yet, no fear. He feels no different from yesterday. Hardly different at all. Life goes on, but in careful, slower motion.

*   *   *

John-Angus is not calm at all. His gear is ready packed, at the foot of his bed. He doesn't want to leave the island. He sits outside the barn as his mother milks the cow. She's babbling happily.

'I'll miss you, lad, but I'm so very proud of you. The Reverend Bethune is too. Didn't you see how he shook your hand? And you volunteering early – he was impressed with that. Impressed with Ewan too. And Myra. We've certainly done our bit, no one can say we haven't. I'll have the porridge on in a minute. Don't go off, John-Angus! What a boy!' she clucks as the lad strides down the machair to the shore, driven by her torrent of self-congratulation. 'What a lad!' she continues. 'Always did spend all his time walking that piece of shore! And the odd thing is, he doesn't even like the water! John-Angus!' she calls. 'What did Flora give you last night? What was it? You didn't say. What a boy! He'll be back when I get the porridge. I'll have to get on, it's getting late. We can't be late today.'

John-Angus has taken some of Flora's remedy already. He's always liked Flora, always found peace and calm in her house, in her company, since Calum took him there after the Battle of the Seas; terrified he was, out of his wits, still screaming, but Flora settled him. She always does. She knows the island herbs, the old ways with them, healing ways. She told him last night she'd given him enough of the remedy to last him to France.

'By then you'll not be needing it,' she said. 'You'll have enough to help you through the first round in the trenches. Don't worry, lad. Just concentrate on doing your best, what you can. You're a good lad, always were. Now, you understand how to take it?'

John-Angus nodded, smiled. Flora patted his shoulder.

'Bless you,' she said. 'Beannachd leat.'

She was gone before he saw the tears rising in in her eyes.

Now he wanders the the beach, blundering from wet sand into surf. Flora has confidence in me, he thinks. And Flora always knows. He begins to feel a little better. Later, Ewan, strolling across the sands towards him, finds the boy much cheerier than he'd expected.

'I wish we were coming on the boat with you,' says Ewan gruffly.

'Mam'll need you,' says John-Angus. 'It's good you're staying. You'd only be with me to Inverness anyway. You and Myra would be off to Edinburgh on the train and me marching to Fort George!'

'I hardly think you'll march,' says Ewan.

'No,' says John-Angus, with a rare streak of humour. 'No, I'd trip them all up! I'd be the Boche's secret weapon.'

'I'm afraid you're right,' Ewan laughs. 'I'm a bit like that myself.'

'What are they like, Ewan?'

John-Angus has hardly mentioned his enlisting before this, never mind asked any questions. Ewan stalls for time.

'What are *who* like?'

'The Germans.'

'Much like you and me, I suppose. You don't have time to gossip in the trenches. Not with Fritz. I can't see why they'd be any different from us, though. They're just soldiers too.'

John-Angus isn't listening.

'The minister calls them monsters of depravity, instruments of evil. He says war is sent to purge the world of sin, and it won't stop till God thinks we've learned enough.'

'I didn't think you listened to sermons!' Ewan laughs.

'I didn't use to listen, but he shouts so loud these days that you can't sleep properly. Ewan, tell me something.'

'What?'

'Are there sermons in the army too?'

'Not so many,' Ewan grins. 'The odd one, I'm afraid. But orders. Lots of orders.'

'A bit like Mam, you mean.'

'Worse,' says Ewan. 'Even more. John-Angus, Iain Murray will look out for you while you're training. We islanders generally stick together.'

'I'm not fond of Iain,' says John-Angus. 'Never was. Calum, now, he's a different fellow altogether.'

'Calum won't be there,' says Ewan.

'More's the pity.'

Ewan glances sharply at his younger brother, more confident now of the boy's ability to cope. They've reached the croft door. Ewan hesitates, decides to speak.

'John-Angus, don't be worrying. The training isn't easy.

But you're strong and fit. You'll do fine.'

'Once I get across the Minch, perhaps. You know how I hate water.'

'Yes,' says Ewan, 'Yes. I have every reason to remember. I'm not that fond of water myself! Breakfast?'

'While I'm able to hold it down!'

FIRST VARIATION

When John-Angus was asked, in his nineties, about the day he left home for Fort George, he shook his head.

'I'm not sure where to start. I'm not a natural islander, or maybe too natural – not a sailor. I always hated water, and the day we left there was a fair swell on. I was very sick, and sometimes I didn't make the rail. I messed up Angus Johnson's new boots. Though I'm thinking those boots will have seen much worse before they got much older.'

His old man's laugh burst out here, through the careful, prepared story.

'He was that angry at me! I didn't care, of course. I was feeling too dreadful at the time. I hardly noticed; though when we got to Kyle his boots still had that stain on them, all damp and spattered, you know? And the smell. He took that all the way to Wrexham!

'Maybe *he* was the start of that tale about the Russian soldiers travelling through Britain with snow still on their boots.. everyone was supposed to have seen them. We thought ourselves the *Russians* must have come from *Ross-shire*, that their foreign tongue must have been the Gaelic we spoke. The snow on the boots was harder to account for.'

He sat forward in the shabby leather armchair here, drumming the fingers of his right hand against loose wrinkled skin on the back of his left. The veins stood out, blue and thick. The camera focused on them as the story unfolded in an old man's voice as distinctly Lewis as the day he left the island.

'But I didn't like the army, not at first. The Fort was so big and heavy. Like a fortified town! And there were so many soldiers; some on their way to the front, rookies like us at different stages of training; and then there were the men who'd been to France and been injured and were coming home to convalesce. Or had been home to convalesce and were going off again. Most of these were very quiet.

'Conditions were very cramped. It was rough, you know, even to those of us from crofts who were used to working hard, used to digging peat and so on. Also I was very shy. And I've never been able to tell my right from left, which made the marching difficult. Forming fours, and all that. I wasn't good at school, terrible at the reading, and I've been thinking, you know, that maybe me and my brother Ewan (he got the Military Cross at Loos).. I've been wondering in recent years if we weren't that lexic.. you know, that makes you bad at reading .'

'Dyslexic?' The reporter's voice offered this, respectful.

'That's the very word. We could neither of us read very well, never; I think that's why we often didn't heed the orders and ended up in sticky situations other people managed to avoid.' He swallowed, drawing breath. 'Folk who read orders, you see, they'd turn and go home when they were told. We just didn't know when to stop!'

Someone off-camera handed him a glass filled with amber liquid.

'Thank you. Slainte!'

John-Angus turned, smiling, his narrow wrinkled face transfigured to the young John-Angus, eager to please. He spilled a little of the whisky raising the glass.

'Damn tremor,' he said. 'Excuse the language.'

He sipped from the glass, savouring.

'Ardbeg, eh? Thought so. But as I was saying, I never got that good at the reading and actually I was rather clumsy too. Didn't know my right from my left. They used to say in the Seaforths that in a formal march I was Fritz's secret weapon – guaranteed to scupper the whole thing!

'When we got out to the trenches, there was no more formal marching. (Except for training periods, that is.) There were route marches, and they were tough in terms of stamina, but easy once you got in step because it didn't really matter which foot you were on and everyone was singing anyway; or groaning. We used to sing to keep us going. Sometimes we were so tired that we'd fall asleep in the ten minute halt. Those packs were that heavy!

'What do I remember most? The cold. The lice. The way the kilt got caked in mud and tore at your legs. Many's the night I've seen my knees and thighs red-raw. Sometimes we'd take off our kilts and work in just our greatcoats and shirts, till the kilt dried out and could be brushed. The lice fair clustered in those kilt pleats, and you couldn't nip them out like you could in a shirt! That's what we called chatting, killing the lice.. you probably know that.'

He paused here, wheezing slightly. 'It's hard, you know, to help you understand how awful it was trying to survive the mud, never mind the fighting. We all should have had the Victoria Cross just for being there. It was a strange thing, the front, very strange when you come to think of it – that long thin line bisecting Europe – four hundred miles long, they say, and only a few miles thick – and all the action in the poisoned centre – an angry river of men pushing, pushing: and sometimes the current went one way, and sometimes it went another. But it hardly moved in four years and it was always noisy and always drenched in blood. Come to think of it, maybe it was more of an artery than a river. I never thought of that before.'

He sank back into silence, staring at his glass, swilling the last few drops of whisky round and round, round and round. He looked suddenly tired and old, as if he might never speak again, but thin and disappear into smoke or fading light. His eyes drooped slowly shut. The reporter leaned forward now, prompting. Her hand appeared on screen, touching his. John-Angus jumped, startled.

'What about your decoration? Will you say a few words about the day you got the Victoria Cross?'

'Oh, I don't think your viewers would want to hear about it. It was so ordinary.'

'Ordinary!'

'There were lots of boys did braver, better things and no

one ever heard about them. All I did was stop a machine-gun and help a few wounded fellows back to our line. Anyone could have done it. Lots of us had to.

'Passchendaele Ridge was worse. Imagine, standing in cold water, right up to your middle, for six days at a time. No latrines. No privacy. The only hot drink, tea that was brought in petrol cans, so it gave you diarrhoea, that's how it was. We all got trench feet and trench fever. It wouldn't have been quite so bad if there'd been proper trenches instead of those shell-holes. That's what they were, shell-holes reinforced with sandbags.

'I got a Blighty, a throat and chest wound. They sent me home. At the time they said I might never speak again. And listen at me! Everybody's tired of my eternal blethering.'

John-Angus looked directly at the camera.

'Actually,' he said, 'I'm tired of hearing it myself. I'd like to stop there, if you wouldn't mind.'

'Okay.'

The reporter nodded to the cameraman who switched his camera off.

'That light,' John-Angus offered, 'is like a star-shell.'

The cameraman clattered round them, dismantling lights, equipment. The young reporter leaned over, nearer to John-Angus. 'I'll come back in a week or two, if that's alright. I'll check it out with Matron.'

'What else is there to talk about?'

'Oh, lots of things. This is just a start. What happened after you were injured, for example. What it felt like in hospital, and when you came home. Then what happened to you after the war, how you found the country when you got back. That kind of thing. Or even, what it was like in rest periods at the front, you know, when you were in support, or in the rear. Or your fellow soldiers, how you all got on, what they were like. And of course, we haven't touched on the Morrison film – how you felt about your character.. when he attempted suicide.'

'Och, Calum wasn't talking about me. It was just a film. It's so difficult to think of island-sounding names that no one actually has! There are so few of them. No, that didn't bother me. Not a bit. I liked the film very much, actually, apart from the accents. But that's Hollywood for you. Maybe if they'd made it in Britain.. but I suppose if they had, the characters would have had English accents, sharp enough to cut butter! Or Irish! Or Australian!'

'You really mean you didn't mind about the suicide attempt?'

'It was a very sad moment in the film. I thought..'

'Yes?'

'When I saw it, I thought many a boy must have felt like that, desperate for peace.'

'Did you know Calum Morrison well?'

John-Angus smiled. 'We were boys together. Calum was the best fiddler this country ever had. Bar none! I often wished I could play like that. And the imagination on him! He was desperate to fight, poor boy. He couldn't, with his foot. He tried to volunteer, the same day I joined up. I envied him, you know. I didn't want to go. And he envied me because I had to! He used to write to me, every single week. I had to get the letters read, of course, and I'd dictate a note back to him when I could. And I wrote that way to Calum's mother more often than my own. A wonderful woman, Flora Morrison. She had the sight, you know, and the knowledge of herbs, and a way that gave you confidence beyond your dreams. She told me before I went off that I would be alright. And she was right. She always was.

'Lassie, lassie, I'm sorry, I'm right tired now. You'll come back and see me another time and we'll talk about the Red Lamps, all the exciting stuff. But not today. Thank you for the dram. Matron need never know, eh? We'll keep that between you and me? By the by, did you tell me your name? I expect you did and I've forgotten it.'

'Zoe. Zoe Wild. Without an E.'

'Good-bye then, Zoe without an E. It's been a pleasure meeting you.'

'The Zoe has an E, it's the Wild that doesn't.. not that it matters. Thank you.' Zoe retrieved her bag then straightened up to follow the cameraman who now stood by the door waiting, holding it open for her with his foot. She hesitated, turned, buckling the narrow belt on her sky-blue coat. 'Of course,' she said, 'you'll have known Iain Murray too.'

'Indeed,' John-Angus nodded. 'Who didn't?'

Zoe and the cameraman clattered along the corridor to the Matron's office. John-Angus heard them all the way. Old he might be, but his ears were still in good order.

'Nice old bugger,' said the male voice. 'How did he get his VC then?'

'Took out a machine-gun emplacement single-handed, gathering three officers and thirty men as prisoners – they'd all run into a dugout.. though I didn't think it was at Passchendaele.. Some of the Highlanders were not noted for taking prisoners, not if you read the books, but there's no doubt that our man did. Then he spent the next eight hours rescuing badly wounded men. One of them might have been your great-grandfather, Eric! And he was a crack shot, John-Angus, one of the best.'

'But he said he was handless!'

'No, he didn't. He said he couldn't tell his left from his right. If you listen to the interview again I think you'll find he says that twice. It's interesting that it doesn't seem to have affected his aim, and nobody who remembers him from the army ever thought of him as clumsy, just this baby-faced expert who hardly ever spoke after his brother died.'

'His brother?'

'His older brother, Ewan. He'd been badly injured earlier – at Loos, I think where he picked up the MC, but he recovered and went back to the front for the later stages of the Somme. He survived Delville Wood, but fell at Arras the next year. You know, I thought it was at Arras John-Angus got the VC.'

'How did the brother die?'

'A sniper's bullet. Days before the actual attack. Shot the top of his head off, brain all over the revetting. Took him three hours to die.'

'God.'

'Yeah.'

'How do you know all this?'

'There's a poem about it.'

'Sassoon?'

'No. It's one of Iain Murray's poems. They're mostly in Gaelic, not so well-known as some of the other World War One stuff. Good though.'

'You speak Gaelic?'

'I read the English. He wrote in English too. I know, I know, it's a cop-out.'

'Hey, Zoe, wasn't that the office?

'God, yes.'

The footsteps slowed.

'You could always take a course.'

'A course?' Zoe's confusion was obvious.

Eric laughed. 'In Gaelic. There's a college in the south of Skye. Sabhal Mhor. They say it's really beautiful.'

'That's an idea Eric. You know, there might even be a film in that.'

John-Angus heard no more. He felt suddenly old; older than the hills, ineffably sad. He couldn't stop the tears. When they came round for his teacup, the care-assistants went running for the nurse-in-charge.

'Are you feeling bad, John-Angus?' Nan fluttered round him, a sweet girl from Benbecula who'd been in Inverness for twenty years but had the island tongue on her still. She bent down, felt the sweat on his brow. 'We'll get you into bed, I think. Are you sore anywhere? Have you a cough? No trouble down below? With the water?'

She eased him into bed, slipped a thermometer under his arm.

'Too much excitement for one day, that's all. Are you needing anything?'

John-Angus shook his head.

'I'll come and check you after tea. I want to hear you've eaten all your tea now! Your temperature's not bad, but we'll check it again later. Now. Are you comfortable?' She handed him the buzzer. 'Ring if you need anything at all. I'm just along the corridor, you know that.'

John-Angus lay back against the pillows, eyes tight shut. Nan reminded him a little of Flora, just a little. She had a whisper of the touch, only a whisper. And nothing could help, he knew that. Nothing helped, not even time. When would they realise that talking doesn't heal? He wasn't lying when he said he could hardly remember the day he stepped aboard the *Sheila*, left home for the first time. He remembered bits of it right enough – all the worst bits, things that frightened, cut into the marrow of you. Any better bits had all gone hazy, like bright summer days when it always proved impossible to see beyond the sun's glaring harshness – all the colours dimmed, all the shapes confused. You had to move into the shade to let your eyes recover.

It was Iain came to tell him about Ewan.

John-Angus was resting, sleeping in a dugout. April 1917. Arras was hard work, the trenches filled with mud that sucked you in and held you fast. It was almost impossible to pull your feet out if you happened to stand still for even thirty seconds. Moving one leg in front of another took enormous effort, and many a boot was lost and sworn about. It was exhausting work just getting around. John-Angus didn't always manage to sleep in the fire-trench, but that day he'd gone out like a light, and would not waken easily. Iain had to shake him quite roughly.

'John-Angus! Wake up, will you? I haven't got long. Wake up, for heaven's sake! STAND-TO!'

John-Angus jumped to his feet immediately.

'What? What's happening?'

He looked anxiously round for his rifle. It was still broad daylight. The Boche wouldn't attack in broad daylight, surely?

'What? Iain! What is it?'

Iain's face gave it away. He couldn't speak. John-Angus took his arm.

'It's Ewan? He's been hurt?'

John-Angus couldn't believe his brother dead; he'd have felt it, known.

'He's gone, John-Angus. Last night. Sniper's bullet.'

'In the head?'

'I'm sorry.'

Iain didn't tell him about the brain, not then; how it had splashed across the trench.

'Did he not have his helmet on?'

'You know how much he hated it. He had just finished sentry duty and taken it off. He stood up on the firestep to let a stretcher past. He was a big man. Every way. I'm that sorry.' Iain had tears in his eyes. John-Angus was crying too.

'Can I see him?'

'Better not. Head wounds..'

'I'm not a baby, Iain! I've been in this bloody war as long as you!'

'Christ, John-Angus, they shot the top of his bloody head off! Do you have to have it spelled out to you? Would it help to see him?'

John-Angus vomited. Iain looked away.

'I'm sorry. Did he.. did he die quickly?'

'I don't think he felt anything.'

'Iain, don't keep lying to me. What.. happened?'

'He.. took an hour or two to die.. but he wasn't conscious. Screaming. We got an injection for him before they moved him to the rear. I don't think there was any pain. In any case, he wasn't there. It wasn't Ewan.'

'Christ,' John-Angus said again.

He sat down suddenly, winded. He could hardly breathe. It didn't seem possible. It didn't seem right that Ewan should be snuffed out, destroyed by one small bullet that didn't whistle past but flew unerringly towards him, concentrating flight and time in final collision. The full stop to end them all. He'd always thought

125

his brother older, wiser, but Ewan was not old; not yet twenty-one.

John-Angus turned his pale, wild face to Iain's grief. 'Iain, what are we doing here? Tell me, for it makes no sense.'

The tears were running freely now down both men's cheeks.

'We're trying to live till it ends,' said Iain. 'Here – ' he held out his water bottle to John-Angus.

'I'm not thirsty, thank you.'

'It's rum,' said Iain. 'It will help, trust me. It's the only thing that does.'

Two days later, 9 April, John-Angus ran amok. Seeing the first men over the top fall prey to enemy fire, he worked his way along the railway under shelter of the bank and did for the machine gunners. He didn't stop there, but ran along the trench killing soldier after soldier, bayonetting them till his uniform was soaked in blood. He came to himself as he pulled the bayonet from a screaming boy who slumped back against the trench wall, coughing blood. His helmet fell off. The boy was sixteen at most. He'd probably lied about his age. John-Angus continued to move forward, quieter now, conscious of possible danger lurking round the traverse. He tossed a Mills bomb round it, waited for the blast, was amazed when they all came out with their hands up, all those officers and men.

'We surrender, Tommy.'

John-Angus knew he was in a difficult position – once they rounded the traverse, they'd see that he was only one against – how many? Behind him he heard clinking metal and guttural Gaelic cries.. Gaelic cries!

'Throw your weapons down!'

He turned the prisoners over to the 5th Seaforth men who'd followed him. The rest of the day he worked at rescuing the wounded. They'd achieved the attack objectives, more than achieved them.

It had been a day of rain and snow. The night was bitter, but John-Angus worked like a horse, like an ox. Like Ewan. As he staggered under the weight of comrade after comrade, he thought of Ewan and Myra in Stornoway that last carefree summer; he thought of them dancing together, all three of them dancing lightly through the hall. He'd have to write to Myra, to his mother. He struggled for words. None seemed possible.

Ewan is dead. Iain told me. I've seen the grave. I helped to put the soil on, made sure the grave was deep enough, if any grave is deep enough to rest undisturbed in this hell. Ewan is dead. My brother.

How can Ewan be dead?

Long into the night he scoured the field of battle, searching.

*   *   *

'Are you alright, John Angus?' Nan's cool fingers swept across his forehead.

'Flora?'

'It's Nan, dear, Nan.'

Her fingers were on his pulse now. 130. Irregular.

'Are you feeling any pain? Any palpitations?'

'I need to write.. to Myra. Will you do it for me?'

'Certainly. I'm just giving the drugs out, but I'll come straight back and bring a pen. You just relax, try and rest. I'll be about twenty minutes. Ring if you need anything.'

She slipped the electric buzzer back in his right hand, sighing as she left the room. If that pulse didn't settle she'd have to call the GP in and it nearly seven o'clock; he'd be in the middle of evening surgery, and not a happy man. But John-Angus had had runs of atrial fibrillation in the past. He was on digoxin. Maybe things would settle.

Nan peered at the kardex, checking drugs for Mary in the next room.

'Do you need your aperient, dear?' she asked. 'Painkillers?'

'Oh, painkillers, nurse. I think the baby's on its way!'

When Nan came back, finally, having given out the drugs, locked the trolley away in the office, fielded calls from one or two anxious relatives, and spoken to the owner of the home about the broken television and the flood in the laundry (they needed a new washing machine, there was now no doubt of that) she found John-Angus lying with his eyes closed. He looked peaceful, was breathing easily enough. She counted his respirations. Nothing wrong there.

He'd been in this home since she first started work here, ten years ago, or is it more? Ten years, because Bobby was seven, in primary three. Yes, ten. And John-Angus had always been a cheery, kind old soul. Bright. It was amazing how mobile he still was for his age, how with-it. His sight wasn't so good, but he'd had one of his cataracts done last year and that made such a big difference to him. Never a reader, he was at least able to enjoy the television again. He had grandchildren in the town; they came up to see him all the time. And no wonder, thought Nan, for he's such a lovely man. She'd never known about his war experiences, though. He didn't talk about them, never had. It came as a surprise to all the staff in the home when the television people first got in touch.

Quite a pleasant girl, that reporter. Not too cocky.

'What sort of programme are you making?' Nan asked.

'A documentary – a record, if you like – of some First World War stories.'

Zoe didn't look nearly as confident as she'd sounded on the phone, but younger, almost vulnerable. Perhaps she just looked thinner, less substantial than she seemed on the box. Aware that her attention was drifting, Nan refocused on the younger woman's words. Zoe was explaining the background to the programme. She was working hard, came over as sympathetic and, somehow, involved. There was passion there. You could feel it, thought Nan. It was as if Zoe really cared.

'So many of these old boys are dead already – there's only a few left we can talk to and it's so important that their stories never die. Most of the recorded stuff is from officers, not ordinary enlisted men. Their view of it is bound to be different.'

'What about their letters home?'

'They're only helpful up to a point. Few of the men seemed able to say in letters how it really was, and people didn't really want to know. It would have been hard for them to understand. Society was different. It was a time when people weren't encouraged to speak about themselves. It wasn't just your Highland reticence; it wasn't just the gulf between those who'd gone to war and those who'd sent them; it was the normal way.'

'Mightn't it be painful for them, going over it all again – at their time of life?'

'I'm aware of that,' said Zoe, slowly. 'Reminiscence work is always two-edged. I won't push too hard. I'm not out for tabloid television, raw emotion. Not that sort of stuff. But what these men experienced when they were – most of them – still in their teens, is hard to believe even now when we have a better idea of the casualties. So many of them didn't survive. Some of them did, though, and through a century of rapid social change.. it would be interesting and informative, I think, to find out what *they* think about it all, after all this time.'

'Well, John-Angus seems keen enough to see you,' said Nan. 'But remember, he is frail – at ninety-six, who wouldn't be? Please don't over-tire him.'

Zoe smiled. 'Thank you. We'll take it very easy. Just a few minutes at a time. That's often the way you build the best stories, I think.'

Nan stood at his bedside. Checked the pulse. Steadier. And slower. 98. She wouldn't have to call Dr Gaitens from his surgery. She pulled the curtains silently across the windows, shutting out the rain and wind. John-Angus's room was homely with its deep leather chairs. Utility chairs at that. He always said he'd never come across another chair as comfortable, and wouldn't do now he'd stopped wasting time in furniture emporiums. The sideboard was quite old too. He'd brought it from home, with the chairs, and the paintings of Lewis, and the photographs of his extending family. There was the photo of him and his wife – John-Angus in uniform, and she clutching an over-sized bouquet; they stood beside a pillar looking ill at ease. Her ankle-length skirt hung plain but stylish, and her waving hair, tucked into a broad-brimmed hat, was obviously thick. Then there were the graduation photos – a whole flight of them, half a dozen young men and women, robed and hooded, smiling awkwardly, clutching their diplomas. He'd told her once who they all were, but she never did remember. The hairstyles were the best clues to the era of each graduation. The latest one – new, was it? – sported a nose ring. Wedding photos, snaps, mostly, stood in front of these. Again the styles gave the age away. The girl with the nose ring wasn't married yet, or hadn't sent a photo. In fact, thought Nan, she hadn't graduated. No robe. No mortarboard.

John-Angus had few books, but he did have his own television and a video. He was perfectly efficient with the controls. Interested in sport, he liked a western and films from the forties and fifties. He had quite a collection, watched them on days when he couldn't get out walking – days like today when the weather was too wild and the reporter came.

Nan switched the light above his bed to dim. John-Angus stirred.

'I didn't mean to wake you,' she said.

'I was only resting my eyes.'

'Are you feeling better?'

'Och, I'm fine,' he smiled. 'But I think I'll take it easy tonight. That wee girl was a bit exhausting, that Zoe with an E, or whatever she said her name was.'

'Serves you right for being such a flirt,' said Nan. 'At your age. Ought to be ashamed of yourself.'

John-Angus laughed.

'I'm thinking,' he said, 'to take up the pipe again and practise my profile now I'm going to be a TV star.'

'You wanted me to write a letter, you said?'

'Och, no, lass. You were dreaming. Who would I be writing to?'

Nan smiled. 'I'm glad you're feeling better. Well, I'll go and do my paperwork, if you're sure there's nothing else?'

'A cup of tea would be grand!'

'I'll tell Betty to get you one right away. See you later.'

She slipped away, closing the door quietly behind her.

A few minutes later, when Betty came in carefully carrying a mug of tea, she found John-Angus sitting in his arm-chair with the TV on.

'How's the light of my life tonight?'

'Desperate to see you. It's a grand cup of tea you make.'

'Cupboard love,' smiled Betty.

'I bet you say that to all the boys.'

'I do.'

She left the tea on his coffee table and picked up some photographs which had come unstuck and fallen from the album on his knee.

'These are old.'

'Yes. The reporter made me think of them. What do you think of these young fellows? Handsome, eh?'

He showed her a photograph taken on the gangway of a ship – two boys in civilian suits and another in khaki. 'That's me,' he said, pointing to the baby-faced blonde boy, 'and that stocky fellow there is Iain Murray. And that's Angus Johnson in his posh new boots. The day we left to Lewis to go off to war. June 1916. Just as well they didn't take the photo half-an-hour later. Me and Iain were both sick as dogs.'

'Who's this?'

'My mother, and my father. There's my brother Ewan too. And that girl is his wife Myra.'

'And this?'

Betty held up a photograph of a girl in khaki breeches and coat, a shapeless cap covering her head.

'That's Constance Smylie.. Connie, she was always called.'

'Was she an army nurse?'

'A VAD, but not a nurse. She drove ambulances. Had a racing motor-bike. too. Took it over to France. That's her over there as well.'

John-Angus pointed to his wedding photograph.

'I should have known. I've looked at that photograph before. It's just.. you all look so young.'

'We were so young,' he nodded.

Betty picked up the last photograph, a soldier sitting in a trench, half in sunlight, half in shade. He held a pencil, but the pad resting on his knee was getting little attention. The soldier stared past the camera into the distance. His fair hair was ruffled by a light breeze, and the muscles in his arms and shoulders, spare but powerful, suggested vitality. You'd have thought the lad would walk off the page any moment, there was so much life in the picture.

'Now he's a bit of alright.'

'Who's that? Oh,' John-Angus laughed, 'you've seen him already. That's Iain Murray again. He was quite a character. Actually that's an unusual photograph.'

'Oh?'

'It was dry enough and warm enough to sit on the firestep when you could have been sleeping in a much safer dugout.. that's a support trench, I think, an unusually quiet one. I'm not sure where or when it would have been taken. Maybe it was posed. Iain did sit for a war artist. There's a portrait of him in a museum somewhere.'

Betty held the image to the light.

'Well, it's great photo. I think this young fellow would have made a rather fine toy-boy!'

'You'd have had to join the queue, Betty. Quite a long queue.'

'Was he killed in action?'

'No,' John-Angus shook his head. 'Not Iain. Though he saw a lot of action.'

'I'll bet,' says Betty. 'Did you keep up with him after the war?'

'I never kept up with Iain! Many's the one tried and failed. He was a conundrum, Betty, handsome but.. a shirker who did more than all the rest of us put together. A liar and cheat, a wheeler and dealer, and yet the most honest man I ever knew, except maybe my brother. The kindest soul you could meet, and the most cruel on occasion.. war did funny things to all of us, but I'm often thinking it brought out a lot in me, and it brought out more in Iain Murray, complex man that he was. He died in 1919.'

'He's a boy, not a man.'

'Don't be fooled, Betty. That's a man. We all were.' John-Angus stopped for a moment, listening. 'What's that noise?'

Betty listened too.

'Och, it's only Mary next door. She thinks she's going into labour. She'll be at the screaming yet.'

'Poor Mary. She can't help it. We all get stuck at the time of life we loved the most.'

'It's good of you to say so, John-Angus. To be truthful, I don't know anyone else who'd cope with Mary as a neighbour.'

'It doesn't happen all that often,' John-Angus smiled. 'Every nine months.'

'Every week, more like. That's why her daughter couldn't manage.'

'Too much life about her, eh? Not a bad thing to be fixed on, birth, new life.'

John-Angus gathered all the loose photographs in his hand, waving them at Betty.

'We were all immersed in death, you know. Not nearly so positive.'

'I'd better go and attend the delivery,' said Betty. 'Shall I put these away for you?'

'No, I'll sort them out. I know the places they should go in. I'll manage fine, thank you.'

'Okay. I forgot to say your grandson Ewan phoned. He'll be late coming in tomorrow. Some sort of meeting. He did say, but I forget what it was. He'll be here after seven.'

'Something at the hospital, probably.

'I think it was.'

Betty left the room. John-Angus heard her slipping in next door to Mary. 'How are you getting on, lass?' Betty asked.

The door closed softly. He could not hear any more, but

hoped it would be a short labour, a quieter night than some when Mary's poor demented mind relived past hopes. She'd told him once she had no live children.

'You have your daughter,' John-Angus said.

'That doesn't count. She's adopted. I had *seven* miscarriages,' Mary sounded almost proud. John-Angus understood that. Life was odd, odd.

He felt tired tonight. It wasn't so much the television girl as the remembering. The trouble with remembering was stopping, once you'd started. He should have said he didn't want to talk to her.

*   *   *

He'd only gone back to the island once, for his father's funeral. Summer 1918. It was after the big German push, but before the final Allied fight-back; early August, an odd time, that. Nobody was sure, even then, we'd actually win the war. Going home was painful.

Connie wasn't with him, though they were married by then. She had taken influenza, and was too weak to travel. She stayed with Myra's family in Edinburgh. Myra, brave lass that she was, saw him off at the station.

'You'll give your mother all my love. I wish I were going with you. I have such good, good memories of the island!'

'Even now?'

'Especially now. It was a golden time, John-Angus. I don't think I've ever been so content, so happy. The island was in Ewan's blood. It was good to see him there. Right. After you left, we stayed on for another week..'

'I remember.'

There were tears in Myra's eyes.

'Most people don't know happiness like that, John-Angus. I'm persuaded they don't. If they did, the world would not be like this, up to its eyes in blood.'

'Most people don't see the results of war.'

'No.'

Myra looked away, round the bustling station. It was busy as ever it had been in peacetime, busier. There were a lot of mourning clothes in evidence, and more uniform, and women doing jobs they'd never done in peacetime. But John-Angus was right. They didn't know, as she herself didn't know, having never been there, in the thick of it. Connie had been there, driving casualties. Connie had a better idea, but even she had not been on the battlefield, up in the front line.

'If they knew,' said Myra, 'do you think it would make any difference?'

'No,' John-Angus shook his head. 'I don't believe it would.'

'But when you think about it,' she said, fighting back the tears, swallowing bravely, 'but for the war I'd never have met Ewan. Or you, or Connie. Even that infernal Iain Murray would never have crossed my path and I'd be the poorer for it. Even for not knowing that *perfidious* crater!'

'What's Iain been up to now?'

'Oh, with his usual aplomb, he has written to Dulcie saying his heart is *with another*! That she must look on their time together as a short but happy fling, and forgive him. He's going to marry some girl off the island!'

'And who might that be?'

'Iain didn't say. Look John-Angus. That's your train now – kiss me! I must dash or I'll be late.'

'Give them all a hug for me when you get back from work! Your mother, and father, and the boys, and Connie, of course. And especially my nephew.'

'Wee Ewan will miss you! '

'I'll be back soon enough.'

John-Angus held her fast, kissed her cheek, and watched his sister-in-law scurry away along the platform before she would break down completely.

What did he remember of the long journey north? Nobody was laughing now about Russians with snow on their boots. He didn't try to talk to the other passengers in his carriage. His neck was stiff and sore; the wound still gave him trouble. And sitting for so long in a third class carriage, not the clearly marked cattle truck the troops were used to, he felt ill at ease.

He had forgotten how beautiful the mountains were north of Perth. Arriving in Inverness station he found he had three hours to wait for the train to Kyle, and made good use of them. He left his luggage in the station, and walked to the castle, then on down Castle Hill to the river, with its islands. On the other bank he saw the fine cathedral and the graceful Royal Infirmary. He passed many stately houses. Inverness seemed to him a fine town, neat and elegant, its busy streets flourishing. Bigger than Stornoway, less confusing than Edinburgh. He wondered if Connie might like Inverness. He'd bring her here one day, a sunny day like today and they'd walk on the islands, and she'd fall in love with it, as he had.

He ate a brief meal in the Station Hotel before retrieving his pack and settling into the train for Kyle. He felt so old, like the pipers in the legend of Tomnahurich; pipers that foolishly went into the hill to play for one night. They left the path to Inverness and followed music from the hill, gaining entry by way of a strong oak door they'd never seen before. It opened on a vast subterranean hall, filled with beautiful women, handsome men, all dancing and these bright folk saw the pipers and welcomed them, drew them in. What a night they made of it! The piping! Music had never flowed so true. As for the dancers, their feet scarce touched the ground, so beguiled were they by the magic in the reels and jigs. The whisky was the best they'd ever tasted. When the dancers could dance no more, there was still whisky and piobaireachd, and the great music filled their hearts, filled the hall, the hill; and the dancers listened now, breathed the music, understanding completely the transformation of the ground, the variations, the truth and bravery and sadness of Ceol Mor.

But when the dawn crept in through the same oak door and the pipers left the hall and went down to Inverness, next morning as it seemed to them, they could recognise nothing but the lie of the land.

They were centuries older. They had played at a fairy wedding, a dangerous thing to do.

Did he know that story then? John-Angus stopped his reverie, intrigued. Did he know that story or had he added the detail in later years to the memory of a difficult journey? It was not likely that he would have come across in Lewis the tale of the Hill of the Fairies, the hillside cemetery used in Inverness from the turn of the century. Now, in the nineties, it was closed. Completely full.

But he certainly felt sad and old. How old was he? Twenty? He had no idea what to do to make his living. Like the pipers, he had delved in the bowels of the earth, and would never be the same. His mother would want him to take the croft on, he was sure of that, but how could he? Connie wouldn't settle on the island. She wasn't like Myra. Connie was a city girl. Maybe.. John-Angus wondered.. maybe after the war, Myra might think about the croft for herself and little Ewan? Who knew what would happen after the war, when things went back to normal, or at least, to peacetime, whatever peacetime would prove to be.

He dozed a great deal of the way to Kyle, missed the mountains. He didn't eat in Kyle though he was hungry again; he was still afraid sea-sickness would overtake him, as it generally did. He didn't want people thinking him a drunkard, a weak returning invalid. The *Sheila* was already in and John-Angus duly embarked, grabbing a bench at the rear of the boat, in the open, where he sat in perfect comfort all the way to Stornoway. The Minch was calm that day.

His mind was not calm. There was too much to think about. He could no longer blot out the knowledge of his father's sudden death. It did not seem credible: but John-Iain had been drunk and fallen into the harbour; couldn't swim, of course. That was the story.

Calum wrote too that John-Iain had never got over Ewan's death.

(It was difficult for Connie to read that bit out to him.)

The strong, silent fisherman never wept, but spent more and more time alone. Drank more every day. It got harder and harder to find him sober. It got harder and harder to get a clear word out of him. Sine, on the other hand, did nothing but talk about the boy, endlessly, to anyone who would listen, and often when there was no one to listen.

What would Sine do? Would she manage on her own? What would she want? What could he do himself, discharged from the forces? They'd talked about sending him to the Depot at Fort George when he was on his feet, that's what the immediate future seemed to promise. But afterwards? What could he do after the war when, if, it ever stopped? He was a soldier, a trained killer. There was nothing he was equipped to do apart from that, except go home to the croft, and that would not be an easy option.

John-Angus sat and worried himself throughout the journey. He talked to no one. Oh, there were people on the boat he should have talked to, men he'd known all his life. They kept their distance, didn't even look at him.

Maybe they didn't recognise the taut face, the ginger moustache. They would all know, of course, about his father drowning. The island worked like that. News travelled at great speed, even without telephones.

Or maybe John-Angus looked as worried as he felt.

Or maybe there was something of the darkness of war still lingering about him.

He didn't know which if any of these theories might be true, but he was left in peace throughout the journey: and for the first time in his life, he was not sick on a boat.

Calum was waiting for him on the pier, his thin, slightly skewed figure unchanged. Alec Stenhouse stood with him. He was taller, broader.

'John-Angus, cove. It's good to see you.'

'It's grand to see you too, Calum, Alec. It's been that long.'

'It must seem longer to you,' said Alec. 'Fit like, eh, man?'

'Oh, chavin awa',' John-Angus laughed. 'You'll see I've

profited from my time away – learned French.'

'Sounds Dutch tae me,' grinned Alec.

'I saw Bob in Edinburgh,' said John-Angus. 'We were in the same ward. He's out of the war now.'

'Aye. One leg the shorter.'

'A great lad. You should see him fly about on those crutches. Once he gets the wooden leg, he'll be off like the hammers!'

'That's Bob for you!'

'You look very alike,' John-Angus said. 'He didn't have to tell me he was your brother, I knew he had to be.'

'It was terrible,' said Calum, 'about Ewan.'

'Aye. Myra's wonderful, though. And you should see the wee lad. So like his father, even now.'

John-Angus picked his pack up, slung it carefully on his shoulder. 'Well, we'd best be off, eh? It's a fair stretch to Sandwick.'

'We'll stop at my house first, cove,' said Calum. 'My mother asked to see you; and you'll need a drink before we walk you all that way.'

'A few months ago you'd have done it in your sleep nae doot, but still,' Alec nodded, 'you must be hungry and tired efter the boat.'

'Or are you feeling sick?'

'Actually,' John-Angus preened himself, 'I wasn't sick, not once! I sat on the open deck all the way. It seemed to do the trick.'

'You'll be famished, then.'

'I am that.'

'Then it's settled.'

'But what about my mother? She'll be worrying..'

'Actually, she's at our house,' Calum said. 'We thought it better.'

'And the animals?'

'Alec Murray's looking after them, they're fine, man, fine.'

'What about my mother? Is she ill?'

'No. She'll be glad to see you. She took it hard, losing your father. She wasn't fit to stay on her own.'

It was just a step to the Morrison's. Flora came running from the house, grabbed John-Angus, giving him such a hug that the breath was nearly out of him.

'Let me look at you? Is this the poor wee boy that went away? You're a grown man! And married, I'm hearing! I'll have to see the photograph, see if she's good enough for you, this Constance Smylie! I'm sure she won't be!'

'She saved my life,' John-Angus said.

'We'll hear more of that later! Come away in now, a' bhalach. Your mother's waiting!'

Sine was hunched in the wooden armchair by the stove, the same one Myra sat in the night Ewan went missing. It came to John-Angus then that this was a special chair Flora saved for those in trouble.

Sine was struggling, anyone could see. This was not the round-faced, cheery woman he'd left two years before; this was a thin little body with sunken eyes, a woman whose face reminded him of boys he'd seen in the moribund tent at the field hospital at Passchendaele.

He didn't like to think about that time, the hopelessness of it. He knew where he was, knew he was dying. It was Connie coming to look for him that saved him from the lethargy of near-death. It was Connie who had dragged the doctor in, insisted he be moved, be treated. She had brought him from the rear of the trenches to the hospital, was not about to give up, though the doctor shook his head.

'Look at him,' the doctor said. 'The boy can hardly breathe. He's virtually unconscious. If we move him, that lung will bleed again.'

'He's not unconscious,' said Connie, 'just in pain. John-Angus, raise your hand if you can hear me.'

John-Angus opened his eyes, took hold of her hand.

'See?' said Connie. She didn't let go of his hand for the next two days. He owed his life to her. What she was doing that far forward, he never quite understood. She should not have been so near the line of fire.

Looking at his mother now, John-Angus nearly wept. He put his arms around her, held her.

'Och, my boy, you're too thin. Too thin.'

It was all she'd say. In a little while, Flora gave her a cup of good strong tea and helped her up the stairs to bed.

'You'll stay with us, I hope, John-Angus. You can double up with Calum – if you don't mind.'

'It's very kind of you,' John-Angus choked. 'Though I could manage on the croft, you know.'

'No, your mother needs you near her for the moment,' Flora said. 'What we do need to do now is sort out the burial. I don't know if Calum found the opportunity to break it to you.. we have your father laid out in the other room. There's a problem with the church.'

'A problem?' John-Angus was mystified.

'The Reverend Bethune,' said Calum, 'took it upon himself to tell your mother he would not give Christian burial to a suicide.'

'Christ.. my poor mother. Was it..?'

'Probably not. Who can say? On the one hand John-Iain wasn't himself. On the other, he was drinking. It was dark. He didn't leave a note or anything like that.'

'Then why?'

'Och, someone in the bar, one of the sailors from the Depot, very religious, religious enough to be in the bar at closing time, swore he heard him mutter about doing away with himself.'

'But John-Angus,' said Alec earnestly, 'that doesnae mean he did. Naebody saw anything.'

John-Angus turned to Flora. 'What do you really think?'

'I think his heart was broken,' she said.

John-Angus wept then. Flora came to hold him.

'It's the war,' he said. 'The bloody war.'

Calum took out a bottle of whisky, poured them all a glass. Alec handed them round, patting John-Angus on the shoulder.

'The thing is,' John-Angus said, slowly, 'you don't need a churchyard for a burial. We'll bury him tomorrow. We can do it on the croft, on the boundary, up on the hill beside the burn. He often sat there. We can dig the grave ourselves. I'll do it. If there's one thing I've learned in the army it's how to dig. Then we'll let people know. The ones who'll want to come. We'll manage without Bethune. We'll manage fine.'

And so they did. John-Iain was carried to his last rest by his son, his neighbour Alec Murray, Aeneas MacDonald, Alec Stenhouse and Calum too, and Colonel Johnson, who was taller that the rest of them which made it a little awkward, but by no means impossible. The Colonel read from the Bible and commended John-Iain's soul to God. Flora sang two psalms in Gaelic, and everybody joined in, and wept because her voice was so beautiful and they could feel the love in it.

Everybody in the township came, and all the people between the croft and Stornoway; everyone who knew the man came to the hill to pay their last respects, to shake Sine and John-Angus by the hand and tell them how much they'd loved him, how good he was.

It was balm to Sine's heart.

When the last mourner had taken their leave, she turned to Flora.

'You've been that good to me, lass. I thank you. I'll be managing better now. I'll be fine here tonight.'

'You're sure?'

'Och, yes. If there's any doubt about it, I'll send this young man to get you. And there's Alec and Catriona just over the hill.'

'I'll go and get my pack then, mother.'

'You do that, my boy. Take your time. I'm fine. My man is here, at rest, God bless him.'

She looked towards the hill, in perfect ease.

John-Angus walked into town with Alec. Calum had disappeared, and Murdo and Flora were to wait with Sine till John-Angus got back.

'Where did Calum get to?'

'I dinna ken,' said Alec. 'He's.. he's a mite unhappy at the moment.'

'So I've noticed.'

'It seems to be off wi' Mairi,' Alec said, making no bones about it. 'He's never that great when it's off wi' Mairi.'

'She doesn't look that happy herself.'

'No.'

'What about Effie? What's been happening with you and Effie?'

'Och, we're just good friends,' said Alec. 'But we are good friends. We're only eighteen, man.'

'I feel more like a hundred!'

'Look what ye've come through!'

'Sometimes, Alec, I feel as if the war will never stop.'

'It'll stop.' Alec shook his head. 'Ye're nae just the wee boy folk hereabouts used tae think ye!'

'Maybe,' said John-Angus, 'I never was.'

Or did he say that? That sounds more the gift of time, that insight. But certainly, Alec nodded, clapped John-Angus across shoulders where the wound, not fully healed, was now aching with the digging of his father's grave, the weight of the coffin. He remembers that quite clearly because it hurt so much he nearly choked with the pain of it.

Alec was truly horrified.

'Sorry, man, I clean forgot!'

*   *   *

'What's this I'm hearing about TV programmes, eh?'

Ewan smiled down at his grandfather. John-Angus was, unusually for him, in bed. He looked bright enough, though his pale skin seemed sallowed by electric light and the orange/yellow paisley of his dressing gown.

Nan had stopped Ewan on his way along the corridor.

'He's not so good today,' she said. 'Had a bad night, after the TV interview.'

'What interview?'

'Zoe Wild from Channel Four. She's doing a programme on

the First World War. He was keen to do it,' Nan stressed. 'I wasn't sure it would be a good thing. I never knew he had the VC.'

'No,' said Ewan, 'he doesn't talk about it. Never did. When we were kids he'd change the subject every time we asked him, even if it was for a school project. It was that frustrating. Not many kids have a grandad with the Victoria Cross. We'd like to boast about it. So.. was this a long interview?'

'No,' said Nan. 'Zoe Wild seemed very thoughtful. I quite liked her. She only stayed a short while, said she'd like to come back, if possible. But John-Angus got a bit excited and breathless afterwards. I asked Dr Gaitens to cast an eye on him today. He did an ECG. Nothing new.'

'He's ninety-six, I suppose,' said Ewan.

'Only in years,' said Nan.

'I know what you mean. I'd better get in there, before I'm in trouble for being late again!'

Nan watched Ewan swinging down the corridor. When she was a student nurse he'd been surgical house-officer. She'd liked him then, a hard-working down-to-earth resident. He'd never changed, never got high on it, though he was now one of the senior surgeons in the hospital. He'd even asked her out once, but she had just met Dan. They were carefree days. Ah well, she thought, back to the paperwork.

Ewan knocked gently on the door of his grandfather's room, and walked straight in, sat himself down on the bed.

'Well,' he said. 'Was she nice, this interviewer?'

'Who told you? Who spoiled my surprise? Betty? Nan?' Ewan nodded. 'Nan. I might have known. I should have sworn her to secrecy. She was lovely, Zoe Wild. She's famous.. don't you watch TV?'

'Chance would be a fine thing! I know the name, though.. can't put a face to it. What does she look like? What did she want to know?'

'All the stuff I can't remember. She's small and dark like your Emma, but she hasn't got the nose ring. Quite pretty, I suppose.

Smaller than she looks on TV.'

'Emma hasn't got the nose ring any more. Got allergic to it. We were jolly glad. Her nose was a mess for a day or two but it's settled down now.'

'I thought the tiny diamond was just fine!'

'Well, me and her mother didn't! We told her time and time again..'

'I think,' John-Angus interrupted, 'it's Calum Morrison's film they were really interested in; that and Iain Murray.'

'Did you tell her about the poems?'

'She already knew.'

'Did you show her the notebook?'

'No. It's funny, you know. I was thinking about Iain, the contradictions in that man.. when a man has the ability to put words together like that on the page, all those wonderful ideas, the humanity and all that sort of thing.. well, you don't somehow expect him to have flaws, to be a ruddy pest! As Iain could be, often was.'

Ewan nodded. 'Still, one of these days you'll be able to sell that notebook for a fortune!'

'I don't think, so, Ewan. And what would I do with a fortune, at my age?'

'Run off to the Bahamas and die like Robert Service, with a nubile blonde on each arm!'

'Don't know if I could be bothered. Too much effort.'

'We could import the sand,' said Ewan. 'And the swimming pool, and the blondes, come to that..'

'For whose benefit?'

'The greater benefit of mankind! And mine. I could come with you!'

'Just as well Julia isn't here. Why, Julia! Good evening!'

'You don't catch me like that!' said Ewan, laughing; but a small hand gripped his shoulder.

'Move over, darling. Nan said I'd find you here!'

Ewan's wife bent to kiss John-Angus. Ewan shook his fist at the old man.

'I'll get you for that!'

Julia settled herself on the edge of the bed. Forty-five now, and still beautiful. John-Angus thought she always would be.

'What are you doing in bed, you old fraud? Are you on strike?'

'He only overdid things with a TV interview yesterday,' said Ewan. 'TV interview, eh? What do you think of that?'

'Doesn't surprise me at all,' said Julia. 'What was it for? Europe's most glamorous great-grandad?'

'Actually,' said John-Angus, 'it was the whisky did the damage. They gave me a wee dram. Well, I asked them for it. I know it puts the heart wrong, but I do like one occasionally.'

'And why not?'

'He knows why not. Grandad, you're the pits!'

'It was my decision. Perfectly rational. If I can't make decisions at ninety-six there's not much hope for me.'

'I bet you didn't tell Andy Gaitens! No, I thought not. Well, don't make any more rash decisions like that. The last time you had supraventricular tachycardia it was almost impossible to stop it. And you didn't like it much. Remember that!'

'Till you're feeling better,' Julia added.

'I was fine yesterday!'

'Listen to it! Julia,' Ewan turned to his wife, 'when you came in, this reprobate was telling me how he planned to run off with a nubile blonde to the Bahamas!'

'I'm surprised,' said Julia to John-Angus, 'Ewan didn't suggest it to you.'

'Actually, he did. Offered to be my escort.'

'Then you'll know that it was good advice. That's Ewan's maxim, you know. Never make a patient do anything you wouldn't do yourself. If you throw in the odd toyboy, I'll come too!'

John-Angus laughed. 'I'm more like to throw in the towel!'

'You are out of sorts, aren't you? What is it?' Julia took his hand and John-Angus felt his eyes fill with tears.

'I'm tired, that's all. Didn't sleep.'

'Has it set you off thinking.. about the war?'

John-Angus shrugged. Julia sighed. 'You were so brave, all of you. I really don't begin to understand how anyone could have lived through what you did – your generation – but you don't have to share the stories, you know. You don't have to relive it, unless you want to. Tell these folk to fuck off!'

'Julia!'

'John-Angus knows I swear. He taught me!'

'It's just..'

'I know,' she said. 'All that stuff you don't want to remember.'

Ewan was bright enough, John-Angus thought; but Julia always *knew*. Exactly. And she didn't humour him like the rest, talked to him, not at him; Julia saw him as a person, not a collection of years and wrinkles. Zoe Wild had been like that, a little. Maybe that was why his mind had been so resolutely set on dredging up the buried past.

'Focus on the happy times,' Julia advised. 'The rest can't be changed. Nothing can be. Alter your perspective on it. Use a different lens.'

'You're not a photographer for nothing,' said John-Angus.

'As you well know!' she laughed. 'I'm more like one of those animals that changes its colour all the time. What do you call them?'

'Chameleons?' guessed Ewan.

'That's it. Thank you, darling. When you're a chameleon,' said Julia, turning back towards John-Angus. 'Like you or me, or even Ewan up to a point – when you're a chameleon it's best to pick your background.'

'That's complicated,' John-Angus shook his head. 'But there's something in it. You're a philosopher, my girl.'

'I get it from you. All these years of living with unholy optimism..'

'That's from Ewan, surely.'

'It's poetry I get from Ewan.'

'I'm leaving now,' said Ewan. 'That's enough flack for one

night!'

On the way out, Ewan stopped to speak to Nan.

'If the TV crowd come back, and he still wants to speak to them, make sure they don't give him any more whisky. That's what set it off.'

'Ah,' says Nan. 'I'll let Dr Gaitens know.'

'Not that I'd want you to bring it up with the old man,' frowned Ewan. 'He has to feel he still has some power over his life. It's a fine balance, isn't it?'

'I don't see why he shouldn't have the odd dram,' Julia said.

Nan smiled diplomatically, did not answer. She omitted the whisky from her evening report.

Ewan and Julia drove home, bickering amiably.

'Don't disappear,' she said, unlocking their front door. 'Dinner will be ready. I left it in the oven.'

'I'll only do five minutes in the study.'

'No. I know your five minutes. Go and set the table Ewan. Open a bottle of wine.'

'What's for dinner?'

'I took out some of that marvellous lasagne you made the other weekend. The salad's in the fridge. I bought some ciabatta too, but that'll take a few minutes.'

'Red wine, then?'

'Great. Ewan!'

'What?'

'Put your coat in the hall cupboard, on a hanger! Shoving it in the stair like that will ruin its shape!'

Ewan lifted the coat from the pillar at the end of the stairs, opened the cupboard, reached for a hanger.

After his second glass of wine, he began to relax. Julia handed him his plate.

'Was it a dreadful meeting?'

'Just the same as always. I hate politics. Sometimes I think the world's gone mad, the whole world, not just medicine.'

'I don't suppose it's ever any different.'

'It's the rate of change, Julia. The lack of concern for ordinary people.'

She refilled his glass, saying thoughtfully, 'There's never been much concern for ordinary people. Look what happened to ordinary people in the First World War – people like your grandad. It wasn't very different in the Second, for that matter. Or any of the conflicts that have spattered on since then. They're about power, not people. Greed. Money.'

'Sometimes it's the power of ideas, surely? Bad ideas?'

'There's a greed there too, a greed for the power attached to ideas..'

'I'm a medic, Julia, not a historian. Would you argue with the Second World War? With fighting Hitler?'

'No, of course not. That had to be done. But it strikes me it's difficult to argue against any war when you're in the middle of the notion of it. Anger is a powerful emotion.. like jealousy.. an *active* emotion.. it drives you to do things, strike out, hit, hurt. Happiness is much more passive.'

'Sex isn't passive,' Ewan raised his eyebrows at Julia, thinking she looked particularly young in candlelight. Now the children have left home she's started dimming the kitchen lights, using candles at table like they used to do when they were newly married. 'No,' he said, 'lust isn't passive!'

Julia rejected this. 'It is once it's sated. And lust, denied, primes jealousy. No?'

'That's too simplistic,' Ewan was irritated now. 'And if war isn't simple, peace is even more complex. If you think of it as a system of atoms interacting, the world as that single system, or system of systems, then we're bound to tend to chaos because of entropy. War becomes inevitable.'

'But you just said war was the simpler state.'

'It is in some ways,' Ewan insisted. 'See, it clarifies ideas. Right, wrong; black, white. Political issues are much simpler in wartime.'

'I don't accept that.'

Julia put her wine glass down. Ewan noticed the faintest smudge of red wine on her upper lip. He always looked for this. He'd like to lick that off..

Julia, unknowing, carried on. 'Alliances are more complex in wars; more is at stake in them. And the action of the individual, always unpredictable, surely underlies the outcome of any battle, or series of battles.'

'No, the power of the weapons does.'

Ewan tried a forkful of lasagne. Still too hot.

'It takes an individual to use those weapons.'

'Talking of which,' said Julia, handing Ewan the salad bowl, 'John-Angus isn't great. I've never seen him look so frail. Almost ethereal.'

Ewan helped himself to salad, handed the bowl back across the table, reached for bread.

'He didn't seem that bad to me.'

'I got a shock when I saw him.'

'He's tired, that's all.'

Julia, seeing how much he needed to believe this, said no more.

'You're a wonderful cook, Ewan,' she said. 'This is great.'

*   *   *

John-Angus was exhausted. There was a heaviness about him he hadn't felt since Connie died. Fifteen years ago. He'd never have imagined he would last this long without her. Fifteen years. And he went on, day after day, lurching through life. How did he fill the weeks?

Life was like that, worked until you tried to analyse it. He'd never been much of a one for pulling things apart, preferred just to get on with them. And people were interesting. Living in the home there was always someone he could talk to. After years in the shop, he missed the people, the customers, their bits of news, even their unreasonable requests. When he turned the shop over to Ewan's father Iain it was the best and biggest field-sport shop in the Highlands; MacLeod and Johnson, Station Square. People came for miles to see it. The name was still there, ghosting the stonework.

He'd been pleased to get that site. Colonel Johnson had suggested it; became his first partner. Connie did the books of course, helped him with his letters. Though he talked about his problems with reading, he did get a lot better, managed the shop perfectly well. When folk asked him how he could bear to handle guns after the war, he shrugged. He had to earn a living. There was many an honest living still made on the land in those days, ordinary folk came to his shop as well as the county set. He taught a bit of shooting too. That was all he was trained for.

When Connie's father died, and his estate was realised, John-Angus bought Colonel Johnson out. Didn't fancy the notion of Kirsty as a partner; he could see the way the wind was blowing there. Not that he wasn't glad the Johnsons had taken her and the girl she'd borne Angus into their home. There was something hard about Kirsty – though there was no doubt the wee lass brought a deal of happiness to the Big House after Angus died, killed in a foolish accident at Harfleur, where he was training the newly-arrived drafts.

It was an unnecessary death. Colonel Johnson had the details from the Commandant himself who wrote apologetically, explaining the debacle.

The day it happened, Angus had been late arriving at the drill-ground, nobody knew why. The men were ready, standing round the table where all the bombs were laid out waiting. His sergeant had already started. As Angus approached, the man reached forward picking up a No.1 percussion grenade. He swung it over the table, round all the men, green recruits, who backed away. *Now lads, you've got to be careful with this one! Remember, if you touch anything at all while you're swinging this chap, it'll go off.* Round and round the table went that arm in a slightly crazy fashion..

'Sergeant! What in blazes do you think you're doing?'

Angus shouted, stretched towards the man, and to his

horror, saw him drop his arm, rapping the grenade against the table edge. They were both killed, a dozen of the trainees injured.

'Sheer bad luck,' said Colonel Johnson. 'One of those things.'

He didn't tell anyone, not even his wife, that he'd written Angus only days before, telling him Kirsty had applied to them for maintenance for herself and her child, now two years old. He didn't say he'd given free rein to his anger in that letter, demanding an explanation, threatening to cut the boy off, strike him from his will. He didn't say he'd told his son in no uncertain terms how disappointed he was in the event, in him.

'These things happen all the time,' he said. 'Unavoidable.'

It was obvious he did not believe it.

Life was ruled by chaos, thought John-Angus, dizzily. Nan had given him a sleeping tablet, he asked for one, though he didn't usually bother, didn't need that much sleep. He hadn't slept at all for three nights now, needed space from the past, from the sudden sweeping flood of too-vivid remembrance that left him paralysed, the pain almost as sharp and fresh as it had been the first time round. Not that sleeping tablets were the answer; he kept dropping off to sleep and waking paralysed – or he felt as if he was – unable to open his eyes, to talk. And he couldn't open his mouth, couldn't get his throat to make any noise at all, it was just like it was in the field hospital, in the moribund tent. He could hear everything, the groans, the cries; and he could smell – the smell was worst of all. First time round it wasn't so bad; you were used to the stench of death, of diarrhoea mixed with chloride of lime. Now when the smell came, he retched at its foulness, or would have retched if he could, if he weren't paralysed.

They were going to leave him to die. He'd been written off. Connie was standing at his bedside; he could hear her, couldn't see her.

'This one's done-for, poor lad.'

'Yes,' said Flora. 'Nothing we can do.'

'Throw him on the pile,' said Iain Murray. 'Throw him over there with Angus and Ewan.'

'I'll get brain all over me,' John-Angus struggled against them as he felt them lifting, lifting.. 'I don't want Ewan's brain over my face, my fingers.'

But he felt the spongy wetness in his eyes. He choked, lay shivering, and still he could not open those eyes.

'There, there, John-Angus, we'll just sponge you down. You've had a wee rigor. You must have some sort of infection. We'll cool you down, don't worry, get the doctor over.'

'Cold,' John-Angus said. 'I'm cold. Too cold.'

'You're burning up,' said Nan. 'Call Dr Gaitens, Betty.'

Next morning he felt better. His temperature was down, but when they sat him up he was too weak to walk to the toilet. Nan brought him a commode.

'It'll take a day or two,' she said. 'Now you're on the antibiotic it won't be so bad.'

'I was paralysed last night.'

'No, dear. It was the sleeping tablet made you feel like that. You weren't paralysed. There's no sign of stroke, don't worry.'

'I feel that weak.'

'It's the temperature. High temperatures do that. It'll probably flicker up and down for the next day or two. Hopefully it won't be so bad as last night. These urinary infections are terrible. Probably what was wrong with you all week.'

'I could do with a whisky.'

Nan slipped him a small one. Very small. John-Angus appreciated the gesture.

'I didn't know you had a Victoria Cross, John-Angus.'

'I have an Iron Cross as well. I didn't win that; stripped it from a boy whose body wasn't even cold. Pleasant, eh?'

'It's war,' said Nan.

'There are things we did – we all did, Nan – I'm too tired to talk about them. Dreadful things. We got into the habit of them, thought they made us men. Both sides. How can you be a soldier and stay human? Back at home, we tried to forget what we knew was in us.'

'Shh. You're over-tired, John-Angus. That's all.'

'The thing is, Nan, the killing was so easy. It wasn't hate, it was a job – except after Ewan died – a job you got good at if you were lucky and didn't meet the shell or bullet that had your name on. I don't know which was worse – killing in anger or the sniping – you needed a cool head for that.'

'Shh, now. You need some rest. Listen, I phoned the TV girl and told her you were ill. She'll not be bothering you. She sent her love, actually. And aren't the flowers from Julia and Ewan lovely? They'll be in tomorrow too.'

John-Angus's eyes fixed on the tied bouquet of variegated cornflowers, dried thistle and thick red poppies.

'Beautiful,' he said.

*   *   *

When he sailed from Stornoway harbour a week after his father's burial, no one came to see John-Angus off. And really he preferred it that way. He lounged on the deck in his corporal's uniform, not realising this was his last sight of the island. He made no special farewell, paid no special attention to the low brown sweep of land, the clustering town.

Calum and Alec, working, said goodbye to him the night before, fully expecting to see him back before too long; Calum, still depressed, would not mention Mairi, though he read them the latest letter from Iain, recovered from his chest wound and back in Flanders with the 7th Seaforth, cheerful as ever.

Sine was fully absorbed in the croft, in her animals. She'd decided a brother from Breasclete should come and live with her, till after the hostilities. John-Angus, relieved, didn't say so.

'Now, look after yourself, Mam. Flora will be watching!'

'Edinburgh!' Sine sighed. 'Edinburgh! It's so far away, that Edinburgh.'

'Not so far,' said John-Angus. 'Not when you think about it.'

She went back to church the day before. He did not go with her.

He remembered that last leaving as a bonnie day, the sea flat calm, the warm wind kind. On the way into town he stooped to pluck seapink and harebells and all the other different flowers of the machair, as many as he could find, to press in a notebook for Connie, unashamed now to walk carrying flowers.

It may, of course, have been a day of island rain, wet and fierce, the flowers on the machair withering beneath the angry raindrops.

And the *Sheila* always ready to sail.

This bothered him too. When he stopped to think of it – these memories could not be accurate. How could he leave the island at midday and settle in Edinburgh before five? It was the same when he relived his journey back to the island; midday, an unbroken journey, no-time. So much of his life was fixed as no-time, past time, waiting for zero hour.

He settled himself on the bench at the stern. This time there were nods, kind words from the crew and more especially the captain.

'Poor John-Iain,' he said. 'I went to school with him you know. I was sorry to hear of your sad loss. A fine man, to the end. Your mother..?'

John-Angus sighed. 'She's brave, you know.. bearing up.. Alec is coming from Breasclete.'

'Good idea. And you? What next for you?'

'Back to Edinburgh first, to the hospital; then maybe a posting to Fort George. I doubt I'll make the France of it this time.'

'From what they say,' the Captain smiled, 'you MacLeod boys have done your bit.'

The boat would be off in a moment or two. John-Angus sat with closed eyes, the hard wood of the bench pressing into his back wound, scouring the scar, reminding him he was alive;

the skin drenched in air, in warm wind, the oil and fish smells jostling with the odour of kelp from the castle shore, a strange mix, a fresh mix.

'John-Angus.'

He didn't quite recognise the voice, though it was familiar. An island voice.

'John-Angus..'

He opened his eyes to find Aeneas MacDonald and Mairi before him, both dressed for travel, Aeneas unusually tired-looking, the girl pale, her eyes pink and swollen as if she had just stopped crying.

'John-Angus,' Aeneas said, 'you're going all the way to Edinburgh, aren't you? Would you, could you please, escort our Mairi? She's going to an aunt in Leith. I know it's a lot to ask. I'd planned to travel myself. But Maisie's that unwell today, and..'

'I'd be delighted to travel with Mairi, and to introduce her to my Connie. It's a pleasure, Mr MacDonald.'

Aeneas did not linger. The boat was on the point of sail. He stood on the pier, waving sadly to his only daughter. John-Angus was clear about this. Aeneas hardly noticed him. It was the girl his farewell was directed at.

'You'll be excited,' he said, 'going off to the big city. Have you been out of the island before?'

Mairi's smile seemed somewhat strained. 'No. Not ever. As for Edinburgh, I don't expect I'll see that much of it.'

'Oh?' John-Angus was surprised. 'Are you not staying long, then?'

'Six months,' she said, looking away from the town, staring out to sea.

'That's plenty of time to see Edinburgh. It's not that big a place; not like Paris or London.'

'Have you seen Paris and London? Have you been there?'

'Not Paris,' John-Angus admitted. 'London's just a mess of smoke and grubby buildings. I was in hospital there for a while. Didn't like it.'

'I'd love to go to Paris,' Mairi whispered.

'Maybe you will, one day. But Edinburgh's lovely, as cities go. Leith is fine. You'll feel quite at home there,' he tried to reassure her, feeling this somehow necessary. 'It's near the sea. Nowhere in Edinburgh is that far from the sea. You can climb up the Castle hill and see the sea, any time. Or Calton Hill. Or any of the hills.'

Mairi offered him another of those tight unhappy smiles. 'Where does your Connie stay?'

'With Myra, Ewan's Myra, in the New Town.'

'Where's that? '

'Oh, it's not that far from Leith. Does your uncle keep a motor car?'

'I don't know. Actually I've never met this aunt and uncle. She's my mother's youngest sister. But your folk – they are all quite well?'

'I don't know,' John-Angus frowned. 'Connie had the influenza when I left. Now Myra's got it, and wee Ewan too. I'm rather worried about them. That's why I'm going back so soon. Though I must say that since your father and the Colonel helped us with my father's burial, my mother has been much better. Much better. The difference in her is amazing.

'It was just like the change in the men after a battle, Mairi.. we're doing better now, but so many of the battles were so terrible.. and we'd come back exhausted, flat, feeling we could never lift a rifle again. There'd be so many of the boys missing.. fine men, gone.. and you'd fall down in your tent, or barn, wherever you found a place to sleep.. exhausted.. but after a good sleep and a meal you'd find your spirits rising despite everything.. you'd share your battle-stories with whoever else got back.. somehow, you had the will to go on living, go on fighting. It's amazing what we can cope with, Mairi. With my mother, I think it was the feeling of being – I don't know – an outcast maybe.. yes, that's what I mean. Outcast. It overwhelmed her. Not that anyone was deliberately unkind, except that withered minister. With the help of the community, she found strength to go on.'

Mairi's lip was trembling.

'I don't mean your family, Mairi. You know I don't. And your poor mother so ill and your father run off his feet. They're so lucky to have you. Everybody says.'

Mairi turned away now, obviously crying.

'I'm sorry,' said John-Angus. 'I always put my foot in it. I shouldn't have said a word.'

'No, it's me,' said Mairi. 'I'm a bit emotional just now.'

They sat in silence for a long time, as if lost on the open sea, the island far behind, the future riding on the wood and metal of the boat's sturdy plausibility.

'When we get to Edinburgh,' said John-Angus, 'I'll take you directly to your aunt's. We should take a cab, I think. I'd bring Connie to see you tomorrow if I could; but I think it will be better to wait until we're sure she's over the influenza. It's been such a rotten illness. There's no point in putting you at risk.'

'That's good of you, John-Angus,' she whispered. 'But I'll not be needing visitors in Edinburgh. I'll be taking it very quiet till my time.'

John-Angus could only stare, seeing now how round she had become, recognising the change in her complexion.

'My Connie will want to visit you, however things are,' he said at last. 'And Myra. And her friend Dulcie. Dulcie's a nurse too. They're lovely girls, both of them.'

'I've.. heard of Dulcie, I think,' Mairi said, blushing.

'Of course! Myra will have talked of her when she came over!' John-Angus was glad to have stumbled on a neutral topic of conversation.

'Dulcie's such a fine person, Mairi, blonde hair, lively.. and a wonderful nurse. She and Myra worked together from the start. You'd get on with Dulcie. She's every bit as clever as you. The only thing is..'

'Yes?'

'Well.. she's had a bit of a blow – she's heart-broken, Myra says. I don't know how she'll be, if she'll be quite herself yet.'

'Oh?'

'When I get my hands on Iain Murray!'

'Iain Murray?' repeated Mairi.

'She's been walking out with him since he was in the hospital,' John-Angus nodded. 'Way back in the winter, January, was it? When he was in hospital in Edinburgh. Anyway, they were supposed to be informally engaged. Now Myra tells me, he's written saying he's going to marry a girl from the island! And that can't be true. I haven't heard sight nor sound of it since I've been home, not from Catriona or Alec or anyone. Of course they haven't heard of Dulcie either! It's just another of Iain's lies. I don't know why he does this kind of thing, really I don't. He's not all bad. There's a good side to him..'

'He hides it well,' Mairi said. 'Poor girl. I can well imagine how she must be feeling.'

Her voice was oddly bitter. Silence fell between them once again, not a comfortable silence, though to any observer, even to John-Angus looking back over the decades, they seemed romantic; two young people lost in conversation, the girl as dark and pretty as the boy was thin and fair, his uniform a foil to her long dark cloak.

John-Angus suddenly remembered his manners.

'Are you hungry, Mairi? Do you need something to drink?'

'Oh no,' she said. 'I mean, no thank you, John-Angus. To tell you the truth I'm feeling more than a little queasy. I'm not the best sailor in the world.'

'Well, I'm the world's worst! Except for Iain Murray.' John-Angus shook his head. 'We always come back to Iain Murray, don't we?'

'Too often,' echoed Mairi. 'I don't know why.'

'Do you remember,' says John-Angus, 'the year we had the Battle of the Seas?'

'Do I not! That was such great fun.'

Mairi saw John-Angus's face grow more animated in talking of his brother than it had been throughout the journey.

'Ewan was that proud of the Battle of the Seas. It wasn't my finest hour, as you know, but it was his greatest achievement, the best summer of his life. He was so sure of himself, so much more confident afterwards.'

'He was wonderful,' said Mairi. 'Wonderful. And I must tell you, John-Angus, that bitter though you must feel towards the minister now, he made a lovely service for Ewan after Arras. You'd have thought it was his own son had been killed.'

'I heard about his son,' John-Angus said. 'I heard about his son, the doctor.'

'What about him?'

'You didn't know? The boy that was the doctor – Alexander, was it? – poor fellow, he was shelled several times in the Dardanelles. Broke down, lost his nerve completely. They call that neurasthenia when officers get it, send them to hospital. Sometimes they get over it. But Alexander hung himself in the grounds of Craiglockhart, the hospital in Edinburgh where they were treating him.'

'How could that happen?'

'He used his dressing gown belt,' John-Angus said, unthinking.

Mairi felt sick, stood up, rushed to the rail, and leaned across it, retching. John-Angus hovered in the rear, cursing himself for telling her, for coming out with all the details just like that. He couldn't stop himself, heard his voice rattling on.

'I can't imagine Mr Bethune coping with it. He's probably pretending it hasn't happened. And what good is pretending? It doesn't get you far.'

They both leaned on the rail then, staring at the passing shore, the swiftly rising land.

When they sighted Kyle, he turned to her more cheerfully.
'So when will Calum be coming down to Edinburgh?'
'He won't. Calum.. doesn't know.'
'You haven't told him?' John-Angus was shocked. 'Surely you should..'
'No doubt he'll hear,' said Mairi.
'You mean it's not..'

Mairi closed her eyes. 'I wish it was, John-Angus. I wish to God it was!'

'Calum loves you, you know. It wouldn't make a difference.'

'You think not?'

'It wouldn't make a difference to me.'

'John-Angus. You're unusual. You've been through the mill. You've been away for longer than the years and months of actual time. You've changed. You've grown. But the rest of us are shrivelling. It would make a difference, believe me.'

Mairi went on, her voice slightly unsteady. 'Promise me something.'

'Of course, Mairi. Anything.'

Her face was solemn. 'You won't tell anybody.. what I've told you?'

'Not if you don't want it.'

'Nobody we know. Nobody. Not Calum. Not Iain. Not even Alec.'

'Alec would understand.'

'Yes, I know Alec would understand, but he would tell Calum right away. I know that boy.'

He noticed her lips, pale as stars rising in the evening sky, or a cow's first thin milk, almost as pale as snow.

'Alec would just tell Calum and Calum would come and find me and I don't want that.'

'But you love Calum, Mairi. You always have. Anyone can see..'

'All the more reason.'

John-Angus laid his hand gently on her arm.

'Mairi, there's no sense in this.'

'Promise me,' she said.

'All right. I promise. But..'

'But what?'

'I'm going to bring Connie round to meet you. You'll need your friends, Mairi.'

She took his hand in hers, holding it grimly, as if it were a

161

lifeline thrown into the Kyle for her.

'John-Angus, there's so much of your dear good brother in you,' Mairi sobbed. 'And so much of your own dear self.'

Sometimes now he wondered if he really said these things, young as he was, experienced only in war, but that's how he remembered it; and not another word till they were in the cab arriving in the street in Leith where Mairi's aunt lived. Just before the cab drew up, exposing him to the aunt's initially suspicious eye, Mairi turned to him, oddly casual.

'John-Angus. Will you do one last thing for me?'

'You have to ask?'

'Will you give this.. this envelope.. to Dulcie? I want her to have it. She'll understand.'

John-Angus didn't, puzzled over the envelope as he carried it all the way back to the New Town.

'No,' Connie said. 'It can't be..'

'Surely not,' said Myra.

John-Angus still didn't understand.

'Look in the envelope,' said Connie. 'It's open. You're supposed to.'

John-Angus resisted at first. Eventually he unfolded the unstuck flap and pulled out the contents of the envelope.

'How very odd,' he said. 'It's a book of poems.. Iain's poems.. they must be. They're all in his writing. And a photo too. A photo of Iain in the trenches.'

'I'm not,' said Myra, 'going to give this to Dulcie. She wouldn't cope. Leave it with me, John-Angus. I'll take it back to Mairi as soon as we're both up to it.'

She never did; and that was how how John-Angus came by Iain's notebook and the first of the wartime photographs. They seemed to mount up year by year, filling out the memories, fleshing them.

He never did tell Calum. And Calum never heard it was John-Angus squired Mairi on her journey south.

That was the really odd thing.

*   *   *

His temperature was up again, worse than ever. John-Angus felt icy, cold; his mind busy, too busy. He was sitting on the machair at the croft, throwing stones that failed to reach the striving water; he was cleaning his rifle in a sandbagged trench while Eddie Shields boiled tea, and there was bacon frying too, German bacon, it had to be. The Seaforth bacon was not yet on the go. Odd how the smell of bacon eased anything, even German bacon, eased even this dull and heavy aching in his chest, soothed his racing heart. And the heart stuttering faster than the machine guns used to play.. what was it they used to say the machine guns played..? MEET me DOWN in PICC-A-DILLY.. was that it? He used to tell the gunners mouth music would be better, had better rhythms, but they never got the rhythm right.

MEET me DOWN in PICC-A-DILLY.

They pulled cartridges out of the ammunition belts to get that rhythm, and in some parts of the line the German boys would answer, slower, for their guns were slower.. YES without my DRAWERS ON. Angus Johnson told him that. When? When had they met and where, for Angus Johnson to tell him? Or had Colonel Johnson passed it on?

That must be it. John-Angus never saw the son after that first aching trip across the Minch. Were Angus's new boots ever the same after it? Was he wearing them that last day in the Harfleur Bullring?

John-Angus felt suddenly lighter, lighter all over, and dizzy. The world was thinning, disappearing into sky. The sky was falling. Maybe he should tell someone about it.

He reached for the buzzer, knocking over Ewan's flowers, spilling flowers and water all over his bedside table. Nan, rushing in to switch the bell off didn't seem to see him standing there beside her.

He could see from her face she was upset. She dropped

into the leather chair beside the bed, gazing at the still form lying there. She was weeping as she closed the old man's staring blue eyes, brushed poppy stamens from his striped pyjamas.

SECOND VARIATION

Calum Morrison's uncle is a sailor; since 1914 all his efforts have been on behalf of the Royal Navy, first in shipping men to the Dardanelles, later in Atlantic convoys. Sublieutenant James-Alec Morrison has served as First Lieutenant in several of His Majesty's destroyers, bringing to them all his many talents – navigation, coolness under fire, an ability to work through sea-sickness, considerable agility on the mouth organ, and, last but by no means least, an earthy sense of humour.

Most island men his age – he's just turned thirty-six – are sturdy, steady and rather devout. James-Alec is all of these, up to a point; has his own religious tract copperplated above his bunk – *The wages of gin is breath*. Unmarried, he spends most of his time shepherding merchant ships across the grey Atlantic, praying for good weather, acting calmly in the flurries of activity that follow sightings of a U-boat (luckily more rare than he thought they might be); but often he finds himself wishing for the calm unhurried pre-war days he spent sailing in the East. Those Asian girls!

When the war is over he ought, he supposes, to go home, choose a wife. He's getting past the age. But those Asian girls..

When one of the survivors of a newly 'zonked' merchant-man is pulled from the pulsing waves clutching an unmarked chinese vase that somehow came undamaged through the conflagration, James-Alec quickly offers to trade a week's supply of cigarettes for it. The survivor thinks he's had an excellent deal and James-Alec doesn't really enjoy smoking anyway.

It's beautiful: sixteen inches high, blue and orange, flecked with gold. Medallions, front and back, show the same delicate picture of a chinese maiden, rich, (perhaps she's a bride?) walking with her women through a calm green garden from the wooden boat she's just arrived in, just stepped out of. Her topmost robe of white and green silk (James-Alec is sure it must be silk) is closely embroidered with storks and spreading trees. She is walking in the shade of a gilded parasol held by one of her equally charming attendants. Two more arrange her robe, smooth the train, shake wrinkles from her sleeve; and as she walks, the inner robes, red and gold, black and blue, shine richly. He can almost hear the sensual swish of silk against grass.. there is not even a glimpse of shoe.

There are, however, subtle differences between the front and back: the flowering tree across the river is here green, there blue; the maidens' faces paler now, and now much redder; the girl who walks before her mistress carrying a lacquered casket frowns anxiously on one side, smiles on the other. The same scene, almost exactly, but two very different narratives.

It troubles James-Alec that this fragile thing should have survived what steel and muscle did not. It fascinates him. When they next pull in to Bucrana, he has the vase carefully wrapped, sends it home to Flora, asking her to put it in his bottom drawer. Or, as he writes, 'you can leave it on your dresser, if you like, but don't let Murdo knock it over! I've taken a great fancy to it somehow. If the war does ever end, if I ever do get married, I'd like my wife to have it.'

Murdo shakes his head.

'Wife? The boy's run mad, at last. We all knew it would happen.'

'Oh, it's beautiful,' says Flora. 'Beautiful.'

Calum agrees, has the vase photographed for the front page of the *Oran* where the story is told of how this treasure survived the U-boat's onslaught and was rescued from the sea. Calum makes light of the sinking, emphasising that the losses of merchantmen have decreased steadily with the convoy system, with our brave boys (so many of them from Lewis too) fighting the U-boats.

Murdo is not sure it is a wise thing to do, advertising the vase. Calum laughs.

'Who'd want it back? The Admiralty? I don't think so. They're much more like to take the line that it's encouraging morale, a pat on the back for the convoy system.'

And Calum's instinct is the surer. There are no complaints from the Admiralty; the commander from the Depot even congratulating him on the delicate nature of the illustration, the tenor of the piece. James-Alec's vase is, for the moment, safe.

Like his uncle, Calum is utterly beguiled by the vase. Alec can't see what all the fuss is about.

'Ken, it's jist a lump o' clay,' he says.

'Philistine,' says Calum, lifting his fiddle, drawing his bow across the strings. 'What tune will we stairt wi'?'

'Noo, dinna you mak fun o' my accent, or ye'll ken whit's at ye!' Alec threatens, waving his bow at Calum. 'Ane o' these fine days I'll get the Gaelic man, that'd gie ye a start, eh?'

'Certainly would,' says Calum, working on the A string.

'Talkin' o' which..'

Alec doesn't go on. Calum finishes his tuning and looks up at Alec who hasn't even opened his fiddle-case, but is sitting looking anxious, almost sad.

'What is it?'

'Something Effie wis tellin' me the day. Fair gave *me* a start. You've no heard the news?'

'Sorry, Alec. I don't follow. What news?'

Calum is not concentrating on the conversation. He's plucking at the strings again, retesting; he decides his E string is not absolutely perfect, starts to retune it.

Alec hesitates, but decides to go ahead. He hasn't been looking forward to discussing this with Calum; was surprised Calum looked so bright when he walked in. He cannot know, then.

'You havenae heard.. about the MacDonalds? You havenae heard frae Mairi?'

'Poor Maisie's bad. I know that. Come on, Alec, we've all known for months that she must have galloping consumption. We've all seen the flesh dropping off the poor soul.'

'No, not Maisie..'

'What then? Is Aeneas selling the shop?' Calum is flippant.

Alec's pained expression brings him back to seriousness. 'Is Aeneas ill? What is it, Alec? It's not like you to be so backward coming forward.. have you got a liver after last night at the bothan? Is that the problem?'

Alec shrugs. Calum will hear it soon from all sides. Best for him to find out from a friend. If the bairn's not his.. though who else's should it be?.. he'll shout and scream, he'll be struck to the marrow, there's no doubt of that; but he'll be prepared, at least, to face the world. And Alec is that sorry for him and for Mairi, heart-sorry for them both.

'It concerns Mairi,' Alec says, feeling his way.

'What about Mairi? She's had an accident? Alec, she's not hurt?'

So Calum doesn't know. Alec's voice is very quiet, very soft now.

'Nae hurt, exactly. But she's awa' frae the island. She took the boat today. They *say* she's going into service on the mainland, but that's always what they say.. is it no?'

'Alec, what are you implying?'

Alec sighs.

'Effie thocht ye didnae ken. She telt me tae tell ye. Nae even Effie kens where they're sending Mairi, man. Nae even Effie!'

Calum looks stricken, now; wild. He clutches Alec's forearm, digging his fingers so tightly into the flesh that Alec winces with the pain of it.

'Careful, my loon.'

'When did you hear this?'

'Effie came to tell me this efternoon, when the boat had sailed. Her eyes were that red.. poor lass.'

'Why did you not come for me right away?'

Alec looks directly at Calum.

'Man, how could I? I didnae ken if ye kent already, micht be keepin it tae yersel. And.. ye ken very weel I couldnae even see John-Angus off today, wi' the manager being off and Bennet awa' on holiday. I wis that busy.. I kept trippin ower my own shadow, I wis that rin aff my feet! But this evenin',' says Alec. 'An' I dinna like this, Calum, I dinna.. your cousin Peggy meets me on the street and stops me and says hae I heard the craic?'

Alec pulls a face as he says this, a face that makes him look uncannily like Peggy.

'She speirs, hae I no heard the latest? Mairi MacDonald's quit the island five months gone! Of course I put her in her place. I cannae stand that besom, Calum. How can you be related to a gannet like thon?'

'Not by choice,' says Calum. 'Not by choice.'

Calum shakes his head. He cannot breathe, he finds he cannot breathe. He knew there was something.. knew! He knew fine! It's not his child, they haven't.. but why didn't she come to him? Why didn't Mairi feel able to tell him?

There is such an anger in him, rising. She should have trusted him. She should have told him. Anger threatens now to overwhelm him, black and raw, spilling from every corner of him, spitting deep and dark, fiercer even than the night he lay and watched Angus Johnson flitting from the MacDonalds' garden.

But this time the anger isn't at Mairi.. no, the anger's at himself. He should have helped her, should have protected her. He knows fine what must have happened.

Alec is frightened. For many minutes Calum says nothing, goes on saying nothing. He stands stock still, barely breathing. He closes his eyes, his fingers clench and unclench the neck of his fiddle. Suddenly he lifts the fiddle, swings it down towards the wooden chair.

'No, Calum, no!' cries Alec, breaking the fiddle's fall with his right arm, groaning with the pain of the impact and the fiddle's banshee wail. 'Ye cannae dae that! That's a very fine instrument.. And I doubt,' he adds wincing, 'but ye've broken my airm, and my right airm tae. Whit on earth am I tae tell the manager? Don't cry, Calum.. don't.. it's alright.. he'll be alright, Mrs Morrison,' says Alec weakly, as Flora flies into the room, wondering at the noise. 'Calum has had some bad news, that's all. But I had tae tell him..'

'Tell him what?' says Flora, sharply. 'What was that terrible noise? Why is your face bleeding, Alec?'

Alec has not been aware till now that his cheek is bleeding, neatly flayed, scoured in three parallel lines by the flailing strings.

'I was trying to destroy my fiddle,' Calum giggles hysterically, 'and Alec.. Alec was trying to stop me.'

Flora looks from one to the other.

'What's going on? Out with it! Who's going to start?'

Alec's never heard Flora so upset. He doesn't open his mouth, though it's odd how sorely he's tempted to join Calum's ill-timed laughter. Flora frowns, speaks firmly to her son.

'Put that fiddle away, Calum, and come and sit down. Now!'

'Is it badly damaged?' Alec asks.

Calum turns it over and over. The sounding board has cracked along its full length, and the bridge become detached. The strings hang limp, the tail piece swinging loose. The neck seems sound.

'It's in better condition than you, I think, Alec. It's mendable,' Calum whispers. 'I'm really sorry.'

Alec moves his arm. 'I think the airm is just bruised.'

'What has been going on?' asks Flora. 'What on earth has been going on?'

Calum does not sleep that night, or for many nights after, refusing Flora's mixtures.

'I'm not ill,' he says.

All through the dark hours she hears him tossing, turning. When was it ever different? Calum always takes life hard, will never change. Music helps, the dance of notes seeming to compose him. It's the only thing that does, that and the writing.

At work he finds some measure of rest; at home, the journal he'd started when the boys went off to war is growing now, faster than ever. There's even a element of wry humour creeping in. This cheers him, gives him hope, though the minute the pen or the fiddle are laid by the old anxieties return to haunt him.

Where is Mairi? Where can she be? How is she managing? He goes to ask Aeneas, but gets short shrift there.

'I'm sorry, Calum. Mairi asked me not to say. She doesn't want to hear from you. We know,' he says now, pitying the lad, 'it's not your doing. I'm as sorry as I can be.'

Calum almost cries to see how thin Aeneas has become, how the eyes on him are sinking into the never-round face. Worry and age have settled on Aeneas, though he can't be any older than Calum's own father.

'And how is Mrs MacDonald?'

'Not so good. Still, your cousin Peggy's starting with us in the shop next week,' Aeneas said. 'That'll help a bit. She's an efficient girl.'

'If I wrote to Mairi,' says Calum, 'brought the letters to you.. you could maybe send them for me.'

'No, lad,' Aeneas says. 'I can't do that. I'm sorry.'

On the way home, Calum remembers having advertised seeds in the *Oran*, for some of Mairi's family.. they lived in Edinburgh.. the address may still be in the ledger. He knows, or thinks he knows the Glasgow aunt emigrated the year before the war. They wouldn't risk Mairi travelling to Canada in her state, with hostilities still so rife. Maybe..

He stops off at the office and after a good hunt finds the old advertising ledger. There is an address; the only possible address. He does not recognise the name – Maitland of Linlithgow. He'll have to look through back copies, checking the advertisements.

The relevant week's *Oran*, however, is not there. It's his own fault. Often, he forgets to keep one.

He writes the letter many times. In the end he sends a simple note which seems to say it all.

Dear Mairi,
Write and tell me you are well, and that you want me to come for you. I love you, Mairi. That's all that matters.
Ever your,

Calum

It comes back two weeks later, marked NOT KNOWN AT THIS ADDRESS.

He writes to Iain then.

Iain,
You will no doubt have heard that Mairi is with child, has disappeared, it seems, off the face of the earth. I have not been able to make contact with her. I have an idea now of what happened between you, why Mairi was crying, why she couldn't talk about it.

I know about Dulcie too. John-Angus was home, and told us all about your supposed engagement. The poor boy was surprised your parents didn't seem know about it. Did you think we wouldn't hear, Iain? Did you think we wouldn't put two and two together?

How could you do this?
Don't write back with excuses. Don't bother writing.
Calum

This produces a flood of letters Calum will never open, some of them addressed to Mairi. He throws them in a shoe-box under the bed, feels like tearing them to shreds, burning the fragments. He does not do this, held back by a superstitious notion that if he were to burn them he'd be somehow responsible for any hurt or harm that came to Iain.

Autumn is upon them. Even on the gentlest, most golden of days, Calum cannot see the sky. The equinoctial storms are nothing to the torment in his heart. He eats little, sleeps less. Flora is worried about him. Seonaid from the teashop, walks round to the *Oran* office every day, bringing him all his favourite sandwiches; to no avail, as she tells Alec over his cream-laden cocoa.

'I ken,' says Alec. 'Seonaid, I'm clean oot o' ideas. I've tried makin' him talk, tried lettin him sit quiet. I've tried takin' him oot for long walks, and swimmin' an' that. I've tried philosophy, religious argument and beer and whisky. Naethin' works. I dinna ken whit tae dae next. I'm rackin' my brain, quine.'

Calum realises all of this. In a distant way he's grateful for their efforts, Seonaid's food, Alec's listening ear. But Calum can't discuss the problem with Alec. Alec is too partisan, takes Calum's side too fiercely.

Finally the boy from Cullen tries a different tack, asking Calum to teach him tunes of his own composing; this is better. The mended fiddle sings as well as ever, tunes flowing freely, new tunes, sad tunes, many of them, but so beautiful that Alec is often overcome.

One Friday evening, he comes with a specific request.

'Calum, I wondered if ye'd feel able tae mak a tune for me.. and Effie? A kind o'.. engagement.. tune?'

'Alec, man, congratulations! This is such very good news!'

Calum hugs the astonished Alec, who bursts into tears.

'It's so wonderful! I'm that happy for you both.'

'It's grand tae hear you say it! I ken, man, whit it must mean tae ye.'

'I'd be very small indeed if I couldn't celebrate a friend's happiness – two friends' happiness,' says Calum. 'If Mairi were here..'

'You were never small,' Alec interrupts. 'But the tune? Will ye nae dae it noo?'

It's October now, the worst of the fighting once again at Ypres. Calum knows the Highland regiments are in the thick of it, the Camerons, the Seaforths. If Iain falls.. but Iain, he reassures himself, has seen fiercer fighting.

*   *   *

At twenty, Calum has never known a woman, not in the biblical sense, though he loves the shape and feel of the female breast, the wondrous softness gentling the hand that slips below the opened buttons of a blouse and under the chemise. The blackberry coolness of the nipple excites him, and its changeable nature – now soft and wide, dissolving into generosity of breast – now well-defined, firm, like hedgerow fruit.

Not that he knows many pairs of breasts. The odd girl, after a dance, seduced by his music, had let him kiss her, stroke her cotton covered bosom. And Mairi, once. He never felt the urge to squeeze and bite these offered breasts, as some boys did; nor the need to divulge his pleasure afterwards, recounting, as too many would, the incident in sensuous detail to the eager audience in the bothan, the bottle passing from hand to hand. Even Alec sometimes fell prey to the bothan's atmosphere, like the night they took John-Angus there.

'John-Angus, loon, tell us whit like are thae French quines?'

'Oh, Alec,' John-Angus blushes, 'I'm a married man.'

'Ye're nae that lang merrit.. hic.. married, cove!' hiccoughs Alec. 'Come on, dinna be a spoilsport. Tell us. We'll no' spill the beans.'

John-Angus shakes his head.

'I'm out of the war. And I'm happily married. There's nothing like it, nothing like it, I tell you. If Connie was here, you'd see.'

'Quite right,' says Calum, standing up, stretching his legs. 'Time for home, I think. We've all had too much.'

'When Iain was here in March,' says young Hamish McGillivray, ignoring Calum, 'he told us the French lassies think the English all have tails, and save themselves for Highlanders!'

'Sounds like Iain right enough,' says John-Angus drily once the laughter has settled. 'He'd do better to tell you about prophylactics! I haven't noticed too much saving, not in the Red Lamps.'

'I'm thinking he did mention prophylactics,' Alec muses. 'But I cannae for the life o' me remember fit ye dae wi' them.'

And Alec puts on such a look and tone of wheedling innocence that even Calum joins in the general laughter. But he's not drunk enough to catch the bothan's mood.

'It's that time,' he says. 'I have to go.'

The boys have got the giggles now and much is made of Calum's having to go, and where. He ignores this ribaldry.

'John-Angus, Alec.. I'll say goodnight.'

'Calum,' says Alec. 'I think I might bide here a wee bit. My head's nae jist straight on my shoulders.'

'Aye, I can see that,' Calum smiles. 'I'll see you tomorrow then.'

'I'll come with you, Calum.' John-Angus rises, a little unsteadily. 'I've the boat to catch, could do with an early night.'

'It's nae that early,' Alec laughs. 'John-Angus, I'll no' mak the pier, I'm thinkin',' he stretches now to shake John-Angus's hand. 'We're that short at the bank. But it's been grand seein' ye, man. Keep in touch, now. I'm hopin' it'll nae be long afore ye're back on the island, and I'm fair dyin' tae see your Connie. Tell Bob tae come an' visit me, once he gets that sea-leg!'

'I'll tell him. Thank you for all your help, Alec.'

Calum is at the door now, throws it open to the peaceful moor.

'Fine moon for poaching, eh, John-Angus?'

'You brought your rod?'

'No.'

'Well, the keeper can sleep easy,' John-Angus laughs. He turns on the threshold. 'Goodnight lads!'

But the boys in the bothan are locked in fevered musings about girls and what they will and won't do; apart from Alec, they fail to notice, far less acknowledge, the older boys' parting. John-Angus closes the door, sets off with Calum.

'What was Iain like in March?' John-Angus asks, slightly out of breath even at Calum's pace. He's still not up to fitness. They'd told him at the hospital he might never be, but he hopes it will just be a matter of time. 'What was Iain like? Was he quite himself?' he asks again.

'He was distinctly odd, if you want to know,' says Calum. 'We were all affronted at him.'

'How come?'

'Well, first of all, there was the day we went to meet him at the boat. Mairi and I waited and waited for it. We were to drive him home, you see, in Alec's dog-cart. And the boat was late, well it often is, but when it finally arrived and all the passengers came off, there was neither sight nor sound of Iain. We couldn't see him anywhere. He didn't come and he didn't come. We hung around for ages. Finally we asked one of the stewards what was holding him up; we were worried, you see, in case he might have got ill on the journey. Truth is, he wasn't on the boat. He hadn't sent word to anyone. His poor mother and father had the house all ready, and a dumpling too; the little girls had made a banner out of flour bags and painted WELCOME HOME IAIN on it; the Murrays had told all the neighbours to come round and celebrate his homecoming, they were that proud of him. And he didn't come.

'No one could understand it. Catriona was so worried she sent Alec to the Big House to ask Colonel Johnson what to do. They wired the hospital, in case Iain might have had a setback. But he'd left the hospital the week before! That was terrible for Alec and Catriona, they couldn't put a face on it, no matter how they tried. Colonel Johnson said to Alec that it's sometimes difficult for soldiers coming back from the front. They can't face normal life. He told him not to worry, if anything had happened, they'd have heard. Iain would turn up; there'd be news, one way or another. Even if he'd gone straight back to the front, as sometimes happened, they'd hear. He said to Alec he thought himself that Iain must have gone on a binge, or be holed up with a woman, but not to tell Catriona; because mothers never understood these things, not like men. He said it was quite a common thing, perfectly understandable. That made Alec feel better, but poor Catriona was still out of her head with worry.'

'When did he turn up?'

Calum sighs.

'Oh, three days later this soldier breezes into the office, where I'm typesetting the front page of the *Oran*, and bangs the counter and shouts Service! and it's Iain. No notice, no explanation.'

'Come for a drink,' he says. 'I'm just off the boat. I'll see you at the County.'

'Just like that?'

'Just like that.'

'So what happened next?'

'He drank like a fish all the time he was home. Everyone pretended not to notice. The Murrays held open house and everybody came and no one asked Iain what had happened to the missing week. They probably,' says Calum slowly, 'wouldn't have got an answer, he was not very communicative. Good at holding the floor, yes. He talked all the time. Got the lads excited with all his nonsense about the tricks French girls get up to when you sleep with them. He has the boys thinking all French girls are tarts!'

'In some of the towns in the war-zone,' John-Angus says, 'it almost feels like that. It's not ordinary life.'

'And I don't know what he did,' says Calum, intent on his own tale, 'but he upset Mairi too. I don't know what happened. I found her on the beach, crying. Iain had gone off by then, up to the bothan. I didn't see him again. He left on the next boat, left as suddenly as he'd come. I don't know if he even said goodbye to his family. No one could make head nor tail of it.'

'Och,' says John-Angus. 'Difficult. He didn't, by any chance, get engaged when he was on the island?'

'He was hardly here long enough to get his boots dry!' says Calum. 'Far less get engaged.. why do you ask?'

'Just, I heard.. well, actually.. Myra, Ewan's Myra in Edinburgh, heard.. that Iain is to marry some girl off the island.'

'Not that I know of! How on earth did Myra come across news like that?'

'He was supposed,' says John-Angus, 'to be.. informally.. engaged.. to one of the nurses she works with.'

'Ah.'

'And he wrote to her the other day, breaking it off. Leaving the poor lass in such a state!'

'That's our Iain,' Calum says. 'She's probably a nice girl too.'

'Lovely,' says John-Angus. 'Wonderful, actually.'

'I've never been able to understand,' Calum says, 'what women see in him. It's always the same, they cluster like wasps round a jam-jar..'

'Till they get stung,' John-Angus nods. 'So it's another lie, this story of him marrying an island girl?'

'I'm afraid so,' says Calum. 'I hope so. I wouldn't wish him on any of them!'

'But it's not just girls,' John-Angus says. 'Men like Iain too; folk are really drawn to him. He stays popular, for all his ploys, for all the times he lands you in it. But you're taken in every time. You can never trust Iain.'

'That's going a bit far,' Calum protests.

'I don't think so.'

'Is he not in your platoon?'

'No, luckily he never was.'

'Luckily? Couldn't you trust Iain in a battle?'

'In battle? Yes, probably. On patrol, or in a push, I think there's probably no more sturdy a fellow; he's brave enough, a fighter if ever there was one. But that's a different side of him. That's not like life. In the ordinary run of things, the everyday work in the platoon, or the politics of it, for example, if there's any way Iain can see something to gain, some advantage to claw from the situation – any situation – then you can't trust him, not an inch.'

'So you'd trust him with your life on the field of battle – but not with your heart, nor the key to your business?'

'That's about the size of it,' John-Angus says. 'Iain would buy you and sell you. He'd take the eye out of your head and tell you you looked better without it. He'd rescue you from under the nose of the Hun, then tread you into the mud in your own trench to gain some minor advantage with the captain!'

Calum looks at John-Angus, laughs. 'I somehow can't imagine,' he says, 'anyone treading you into any mud. Not any more. You've taken on Ewan's mantle.'

'Calum, don't.'

'I'm sorry,' Calum sighs.

He looks up at the stars, bright against the early autumn sky; thinks how odd it is to be able to walk in comfort watching them. There's no wind tonight, not a breath. In the distance a cow is lowing as if she's lost her calf, the mournful noise echoing across the moor, above the sheep's more scattered recriminations, and their own footfalls.

'You know, Alec has a theory that we all become the person the world wants us to be, predicts for us; he says we grow to fill the space the world allows.'

'That's too difficult for me,' John-Angus smiles. 'I wonder how would he fit Iain into that scheme of things?'

'I'll ask him,' Calum says. 'Next time he brings it up! Actually, I remember,' he says, 'what happened the very first time I saw Iain.. but it's quite a long story, and this is where our ways part..'

They've reached the shore road. Calum turns towards John-Angus, wondering what happened to the worried, clumsy boy he knew at school. He wonders if John-Angus realises the extent of change within himself as he stands there in the August night, confident, composed. Iain, when last seen, had been utterly inscrutable; brutal, almost. John-Angus is calm, even gentle, but equally dangerous. Calum can sense a darkness in him. He's not sure which of the two he finds more worrying.

'I'll say goodnight, then, and Godspeed.' He holds out his hand.

'No, tell me the story,' John-Angus says. 'I'd like fine to hear it. It's such a grand night, isn't it, still warm..? Of course you're at work in the morning, I know.'

'Well, if you're sure,' says Calum.

'We'll have a drop of the cratur.' John-Angus pulls a whisky flask from his pocket.

'My, that's grand,' says Calum, savouring the malt.

'Comes from Oban,' says John-Angus. 'Connie gave it to me.'

There's a huge black rock on the machair below the path, a rock they climbed on constantly as children. Calum remembers how often he's fallen off it, grazing his knees, his hips and his elbows too, though he persevered. He was determined to conquer it, and did in the end.

They sit below the rock, watching the ebbing tide, the moonlight dancing on the whispering water.

'Do you know something?' says John-Angus.

'What?'

'I can't cope with the stillness here. It feels ominous. It feels like something terrible is going to happen. The city's not as bad. It's noisier. Where Myra lives in the centre it never gets quiet. Even at night, you'll hear carriages and cars rumbling over the cobbles, and the streetlights on of course, all the night long. I got so used to sleeping through the noise in France, I can't sleep now without it.'

'I don't understand,' says Calum. 'The noise can't be very regular, surely, the shells and that? Is it not disconcerting?'

'No, except in a bombardment, when it's regular hell. We sat through this bombardment once in a thunder storm at night, with Very lights flashing and shells whining and exploding and lightning lacerating the upper skies as if heaven was mirroring the chaos below. You couldn't tell what was one and what the other. It was very odd. But the odd shell.. you get used to that, just as you get used to the tinkle of rats moving through the mounds of tins flung away over the top of the trenches.'

'Rats..'

'They're everywhere. Shell-fire doesn't seem to touch them. And you learn to recognise shells, tell by the sound what sort they are, where they're going to fall, whether or not you need to duck. You learn this fast. You have to.'

'Bullets must be harder,' says Calum.

'No,' John-Angus shakes his head. 'A bullet either has your name on, or it hasn't. If it's not for you, you hear it whistling. If it is, you don't. You don't duck bullets.'

'Give me quiet, any time,' says Calum. 'It must be quieter in billets, no?'

'Even in billets, you hear the big guns roaring.'

'How do you ever sleep?'

'I find it harder sleeping here with the waves and the gulls and the animals lowing. The beds are all too soft. You don't feel safe.'

'You'll get used to it,' Calum says.

'I know that theory. When I first went to the Depot,' John-Angus says, 'I was terrified. Have you ever seen Fort George, Calum?'

'No.'

'I think it was built to subdue folk by its very vastness.. huge, sculpted walls, and ditches and streets as big as Stornoway, and square after square, and parade grounds.. I thought, *If this is what war's like, I'll never manage.* War's not like that, of course. Fort George is a palace to the trenches. But it's colder and windier even than Lewis. The gales funnel up the Great Glen, scouring at the Fort as if they're trying to pluck it from the face of the earth. It can be warm everywhere else, but Fort George will be freezing. And it's as busy as Inverness! Can you imagine the comings and goings?'

'It must be hectic right enough,' says Calum.

'I thought I'd go out of my mind. I was hopeless. I couldn't march, I was the worst runner by far in the whole section; I seemed to take twice as long to get my uniform clean; my kit kept being pinched, and what could you do but swipe someone else's? You couldn't afford to keep paying for it, not when you needed all your pay to spend in the canteen making up deficiencies in the ration. I was always broke, always hungry. And I kept falling foul of this fisher lad from Buckie – Eddie Shields. He didn't like Iain either, I'm not sure why. One night he and a couple of his east coast pals jumped us in the barrack room. Iain, great fighter that he is, ran off and left me at their mercy.'

'No,' breathes Calum.

'He didn't come back for hours, said he'd been looking for the Corporal. Shite. I told him that, told him to his face. But I knew, after that, if I was going to survive at all, it would all be up to me. I'd get no help from Iain. He'd told Ewan he'd look out for me, but far from doing that, he'd drop you in it if he could. I cried myself to sleep that night, and my ribs were sore for days, but there was nowhere I could go, nothing I could do but somehow pull myself together and survive.'

'How did you manage that?'

'I got better at soldiering. Struck lucky with my platoon, too.. no Iain, no Eddie. And I turned into the best shot in the section, which gives you a certain reputation. What I couldn't teach you about shooting people in the head is not worth knowing.'

John-Angus's voice is as gentle as ever, slightly proud. Calum shivers.

'And you should see me with a Bowie knife. Artistic. Sculptor of human flesh. That's a consideration, eh? You think I'll get used to that in time?'

'You'll learn to live with it,' says Calum.

'It's not all Iain's fault,' John-Angus says, sighing, 'but I blame him for it. And I blame him for Ewan's death, because he came to tell me about it. And I lost my virginity in Iain's company, and that's a better story, Calum, but you haven't told me yours, and all three of mine are as sad as the times we're trying to survive. That's Iain's phrase, by the way. He said that to me after Ewan died. I was crying. I asked him what he thought the point was.. no, I asked him what we were all doing.. he said, *Trying to survive.* In his own way I think he finds it just as hard as I do. There are, of course, different levels of survival.. So tell me your story, Calum. Tell me your version of Iain. I'm interested to hear it.'

'It's odd,' says Calum, 'I've never told anyone this, for all it was so important to me at the time. You might know this story, might have different memories of it; you may have been there in the background when it actually happened.. it was the day I started school. Do you remember how scared you felt that day? Did you feel scared?'

'Oh yes,' says John-Angus. 'Terrified. You knew they wouldn't speak to you in Gaelic and you were so afraid the teacher would make you feel stupid.'

'I was anxious about the teacher,' says Calum, 'right enough, but I was even more worried about the other pupils. Children had not always been kind about my leg, you know. I'd been teased already by youngsters from other townships. I hated it when they stuck their tongues out at me, called me Limpy Calum.

'For weeks before, I told my mother I was not going to go to school, but she said I had to go, and that was all there was to it. She said it might not be easy at first, but in the end I'd manage. She combed my hair and washed my face and knees and took me. I was six.

'Well, I sat there terrified, hardly opened my mouth.. the teacher was so strict, you weren't encouraged to! And I got a splinter in my knee from the rough wooden benches, and a row from the teacher when I dropped my slate. I was that glad when he told us school was finished for the day, thought the worst of it was over. But that was when the worst of it began. It was a lovely day. I remember; it was sunny. I remember yet the sun in my eyes, and the heat of it on my neck, as the other children pushed me round and round the circle of them, laughing at me, calling me club-foot, cripple, Limpy Calum.

'Then a stone hit me, hit me on the head. Nobody had ever hit me. Nobody. I didn't believe it till the jagged edge cut deep in my skin, knocking me sideways. It was sore, and I felt dizzy. But I didn't cry. I was used to falling, used to hurting. You can't see it just now, but there's a pale scar just beside my eye where the stone hit me. I didn't move, not at all. Blood was trickling down my cheek, but I ignored it. And I hated those children, all of them; if you were there, John-Angus, you and Ewan, standing frozen in that raucous, diminishing circle, I hated you too, cursed you silently. Sometimes I wonder if I damned our whole generation at that moment.

'I don't think I really felt the pain. I didn't move, didn't utter a word, not a single sound; just stood, not frightened any more, waiting and hating, watching. Suddenly, this wiry boy with a shock of fair hair pushed across the ring right up to me, a stone in each hand. I held my breath as the boy came closer, closer.. watching those hands, and the jagged stones. I glared straight at him, daring him to throw them at me. He couldn't have been more than two feet away, when he raised his right arm, screaming. "This boy's my friend! Leave him alone!" He turned to the crowd screaming at the top of his voice. "This boy's my friend, right? He's brave. Fight him, fight me!" And the crowd looked at the boy, at the cutting, jagged stones, and simply melted away. I didn't see where they went. I sat down against the school wall, weak as a pool of milk. I remember thinking, *At least I didn't wet myself.* It had been quite a possibility. "Is your eye alright?" the boy asked. I noticed, for the first time, blood dripping on the jumper my mother had knitted specially for school. I took my handkerchief out and held it to my temple. "I'm Iain," said the boy. "I'm Iain Murray. You're Calum, right? Don't worry about those sheep, Calum. They're all frightened of me. I'm the best at fighting."

'Well, we sat there for a while, till my eye stopped bleeding. I didn't speak. It had been the worst day of my life, from the teacher's loud English, and refusal to answer even simple requests in Gaelic, (so that several children wet themselves, not remembering the phrase that unlocked all doors – *please, I need out!*) to this afternoon's assault. My mother had thought to teach me that necessary phrase, so I had not been one of those children sent home for dry trousers, as if we had more than one pair at a time; but I felt ill at ease in the stern bemapped classroom after the warmth and freedom of home. And I had every reason now to doubt my fellow pupils. Iain watched my silence for three, maybe five minutes. It seemed a lifetime. "Honest," he said. "Honest, I'm the best at fighting. I'm the best at English too." I may have looked impressed at that. It had seemed to me that the way to survive the classroom was to master the English, even if it was a crabbit tongue.

"Tell you what," said Iain. "I'll teach you a magic word."

"Will you?" I spoke at last.

"Mind, you have to say it loud. It's much better loud.. listen, shite.. shite.. shite!"

"Shite shite shite," I shouted.

"Shite! Shite! Shite!" we chanted together, louder and louder, so loud that neither of us saw the teacher coming out of the school. He walked up to us, and pointing a dour accusing finger, proceeded to march us directly to the classroom. If you'd been loitering outside the school, John-Angus, climbing the wall (and perhaps you were?) you'd have seen through the high school window the brown tawse swinging. You'd have heard it fall six times. And you could have followed us home, along the shore path, blowing on our hands. "Shite! Shite! Shite!" said Iain. I thought dock leaves might help, and said so; and we found some, and spat on them and duly applied them. "No use," I said to Iain, hobbling happily after him. "They're just shite!" He turned to me then, and I think it's the only time I ever saw Iain think ahead for another person. "Remember," he said. "It's a magic word, a secret word. Don't say it at home!"

   "I'll say," I told him, "you're the best at fighting!" "Shite," said Iain.'

   John-Angus laughs. 'I like your Iain story.'
   'That's not quite the end,' says Calum. 'I was lying in bed that night, going over the day's events, as you do when you're young, or I did anyway. And I frightened myself, couldn't help it; I frightened myself remembering how helpless I'd been as the children crowded nearer and nearer; I could see the sharp stone coming, feel it's cutting edge; trace the taut ellipse as it whipped from the throwing hand. I could see that stone and the boy that threw it too. He was wiry, with a shock of fair hair. He was screaming louder than anybody. "Limpy Calum. Limpy! Hey Limpy! Take that, Limpy!" '
   'Ah,' John-Angus searches for a pebble to skim across the waves. 'Just as well you had the magic word.'
   Calum and John-Angus sit in silence, staring at the waves, studying their rhythm as they roll against the moonlit shore; always the fath of seven smaller waves is followed by the claith, three bigger ones. John-Angus turns to Calum.
   'What if it's the same for us? Seven small, safe waves, then danger?'
   'Maybe it is,' says Calum. 'Maybe that's why misfortunes come in threes – though I can't say I've ever noticed the seven good things..'
   'You're an optimist, right enough,' John-Angus says.

*   *   *

Calum walks home heavy-hearted. Will not sleep. His mind is active; there can be no rest for him tonight. There's too much in his head. John-Angus's words keep pounding in his skull.

'In the trenches, on sentry duty, you can persuade yourself you see the land slip back and fore, the bushes ebbing and flowing. Trick of the dark.'

'I'm not sure I'd cope with that.'

'Aye, you would.'

'What it must feel like.. day after day..'

John-Angus said nothing. He unscrewed the cap on the whisky flask, offered it to Calum. After his own slug, he sighed. 'Mind you, maybe I was looking the wrong way. Land is static, more or less. It's men that are the tide; it's men that vacillate, and all their movement under cover of darkness. We can't see what we're doing.'

The street is silent until Calum walks past the Munro's house, setting off the collies.

'Quiet!' Old Alec yells.

'What is it?' shouts Neilina, so loud Calum can hear her. She's that deaf, she can't help shouting.

'Just the dogs going daft. It's nothing. Go back to sleep!' her son shouts now.

Calum smiles, slips into his own house as quietly as he can, managing, he thinks, to disturb no one.

John-Angus had shaken his head at Calum.

'You've got it bad, haven't you?'

'What do you mean?'

'Speak to the girl!'

'I can't. She won't let me near her. I don't know what to do about it,' Calum said simply. He tried to control the emotion in his voice, 'I'll be bursting into tears next. You'll be saying it's the whisky talking.'

'If only it could.'

Flora, who never sleeps till Calum's home, hears her son

trip on the rag-rug, then blunder up the stair: she turns over in bed, huddling against Murdo's serene, snoring, back. She can relax at last. It's after two.

Calum does not go to bed, but drags his bedside chair over to the table at the window. She hears him strike the match to light a candle. All through the growing dawn she hears the scratching of his pen. That pile of stories in his drawer is growing. She does not understand (and neither does Calum) why every one is written about Iain Murray.

Drapeau Blanc

Iain Murray is billeted with the rest of his platoon in the Drapeau Blanc, or what is left of it. He can't use this address on his letter though; can't use any address but BEF FRANCE.

My Dear Mairi, he writes

It is a lovely spring evening here. The sun is warmer than it is in summer at home! It's glaring through the poplars at me.

In fields next to this village you can see the young wheat, well on its way already; and the fruit trees are all in blossom, apples and pears. It's like June in the walled garden of the Big House..

Iain's been stuck on this sentence for the last hour. He frowns at the cracked and fading photograph propped against the window sill he's leaning on.

Three figures squint from the picture into unaccustomed sun: Calum, almost elfin, almost puckish, his dark hair and pointed features exaggerated by the camera; Iain himself, a smudge at the back, out of focus (he moved – had Angus not called out to him while they were posing?); and Mairi unusually solemn, her dark curls caught effectively for once at the nape of her neck, not a single hair straying. You could never tell the lively intelligent girl she is from this likeness. She looks every inch the model of solemn propriety. Mairi! He lifts the photograph, examining it closely. She has such clear skin, such good features, but you could never tell. The three of them might have been at a funeral.

He puts the photograph down on the letter, leaves the pencil rolling on the uneven sill, opens the window wide; breathing the fresh sweet air of spring. Spring in France. He'll postpone the letter till tomorrow.

The building doesn't help, isn't conducive to writing to a childhood sweetheart. With a name like the Drapeau Blanc (the sign still crooked on the half-shot door) how could it be? Its damp and damaged walls still endure the colourful, peeling murals that once helped the brothel's clientele into the mood for speedier achievement of the business in hand. The wall next to Iain bears a voluptuous blonde with impossibly large and slightly too pink breasts. Her disintegrating eyes seem trained on him.

– How long is it since you've done it, Iain? asks John MacPhie, the dark boy sitting on the right, his back to the wall. John MacPhie comes from Mallaig, has been in the platoon for four months now, making him almost an old hand. He's leaning against a painted peacock, staring at the naked arms and legs of Venus rising from the waves, or at least, an attempt to reproduce this famous vision.

– Done..? Dunno. It's not something you count..is it?

– I wouldn't tell the others, John says. I know you wouldn't split on me. I've.. never done it, actually.

– Never?

– I was brought up Catholic.

– What's that to do with anything? They're Catholic here.. and look at this!

– I'm looking says John. I'm looking..

Iain picks up his jacket, cap.

– Come on!

John looks askance at Iain.

– How can you ask me to leave..her?

Iain laughs.

– Let's go for a drink.

– Take your belt as well, says John. The Colonel's on the warpath. John Munro was put on a charge for being improperly dressed in the village street last night.. he got field punishment No.1..

– John Munro was drunk! And half-naked!

– You wouldn't want to risk it.

Iain takes his belt.

– Let's go! Dew van rouge!

– What's the French for wine again?

– I don't speak French, says Iain. You're the Catholic!

– They seem to follow your Gaelic better than my French, says John. He lingers by Venus, running his finger down her loins.

– The girls that worked in here, Iain, in the Drapeau Blanc.. Eddie Shields told me they're still in this village, in the estaminet.. or one of them is, at least. A Mademoiselle Bernadette.

– Dew van rouge would be cheaper and last longer, Iain laughs. If that's true. Don't believe everything you're told. Wait till we go to Amiens, John. Or Béthune. There's a Red Lamp there. You'll get your three minutes of heaven then.

The village they walk through is in the odd state of decay typical of the hamlet that has billeted first one side, then the other. Presently, it lies behind the Allied line, though the artillery has not moved far enough away to be inaudible, and the occasional shell flies too close for comfort. Sometimes it is honoured by visits from American politicians, driven from Paris in fast staff cars, thrilled to feel they're at the front, under fire. They pay through the nose for souvenirs, the sort all the men have gathered, pieces of spent shell-cases, Boche caps, medals. Iain keeps a look-out for his usual contact, an American liaison officer, but there's no sign of him.

The estaminet has a large sign at the front proclaiming Business As Usual. It has recently been shelled. The back wall now opens directly on to the orchard at the rear. Iain and John sit at a small round table by the shell-hole. Someone has stuck a candle in a wine-bottle and propped it in the gaping wall.

– What do you think? says John. Romantic, eh?

– There's nothing, Iain says, like giving them something to aim at, is there? Van Rouge, he says to the waiter, holding up two fingers. Poor Doo.

– Speak for yourself, says John, I think it's fine.

The estaminet is full. Several regiments are currently billeted in the area. The local folk, those that remain, do well out of the troops, selling eggs and bread and wine and watered beer at hugely inflated black market prices. While their money lasts, the troops don't seem to care. As long as the Canadians and Australians , those fuckin' five-bobbers, aren't around to make them feel hard-done by. And as for the Yanks! It's solid British troops tonight, better for morale, easier all round.

Iain is looking for the waitress he was working on last night. Like Eddie Shields, he'd heard the girl had come to the estaminet from the Drapeau Blanc. Mademoiselle Bernadette is plump, looks good-humoured. He has high hopes of their burgeoning acquaintance.

He smiles as the wine arrives, borne on a tray of woven wicker by the very image of the painted blonde whose eyes had interrupted his letter to Mairi. She's hard to age. She could be thirty.. thirty-five.

– Ma chère Mamselle, says Iain, offering her a chair. Asseyez-vous.. Bernadette?

She sits down, smiles.

John can't take his eyes off her.

Bernadette's room is simple, almost austere. The white unadorned walls have not been damaged by the shell that rocked the rest of the estaminet. There is a crucifix above the bed, and by the door, a picture of the Sacred Heart. Iain doesn't like it, hung his cap on it. He's seen too many opened chests: it's far from realistic. Or perhaps (and he doesn't ever admit this to himself, not even when he's struggling to sleep in the flimsiest merest scrape of an excuse for a dugout), perhaps the thorns round the exposed heart remind him too closely of the barbed wire facing all of them beyond the parapet.

– Why do you stay on here, Iain asks, after the shelling? The Boche have obviously marked the place. They'll have the map-reference from when they used this area. It's the obvious way for them to catch our troops off-duty.

– It would be bad for business to move suddenly, says Bernadette. I do not think that one shell anything but accident. I have my sources.

– *I'll bet you do, says Iain. He's lying on her bed, naked, fighting off a strong post-coital desire for sleep. He knows he's unlikely to get the opportunity. It would be bad for business.*

– *Actually, I've slept with you the last two nights, he says. In the Drapeau Blanc.*

– *Ah, she nods. The paintings.*

– *Don't do you justice, Iain says, stroking her breasts.*

There's a crash on the stair outside as if a table has been knocked over. The door handle rattles. Someone roars.

– *Your husband? Iain jumps to his feet, pulling on his kilt, his boots.*

– *No, says Bernadette. He's downstairs, serving in the bar.*

The locked door now bursts open, thrown half-off its hinges, and a huge kilted private, red-faced and red-haired, explodes into the room.

He stares at Iain, shaking his head as if disbelieving the evidence of his eyes. He turns to Bernadette and scoffs, Ken, ye'll be needin' a real man noo, efter that wanker!

– *Go back to your pigsty, Eddie. You're drunk, says Iain, coolly, slipping on his shirt, fastening it.*

Bernadette pulls the sheets up to her chin, wraps them tightly round her. She says not a word.

Eddie raises his eyebrows, pulls his belt off, wraps it round his wrist.

– *Has this criminal been troublin ye, missis? I'll sort the wee runt oot, he says, swinging the belt at Iain, missing. It lashes the bed, catching Bernadette's feet. She cries out, draws her legs up.*

– *See whit ye've done? cries Eddie. Gone an' made me hurt the quine. Ye juist cannae take it, can ye? Nae bottle. The ither wee island runt wis the juist same. Ye ran awa' that time. Nae chance o' that the nicht..*

He swings the belt again, whipping Iain round the face, raising a broad weal that darkens quickly. Eddie swings the belt once more, round and round his head..

Iain stands quite coolly, waiting, watching the arcing leather; suddenly he pounces, snatching the buckle sharply, pulling Eddie so far off balance that he falls, his head cracking smartly on the iron bedstead, starting to bleed. Eddie seems a little dazed. Iain strives to compound his advantage, pushes his opponent towards the door, but Eddie's greater weight is a serious obstacle, his brief confusion lapses into reflex ferocity. The two Jocks clutch each other, tumble over and over, out the door, kicking, scratching; they roll down the stairs one over another, swapping punches when they can.

Iain is winded, but Eddie, three quarters drunk, fights best in this glorious condition. He's had practice. All the time he's goading Iain, taunting him about John-Andrew. Ye should hae let him swing.. why did ye cut him down, ye bastard? Whit guid wis that loon tae onybody?

He shakes Iain off at the bottom of the stairs, shoving him hard against the wooden shutters of the single remaining window in the estaminet. The shutters splinter like match-wood. The crowd has drawn back quickly to the relative safety of the corners. The youngest waitress screams.

Iain picks himself up, charges Eddie, butting him in the groin. Eddie crumples. Iain seizes the moment, jumping on top of him, grabbing him by the throat: he is successfully squeezing the life out of Eddie when he's pulled off him by John MacPhie.

– Red Caps on their way, says John. We'd best make ourselves scarce.

Iain, out of breath, blows a kiss up the stairs to Bernadette,

– Sorry. C'est la guerre.

– It's business, she shrugs, slinging jacket, cap and belt over the banister. Good luck! Go. Go!

They slip through the shell-hole into the safety of the orchard just as two burly Red Caps rush in through the door, and are shown upstairs to Bernadette's plausible tears. Eddie Shields is nowhere to be seen.

Back at the Drapeau Blanc, an anxious John MacPhie examines Iain's face.

– Word is we're for the the front tomorrow. Do you think they'll let you go?

Iain stretches his jaw, fingers it gently.
– Why not? I'm just warmed up.

'Why did ye cut him down? Ye should hae let him swing.'

Calum remembers the story about the poor Bethune boy found hanging in an oak tree at Craiglockart. They didn't put it in the *Oran*. In fact, if he remembers right, any national newspapers mentioning the death were sent straight back to the suppliers on the mainland. Alexander. That had been his name. Defender of men.

The dawn is rosy now. Calum stares out of his window at the glowing clouds. He should lie down, try for sleep. He puts the pen down, falls into his bed, closing his eyes. It's going to be another lovely day. He'll have to get through it one way or another.

He can hear his mother rising, moving round the kitchen, lighting the stove. His father will be sleeping sound; it's not from his father he gets his lack of sleep.

He dozes, waking in midsummer lack of darkness.

Callanish again.

This time he's the farmer, trying to dig stone from Callanish to mend the drystone wall round an exposed field: the central megalith is just the size of stone he needs to fill the gap through which his sheep are cascading nightly to the rocks below. He never seems to reach the bottom of the stone, though he digs deeper, deeper into the peat moss. His hands are blistered.

Every morning there are three or four newly-dead sheep on the beach below the high cliff. Every morning blood-stained remnants are smashed against the rocks by the tide, picked clean by gulls, circling, calling. His flock is getting smaller, the swathe of skulls at the cliff-foot deeper.

Every day he toils, digging at the stone's foundation. There must be an end to it.. at night he slumps exhausted by the wall, the gap unfilled. He wakes to new destruction.

One day he climbs down to rescue a fallen lamb; it's baaing piteously, wriggling its head. He curses himself for a fool as he goes carefully down the cliff. He won't be able to save the lamb, there's not a chance of it. Its legs are broken, you can see by the angle. The lamb is dead already, as good as dead, but still he lowers his own weight carefully down the crumbling cliff, works his way towards it. There has been snow; touches of white highlight cracks and gullies in the rock, make footwork difficult.

The lamb is lying on the jagged shore beside its mother, bleeding on snow and kelp-lined rock. Its legs are shattered and a sharper edge has pierced its abdomen. Why it should be calling, crying, when other larger sheep lie in silent death, Calum does not know. He raises a large smooth boulder high against the now-blue sky, brings it down smartly on the lamb's small skull, crushing it. There's blood on his hands the salt sea seems only to congeal. He leaves a trail of bloodstains all the way up the cliff.

As he digs he is tortured by the notion that the littering skulls might not be sheep, that the footholds in the cliff resemble human limbs, that the wet, slimy foliage is not snow on vegetation but decay on weathering flesh.

He works on till his spade cuts sharply, neatly – too easily – into a bloated abdomen. The stench is foul.

He retches, moves round to the other side of the obelisk, starts digging again.

'Calum,' says Flora. 'Calum, you'll be late if you don't get up in the next five minutes. Your father's away already! If you get going now you'll just have time for breakfast.'

'I'm not hungry,' groans Calum, pulling the covers further over his head. 'I need five minutes longer.'

'Get up,' says Flora. 'Isn't this the day you go to press?'

He pulls the covers down at that, sits up blinking.

'Look at the state of this room,' says Flora. 'All those papers on the floor.'

'Leave them!' shouts Calum. 'I mean, I'll do that.'

He slides out of bed, starts gathering the scattered, scribbled sheets.

'I thought I taught you,' Flora says, 'when you were three, or younger, to get undressed *before* going to bed.'

'I was late,' says Calum. 'Tired.'

Flora turns, goes downstairs, tutting.

'You'll barely have time to shave! Give me those trousers. I'll press them. What state is your jacket in?'

*　　　*　　　*

Calum works steadily through the morning. He loves his work. He may, at times, deny the art in it, even the craft.. but words are what he lives by, what he lives for, even when he's as tired as he is today. His love for Mairi would be sun to him, spring – if all would suddenly come right – but words and music are meat and drink; they make life possible. You can change the world with words.

Calum wonders if ideas can exist without words, without language.

He considers this.

There could be emotion, certainly; there is emotion in music.. music can convey any given emotion in a visceral, more sensual way than words alone. And you can have a conversation of tunes between musicians, a flyting, as, indeed, he often had; yes, and music could paint landscape, describe it, just as paint might stimulate physical emotion, either by its style, or the quality of brush-work or image represented, or simply by its shape and colour.

These forms of communication were just that; conversations in paint or sound, bodily sensation whose meaning was conceived and transmitted by the artist – painter or composer – on the canvas, or in the tune; and usually it was a one-way conversation, a statement received, stimulating a reaction the original artist did not necessarily observe. Whereas language, thinks Calum, spoken language, can be two-way because words are quicker, more precise, more easily shared.

He is momentarily beguiled by the thought of a world where ideas and emotions may be sung or somehow played, in wordless music. Would it be possible to cope with such a spectrum of immediate physical interaction?

And what about colour, soundless language, played in light? It would be possible for a myriad interweaving of colour to communicate meaning, yes it would; but would such language travel, as sound did? Would it work at night?

Was language a cooler, more acceptable music, translating experience into manageable code?

He must talk to Alec about this. Alec would have an opinion. Alec would probably say it would all work fine, be more precise, with numbers instead of words.

Calum wonders if the war would have happened without words. Did the fact of different languages.. of possible confusion, of endless misinterpretation.. predict war? Or, say, if there were suddenly just the one language in the world, a single human language; would it stay like that, single? No, thought Calum. Not a chance. Individuality would soon make sure that differences arose, that language once again became diverse. There is strength in that, he thinks, in the possibility of richness, or chaos.

Did words generate ideas? Or did ideas ripple like waves through the different languages used by human populations? That's a possibility. Ideas of peace, of war; ideas of love.. but love is tied to person, usually, to sensual attraction, more emotion-led than intellectual, or at least, lust is (if physical love must all be lust, as Calum is inclined to think it).

But love for parents, for children, isn't lust. Surely family love is based on care and kindness, on belonging? That child is *mine*, that mother *mine*, that father *mine too*.. belonging, based on sameness. They are like me, *mine*. My community is me. Friendship must come into that bracket.

And difference.. not-me.. is attractive and disturbing, both. Like women.

We couldn't kill the Boche if they weren't different, thinks Calum. If they weren't *seen* as different.

Nor could they kill us.

We're the same stock, more or less.. and yet all of us, and especially those who work with words, try to influence opinion – journalists, writers, politicians, propagandists, all – echo this notion of difference.. where it isn't true.

And what, after all, is truth? Truth is how you see it from where you're standing. More or less. It's odd, isn't it that he's writing so many stories about Iain, about the war; the war he has no chance of seeing.

What's *story*, then? He doesn't know. A story, for the *Oran*, is something that's happened (substantiated by given information) reflected and deflected by the lens of his own personality and language; probably his culture too, Calum concedes that. But the war stories he makes up, the traditional stories his mother tells, the books he reads (*Dubliners*, for example) what, then, are they but *What happens if..* reflected and deflected, as before.

Calum can't improve on that. A story is *what happens if.* And stories can be true, some stories are more truthful, more honest than what happened *next*.

He listens to himself and laughs.

'Calum!' calls John from the print-room.. 'There's a problem here..'

In the early afternoon, Calum thinks it might be possible, after all, to see John-Angus off on the boat. Everything's gone well. He unties his apron, leaving the apprentice working away.

'I'll not be long,' he says. 'Ten minutes. I'm going to see the boat off.'

'Calum..'

John's words are lost. Calum nods, smiles.

'Ten minutes. I'll be back, if anyone's looking for me.'

It's a wonderful day for sailing, he thinks, the sky so blue, the sea so calm. He glances across the bay, sees the *Sheila* steaming, almost at the Arnish light.

What time is it? He sighs. He's missed the sailing. Goodness only knows when they'll see John-Angus back, and he owes him such a debt of gratitude.

He stands for a moment, watching the ship strike south across the Minch. She'll pass the Milaid light and then the Shiants.. such a wonderful name. So many tales have focused on those treacherous waters round the Shiants; the story of brown-haired Alan, for instance, best of all seamen, who drowns when he sails south to his own Reiteach. The ship is lost with all hands, and Alan's body is never found. Still, he meets his true-love, black-haired Anna, there is a Reiteach, all agree; for she throws herself into the waves, giving herself up to them (another version has her coffin lost at sea), but in all versions, every one, Alan and Anna will not be denied. They come together in the swirling currents round the Shiants. So many of the old tales have unhappy endings.

Once, he had told Mairi this story, and she sighed.

'It's not sad,' she said. 'The sea is love. The sea is just a metaphor for leaving your old life behind, immersing yourself in the new.'

Calum wasn't sure.

'Might it not be a warning against love?'

'No,' said Mairi. 'It's a metaphor. Sea is always a metaphor. It's dangerous, the sea, but then metaphors can be! Seductive too, like the snow falling softly in *The Dead*. Like the sadness in it. Not that death is seductive,' she sighed. 'So many dead. Too many.'

And he bent down, kissed her then. He can still remember the sweetness in her lips, the joy in his heart.

They were, that particular day, walking round the stones at Callanish, the monoliths pillaring a grey and heavy sky.

'These stones,' said Calum, who had been researching the subject for the *Oran*, 'were giants who lived on the island and would not convert to Christianity. St Kieran, bless his cotton socks, turned them into stone.'

'And a good job he made of it,' said Mairi. 'Very.. stone.'

'Indeed. And if we'd been here at sunrise,' said Calum, 'we'd have seen *the shining one* walk the avenue, preceded by a cuckoo's call. I'm not sure who or what the shining one might be, though.'

'We should have been here at sunrise, then,' said Mairi. 'We'll come next year. We'll come every year.'

'They say,' said Calum, 'it's a lucky place for a wedding.'

'A bit draughty for the guests,' said Mairi.

'No, not that bit of a wedding..'

'Very draughty indeed!' Her eyes were dancing.

They huddled by the highest obelisk, in the middle of the circle of thirteen stones. It shielded them from the wind, also the road. Even with the grey sky, this would have been an excellent place to view the Harris hills. Calum didn't notice them. Mairi pulled him closer; and he bent to kiss her, and she kissed him back and held him tight, so tight. And she pulled away for a moment; and when she turned back to him she'd opened the buttons on her blouse and she pulled his head down then, over her shining breasts and Calum buried his face in them, kissing them over and over, and she bent her head towards him and her fingers rippled through his hair, and she stroked him, soothed him like a child, as he fastened on the nipple.

When they heard children on the road, Calum jumped. Mairi laughed, swung her shawl across the open blouse, and did not fasten it till they were in sight of Stornoway. All the way home he'd driven with her open to him, wanting him to touch her soft, white skin.

'Mairi,' he said, 'you're the shining one.'

'No,' she touched his lips. 'You are.'

When they got back to Stornoway there were letters waiting for both of them. Ewan's death, said Iain, had made him conscious of life, of human purpose. *It's in my mind to marry Mairi*, he wrote to Calum. *She's the one thing makes this all seem possible.*

I've come to see, he wrote to Mairi, *that you and I should get to know one another better, for life, perhaps.*

'I don't like this, Calum,' Mairi said. 'We'll have to write to

Iain now, jointly, tell him we're in love.'

'How can we do that?' said Calum. 'You know what happens to men who get that sort of letter at the front. They go out looking for trouble. They get badly injured. They get killed.'

'But it's not honest, to go on letting him think..'

'What else can we do but wait? How would we feel if Iain died?'

'It's a bad idea, Calum.'

'It's just a matter of waiting, Mairi. We'll tell him when the fighting ends. How can it change what's between us?'

But Mairi was right. Over the months, Iain's letters to her became openly amorous; often his letters to Calum were full of Mairi. He seemed to imply she was his by right. This drove a wedge between the pair that had no root, no basis in reality, but was none the less effective, even after Iain's disastrous leave.

As Calum stands in the harbour now, watching the *Sheila* steaming away into the blue distance, he thinks John Angus was right. He'll have to go and see Mairi, tell her how he loves her.

He turns back to the office with a new sense of direction, waving to Effie over on the far side of the street. Her eyes are red. She's been sobbing her wee heart out again. That blackguard Angus! Calum holds him responsible for everything. He'd cross the road, go and talk to her, but she disappears into the bank.

Alec will help her, Alec's a helpful sort of boy.

In the window of the ironmonger's, Calum sees a blue vase, similar in shape to the one his uncle rescued from the sea, though the central picture has no maidens in it, no garden, no boat, no flowering tree; just a blue mountain, snow-capped, and a stormy sea, higher and more treacherous than the calm volcano.

THIRD VARIATION

Mairi's aunt, Esther Maitland, lives just off the Leith Road, not in Leith itself, in a heavy-looking terraced house of pinkish stone, screened front and back by privet hedges six feet high. The house is new to them; and smaller, more cramped, than the house they'd lived in previously in Linlithgow. It's large enough by Edinburgh standards. There are maples in the garden, a tall copper beech, and rowan and hawthorn trees, and tiny patches of grass the two young children are not encouraged to play on.

Esther and her husband John have tried to make Mairi as welcome as possible.

The wash-stand in her room is furnished with lavender-scented soap, and the table by her bed offers a selection of books, Henry James, DH Lawrence, *Sherlock Holmes*, none of which Mairi is inclined to read. It's a small room, high and narrow, but the wallpaper is pretty, pink roses trailing trellis-like over figured vellum. The curtains, blue velvet tied with crimson cord, contrast gently with cream lace nets, and a Persian rug, deep blue, lies beside the bed. This rug is wonderfully thick; Mairi's feet sink inches into it. The bed itself is high and narrow, lightened by a plain cream quilt, thickly embroidered cushions and bolster; the curved brown bed-head matches the polished wardrobe and narrow tallboy jammed behind the door. There's one chair at the window, a small armchair, upholstered, also blue.

'I hope you'll be comfortable here,' Esther smiles. 'We want you to feel quite at home.'

Mairi thinks of her large attic room in Stornoway, with its grey light, uneven plain walls and scrubbed pine furniture. This room is much too narrowly grand for her to ever feel at home, she thinks, but she thanks her aunt, and says she's tired, and sits down on the bed. When Esther looks in later she finds the girl fast asleep on top of the covers. She has not unpacked. Esther slips to the linen cupboard on the landing for an extra blanket, drapes it over Mairi and tiptoes away.

For the next three days, Mairi keeps mainly to her room, eating little, saying nothing, much to Esther's consternation. She does, prompted by Esther, eventually unpack; then slumps back in the chair by the window staring blearily ahead.

'Come downstairs, Mairi. Hannah and little John are dying to see you. You're one of the family. You can't sit alone here all day, every day.'

Mairi closes her eyes. Her aunt removes the untouched dinner-tray, gives up, for the moment. That night, as she sits in bed supposedly reading, she lays the book down, turns to her husband, hesitates.. John looks up, smiles.

'What's bothering you, Esther?'

'That lassie. It's three days now. And she sits there hour after hour, John, staring at the wall; doing nothing, saying nothing, seeing no one.'

'Well, apart from anything else, she'll be homesick. She's bound to be. And she must be uncomfortable about the baby... about her prospects.. you can understand it. It's all such a mess.'

Esther sighs. 'I think she's fretting over Maisie.'

'We all are.' John reaches over, takes Esther's hand. 'What's the latest there?'

Esther looks up at him, her blue eyes full of tears.

'Aeneas writes he doesn't think she'll make it through the autumn.'

John slips his arm around her, soothing her, knowing how near the tears are.

'Poor Maisie. Poor Mairi. Poor foolish lass. No wonder she's in a state. We'll have to give her time.'

'Yes. Maybe time will help. At least she's got time.'

Esther leans against his shoulder, closes her eyes.

Mairi does not know what to do. Cut off from the island, from Maisie and Aeneas, she is sinking in a lethargy that threatens to overwhelm her. She misses her home, her room, her work. She dare not think of Calum; cannot guess her future. She does not recognise herself when she looks in the mirror.

The changes in her body are difficult, uncomfortable. She hates the swelling abdomen, the engorged breasts. It's disconcerting to have another human being fluttering within her. It seems inappropriate. She's on the point of losing her own mother, whom she loves. How can she take on the role?

Yet, she's very conscious of the baby's movements within her, gentle as they still are. Maisie tried to prepare her, tried to explain all the changes to her, what would happen over the months.

'Ask Esther about the labour,' she said. 'Mine wasn't good, not typical. I'm not going to fill your mind with that, Mairi. Ask your aunt about it. She'll find you a good midwife, I've no doubt.'

Maisie sat up in bed as she said this, propped on four pillows; she was very thin and weak. These days the hacking cough produced more and more blood. Her poor white face had shrivelled almost to the bone, and her hands lay wrinkled, sallow on the coverlet she and Mairi had painstakingly worked some years before. Just to speak exhausted her. Mairi took one of her mother's hands tightly in her own.

'Let me stay here with you,' she cried. 'Don't send me away, Mam, don't.'

'I'll be here when you get back,' Maisie whispered. 'Be sure of that. But I can't look after you when it's your time, not like Esther would. I don't want you left, Mairi, like I was, without proper help when you need it most.'

'But I'll miss you. And I don't *know* Esther.'

'You'll be fine, Mairi. She was the sweetest of us; and her John's a right nice lad. They won't harass you.' And now Maisie produced her final argument, the one that swayed Mairi, got her on the boat. 'And your father won't worry the same. Nor will I. We'll know you're in good hands.'

For three days, Mairi sits alone in the narrow high-ceilinged bedroom staring blindly, as if in deepest mourning. On the fourth, her aunt shows two young ladies upstairs to the parlour.

'It's good of you to come,' she says. 'I'm at my wits' end with her.'

'Mairi!' she knocks on Mairi's door. 'Mairi – visitors!'

Mairi opens the door. She looks pale and and miserable.

'Mairi,' says Esther, 'here's two young ladies come to see you. Margaret will bring us all some tea.' She flounces into Mairi's room. 'I'll help you fix your hair!' she says, and with a few deft strokes, transforms the untidy knot into a neat arrangement. Next she looks at the grey blouse and skirt the girl is wearing. 'That colour isn't right.. wait a minute, I have an idea.' She scurries from the room, returning with a sky-blue paisley shawl. 'There. That's better. Now we see what a bonnie lass you are!'

'But who is it?' Mairi asks, submitting passively to this whirlwind of activity. 'Who's here? Who are these young ladies I have to see?'

'Didn't I say?' Esther fixes the shawl with a silver pin. 'Myra and Connie MacLeod. John-Angus's family. What a nice boy he is! You could see that straight away. Now, let me look at you. That's good! Through we go. What's wrong now? Why are you crying?'

'Oh, nothing,' says Mairi. 'I thought..'

'Yes?' Esther waits.

'I thought it was a deputation from the church!'

'Let's get you better first, then we'll worry about the church!'

Esther's parlour, as in many Edinburgh houses, is on the first floor. It faces west, overlooking the front garden with its spreading copper beech. Late afternoon sun, dappled by the burning leaves, dances through the fine bay window, dazzling Mairi as she comes in, hovers on the threshold. Myra rushes forward to greet her.

'Mairi, dear!'

Mairi finds herself held warmly.

'I'm sorry it's taken us so long to get here, but we wanted to be absolutely sure we were free of influenza. How are you, my dear?'

Myra's voice has lost none of its warmth. She holds out her hand now, indicating the tall, loose-limbed girl on the couch. 'Let me introduce Connie, John-Angus's wife.. Connie, Mairi.'

'Do sit down, please. Can I offer you all some tea?'

Esther's back upstairs now, with Margaret, the maid. Esther carries the teapot and water-jug, Margaret a tray of china, sandwiches and little cakes.

'Wonderful,' says Connie. 'I'm starving. It's been ages since we've eaten.'

'Half-an-hour,' says Myra, raising her eyebrows. 'If that.'

Connie sits down, reaching for the sandwiches as soon as decently possible. 'In France, you never know when you'll get your next meal.' She sweeps three sandwiches on to her plate. Myra shrugs. Esther and Mairi smile. Teacups are filled and the soothing ceremony of balancing cup and saucer, plate and napkin soon overcomes any shyness in the group.

'Where are you from, Connie?' Esther asks.

'Oxford. But I don't think we'll be back there. Too far from Lewis. John-Angus wouldn't cope.'

'Actually,' says Mairi. 'I think he'd cope with anything!'

'I've made him my excuse,' frowns Connie, 'for not going back. I've always hated Oxford. Except the Botanical Gardens. They're good.'

'The Edinburgh ones are better,' Myra says.

'You think everything in Edinburgh is the bee's knees!' Connie turns to Esther. 'Are all Edinburghers like that?'

'Don't ask me,' laughs Esther. 'I'm Glaswegian. I think Glasgow is the centre of the world.'

'What about you, Mairi?' Myra makes an attempt to draw Mairi into the conversation. 'Where's your centre of the world?'

'I used to think it might be Paris,' says Mairi. 'Now I'm not so sure.'

'Are you enjoying your work as a VAD, Myra?' asks Esther to cover the silence that has fallen on them.

'I've not been able to work since I had the influenza, but I do enjoy it, yes. Though it's very hard. And now that little Ewan is running around, it's more difficult for my mother to manage him – she's at that age when young children are not the easiest thing. Don't you forget,' says Myra blithely, 'what a lot of work babies are? Good grief!' she breaks off. 'Mairi, please forgive me! How tactless!'

'No,' says Mairi. 'Don't be silly. I'm not a fool, Myra.' There's an edge to Mairi's voice, a suggestion of tears, but she controls it. 'Please go on. Are you giving up your work?'

'It looks as if I'll have to. On the bright side, it means I'll be able to visit my friends more often!'

'And you, Connie?' Esther asks. 'What are your plans?'

'Oh, we're waiting to see what happens with John-Angus. If he's billeted in Fort George, I thought I might go up there, maybe stay in Ardersier or Inverness, try to find work nearby. He has another Medical Board next week. In the meantime,' says Connie, 'poor Myra's stuck with me and my unquenchable appetite!'

'If I hadn't children,' says Esther, 'your type of work is something I'd have loved to do! I do so envy you both. One of my friends went off to London right at the start of the war to look for war work. She went on her own motorbike, mind you, a powerful thing, dropped handles, the lot – became a nurse on the Belgian front; she and another girl run a first-aid post. They call them *Les deux madonnes de Pervyse*.

'Or they did,' says Esther, remembering. 'They were both badly gassed in March, and though my friend recovered, the other nurse – the trained one – was so ill they've had to close the post.'

'Terrible stuff, gas,' says Connie.

'Isn't it wonderful,' says Myra, 'what women are doing these days? We're capable of so much.. we've really proved it.'

'The problem will be,' Esther nods, 'to ensure these opportunities for women survive after the conflict.'

Esther and Myra are soon deep in conversation about women's suffrage. Connie chips in now and then, polishing off more sandwiches and starting on the cakes. Mairi, gradually relaxing, drinks her tea and watches, fascinated by the gently waving shadows cast on floor and wall by the copper beech. Her panic is beginning to settle; this strange world of bricks and noise and trees may be possible. May be.

'Don't you think so, Mairi?'

'Sorry, Esther. What did you say?'

'I was saying it would be good for you to see the city properly while you're here; get a little exercise.'

'Well,' says Myra, 'why don't we start with the parks, while the weather's good?'

And the conversation turns to Edinburgh and its sights: the Royal Mile, the Castle, Princes Street Gardens, Holyrood, Cramond, the Marine Gardens at Portobello with skating rink and menagerie.. Mairi's head is spinning with names.

'Where would you like to go?'

She shakes her head. 'You choose.'

'Mystery tours,' says Connie, 'are the best of all!'

'What nice girls,' says Esther, as she and Mairi stack teacups and plates and saucers on the tray. 'They'll be good for you. Where are they taking you tomorrow?'

'The Botanics, I think.'

'You'll enjoy that,' Esther nods, adding, 'the Glasgow one is better, though. More modern. Mairi.. have you written to your parents?'

'No.'

Mairi's voice is tight, controlled, but Esther goes on. 'Don't you think you should? They'll be worrying about you. I dropped them a note to say you got here safely, but it's four days now..'

Mairi blushes, nods. 'I'll do it straight away.'

'And Mairi..'

'Yes?'

'Keep that shawl. It's never suited me, and you look perfect in it.'

'Thank you, Aunt Esther.'

'Esther, call me Esther. Not Aunt. You'd have time to do that letter before tea, then we could get it off tonight. The post box is just across the road there, at the end. See?' She points out the red box in a distant wall.

'I have no stamps.'

'No problem,' says Esther. 'I have plenty.'

Mairi finds it hard to start the letter, keeps it short.

Dear Mother and Father,

I'm settling in here. Esther and John are lovely, very kind; and the children really sweet. John-Angus's wife Connie and Ewan's Myra came to see me this afternoon; and we're going to the Botanic Gardens tomorrow.

I found the journey tiring, of course, and I miss you both. Very much. Edinburgh seems enormous. So little sky. There are a lot of trees too, even in the city. I expect I will get used to it.

I really do miss you both very much indeed. Don't worry about me. Write and tell me how you are. I'll write to you every day.

Your loving

Mairi.

She slips downstairs to find her aunt busy in the kitchen, supervising tea for Hannah and little John.

'Stamps?' says Esther. 'Top drawer in the bureau – yes, that's it. If you could pop those other letters in the post as well, I'd be most grateful.'

Mairi feels a little odd, exposed, as she walks along the street towards the post box. It's not logical, she argues with herself. No one knows her here, and even if they did, what difference would it make? None. None at all.

It's good to feel the sun on her neck, on her hair, as she walks on the clean hard pavement, peeping through the hedges at the city gardens, gardens full of roses, pansies, hollyhocks and strange bright flowers you never got on the island. Odd, Mairi thinks, that all the hedges should be quite so high – the folk living here must all feel vulnerable, when they're trying to hide like this, behind a few twigs, a swathe of green. It doesn't work. Nothing in this life can remain hidden.

Over the next few days, she gets into a routine of helping Esther and Margaret round the house, walking with Myra and Connie, and playing with Esther's children, who at four and seven still need a surprising amount of care. Myra's Ewan, at eighteen months, needs even more. It's difficult, Mairi notices suddenly, to come to terms with Edinburgh's lack of sea. Oh, you can see sea in the distance, but it isn't the defining substance it is on the island.

She is surprised to find she misses the sea.

She writes home every day, waiting anxiously for news of her mother who has rallied a little, seems better, or so she and Aeneas both report. Maisie is sweating less, coughing less, has expectorated no blood for a week now, which is quite remarkable. Peggy MacLean is proving efficient in the shop, as Mairi had predicted she would be; she isn't gossiping too much either.

Her father includes snippets of news about other people in the town. He never mentions Calum, except the time he writes about Effie and Alec's engagement; how Calum made a special tune for them and played it at Anna's house at the small party she held to celebrate the very happy occasion. They are to be married in six months' time, still a bit young, Aeneas says, to be taking on such responsibility. Mairi lays a hand on her wriggling abdomen, thinks about responsibility.

And the thought of Calum playing what must be, she has no doubt, a sweet and tender tune.. Calum.

She struggles to forget the fine brown eyes, the thick dark hair, the beautiful and tender hands, so true upon the fiddle strings. She tries not to hear his tune for her, but 'Mairi's Waltz' rises up to haunt her, that and 'The Dark Ship'.. Calum's drifting melodies seem somehow to define her past, her future.

She cannot explain what happened. There is no sense in it.

*　　　*　　　*

It's autumn now, October, and the Edinburgh streets are beginning to gather their yearly hoard of fallen gold. For Mairi the autumn has been a revelation of angry colour, sharp winds (snell, the Edinburgh folk call them) and Edinburgh's own peculiar smell, a mixture of malt and soot. Though the war appears, at last, to be going the Allies' way, Mairi does not think about it, seems utterly detached, wandering through the days in a state of blithe dissociation.

'Don't you think it odd,' says John, 'that she never mentions the baby's father?'

Esther's rifling through her wardrobe, looking for her chinoiserie blouse to wear the next day when Myra and Connie come to tea. 'No, I don't think so. Maisie says it's a lad from the island, a soldier – she didn't say much about him but you can tell she doesn't trust him somehow, would rather Mairi didn't marry him. And anyway he hasn't been in touch. If he'd been worth anything he would have been in touch, don't you think? They're able to write letters, even at the front.'

Privately, Esther wonders whether Mairi told him. The girl seems so traumatised by the whole experience that she's denying it, ignoring her condition.. shows no interest even in the baby clothes Esther has been gathering for her, long flannel robes, and shawls, and nappies of muslin and towelling. She has put all these things in a chest at the foot of Mairi's bed, and looked out her old rocking-cot in the attic. It's still in good repair; the muslin and ribbon trimmings are, she knows, safe at the back of the linen cupboard. She doesn't admit it even to herself, but Mairi's presence leaves her wishing for the tender certainty of pregnancy.

Poor Mairi has none of this certainty, but sometimes in the quiet of the night she opens the chest, looks at the tiny gowns with their neat smocking and cross-stitching. It doesn't seem possible that these have anything to do with her. She holds them, strokes them, disbelieving. This cannot be happening. The baby is more active now; she has regular heartburn, worse at night. The small feet pummelling her abdomen seem almost as desperate as she is to be out of this situation, out of it; freed from the cage of rose-laced trellis that Esther's carefully decorated room becomes at such moments.

Why can't she be back on the island? She wants no one but

her mother, and by her actions, by her own actions, she has forfeited the right, the possibility of being there.

What if Maisie should die before the child comes, before she, Mairi, is able to go back? The reaction on the island won't be good, she knows that; but it won't be good whenever she goes back. She might as well get the backlash over now, be with her mother, while her mother has breath in her, surely that makes sense?

She stifles her tears. Sound travels in this house. Esther and John are kind, she cannot let them know her unhappiness. They might write of it to Maisie or Aeneas. Mairi takes her sorrow and forces it behind locked doors with all her other unresolved griefs: with Calum's angry hurt face the day he accused her in the teashop (more or less directly) of sleeping with Angus.. *why didn't he trust her*? Calum's dull compliant face the day they drove back from Callanish, and opened Iain's letters to find Iain announcing that he had decided to marry her (*as if she had no power in the matter, no say*), did Calum not want her after all? Or Calum's face when Iain came home, his grim jealous passivity in assuming she wanted Iain.. *Iain*!

She leaves her grief in this bleak compartment she has reinforced, made rigid; locks it away, offering an apparently untroubled expression to the world, a face reacting passively to all before it, a face that looks blankly anywhere, everywhere, at everything except what really matters.

Walking in the Botanic Gardens the next morning, Connie and Myra ponder the same problem.

'Why do you think she never talks about him?'

'She may not know we know,' says Myra. 'And may not think we know him.'

'She knew Dulcie knew him.'

'Yes, but.. she's not calculating, Connie. When she gave that book to John-Angus for Dulcie, I thought.. I don't know what I thought..'

'Well, I thought here's this girl coming to lord it over

Dulcie.. that's what I thought!'

'Do you still feel that way?'

'No. She's a nice kid. Not awake. Going round as if she's in a dream. John-Angus says she's not usually like this.'

'I don't think she is,' Myra nods. 'When I was in Lewis, Mairi seemed vivacious, bright. Intelligent. I didn't see much of her, of course. She was generally with her cousin or the lad with the withered leg, Calum, the one that plays so well. I've told you about him.'

'Were they..?'

'John-Angus would know. We should ask him, maybe.'

Connie strides in worried silence for a few minutes, then turns to Myra.

'Why do you think she gave him the book?'

'Which book?'

'The poems.'

'Have you looked at it?'

'No.'

'It's dedicated to Dulcie. That's written on the first page.'

'Then how did Mairi come to have them?'

'That Iain,' says Myra, 'is a complicated fellow.'

'And I quite liked him,' Connie says. 'Isn't it odd? I thought he was a nice lad.. simple, straightforward, and charming.'

'Charming he can be. Simple? Straightforward?'

'That's how he seemed to me. D'you fancy a turn in the hothouses?'

'Not today.' Myra stands still now, looks anxious. 'I.. want to call past Dulcie's house. I met Angie yesterday..'

'Angie?'

'The VAD from Ward 11. She tells me Dulcie's ill, has been off work for two weeks now.'

'Funny that she never wrote.'

'That's what I thought. That's why we're going to see her.'

'Where does she stay?'

'Not far. Fettes Row.'

They walk up a narrow path, edged with low box hedging.

'Are you sure this is Dulcie's house?'

'Yes. Her grandmother left it to her.'

'Ah.'

Myra rings the bell. Connie looks round at the neat grass, the autumn crocuses, the late-flowering primulas. 'She must be out.'

Myra rings the bell again. There's no sound within, no footfalls, no pulling of bolts.

'Come on, Myra, let's go.'

Myra rings the bell again. When there's still no answer, she raps on the ground floor window. The curtains have not been opened.

'She's not in, Myra. Come on. We'll come back tomorrow.'

Connie starts up the path. Her hand is on the green-painted wrought iron of the gate when the front door opens stiffly.

Dulcie shows them into the darkened front room. A fire is half-laid in the grate, and two or three empty cups sit on the mantelpiece. A small white terrier sits in the corner, growling.

'Be quiet, Jock,' says Dulcie. 'To your basket!' Tail down, the animal obeys, still looking at Connie and Myra with distrust.

'What a delightful fellow,' says Connie. 'I didn't know you had a dog, Dulcie. How long have you had him?'

'Since February,' Dulcie says. 'He was a birthday present.'

'He's very fine.'

'I wish Mrs MacConnochie thought so! Whenever she comes in, he growls and nibbles at her ankles.'

'Maybe she's not good with dogs?'

'No. I leave him in his run at the back the days she's in. It's hard to get good help; she's very trustworthy. And he's a bit over-protective of me, always has been.'

'Shall I pull the curtains, Dulcie?'

Myra's halfway through the act as she asks this. Clear light floods the room, shines on Dulcie's dressing-gown, stretched taut across her burgeoning.

'That's better.'

Myra turns.

'What can we be doing for you, Dulcie, now we're here?'

'There's not a lot,' says Dulcie, 'to be done. At this stage.'

'Christ, Dulcie, no!'

'Shut up, Connie. Dulcie, how long.. ?'

'Mid-January, the doctor says. I'm fine, honestly. I'm really well. I didn't show at all till the last few weeks.. I don't care anyway! Bugger them if they talk.. I'm going to love this baby like no other baby's ever been loved. I'm going to call her Elinor.'

'Not if she's a boy,' says Connie.

'She'll not be a boy. She wouldn't dare.'

Dulcie looks at Myra.

'I can read your mind, you know. But I'm really fine, not being brave, nothing like that. I like to sleep late, Myra, when I can. VAD work doesn't leave much room for that. Now I've stopped it, I can stay up late and sleep late. And as for Iain Murray – if he comes back he comes back. If he doesn't, tough. He hasn't any money, I don't need him for that. And I knew what he was like, I did. I knew him to the bone. He loved me, Myra. That was all that mattered then; it's all that matters now.'

'But what about the world, Dulcie? How will you manage?'

'When you've money, you can do anything. Folk are always respectful of cash! And even if the freedoms women have gained in the war should disappear in peacetime, it won't matter. Money, I suspect, will matter more and more in the fine new world we've made.'

'Don't be so cynical!'

'It's not cynicism, Myra. It's fact.'

'She's right,' says Connie. 'The Russians may be Bolshevik, but there aren't many nations likely to follow them.'

Myra moves to the mantelpiece, lifting down a photograph of Iain. 'That's a lovely frame.'

'Thank you. Margaret MacDonald made it for me, to her husband's design. I like their work. It's not so fashionable these days, though. They showed in Germany before the war..'

Myra isn't listening, she's looking intently at the picture which shows Iain sitting at the table in this very room, lost in thought. The pencil in his hand, the tattered notebook, are in shadow. There's a sense of peace, of stillness, Myra never saw in him.

'Is this your work, Dulcie? Did you take this photograph?'

'Yes. The day before he went back off to France. It's good, isn't it?'

Myra looks at it again, this image of a man at peace, in equilibrium; a happy man.

'If you feel like that about him,' she says, 'write to him, telling him; and about the child.'

Dulcie's eyes are bright, too bright. 'I have. He didn't answer.'

*   *   *

Mairi lies down in the early afternoons for half an hour or so before getting up and writing home, or walking with her new friends. She's not sleeping well at nights, so the early afternoon nap is welcome, necessary, though she has a tendency to dream then, or to lie remembering..

Lewis seems very far from this tidy room. It's hard for her to imagine what the island air feels like, smells like. But she remembers the Murrays' croft all too well, the seaweed sourness of the boathouse on the shore.

It's a chill day towards the end of March. The wind, which has been fierce, is quiet now, has disappeared. Under her long wool cape, she's wearing her blue silk blouse and skirt, the ones she wore at the dancing the day Iain enlisted. They're her very best things, she feels good in them, loves the feel of silk, loves the colour. The skirt is a little loose. With Maisie's illness, with the worry about her mother and all the extra work at home and in the shop, and also with her own unhappiness at Calum's increasingly taciturn frame of mind, she has lost weight.

Calum picks her up, driving her to Holm in old Alec's dog-cart. She's made a special effort with her appearance, hoping to reassure him, help him understand how much she loves him, but he's had a dram or two already, and is quiet, sullen. Doesn't answer when she talks.

'What have you been up to?'

Silence.

'How's your mother? Father? I haven't seen Alec for ages. What's he up to? Have you been speaking to Iain?'

'I was wondering how long you'd take to turn the conversation round to Iain.'

'Calum, don't be so stupid!

'Stupid right enough,' he says, 'to have thought you cared at all for me. It's always been Iain, hasn't it? Bloody Iain!'

Mairi leans forwards, pulling on the reins. The pony halts, obediently.

'What do you think you're doing?'

'I've had enough of this,' says Mairi, climbing down from the cart, her blue skirt catching on the seat as she does. She loses a little dignity extracting it, but none of her anger.

'Come on, Mairi, don't be stupid. Climb back up.'

'No. I've had enough, Calum. You're impossible. If you don't trust me, we shouldn't be together. I told you last year we should write to Iain explaining the situation – you're the one that held back. You're the one that immediately assumed I was cavorting in my parents' shed with Angus Johnson. Angus Johnson, of all people! And now you've the.. the *ignorance* to imply that I.. *that I..* am the one with eyes on Iain Murray!

'Calum Morrison, you're besotted with the fool and you are a fool, and I've had more than I can take of you. Go to the party yourself. I'm not coming.'

'Don't be silly, Mairi. Look, we're nearly there.'

'I don't care.'

She turns her back on him, makes off along the road. Calum watches her to the corner, then curses, and drives on.

Hearing him driving off, Mairi sits down on a rock at the side of the road and bursts into tears.

How long she sits there she could not say. No one else passes on the road. Calum had been late arriving for her. It's nearly dark now , but the moon's up early and a bright moon too, a huge orange moon bobbing low in the eastern sky; and the night is still, even slightly warm. Today has been the first really spring-like day. Mairi sighs. If her heart is broken, there's nothing but exercise, and good hard work to mend it. She stands up, shaking her cloak and turns for home.

She is still within shouting distance of the croft. The laughter and chatter drift down along the road, increasing her sense of loneliness. And now she hears the fiddle, Calum's fiddle, there's no mistaking it, he's playing the waltz he wrote for her.. she stops walking, spellbound by the real love in the tune. And now he's playing 'The Dark Ship' and it seems to Mairi that it's not about the war, and it's not about the dangers of the sea, but about Calum's own troubled heart, his own inability to trust in himself, in love.. and now he's dipping from the one tune to the other.. Mairi sees now how similar they are, how one predicts the other.

She keeps walking.

'Mairi?'

'Iain. What are you doing here? You should be at the ceilidh. They must be looking for you.'

'Och..' Iain shrugs.

'Goodnight, Iain,' Mairi says, turning.

He stops her. 'I was sorry to hear your mother has been so ill. You didn't say.. in your letters.'

'We didn't think you'd want too much news like that, not in the trenches. Too much reality there already, that's what we thought.'

'In some ways, that's probably right, I suppose.'

'Look, Iain, I have to go. I'm not good company tonight, I'm sorry. Get up to the croft. You'll find better craic there.'

'I'm not up to it myself,' says Iain. 'And you can't walk all the way back to Stornoway, not in those shoes. Let me go and borrow a cart. I'll take you.'

'No. I'll walk, Iain. Good night.'

'Mairi, you're being foolish.'

Mairi shrugs.

'Well, before you go, come and talk to me a while. Before I go back to the house and pretend to be cheerful. Come on,' he takes her hand, 'let's walk beside the sea.'

'What would you like to talk about?'

'I don't know,' Iain sighs. 'Life here doesn't seem relevant, and France is indescribably bad; doesn't make sense. If I were to mention *mud*, for instance, to you it's earth and water, but to us over there it's living hell: it sucks us down, prevents us sleeping, drowns us, buries us. The vocabulary doesn't stretch from one experience to the other.'

'I've heard,' Mairi says, 'that Eskimos have forty words for snow..'

'You're a clever lass.' Iain shakes his head.

'I suppose,' she says slowly, 'you can't even make up the words because of the difference in shared experience.'

'That's right. But images, Mairi, sometimes images can shock people into understanding.'

'Photographs, you mean? Paintings?'

'I meant word-images, poems.'

'You're writing poetry, Iain?'

'I've always loved poetry.'

'Not that I remember!'

'No, I have, Mairi. I used to scour the readers at school for poems. They weren't always all that good.'

'Well! I'd never have thought it. Iain Murray writing poetry. You'll have to send me some.'

'I can do better than that.. look, borrow this. Send it back to me when you've read it. Or keep it, Mairi.. if anything ever happens to me, send it to the girl in the poems.' Iain takes a notebook from his breast-pocket. Mairi slips it into the pocket on her cloak.

Iain hears the swish of silk. 'That's your best skirt, young lady.'

'Yes,' says Mairi, 'and all in your honour, sir!' She curtsies gracefully. Iain takes her hand on the beach and they dance a pretended minuet, scurrying in some disarray from a sudden flourish of the incoming tide.

'Imagine you writing poetry!' she says again.

'I thought everybody did.'

'Iain!'

'Well, you might have.. you're clever enough.'

'You have a slippery tongue, Iain Murray, and I know it well. You'll not bamboozle me as you do those French girls.'

'I don't bamboozle them. It's either one thing or the other; business or strictly mild flirtation. They're either on the make, or virtually in convents! But I shouldn't be saying that type of thing. I've been telling the boys that they're all on the make. You won't give me away, Mairi?'

'Is it likely that I'd be invited to the bothan, Iain?'

'You might tell Calum.'

'Calum knows you as well as I do.'

Mairi shivers.

'You're cold.'

'I should be going, Iain.'

'Don't go yet, Mairi. Look, if we sit in the lee of the boathouse it won't be quite so chilly. It's just the onshore breeze.'

But it isn't much warmer. The wind is still sharp as a knife.

'Come inside,' says Iain, 'and we'll close the door. Better?'

'Yes, it is.'

Mairi's still shivering. Her teeth are chattering too. Iain comes to stand beside her, rubs her arms, her back. He offers her his half-bottle.

'No!' says Mairi. 'You know I don't drink, Iain..'

'It's medicinal, Mairi,' he coaxes. 'Look, you're chilled to the bone. Go on. Just have a little.'

Mairi risks a small sip, coughs.

'Very medicinal!' she says when her breath comes back at last.

'Now try a little more. It'll warm you from the centre out.'

Mairi realises this is happening already. Even the one sip

has made her feel less like a block of ice. She takes the bottle, sips and coughs again.

'Now, jump up and down,' Iain says. 'Stamp your feet! That's what we do in the trenches. But you have to be careful, of course, to keep your head down while you're doing it. Not that you'd have problems, with your lack of height..'

He measures her head against his chest.

'See? You just reach to my heart.'

He looks at Mairi. She's still shaking.

'Come here,' he says, and wraps his arms around her.

And it's warm in those arms, and safe, after the chilly emptiness of Calum's jealousy. Mairi sighs, leans against Iain as if to draw strength from him. She's warmer than she was. Much warmer.

Iain sits down on a half-barrel by the door, pulls her on his knee like a child.

'Better now?'

'Thank you, Iain.'

'Mairi,' Iain says, 'I must tell you in all honesty, I'm in love with someone else, but you are very, very sweet. May I kiss you?'

'Yes. I'm in love with someone else too.'

'That's alright, then.'

And it's not the tiny sips of poitin, not two sips like that.. and it's not the incandescence she feels when Calum touches her, nothing nearly so intense.. but Iain's there, he's warm, and her heart is bleeding.. and his hands are practised, and he knows how to make her feel.. how to make her want..

But it's an odd experience all the same. When Iain enters her, Mairi experiences only an angry heat, a stretching, dull pain that settles gradually. Her own excitement lessening, she watches his dispassionately. Odd to have someone pumping up and down on top of you like that.. and so self-absorbed.

'Dulcie,' he mutters as he rolls off, leaving Mairi wet and cooling. He seems delirious, relaxed. Mairi is discomfited, leaking. The smell is something like the kelp they're lying in. She doesn't like it.

'Iain,' she shakes his sleeping shoulder. 'Iain, I'm going home now. Thank you for the book. Come and say goodbye before you go.'

He doesn't wake. She feels distinctly odd, light-headed. As she wanders along the beach, she feels the slow, cold drip of Iain's tide. There's nothing she can do here to rid herself of the smell, and it will be a long walk home.

Walking up to the road, over the machair, she hears her name called.

'Mairi! What? Are you still here?'

'Go away, Calum Morrison!' she shouts, bursting into tears. 'Have you not said enough for one night? I don't wish to speak to you.'

'Mairi, I'm sorry. Let me take you home. I didn't mean any of it.'

'I did, Calum. I meant every word.'

She's crying now, furious that Calum had not been the one to join with her.. with Calum it might have been exciting.. she might have felt the joy she'd watched in Iain, the act might have meant something. Mairi's tears grow angrier, more bitter. Calum watches, mystified.

Neither of them notices Iain walking on the beach, though Calum knows he's there. Everyone at the croft celebrating his homecoming knows Iain cannot face them, is drifting on the shore.

Mairi and Calum, arguing, do not see or hear him, but he sees them, and hearing Mairi crying, wonders what he's done. He can't remember. He shouldn't drink so much, but how else would he cope?

He cuts across land to the bothan; leaves the island next day. Passing the cliffs of Holm, he takes a photograph from his pocket, a picture of himself and Mairi and Calum, taken on the pier the day he left for the Depot. He studies the carefree faces, they look so young, so innocent.. before tearing the picture into tiny pieces, and dropping them in the angry tide.

He does not look back, makes for Edinburgh, and Dulcie.

*   *   *

Connie arrives alone for tea at the Maitlands' that afternoon. Myra has stayed with Dulcie, knowing she is too upset for Esther's all-seeing eye. Connie is quite happy to visit on her own. Myra and Esther treat Mairi too much like a child; she knows in her heart this cannot be good for the girl.

When she rings the bell, it's Mairi who opens the tall blue door.

'Come in, Connie. No Myra?'

'She had to stay with a sick friend. Last minute thing, you know.'

'Well, Esther's been called out too. Not to a sick friend, but to an emergency tea party for somebody or other's birthday. Someone about four years old, I think.'

'Serious stuff.'

'Do you want to run upstairs,' says Mairi, 'and I'll make tea?'

'As it's just you and me, why don't we find a café?'

'Mystery tour!'

'That's right.'

'Just let me get my cape.'

The two girls wander along the road towards the town centre.

'We'll not take the first café,' Mairi says. 'I think.. the third one.'

'I'd go for the seventh! Luckier number.'

'Depends how far apart they are,' Mairi pats her abdomen.

'Yes, sorry. Forgot. Okay, third café.'

'Seventh if they're *very* very close together.'

'Shall we put rights and lefts in too? Starting now?'

'Why not?'

'Okay.. right, left, right; right, right, left.'

'Third café. Or seventh.'

'What was that again? Right left right; right, right, left?'

'That's what you said..'

There turn out to be very few cafés on this particular itinerary. In the end, they slip into the second. Mairi's quite breathless by now.

'That's a good game, though. A city game. You couldn't play it in Stornoway.'

'Not for cafés, maybe,' Connie says. 'I used to play it in the support trenches with this young officer I knew.. not too clever when I come to think of it now.'

'You were actually in the trenches?'

'I wasn't supposed to be. But I'm a bit reckless at times, always was. I have a reputation for it, I suppose.'

'In Stornoway, you're the girl who saved John-Angus. Everybody knows Connie Smylie, like Kate Barlass, or Grace Darling.'

'Well, he's special,' says Connie. 'Famous really. He'd been pointed out to me several times as the boy who got the VC in Arras. He'd seen me loads of times before I took him to the hospital, but he never noticed me.'

'I expect you were always busy.'

'No, he just never noticed me. That's the truth of it. I noticed him though. I thought he was beautiful.'

'You like plain speaking, don't you?'

'Does it bother you?'

'Not at all. You like plain speaking, you like sandwiches, you like John-Angus. I like all three.'

'You're in a funny mood today.'

'No, it's just.. I'm feeling more alive,' says Mairi. 'I don't know why. I did have a good letter from home, and my mother's a little stronger again, and I'm beginning to hope she'll still be there when I get back. But it's not just that. I woke up feeling better. Stronger.'

'There are days like that.'

'Did you find it difficult coming back here?'

'Goodness, yes. And also no. No, because it's such a relief to be out of danger, and have John-Angus with me.. or nearly with me, anyway. And yes, because no one knows here; folk have no conception what it's like.. well, even the generals over there have no idea. They're well behind the lines, away from the mud, but the boys, they know what war costs, and the RAMC, and the stretcher-bearers and the prisoners and the nurses and the doctors.. you can't say this to most people, Mairi. They just don't want to know, not in detail, not at all. You might be describing the far side of the moon, for all it means to them. So that's difficult. You have this huge gap in your life, this huge thing you can't talk about. And you miss the excitement too, the emotion of it. I know that sounds daft, and I was never in the front line as you know, but when you're under fire, when you're in danger, you're suddenly very conscious of how good it is to be alive. It seems an oddly seductive thing.. for some of the boys it was almost addictive. I didn't believe them at first, thought it was just the *nursey* line.. you know what men are like with nurses.. but quite a few people seem to find it so. It's odd. Seriously odd.'

Mairi laughs. 'I've never heard you talk so much.'

Connie laughs too. '*I've* never heard me talk so much. What did they put in this tea?'

'Well,' says Mairi, slowly, 'I think I understand, a little, how you feel. I've been feeling so down.. you wouldn't like to know how bad.. but today I feel alive. I'm even glad to feel the baby moving. I wrote to my mother telling her that this morning.' She lifts her teacup in both hands, focuses on the tear-blurred rim. 'I love her so much, Connie.. I'm terrified she'll die before I get back to the island. What will I do without her?'

'You'll never be without her. Never.'

'How can you be so sure?'

'I've seen a lot of death, a lot of grief. You'll grieve, Mairi, but your mother will always be with you, in your bones and in your heart. And in your love. She'll be in your baby too, through you.'

'I want to go home,' says Mairi. 'The only thing that keeps me here is the knowledge that she wanted me to come.'

'She'd be frightened of infecting the baby.'

'I never thought of that..'

'*She* obviously did.'

'I don't want her to die, Connie. I'm not sure I can cope if she's not there.'

'You can,' Connie says. 'You will. You'll get the strength you need. You're a very strong girl.. anyone can see that. Look at how you're coping with the pregnancy.'

'I haven't been,' Mairi drains her cup. 'But now I will.'

'Let me see that.'

'You read cups? I didn't know.'

'Actually I read leaves. Everybody's superstitious one way or another in France,' says Connie, taking Mairi's cup and frowning into it for long moments.

'Something wrong?'

'Mountains, or rocks ahead,' says Connie. 'That means problems, not necessarily insurmountable.. I'm sorry, Mairi. I was hoping it would be a harp.'

'What would that mean?'

'Wonderful good news!'

'I've never seen a tea-leaf harp.'

'I have. There was one in my cup the day I found John-Angus.'

'There you go. That proves it then.'

'We should be getting back, Mairi. Esther will be wondering where you are.'

The sun is still quite warm though there's a chill in the air as the girls retrace their steps.

'Have you thought how you're going to manage when you go back?'

'We'll cope,' says Mairi. 'Maybe we can get another maid. Knowing the island, though, I'll have to keep my head down for a year or two. It's a little more conservative over there than here.'

'What about the baby's father?' Connie realises she's been leading up to this all afternoon. 'You never mention him. Will he not figure in your plans?'

'No,' says Mairi. 'No. We'd kill each other inside a month.' She smiles at Connie's silence. 'What? Shocked?'

'Frankly, yes,' says Connie. 'I hadn't realised.. how ill your mother was. I thought.. I thought you were unhappily in love.'

'I am,' Mairi sighs. 'But that's another matter.'

Esther is panicking by the time they get back home, and Mairi is exhausted, though obviously happy. When she hears how far they've walked, Esther raises her eyebrows.

'Mairi, you're seven months pregnant. If you want to bring on early labour, that's the way to go about it!'

'Sorry,' Connie excuses herself and leaves. Mairi sees her to the door. 'Don't worry,' she whispers, 'I'm fine.'

She repeats this to Esther. 'Honestly, I'm fine.'

'I'm not,' says Esther. 'I was very worried, very worried indeed, about you. Sit down and put your feet up while I think of something cross enough to say..'

'Esther,' says Mairi, 'A lady does not swear except in childbed. My mother told me that!'

Myra takes the same line as Esther.

'That was too far, Connie. Mairi isn't all that fit. It could bring contractions on, you know. You should have had more sense!'

'And she's not in love with Iain,' Connie runs on, oblivious. 'She's in love with someone else. Calum. It must be. Can I see those poems?'

'Iain's poems?'

Myra fetches the notebook from the back of her bureau. Connie bends her head and reads in silence for a full twenty minutes. Myra is amazed to find her weeping at the end of it.

'I wouldn't have let you see it if I'd thought the poems would upset you.'

'They're good,' says Connie. 'Wonderful, actually. You should give this book to Dulcie.'

'How can I do that? She'd ask where I got them. If I tell her

Iain is the father of Mairi's baby, is that going to help her?'

'I think it would be better than her thinking he doesn't love her. It's obvious from these that he does.'

'She knows he *did* love her,' Myra says. 'It's obvious from the photographs she took of him, of them together. What she doesn't know, what none of us can ever know, is what he's feeling *now*.'

'War doesn't help.'

'No,' says Myra, 'too much of the moment. And living in the moment, or dying in it, has its consequences.'

Connie closes the notebook, hands it back. 'I still think you should give it to her.'

'No. It wouldn't help. I spent the whole day in Dulcie's company. She's completely alone, you know. Her brother was killed at the Somme; their parents died of fever on the way back from India ten years ago – the children were at boarding school in the city here. All she had in the world was her brother.'

'And Iain,' Connie insists. 'You should give her that book. There aren't many things we disagree on, Myra, but you're wrong in this. I know.'

'I don't think so,' says Myra, slipping the book back into the envelope and pushing it once more to the back of the bureau. 'I'll leave that decision to John-Angus. When is he getting back from training school?'

'Two weeks,' says Connie. 'We should know by mid-November where his posting is.'

'Good.'

'You're fed up of my appetite. I warned you!'

'No. I'm trying to work out how we can see enough of Mairi and Dulcie. The longer you're here, the better. I'll miss you when you go north, you daft thing.'

'We might go south,' says Connie. 'But I hope not.'

*   *   *

Mairi is frightened that night by a series of contractions, the muscles in her abdomen spasmodically tightening; at times they grow so hard and sore her belly feels like wood. She panics, thinks the baby may be damaged. The pain of each contraction makes her shiver and sweat. She doesn't want to disturb Esther, keeps leaving it, giving it another ten minutes, worrying. The contractions eventually settle down.

As she's drifting off, at last, to sleep, she thinks she smells her mother's perfume. Guerlain. She's sent to Glasgow for it since Mairi can remember. What is it called? Samsara?

Mairi thinks she smells the perfume, feels her mother's cool light hand against her fevered brow.

The contractions settle down, do not return, and she wakens to the first frost of autumn. The petals of the clematis blooming unseasonably by her window are encased in shining crystals, their velvet blue deepened almost to navy. Sugar flowers. Glass flowers. Fairy flowers. When the ice burns off in early morning sun, the plant emerges, wrinkled; the dead blooms shrivelled, limp. It's weather, not an omen, Mairi tells herself.

And the sparrow trapped in the inner hall late that morning, that's not an omen either.

She's not surprised, none the less, at the telegram. MOTHER DESPERATELY ILL. FADING. Esther and John catch the first train. By the time they're in Inverness, the news has reached Edinburgh of Maisie's death. Mairi wires them at the station. They carry on to the island for the funeral, confident that Margaret and Mairi will manage the young ones.

'You'll keep Mairi till she's settled with the little one?' Aeneas asks, anxiously.

'Don't worry,' Esther says. 'She's like a daughter to me. But write to her, Aeneas. Come over and see her.'

'I will,' he says, 'just as soon as everything is straight here.'

He's a shadow of himself. Looking at him, Esther thinks he'll run himself into the grave if he's not careful. The shop is surviving, thanks mainly to Peggy. Colin, though senior in time served, is much less able, less hardworking, never sees what's to be done unless he's told. He has beautifully soft hands, which he looks after obsessively.

Peggy, who has grown fond of Aeneas (and was always fond of Mairi and admired Maisie) understands the business. She understands Colin too, manages him very well. The week of Maisie's death, she manages a shiny emerald ring from him, but doesn't wear it then, in due respect. They announce their engagement two weeks after the funeral. On Armistice Day. It's the first bit of good news Aeneas has to send to Mairi.

FOURTH VARIATION

Julia sighed as the phone rang for the twentieth time that morning. She hadn't been able to get on with anything, not a single thing. Ewan was right, though she hated to admit it. They should have had caterers to do the funeral. Emma, home for the funeral, slouched around the kitchen in leggings and teeshirts, not even troubling to answer the phone.

'Get that for me, would you darling?'

Emma shrugged, ambled into the hall and slowly lifted the phone. 'Hello. Yes. No. He's not at home. Would you like to speak to my mother? Mum! It's for you.

'I told you it would be,' she grumbled, handing the receiver to Julia. 'There's no point in my answering. It's for you every time.'

'Who is it?'

'Don't know.'

Julia sat down on the stair, sighing.

'Hello? Julia MacLeod. What can I do for you?'

'Hello Mrs MacLeod,' a bright female voice sang out from the other end. 'You don't know me, but I met your grandfather, and I was very sorry to hear about his sudden illness. Excuse me for a moment, please.'

The voice stopped there. In the background Julia could hear a muffled *No, I'm just on the phone to her. Hold on. I don't want to push it, Jane.*

More reporters. John-Angus had been well-known, if controversial at times.

'Sorry about that,' the voice was clearer again. 'I haven't introduced myself. I'm Zoe Wild.'

'Oh,' said Julia, 'I knew I'd heard the voice somewhere. You sound a lot younger on the phone!'

'Everybody says that.'

The girl was blushing as she answered, Julia could tell. 'What can I do for you?' she asked again.

'I know it's a bad time,' said Zoe. 'But we have some lovely footage of your grandfather..'

'My husband's grandfather.'

'Yes, sorry.. I met him a couple of weeks ago in the Meredith. I really took to him. But I didn't want to tire him, and we didn't get round to discussing many of the issues I'd have liked to explore. The thing is.. I wondered if I could speak to your husband? And yourself of course. I gather your husband's father is dead?'

'John-Iain's been dead, oh, ten years at least. His wife is still alive, but she doesn't keep well, I'm afraid. I don't think she'd agree to see you. But I'll ask Ewan to get back to you. What's your number?'

'Excuse me, Mrs MacLeod. I'm sorry about these interruptions. This place is like a fairground.'

More muffled speech. Julia thought she heard *yes, I'll ask her, but I'm not..*

'The thing is,' Zoe continued, 'if you didn't mind, I'd like to come to the funeral. I'd like to come, for myself. And my producer has asked me to ask if we might film some parts of it. To contrast, you know.. with what might have happened in France.'

'Oh,' says Julia. 'I don't know. That seems a bit intrusive.'

'Well, I'd like to come anyway,' says Zoe. 'Mr MacLeod made a profound impression on me. He was a lovely man.'

'Yes,' said Julia, 'he was. Look, give me your number, Zoe. I'll discuss it with my family and get back to you.'

As she wrote the number down, Julia's mind went into overdrive. Film the funeral? Her instinct was to say no, firmly no. But it was not her decision.

'I'll get back to you about the filming,' she promised. 'The service itself – cremation actually – is tomorrow, Thursday, 2pm, at Inverness Crematorium; that's at Kilvean, next to the new cemetery. It's easy to find; you head out of Inverness on the road west, and it's just beyond the golf-course, below Craig Dunain. It's clearly signposted. You can't miss it.'

She put the phone down. It rang immediately.

'Hello?'

'Is that you, Julia?'

'Mamie, hello. How are you today?'

'Sore and stiff, if you want to know the truth. I need a black hat for this funeral.'

'I wasn't going to wear a hat.'

'What? Not wear a hat? That's not proper.'

'People don't really wear them any more.'

'I'm not *people*. I need to go into town this afternoon. When can you come and pick me up?'

'Emma's home.. she could come any time.'

'Not Emma, you. That girl is so blooming fidgety, I'd never choose anything.'

'But I've all the baking for the funeral to be getting on with, Mamie.'

'Can't you get caterers to do it? Use some of that senior consultant's salary.'

Julia sighed. 'I'll come after lunch, then. One forty-five?'

'I'll be ready.'

She put the phone down. It rang immediately.

'Hello?'

'Oh hello, Julia, this is Nan from the Meredith. I know this probably isn't a good time to phone, but I wanted to let you know that John-Angus's things are ready for collecting. We've managed to get them all into the trailer Ewan brought.'

'Great, Nan. I'll call round for them later this afternoon. See you then.'

'What time's the service? There's quite a few of the girls want to come.'

'Two, at the crematorium.'

'Grand. I'll maybe see you later.'

The line went dead. Julia replaced the receiver, stood waiting with her hand in mid-air. The phone didn't ring. She slipped back to the kitchen and was just starting to rub the margarine into flour for the sausage-roll pastry when the phone erupted again. She heard Emma's slow amble across the hall's beech flooring, her laconic *Hello*.

'Mum! Phone!'

'Who is it?'

'Don't know.' Emma put the phone down and wandered back through to the blaring CD in the front room.

Julia wiped her hands, running them under the tap. Flour had stuck under the rings, as it always did. She'd have to sort that later. She should have taken them off, never thinks of it in time.

She rushed through to the hall, picked the phone up.

'Hello,' her tone was business-like. The voice at the other end seemed elderly but brisk.

'Hello, Mrs MacLeod, Elinor Hershaw speaking. You won't know me, but my mother knew John-Angus very well. I saw in the paper he had died and wanted to offer my condolences. If I can, I'd like to come up for the service – the details weren't in the *Scotsman*.'

'Of course, Mrs Hershaw..'

'Miss.'

'I'm sorry, *Miss* Hershaw. The service is at Inverness crematorium at two, tomorrow Thursday. Where will you be coming from?'

'Edinburgh. I expect there'll be trains that fit?'

'I don't know, I'm sorry. You'd have thought so.'

'You must be Ewan's wife.'

'Yes,' said Julia, surprised.

'Thought so, though you don't sound Italian, not a bit!'

'I speak Italian,' Julia laughed. 'My mother was Italian. How do you know all about me?'

'Mother kept track of all the children, one way or another. Probably sent you a wedding present.'

'You have the advantage of me. I don't remember the family history so well – how did your mother know John-Angus?'

'Actually,' said the voice, 'I'm Dulcie's daughter .'

'Dulcie's Elinor! I should have known, I'm so sorry. We have a photograph of you.. you must come and stay with us after the service. You won't be wanting to go back to Edinburgh tomorrow night.'

'That's very kind.'

'Come up to the house with your luggage first. If we're already on our way, I'll leave the sun room door open. It should be safe enough in there. See how the trains go.'

'Very kind of you.'

Elinor rang off. Julia did not immediately replace the telephone receiver.

'Who was that then?' Emma was leaning on the wall opposite Julia.

'Dulcie's daughter.'

'Dulcie who?'

'The Dulcie – the VAD.'

'*The* Dulcie?' Emma's eyes lit up. 'I wonder what she'll be like? She must be ancient.'

'Seventy-odd,' said Julia. 'She was born just after the war ended. She sounds very interesting. We'll soon know. She's going to stay tomorow night.'

'How will she get on with Eilidh?'

'Why Eilidh in particular?'

'Well.. Iain..'

'Och, Emma.. that won't be a problem. Mairi and Dulcie liked each other. It wasn't like the film.'

'Do we have a copy of the film?'

'Somewhere. It's not life, remember, Emma, not *literal* truth. The John-Angus character.. John-Andrew, I think Calum called him.. is bullied so badly in the training for the trenches that he tries to commit suicide. He's killed on his first foray over the top.'

'What crap!'

'Well, it works in the film. John-Angus didn't mind a bit. He only ever used to complain about the accents.

'They had Bogey for Iain, and Ingrid Bergman for Myra – she was particularly good. And a girl called Kathleen Ryan, not so well-known now, as Mairi, and James Mason as Calum.. and they had to have Bacall, or Bogey wouldn't come, so Bacall did Effie, not that successfully. She was too hard. But Gregory Peck was Ewan, and Dirk Bogarde played John-Angus. And David Niven was just right as Angus Johnson.'

'Who played Connie?'

'There wasn't a Connie. It wasn't true to life, remember? Calum Morrison wrote *The Dark Ship* in the forties, thirty years after it all happened; but some of the events still seemed so real to him, Emma, so difficult that he found he had to change them. Others didn't make narrative sense, and sometimes, I expect, the characters themselves took off in unexpected ways, came alive, refused to stay in solid history.'

'He still shouldn't have done it.'

'Lots of people thought so. The island never forgave him. That's why he left, I think.'

'I thought he left to go to Hollywood and Pinewood, and all these places.'

'That too.'

'Make up your mind!'

'I have.'

Julia put the receiver down. The phone rang immediately. She sighed.

'Phone your father, Emma, on the mobile, and ask him which caterers he thinks are best. Oh, and I need to speak to him too.'

Julia didn't get back home till nearly seven, drawing up carefully in front of the garage doors so it would be easier for Ewan to lift the chairs and sideboard out of the trailer. The pictures and John-Angus's clothes and books were all stowed in the car. She found two strange cars already parked in the drive, or rather, two cars strange to her. This would, she supposed, be the order of the week.

She struggled into the house under the weight of the box containing most of John-Angus's books and photographs. These she carried to her studio, leaving them behind the door, and went back for the paintings. It was dark, but not raining. The furniture was safe enough for the moment in the open.

As she boiled the kettle in the kitchen, Julia wondered about the cars. She couldn't hear any unknown voices in the lounge, though it sounded as if the television might be on. She wandered through with her cup of coffee to find Emma and Finlay and a girl with short dark hair all sitting on the sofa engrossed in the video copy Ewan made of *The Dark Ship* last time it was shown. The quality was poor; the sound, in particular, fuzzy, which ruined it for Julia. Music was so important.

She bent to kiss Finlay on the top of the head.

'Good to see you home, boy. New car?'

He looked up, smiling. 'Hired. I don't have to go back till Monday. You okay?'

'As okay,' she nodded, 'as anyone can be who's just spent the whole afternoon trying to buy a black hat for Mamie.'

'Ah,' he sympathised. 'Rather you than me. Mum, this is Zoe. She's come to see Dad.'

'Of course! I'd forgotten,' Julia stretched across to shake hands. 'I'm sorry, Zoe. I hope they've been looking after you?'

Zoe smiled. 'It's really good to meet you, Mrs MacLeod.'

'Call me Julia. Ewan's late.. hospital time can be a bit unpredictable.'

'A *bit*!' echoed Finlay.

'Shh. We're coming to the bit where John-Angus goes over the top..' Emma glowered.

'I'll go and put the dinner on. '

'Mum..'

'Yes, Emma?'

'Could I have a coffee?'

'What about you, Zoe? Have they offered you something?'

Zoe raised her wine glass. 'Finlay opened a bottle.'

'Shh,' said Emma, again. 'You're ruining the film, Mum.'

Julia was tempted to tell Emma to bloody well fetch her own coffee; tempted to ask her where the dinner was.. it was laid out, after all. It wouldn't have taken Emma more than ten minutes to pop it in the oven and prepare a salad. Zoe Wild's presence made this retort impossible, so Julia bit her tongue and slid back to the kitchen.

She poured herself a glass of the opened Chardonnay. What an afternoon.. steering Mamie round town, through every single shop, it seemed, from the cheapest of chain stores to the tiny boutique on Lombard Street that specialised in hats and was the place Julia originally suggested.

Mamie shook her head.

'Too expensive.'

But the chain stores had nothing suitable, the department stores were all out of black, and the specialist dress-shops weren't catering for funerals.

'Monsoon!' said Julia.

They trailed through heavy rain all the way back along the High Street, waiting fully five minutes for the shopping centre's slow lift because Mamie hated escalators and couldn't manage stairs. There was nothing in Monsoon that took Mamie's eye, though Julia thought their little black pillbox would have been just fine. Very Jackie O.

At five o'clock, desperate, Mamie at last agreed to go back to the hat-shop where, with the patient help of the owner, a simple black broad-brimmed straw was finally chosen. It was expensive, but Mamie didn't comment on the price.

'We'll go out for tea now,' she said, as they reached the car.

'Can't, I'm sorry. I was due at the Meredith an hour ago to pick up all the bits and pieces. And Ewan has a television interviewer coming to see him tonight.. you wouldn't fancy speaking to her? A Zoe Wild..'

'Never heard of her. What does she want?'

'She's doing a programme about the Great War, spoke to John-Angus a week or two back, filmed him. He seemed to like her. She was asking about all of them, John-Angus, Ewan, Calum, Iain..'

'They're always interested in Iain.'

'Well, the poems.. I suppose. Do you want to talk to her?'

'Certainly not!'

'She'll be at the funeral. They wanted to film it, but Ewan thought that too intrusive.'

'Quite.'

'Doesn't it get dark so early these nights?' Julia started the engine, switched on the lights. 'Fasten your seat-belt, Mamie.'

'I hate them. Oh, okay. Don't look at me like that.'

Julia felt her way along the one-way system, hating the rush hour traffic, always so bad-tempered, or at least, bad-mannered; angry lights reflecting on wet streets in the dusk stabbed her tired eyes, made them water a little. Out of town, the traffic was calmer, and the lights less urgent. They swept up the hill by Inshes, then up past Cradlehall to Mamie's cottage at Nairnside. Mamie refused point blank to think about moving into town, though she'd long stopped driving and never used buses.

'I'll have to dash,' said Julia. 'Sorry.'

She carried the precious hat through to the front bedroom where a black dress and coat were already laid out. Mamie followed.

'Do you think those shoes will do? And that bag? I've got some black silk gloves.'

'Yes,' said Julia, firmly. 'Wonderful. You'll be the smartest woman there. Now, remember, the taxi will come for you at one o'clock precisely.'

'I thought Ewan was coming.'

'He has to be at the crematorium. He'll be nervous enough.'

'That boy hasn't a nervous bone in his body! He takes after me!'

Julia laughed, kissed Mamie on the cheek and made her exit.

If it was hard helping Mamie to find a hat, it was harder picking up John-Angus's possessions. Both Julia and Nan were close to tears as they hitched the trailer to the car.

'You'll be more used to this than I am.'

'No,' said Nan. 'I never get used to it.'

Julia hugged her. 'Thank you for everything. We'll see you soon. Not just tomorrow, I mean. It'll be so odd not coming here every other day.'

'So many of the girls wanted to go tomorrow we had to pick the names out of a hat. We all loved him.'

'I know.'

'Take it easy, now. Take care.'

Julia waved, drove off slowly. She'd never liked towing, and worried about steering the trailer through the Meredith's narrow arching gates. She did, in fact, scrape one end slightly.

What does a life amount to, she wondered now as she swept round the kitchen throwing the evening meal together. What are you left with? One or two pictures, a handful of stories.. the odd person to wear a black hat for you. Mamie must be thinking that the next funeral, or the next, will be her own. Perhaps that was why the hat was so important.

How many folk did John-Angus touch in a life that spanned nearly a century? And what had they to show for it? Take his chair.. he had loved that chair, felt comfortable in it, sat in it for almost fifty years.. what is it now but wood and leather? Still, she was going to have that chair in her studio. Ewan could have the sideboard and the other chair. He wouldn't know the difference.

She slipped back into the living-room.

'Finlay.' She beckoned to her son, who followed her through the hall into the garage. 'If we get this stuff in now, it'll save your Dad having to do it when he comes in. I'm worried it might rain.'

'What stuff?'

'Your Grandad's stuff, in the trailer.' She pushed the garage doors up.

'Mum,' said Finlay, 'these are too heavy for you.'

'Look, I'm not quite so feeble as all that.. the sideboard, maybe, I'd have trouble with. We can leave most of it in the garage till the weekend. Just give me a hand, and less of the lip, please.'

'Listen to it!'

Bickering pleasantly, they removed the furniture and boxes

from the trailer. Julia took the special armchair through to the space she'd cleared. This was the one he used, she knew that from the small tear on the chair's right arm. She sat down, lay back, closed her eyes.

A good chair, simple. She could almost feel John-Angus in it. And she could smell the fish-pie, almost ready. Better get on her feet, or there would be no dinner for any of them tonight.

She checked her watch, wondering where Ewan was.

Just as she was about to call the young folk through for dinner, she heard his car on the drive, saw his headlights sweep the length of the back garden, glancing off the white summer house at the far end, lending its trellised walls a ghostly transience. The rotary washing line beside the patio, caught in the side beam, swirled sharply, focused lightning. Next minute all was dark. Julia switched the oven off, laid the last napkin on the table.

'Ewan,' she called as she heard him open the door. 'Ewan!'

She came into the hall as Ewan, having slung his jacket on the stairs, turned towards the living-room door. Zoe Wild was standing there with Finlay and Emma.

'Miss Wild, I presume,' Ewan said, advancing towards her, holding out his hand.

'Mr MacLeod?'

Zoe was formal, cool. But Julia, seeing Ewan's eyes, knew they were in trouble. She'd seen that look before.

Dinner was not a great success. Emma refused the fish-pie.

'You know I'm a vegetarian!'

'This is *fish*-pie, Emma.'

'I don't eat fish.'

'You were eating fish the last time you were home.'

'I'm not eating fish now.'

Ewan raised his eyebrows, smiling at Zoe. Zoe looked down at her plate.

'Then, Emma,' Julia said evenly, 'you should go to the fridge and see if there's anything you think might be appropriate for you in there.'

Emma glowered at her mother. 'I'll just have the potato.'

'Fine,' said Julia. 'There's plenty of bread and salad.'

'Just as well you're on the mainland,' Ewan nodded. 'I was speaking to Bob Findlater on the phone today and he was telling me about his son – Bob's a GP on the island – his son came back from university with green hair, an earring and a notion to be vegetarian! Bob didn't mind the hair so much – he knew the colour would grow back, and he's sure the boy will come out of the earring phase – like you and that nose-ring, Emma – but the thing that's really bothering him,' Ewan carried on, oblivious to Julia's frown or Emma's glowering, 'is the idea that his son, his sensible theology student son, might *stay* vegetarian!'

'Medics,' Finlay smiled, his brown eyes dancing, 'are so open to new ideas! Have you ever been to Lewis, Zoe?'

'No.'

'It's a remarkable island. You won't understand the people, I don't think, until you've seen the soil, or lack of soil. It's mostly water.'

'This programme's not really about Lewis,' said Zoe, 'but the men that served in the First War.'

'It was a terrible thing for the island..'

'I read once in the *Stornoway Gazette*,' said Ewan, taking up this theme, 'that six thousand, two hundred men from Lewis served in the Great War out of a total population of thirty thousand. And eight hundred had fallen by November 1918, and they lost over two hundred more in the *Iolaire*.'

'You wonder,' said Finlay, 'how it must have hit the rest..'

'The casualty list would have been at least twice that,' Zoe said.

'No, I meant the folk on the island. For such a tightly knit group to lose so many boys, so much energy gone.'

'Zoe, would you like a little more wine?'

'Thank you, Julia. Finlay,' Zoe smiled, 'I take your point. The damage must have been incalculable, even more focused than in urban areas, perhaps.'

'I think,' offered Julia, 'there was great deal of emigration too.. in the twenties..'

'They needed a new start. You can understand that, but it can't,' said Finlay, 'have been easy. Didn't Iain Crichton Smith write about the emigrants' poverty, how hard it stayed for that generation? Didn't we do that at school, Emma?'

Ewan put his glass down on the table. 'That's not relevant.'

'Yes it is. It was direct result of the war.. a social consequence just as shattering as the changes in class structure, or.. I can't think of the right word for this.. the diminishing of the power of the church.'

'No, Finlay. That didn't happen after the First War! The church was still pretty powerful, especially on the island. Still is.'

'But Dad, the groundwork for all the social change that swept the world in the twentieth century was in that conflict! Look at the death rate! Think how much land was destroyed, how many villages disappeared.'

Ewan was unimpressed. 'They rebuilt the villages. And as for boys – while there were more spinsters.. or you get that impression.. the population didn't dip that much. The number of young men in England and Wales in 1921 was higher than in 1911.'

'How is that possible?' Emma asked. 'How does that figure compare with general population data?'

'That's my girl! ' said Ewan. 'Spoken like a true economist! As I remember, the proportions were more or less the same. Only slightly down. I read that somewhere not too long ago.. it staggered me.'

'Though,' said Zoe, 'the numbers are incredible. Nine million people lost their lives; a daily average of six thousand men. And fifteen million more were wounded.'

'And it was only a draw.. that's why we had the Second World War.'

'Who told you that?'

Emma blushed. 'The history teacher. At school.'

'That's wrong! We won,' insisted Ewan. 'The Allies definitely won! We had the tanks, the technology!'

'But were terribly wounded,' Finlay said, 'financially. Both sides were. The war cost both sides much more than they could afford.'

'So what's that but a draw?'

Zoe nodded. 'The costs are what I want to show in the programme, and not just the financial ones.'

'How can we help?' Julia stretched for Zoe's glass, refilled it.

Zoe smiled her thanks. 'This is a preliminary visit. Normally I'd send my researcher. But having met John-Angus, and being here for the funeral, I thought I'd run through the basics with you.. I'd like spend a little time talking to Ewan before we decide whether and what to film.. I know you will be run off your feet tonight, that tomorrow will be impossible. But maybe I could come back next week?'

'We're always run off our feet. Tonight's as good a time as any,' Ewan smiled. 'Come through to my study. Bring your coffee. Julia and the kids will clear up.. if that's okay with you, Jules?'

'Sure.'

Julia set the coffee on the table, poured it, offering milk and sugar. She turned to Ewan.

'Don't forget to phone Mamie, will you.. she's a bit down, I think. Wanted you to pick her up tomorrow.'

'Impossible.'

'I told her that. There's a taxi ordered. It'll be okay. She'll come with us afterwards. But who's doing the eulogy? Have we any more phoning to do about that?'

'No, Eilidh's agreed to do it. And the catering's fixed. I got Ishbel to phone Jackson, get the special rate; it wasn't a problem.. They'll be here about eleven.'

'It's for after the service,' Julia explained to Zoe. 'I'd hoped to do it myself, but there's been so much going on, so many people phoning.. still, we seem to be getting there. Right, Ewan, I'll bring another cafétiere through to the study when the kettle's boiled.'

Ewan, shepherding Zoe towards the hall, stopped suddenly. 'Do I gather you've picked up John-Angus's things from the

Meredith?'

'Yes, late this afternoon.'

'Then maybe you could look out Iain's notebook. For Zoe?'

Julia stared at Ewan in exasperation. He was talking to her as if she were his secretary. In point of fact, she had often said that she had no idea how Ishbel coped with him.

'Ewan, I don't think..'

'Come on, Jules, it won't take that long. It would be so interesting.'

He flashed one of his boyish smiles now, more for Zoe's sake, thought Julia, than hers. She did not give in.

'I haven't time, Ewan; I don't want to pull all those boxes apart when we're going to be so busy tomorrow. We don't even know if the notebook's there. When did you last see it?'

'Where did you leave the boxes? I'll look for it myself.'

'Ewan, please.. the house will be full tomorrow. I've quite enough to do already.'

'I said *I'd* do it..'

'Exactly. Think of the mess you'd leave. You also said you'd talk to Zoe.'

'I can do both.'

'Actually I haven't all that long,' Zoe interrupted. 'My producer is expecting me at nine. It would be lovely to see some of that stuff in a week or two, maybe?'

'Next week,' Julia smiled. 'No problem.'

Ewan's displeasure was almost palpable. 'Come on then, Zoe. Best get started.'

He swept her out of the kitchen towards his study.

'Wow,' said Finlay, closing the door after them. 'Zoe Wild, or what?'

'You're on dishes!'

'Mum!'

'Come on, Finlay. The day I've had! And Emma disappearing, and your Dad playing diva..'

'What's eating Emma anyway?'

'Don't know. She's been like that since she came home last night. There's something bothering her, but I can't get to the bottom of it.'

'Missing the nose ring?'

'Leave it out, Finlay. Your father's bad enough. Actually I liked it!'

She poured herself a cup of coffee, leaned back in the chair, trying to relax her neck, the muscles tight as iron. Maybe she should take a shower. If they didn't improve, she'd end up with a migraine. She shouldn't have the coffee either.

She sat with eyes half-closed, watching Finlay, as he slowly cleared the table. He was growing up, suddenly much older-looking. No longer a boy. The muscles round his neck and shoulders were thickening, his hair changing too, receding at the temples. Twenty-five. By that age John-Angus had been home from war for five years.

'How's the job? How's it going?'

'Surgery's.. not for me,' Finlay said slowly. 'I've decided to opt for general practice.'

'Have you told your father?'

'No. I will though. Don't think he'll like it much.'

'It's your life, Finn. Don't let him run it for you. He should know better.'

Finlay looked carefully at his mother now. Something in the voice, something in the tone.. of course, she was tired. Grieving. She had loved John-Angus like a daughter, had been closer to him than anybody, even Ewan. How she managed to cope with Ewan, day in day out, Finlay had never been able to understand.

'Don't be sad,' he said. 'John-Angus wouldn't want it.'

Julia smiled briefly up at him, sipped her coffee.

Back in her hotel room shortly before ten, Zoe found a message blinking on the answerphone. She looked enquiringly across at Jane.

'Play it.'

Zoe pressed the button.

'Ewan MacLeod here, Zoe. Just to say it was an uncommon

245

pleasure meeting you. I hope.. well.. we'll see you tomorrow, anyway. God bless.'

'Fuck!' said Zoe. 'I was afraid of that. This prize chump has a charming wife, two lovely grown-up kids.'

'Engaged won't work, married won't work. Tell him you're gay,' Jane advised. 'That'll confound him.'

'No,' sighed Zoe, 'he wouldn't believe it. God, I could do with a long vodka.'

'Shall we phone room service? Put it on the bill?'

'Fine.'

Zoe kicked off her shoes, flopped on the bed, flicked through the TV channels, switching off quickly. She sat up suddenly.

'The family won't be useful, not for filming. We'll just have to use the footage we have of the old man.'

'You never know what may turn up at the funeral.'

'True. But.. the thing is, Jane,' she said, stripping off her stockings, 'and this could be exciting.. they *may* have an actual notebook of Iain Murray's poems.'

Jane looked up from the telephone.

'Oh? Excuse me – two long vodkas, please. Room 204. Thank you.'

'Yes.. they think John-Angus had one.' Zoe rolled the stockings carefully, slipped them in the bottom drawer of the dresser between the beds, with all her other washing. 'They're not sure if he still had it. When he went into the home ten years ago, he gave away a lot of stuff. They'll know in a few days when Julia's had time to go through all his books and papers.'

'You know, that might be a better angle for the programme.. focusing it on the island.. on that group of men, the film, the poems..'

'That's what the MacLeod boy was trying to say. You'd have been proud of me, Jane. I was very laid-back. Very cool. They have no idea of the value of that notebook, if it still exists. Not so odd, really. It wasn't theirs. Maybe it still isn't; John-Angus may have given it to someone else.'

Zoe moved now to the top drawer, slid it open, lifting out *A Private View*.

'Wouldn't it be nice to see this stuff in Iain Murray's own writing?'

She opened the book carefully, turning to the back, to the formal, posed portrait to Iain's eyes. Such energy. So much life.. life that shouted, screamed..

'How much did that book cost?'

Zoe blinked. 'Don't ask.'

Opposite the photograph, the single paragraph. She knew it off by heart.

Between 28th September and 25th October 1918, the 7th Seaforth, as part of the 9th Division, took part in the series of attacks that carried the line twenty miles from Frezenberge Ridge outside Ypres to Harlebecke. The final operation was carried out at a cost of 331 casualties. Corporal Iain Alexander Murray was one of these. Instead of finishing the war in the army of occupation, Iain crossed the Channel in a hospital ship, his arm and thigh wounds responding eventually to the excellent care he received in Reading No 4 War Hospital, where he celebrated the Armistice. From there he entrained to the Depot at Fort George, near Inverness. He obtained his discharge papers in December and was travelling home to Lewis when he was lost at sea on 1st January 1919.

It always made her cry.

CEOL MOR
(The Great Music)

The last Sunday in November is foul and dark, a day of gales and driving sleet that cuts into the bones of you. The damp cold has you shivering before you've been outside long enough to pull the house door firmly shut. Flora Morrison is glad she lives so near the church, and does not have to walk miles into town for the service like other members of the congregation.

'Hurry up, Calum,' she calls up the stairs to her son. 'It's time we were off.'

'I'm not coming,' says Calum. 'I told you. I'm not going back.'

Flora looks up anxiously from the dimness of the cramped hall. She climbs on to the first step now, into the light. Calum leans against the door of his room, impassive.

'But you have to go church!' she says.

'I've told you.. all that stuff about the fall of Eve, the snide remarks about feckless women, fatherless children.. not that it can harm Maisie, she's past all that, but Aeneas is the kindest and most charitable of souls! He's grieving enough already! Bethune makes me sick!'

'I know,' says Flora. 'It seems harsh, but it's just his way. And he's the minister after all. It's his job to tell us such things.'

'I don't see why he should be a judge. It was downright inhuman. If that's what Christian fellowship means I, for one, don't want it.'

'Calum! *Aeneas* still goes to church!'

'That's up to him. That's his prerogative. As for me, I'm not going back.'

'That's pride talking, Calum.'

'It's logic.'

'No one can live without God.'

Calum sighs. 'In the last four years we haven't seen that much of him. Plenty of boys living and dying at the front didn't get much help from your precious God.. and don't say the war was a punishment, a purification, for I know you don't believe that! And as for thanking God the war is finally over.. you don't need to make excuses for me, or say I'm ill, or any of the things you've been doing for the past three weeks. If he asks, tell him I won't be back.'

Flora looks at her son in despair. 'You can't not go to church.'

Calum shrugs. 'I can. I'm not going. It's as simple as that. Go on. You'll be late. My poor father is getting more and more uncomfortable waiting for you. You'll need to hurry. You know how cruel Bethune can be to latecomers!'

Flora has come nearly all the way upstairs to Calum. She hovers, hoping he will somehow change his mind. He doesn't.

'If you're going, you'd better be off,' he says, going back into his room. 'I'll see you later.'

Flora minces her way down. Murdo is huddled in the porch, squinting at his watch.

'No?'

'No.'

'I didn't think so.'

They set off down the street, bent double in the wind that claws the flesh no matter how you turn. Flora pulls her cape more tightly round her, holds it with her right hand while her left clings to her Sunday bonnet.

'We'll be late,' says Murdo.

But they slip into their pew just before the minister appears.

'Calum?' Alec asks.

They shake their heads.

As Murdo and Flora fidget with their hymn books for the opening psalm, Calum settles at his bedroom table sorting through the stories that have gathered in his drawer these last two years. Stories of love. Stories of battle. Always the hero – even now – is Iain Murray, or the Robin Hood figure he's become in Calum's mind. You could, thinks Calum, bind these fragments in a grander whole if you could find a linking theme beyond the war. Or themes.

The island, or lack of island.. that's one possibility. Love, another. Jealousy.. perhaps the best of all.. though he is not sure he's equipped to cope with that emotion, nor would he want to share his exploration of the state. Who did he love? Who is he jealous of? (*Whom*, his teacher would have said. And of *whom*?) Calum isn't sure he wants to know.

This week he has been re-reading *The Dead*; in fact he has been re-reading *Dubliners*, all of it, studying how a modern book of stories is constructed. But *The Dead* – what a story.. love lost, leaning upon lost love, falling like the snow, eternal, pure.. how that story holds him. He aches for Gretta and her new-washed hair, her veiled, sad voice drifting into chaste sleep, for chaste she is, will always be. Does Mairi, he wonders, ache for Michael Furey? Calum loves the way Joyce's words have transformed the emotion, the narrative, in crystalline form.. perfect, like water feathering into snow, falling on the world, on the universe.

Mairi is in Edinburgh, must be; the aunt and uncle seemed a fine pair when he met them in Aeneas's front parlour after Maisie's funeral, dazed though they all were by Bethune's unexpected onslaught.

'Calum, hello. Aeneas tells us you've been very kind.' Esther squeezed his hand warmly. 'And I know,' she said, 'my sister was always fond of you.'

Esther reminded him of Gretta, with her elegance, her plenitude of russet hair; she reminded him of Mairi, with her quick sense of humour. Even her voice unsettled him, so reminiscent of Maisie's. *My sister*, she said, *was fond of you*. Did she mean Mairi?

He could find the address in Leith, it would be simple enough, but something holds him back. If Mairi wanted him, she would have written surely? Is she, perhaps, in touch with Iain? Calum's eyes stray towards the box of unopened letters. The new one on his dresser has an English postmark. Iain must be wounded. He does not open the letter, does not wish to know that Iain and Mairi.. if Mairi and Iain..

If she wants him, she knows how to find him.

Calum reaches for his fiddle, plays with all his heart and soul; there being none to remonstrate with him about the Sabbath. As always, he starts and ends with 'Mairi's Waltz'. Oddly, it comforts him, reminds him of the possibility of love, its sweet fragility.

When he's played his emotion into stillness enough, there's writing: he takes his pen and sits here by the window looking down over the roofs of half the town and out across the bay. Calum feels as strong, no, stronger than the next man, more secure on his sea of paper than he ever is on land; like some ancient sailor – Phoenician, perhaps – he sets himself adrift on currents he may not always recognise. The journeying is good. It keeps him tender, sane. He sets course by the stars, hopes for eventual landfall.

The wind is cruel today. It's rattling the roof tiles, whistling through crevices between the roof and wall. It drowns out any possibility of street noise. Never the less, Calum's conscious of movement in the street, of footsteps rushing to the house. The door bursts open, slams.

'Calum!'

'Alec! Come right up..'

Alec thumps up the narrow stairs.

'It's good to see you, cove, but I wasn't expecting you. What are you doing here? Aren't you going to dinner at Effie's?'

'Iain Murray's been wounded again, nae badly, mind,' pants Alec, breathless. 'Catriona wis tellin' me at the church. She a' but asked me tae tell ye. He'll be back at Fort George in a few weeks. Then he'll be hame!'

'That'll set her mind at rest.'

'Och, I dinna think she's worryin' that way. A nice woman, thon. But fit's a' this?'

Alec stares at the stories littering Calum's table. Calum blushes.

'My new religion. Personal. Just for one.'

Alec blushes now.

'Ye ken very weel that I agree wi' ye, man. Totally agree wi' ye. But I cannae stop the kirk till efter the weddin'.'

Calum laughs. 'And then it will be after the christening, and then the next one, then the next! Do what you feel you need to, Alec, not what will please me. Don't worry about it. It won't be a problem between us.'

Alec picks up one or two of the pages on the table, glances at them briefly, raising his eyebrows.

'Bethune was on at your parents about ye, efter the service..'

'He'll soon stop.'

'I dinna think it.'

'Then they'll have to learn to cope.'

'Nae doot! Calum, man,' Alec flushes as he says this, 'the thing is.. ye dinna think.. I mean, giein' up the church.. hae ye thocht that it micht harm yer work prospects?'

Calum nods. 'It's a definite possibility. But if my only reason for going to church is financial, it won't do my living soul any good, now will it?'

'The trouble wi' you, Calum Morrison, is that ye're a born idealist. A perfectionist.'

'There's not much I can do about that!'

'I dinna think,' says Alec, 'we'd any o' us want tae change ye. But why are these stories a' aboot Iain Murray? Is there nane aboot thon blackguard Calum Morrison, or that fine loon Alec Stenhouse, or even John-Angus?'

'They're made-up stories, Alec. Fiction, not truth.'

'As to that, it's been my firm opinion that a lot o' whit they've been giein' us fer truth over the last few years is naethin' mair nor less than fiction.'

Calum laughs, looks at his friend as he stands there in his best suit, his usually tidy hair astray after the running and the wind. He's wearing his favourite shirt under the navy suit, a blue and white striped one bought from Mairi, from her own hands, all because she said that it would suit his eyes. She had been right. The shirt made Alec's eyes an unusually clear deep blue, like sea on the horizon on an unclouded day. That shirt made Alec almost handsome; his integrity inescapable.

How could a shirt do that? Calum scoffs his own conclusion here. Alec's truth is in his heart, his eyes. The shirt, the colours, merely help you see it. Mairi knew all of that.

Calum hears his parents rattling at the door now.

'Alec! You're late! Effie will think you've forgotten your dinner.'

'Christ, I'll hae tae run! Can I read mair o' this later?'

Alec tumbles down the stairs and out into the weather. Calum shakes his head, sighs, takes up his pen.

So much of his time at work is spent celebrating, officially, the end of the hostilities. And he is glad they're over. It's a great relief for the island, not only the families of the returning men. But where will they find work? Where will they find land? Will there be food and jobs to feed these hungry boys?

He is not sure how he'll cope with Iain on the island. It's disturbing, just the thought of Iain coming back. Iain, whom he last saw drunk and lurching on the shore in darkness. Iain, with blood on his hands, blood and more than that..

Calum's not sure what he feels beyond disquiet.. is it envy? Disgust? He thinks about that last time and, as he does, a quiet, gently dangerous echo of John-Angus comes unbidden to his mind. It's not disquiet, Calum thinks.. no, not disquiet. It's fear. Pure and simple.

He's started this private game of trying to remember Mairi, mapping every image for the future: the shape of her head, the depth of russet in her hair, which dresses make her eyes look green, which shoes she might be wearing. He can almost visualise, recreate in three dimensions the girl as she was in the spring. She will be different now. He cannot imagine her.

What will she look like swollen by pregnancy? Does her hair shine, her body sing with new life? She can't be happy, no. She'll be mourning Maisie, torn by the savage and final uprooting of the love that has always been her main support.

He should write to her again.. No. He must wait for her to move. Even Alec says so.

She hasn't written to Effie. Still, her aunt looked kind, would not be cruel, critical. Calum has hated the gossip, the backbiting in the town.

'That Mairi MacDonald, so high and mighty!'

'Pride comes before a fall. I've always said it.'

'Aye, fallen is the word, never truer!'

And for all Alec says that Peggy met him gabbling the news, Peggy, since she started work in the shop, has been Mairi's chief defender. She has such a way of silencing, of snubbing without opening her mouth, almost. Peggy loves the shop, you can see it in the pride she takes in rearranging stock, in helping customers towards the best choice. She is, Calum thinks, a second Maisie. It's remarkable to see the difference in her. And Colin, since she's taken him in hand, is smarter, more awake, works much harder. Aeneas has nothing to worry about there, poor broken soul. He sits at home half the day in darkness, but the business is flourishing.

Death is such a final parting.

There are times when Calum panics, feeling he has lost Mairi for ever, has let his love, the one true love he'll know, slip through his fingers, and for what? He is capable of as much – no, more – love than the next man. His withered leg, his limp, may slow him on the street and on the moor, but his mind is sharp; he is able, knows the world, how to manage better than the next man, better than most. He does not have this feeling of inferiority with any other human being.

Why should Iain disconcert him? Why does he always bow to Iain's blithe assumption of superiority? What has Iain got that he, Calum, has not?

Calum ponders this, plays with the stories on his table, his constructed life of an imagined hero. The answer, and it does not take him long to reach it, leafing through the closely written sheets – the answer stares back, unperturbed. Calum has known this all along.. it's down in black and white, for goodness sake.. what Iain has in bright abundance, what he lacks himself, is confidence. Iain is perfectly, supremely, sure of his ascendancy. He *knows* he is the best.. at fighting, English, sex.. there's no one else. Iain is the centre of his world. And always will be.

'Calum. Come down for your dinner!'

Flora's voice is slightly sharp. Calum, hearing this, slides down the stairs to the kitchen table set for the cold meal they always eat on Sunday. After the bedroom's chill he finds the warmth pouring from the black stove both cheering and too much.

'Will you say grace, Murdo?'

Flora bows her head. Calum does not feel obliged to bow his any more. Sitting in the wood lined kitchen, where he's sat so many times, where he's played his fiddle, laughed and worked and wept, Calum feels free. There are costs, of course. His mother's sadness, the only-partly masked anxiety, the hastily-dried tears. His father's puzzlement is just as obvious, just as affecting. His father does not understand why Calum should question such prime irrelevant authority. His mother understands, but fears the consequences.

'Alec called by,' says Calum.

'Good.'

'He's off to Effie's for dinner.'

'He's a fine boy, that Alec. I wonder how long the bank will leave him here now the war is over?'

'I don't know, Dad. I've been wondering the same thing myself. I'm inclined to think Alec may already have turned down promotion in order to stay on the island.'

'That's love for you, eh?'

'Certainly must be.'

Flora's eyes have not left her plate. She has not lifted her knife and fork. Calum reaches forward, touches her hand.

'Do you need the salt and pepper?'

'I don't need anything from you!' she snaps. 'You're making

us the laughing stock of the congregation!'

'Mother..' Murdo's tone is soothing, warning.

'No!' she shouts. 'I'll have my say. I'm not putting up with it, Calum. Everybody's looking at us, talking behind our backs. Can you wonder? You can't afford to put yourself outside your own community. I've been patient for weeks.. now I'm laying down the law. Plain and simple. It's for your own good. You'll go back to church tonight. And you'll go round to the minister's this afternoon, apologise for missing these last weeks.'

'I'll do nothing of the sort!'

'You'll go back to church, Calum, or you'll leave this house. This is a God-fearing home!'

'Yes,' says Calum quietly, 'I can see that.'

He's now as white as Flora is red. Murdo watches anxiously his wife's set angry face, his son's blank pale one. Calum lays his knife and fork down carefully beside his plate of untouched fo od. He doesn't say a word, but pushes his chair back, rises, and leaves the room.

They hear him stomp upstairs, and moving about his room, back and fore, back and fore.

'That wasn't wise, Mother.'

Murdo takes a mouthful of cold meat. He hates cold dinners.

'You should go up, tell him you didn't mean it.'

'I meant it,' says Flora. 'I meant every word. He needs to hear the truth, Murdo, from one of us.'

'You're too hard on the boy. If it was Alec, you'd be counselling him. You'd be patient.'

'Calum is too much like me. He's in a temper now, but he'll come round. He'll go and see Bethune.'

'I don't think it.'

'Wait and see.'

Flora's more calm now. The drumming in her ears has settled. That boy! Why does he never listen? Why does he always think his own ideas are best?

'Because you've always told him that.'

Murdo's answer startles her. She hadn't realised she'd

spoken aloud.

Flora sips a little water, picks her knife and fork up, starts to cut the meat into even squares. She'll go and see Calum when she's finished. She likes cold mutton, always has.

'Do you want a little more, Murdo?'

'No thanks. I thought I'd go up, see the boy.'

'No need. He's coming down. Listen? What did I tell you? Calum's a realist.'

She looks expectantly to the door, hears fumbling in the hall. Murdo looks at her, frowning.

When Calum comes into the room he's in his outdoor clothes, and in the hall, by the door, his suitcase and his violin case stand together. He plays with his cap, turning the edges round and round.

'I'll be off then,' he says. 'I'll come back for the other books when I find a place to stay.'

'Just where do you think you're going?'

'I'm not sure,' he says. 'But I'll let you know, don't worry. You're perfectly right, it's not fair that my decision should reflect on you. If I leave, it won't.'

'Be sensible, Calum! Who do you think will take you in.. on the Sabbath?'

'Oh, some Christian, likely,' Calum shouts, turning on his heel. Angry now. He hadn't meant to lose his temper.

He sweeps out of the house, into the biting wind.

Murdo rushes to the door. 'Calum, come back! She didn't mean it!'

'I meant every word!' Flora cries. 'Every word.'

Calum doesn't hear either of them. The gale throws their words back into the chilling hall. Flora slams the door shut.

'He'll be back!'

'Flora,' says Murdo, 'go after him. Get the boy back.'

'No,' says Flora, 'how can you live without the church?'

'Sometimes,' Murdo says, 'I wonder how we manage to live *with* it.'

'You're as bad as he is! Out of my way!'

She sweeps into the kitchen, bangs the door, rattles the plates. Murdo slips into the other room, shivering, but not because the room has no fire in it. He hates it when Flora and Calum fall out, the one as stubborn as the other. And this time he can see no easy ending. Faith is a difficult question, always.

Calum has no clear idea of where he might go. His mother's right, of course. None of the town's landladies will take him in on the Sabbath. He can imagine Mrs Harper's response. Mrs Harper is one of those who will be telling the tale, luxuriating in it.

'Just fancy!' he can hear her. 'Anyone putting themselves above the church, above the Lord, above the minister!'

Her voice rising with each succeeding cadence, and the sentence rehearsed, no doubt, in the minister's hearing.

Alec is no longer in Mrs Harper's clutches, but the one-roomed cottage he rents is very small. He could stay there overnight, maybe. That's what he'll have to do; though Alec won't be back from Effie's for hours yet, and the wind and spiteful sleet make hanging round the streets an unenviable prospect. It's so cold. The wind whips every last drop of warmth out of your body. Even with his cap pulled well down, Calum's head feels chilled, almost sore, and any exposed flesh, his face, his hands and wrists, are scoured and stinging. He decides to leave the case at Alec's door and try for dinner at the County. He'll manage if he hurries. He cuts across the back streets into the heart of town. The wind is winning the battle, he thinks, but it's not far to Alec's. No point in turning back now. He presses on, past the Mayhews' solid house, past Aeneas's sleet-covered garden.

He notices that the door of the MacDonalds' house is open, sleet lunging meanly into the hall. The floor looks wet as if the door's been open for some time. Calum tucks his violin case under his arm, opens the gate.

He walks up to the door, and would have pulled it shut; but a thought strikes him that Aeneas may need help. He knocks. No answer. He rings the bell. Still no answer. He sets his case and violin case down, moves forward, knocking on the inner door.

'Mr MacDonald!'

Silence.

The house is freezing. Calum's breath foams before him as he checks the parlour (he knocks gently first) then the dining-room. Each succeeding room seems colder than the last. The kitchen is empty too, though the stove has been lit, obviously some hours since. Calum stokes it up. There's no one in the scullery.

'Mr MacDonald! Aeneas!' he calls again. 'Mr MacDonald!'

He climbs the stair, shivering, checks the bedrooms on the first floor. There's no sign of Aeneas. The bathroom door, open, reveals its emptiness. Calum goes up again, to the attic. The maid's room is bare, empty. Mairi's room gives him a start – this must be Mairi's room, surely, with its lace mats and bright rugs. The wardrobe doors swing open.. and there's her blue silk skirt. Calum buries his head in it, breathing her perfume, her very self. There's a salt tang too, an air of kelp.

He turns last to the dressingtable. All the drawers are open as if someone has been searching through them. In the top drawer, under scarves and handkerchieves there shines a bright blue notebook.. Calum picks it up, weighs it in his hand. He glances at the first page of Mairi's writing.

Friday 2nd June

When is a waltz not a waltz? When it's a love song. I hope you're lying awake, thinking of me, as I'm thinking about you. It's so bright tonight, it won't get dark; it's nearly the longest day. The longest day, the shortest night – the shortest night.

I skipped home from the dance. Aunt Anna thought it very odd, kept telling me a young lady does not behave like that, but Effie and I were both so happy! We said it was the moon. Was there a moon? I don't remember. It was too bright to see. I'm not going to write any more, except, Effie told me Ewan's new wife Myra is going to stay in Edinburgh – imagine that – with her family, when Ewan goes back overseas. It won't be like being married at all! And after the war, it means Ewan will likely go to the city to live, won't come back to the island. It will break his mother's heart. It's just as well she's got John-Angus. He was always her favourite. Ewan knows that. He always seemed glad about it.

Effie was not best pleased when Alec Stenhouse danced with Peggy, seemed to get on with her very well. But that's not fair. I told Effie she can't be possessive about all the young men, only the one she's promised to marry. Effie sighed. Peggy's very taking, she said. It was not a compliment.

His cheeks are salt with tears when he stops reading. How long he stands there, he could not say, but gradually he remembers why he finds himself in Mairi's house, in Mairi's room. He puts the notebook carefully back in the drawer and slips downstairs. Outside the grey afternoon is merging imperceptibly with dusk. If this were war, if this had been the trenches, it would have been stand-to all day, he thinks, the light so poor. He checks the downstairs rooms again. There's no sign of Aeneas. The only odd thing, and he hadn't noticed this before, is the whisky bottle, open in the kitchen. At this time of day? Calum sits down in the rocking chair, wonders.

Anyone filling coal would have gone out the back, but the back of the house is firmly shut. He sits and listens quietly to the empty house. Then he hears it, the insistent rapping, like a shutter rattling somewhere about the place.

He stands up, concentrating on the noise. It's louder in the dining-room, loudest in the parlour. Calum goes into the room and sees only now that the side window is open and wooden inner shutter is swinging back and fore. He walks across the room, skirting the heavy plush chairs and the black ornate Chinese cupboard. The window sash seems stuck. He notices the ladder first, its oddly crooked angle. Maybe..

He rushes out the front door, round behind the screening shrubs to find Aeneas lying, unconscious and cold, below the parlour window.

There's a pulse at least. And shallow breathing. Calum looks round, trying to work out what to do. He knows he has no chance of lifting the older, heavier man, not by himself. He takes his jacket off, pillows it below Aeneas's head and runs across the lane to the Mayhews' door.

'Is Andrew in?'

Jean stares at Calum. 'My, what's at you, Calum?'

'I've just found Aeneas unconscious in the garden. It looks to me as if he's fallen off a ladder and banged his head. He's soaked through, and I can't carry him in, Jean, not by myself.'

'Andrew!' Jean calls. 'Andrew! Come here! Hurry!'

It's a struggle, even with Andrew Mayhew's bulk, to lift Aeneas indoors; he's a dead weight. Andrew takes the head, Calum the feet. They carry him head first into the parlour, lay him on the chaise longue. Aeneas moans. It's the first sound he's made.

'Have you any idea,' says Calum, 'where we might find a blanket?'

'Not a clue. You try and find one, Calum. I'll run for the doctor.'

Calum checks the cupboards in the hall, then climbs the stair again. There was a blanket chest in one of the bedrooms.. he doesn't like this feeling of rifling through another fellow-mortal's unhappiness. Yes, there's the chest, and in it two cream woollen blankets. Calum carries both downstairs, lays one over Aeneas, who's moaning again. Calum sees the darkening graze on his right temple.

He lights the lamp on the parlour table, then goes out to the outer hall pushing his case and violin case to one side. Then he slips into the garden to retrieve his jacket, wet now, and smeared with ground and blood. He takes it to the kitchen, sponges the blood off and leaves the jacket drying before the stove. He fills the kettle, sets it on the hob. As an afterthought, he corks the whisky bottle, pushing it away into the nearest cupboard. Then he rinses out the glass.

He thinks he remembers kindling being stacked in the scullery. Ah. He takes some sticks and paper back and is laying the fire in the parlour when Dr Smith arrives with Andrew Mayhew.

'Just go on with your work, Calum,' says Dr Smith, kindly.

'You've done well. Andrew tells me you were the one to find him.'

'I was going along the road to.. visit Alec,' Calum says, 'saw the front door open. Well, in this weather, I thought it odd. I couldn't find Aeneas anywhere, then I noticed the window and the ladder.'

'Ladder?'

'Aye, see? That sash is broken.' Calum points across the room. 'I think he must have been trying to work at it from the outside and slipped. Can you do anything with it, Andrew?'

Even Andrew's strength finds it impossible to shift the window.

'I'll off and get my tools,' he says, leaving the room.

Dr Smith looks at the ladder.

'How much has he had to drink?' he asks.

'How did you know?' Calum asks. 'I put the bottle away.'

'The smell, man. He's hurt his head, yes, but if you ask me, most of it's the drink.'

'I don't know how much he may have had,' Calum says. 'There was whisky in the kitchen, but I've put it away in a cupboard. No sense in having people talking, is there? Poor Aeneas has more than enough on his plate already.'

'My sentiments exactly. You'll stay and look after him?'

Dr Smith looks quizzically up at Calum. 'I see,' he says, 'you've brought your case.'

'I was going to Alec's..' Calum shrugs. 'My folks and I.. But you don't miss a thing, do you?'

'It's my job, laddie. Just like it's yours. Many another man would have walked right past the open door. It takes someone with a nose for a story to find it.'

'I never thought of medicine like that.'

'Most people don't. You'll stay?'

'Do you think Aeneas would want *me*?'

Dr Smith sighs. 'He needs someone, Calum, and you – you need a temporary roof. Seems like the ideal solution to both your problems. Get the fire going, and I'll clean up his head. If we can get him warm, he'll probably be fine. We don't want him to start pneumonia. In his present state of mourning, he wouldn't survive it. And see if you can find me a clean towel, and some hot water.'

'Ah,' says Calum, 'I put the kettle on earlier.'

'I can see,' nods Smith, 'that you're a natural at the nursing. I'll leave some mixture you can give him when he wakes. It's painkiller,' he says, pre-empting Calum's question. 'Don't let him have any more whisky. If his conscious level deteriorates, send for me at once.'

Andrew Mayhew comes back in as Dr Smith is packing up his bag.

'Calum's going to stay and nurse Aeneas.'

'Wonderful,' says Andrew. 'Jean was going to come, only with Maisie having had consumption, and Jean being in a delicate state, I was a little worried.'

'She's a good lass, Jean. She'll be fine, don't you be worrying. I'll call first thing, Calum. Eight o'clock? Then we can organise some cover for the day if that seems necessary.'

'Chrissie should be in by then,' says Andrew.

'Chrissie?'

'Chrissie MacNeil. She's been helping with the house, the last few weeks.'

'Excellent,' says Dr Smith almost bouncing from the room. 'Don't try to move him, Calum. Best to keep him downstairs overnight. Bye for now.'

When they've seen the doctor out, Andrew Mayhew turns to Calum. They're both shivering.

'Calum, man,' he says, 'I was forgetting – it's the Sabbath. I can't touch the window till the morning. If you wedge the shutters fast that should keep most of the weather out. Come and get us if you need the doctor, or any help at all.'

'Thanks,' says Calum. 'You're a good man, Andrew.'

It takes Calum a good hour to get the shutters firmly closed. The inside catch is broken and was never, in any case, intended to hold back the swirling winds now driving sleet and rain hard against that side of the house. Eventually, he wedges the shutters with towels, though the strongest winds keep dislodging this arrangement. He's afraid to lean one of the heavy parlour chairs against the rattling wood, in case the damp will damage it. He pulls the other curtains in the room and leaves the kitchen door open in a vain attempt to take the chill off the hall.

Aeneas, meantime, has slipped into a lighter, more natural sleep. Calum feels able to leave him long enough to make a cup of tea. He stokes the kitchen fire again and brings more coal into the parlour where he settles at the table with his notebook and pen. The room is almost cosy, though each time the shutters flail, the heat is quickly lost.

Flora and Murdo spend the afternoon in silence. Flora has taken her Bible out. Murdo sits smoking by the fire. The tapping of his pipe annoys her.

'Will you stop it, Murdo! I'm trying to concentrate.'

'It's the terrible temper you have when it's roused,' says Murdo. 'You should go and find the boy and make your peace.'

'He'll be at Alec's,' Flora snaps. 'There's nothing likely to be coming over him!'

'You will regret this day's work, Flora.'

'Wheesht. I'm trying to read the good book.'

'Then it would help,' says Murdo, 'if you held the blooming thing the right way round!'

Flora looks down, astonished. Murdo's right. She covers her dismay with anger.

'You have always spoiled that boy! He's ruined, ruined!'

Murdo does not answer, looks her in the eye. This simple act enrages her beyond belief.

'There's no way,' she shouts, 'that ungrateful blaspheming boy will set a foot in here again till he repents! Unless it's over my dead body!'

Murdo stands up now, walks past her

'Stop playing the fool, Flora.'

He opens the hall door. Flora, having heard the outer door open and shut, as Murdo did during her outburst, looks on the horrified face of Alec Stenhouse.

'I'm s-sorry,' stutters Alec. 'It's nae a guid time, I ken that. I wis lookin' for Calum.'

'He's not here,' says Murdo. 'We thought he'd gone to you.'

Alec looks from one to the other, shakes his head slowly.

Murdo turns to his wife who's standing rigid by the stove.

'I'm off to look for him,' he says. 'When I come back I want you to be ready to apologise!'

Alec shrinks against the front door, pretending he's not there. The tension in the small room is unbearable. He's never seen Flora's eyes so big, so angry. She's furious, but also frightened. Alec is suddenly aware of just how panic-stricken Flora is. He moves towards her, hugs her fiercely. Flora breaks down at this, crying uncontrollably.

'Come on, Alec lad,' says Murdo when the crying settles, 'come and help me find him.. It'll be easier with two.'

Flora sits by the ticking clock for minute after endless minute, her fingers clasped so tightly that the knuckles have gone whiter than the wet snow sliding down her windows. One hour passes in an agony of fear. Two hours. Murdo staggers back wet and alone.

'No sign,' he says. 'We'll try the office in the morning.'

Alec, trudging home, wet and worried, sees the light in Aeneas's parlour, wishes the man well, goes home to spend the long night worrying.

'He'll have gone to the Bothan,' he told Murdo blithely enough when they'd combed the town twice, thoroughly, checked the harbour too, though it was difficult at night to be sure the squirming waves were free of detritus.

'He'll have gone to the Bothan.'

'Aye,' Murdo pretended to grasp that feeble straw. 'That's very likely. Good thinking.'

Alec's fire is still in, just, when he gets home. He builds it up and sits all night in front of it, shivering.

Flora, too, sits in her chair all night, angry at herself, at Murdo, most of all at Calum, the cause of all her worry.

'You started it,' says Murdo, firmly; going off to bed to lie unsleeping through the night of fitful wind. The tiles are rattling. He'll have to check them in the morning.

Calum sits up too, less worried now about Aeneas, who woke naturally once, smiled at him and said, *Why, Calum!* before dozing off again. The wind disrupts the shutters once or twice every hour, and the creaking in a strange house after dark in such a wind is completely disconcerting. His patient's temperature comes up to normal, stays there. Calum relaxes now, thinking they'll have fended off all worries of pneumonia.

At six o'clock next morning, he stirs in the fireside chair, as Aeneas brings them both a cup of good strong tea. By eight o'clock when Dr Smith, true to his word, arrives, Calum and Aeneas have come to an arrangement that Calum will rent two of the attic rooms, at least until such time as Mairi is able to return.

'I fear it won't be soon,' Aeneas says, 'the way things are.'

'Maybe,' says Calum, 'we'll get a better minister.'

'Maybe.'

'I haven't,' says Calum, 'written to her. Nor will I unless she asks for me.'

Aeneas shakes his head.

'She asks for no one.'

*   *   *

Thirty-eight weeks is the time of maximum discomfort in a first pregnancy. The abdomen is by then so severely strained that it is hard to sit down, hard to stand, hard to lie without a pillow tucked behind your back, and one below your abdomen: the skin feels stretched to bursting, the heartburn is unbearable and two more weeks (or more) of like discomfort loom before you. Many an incipient mother becomes discouraged at this stage, wishing desperately for labour to release her from the sentence of growth now ripening within her womb.

Lightening (the baby's head slipping down into the birth canal) comes overnight; easing the burden on the abdomen, but stressing the bladder and the lower spine, and rendering walking even more of a waddle than it was before.

Mairi is, however, glad of the lightening. She can breathe again, a little. The child is packed so tightly now that its movements are painful, almost bad tempered, as if the mite were struggling too for freedom. The small feet – they are feet, she's sure – kick her ribcage painfully, fists pummelling her lower abdomen. Soon she must learn to know this uninvited child.

Her breasts are oozing nightly. Her body seems intent on its own purposes. Even her mind seems less under its own control, determinedly placid, unruffled despite all that life has thrown at it.

She has not even begun to take in her mother's death. In her head, her mother is still there, across the Minch, waiting. She feels this to be true though she knows, tells herself every day, that Maisie is gone. It makes no sense. Not when she's needed, loved so urgently.

And with Esther, there are moments when expressions or a turn of phrase will recall her mother vividly; even with the small children, memories intrude, simple things, like reading a bedtime story, can bring on such a flood that it seems truly impossible that Maisie should be gone.

Talking to Myra and Connie brings comfort and sense. They come as often as they can, though John-Angus is now up north near Inverness, and Connie may leave to join him soon.

'What are you doing afterwards?' Connie asked one day, as they sat in the kitchen, drinking tea.

'This evening?'

'No, after the baby..'

'I'm going home,' said Mairi. 'We'll get an extra maid.'

But the more she thinks about it, the less probable, less possible, this seems.

'You should stay in Edinburgh,' Connie said, unthinking. 'Team up with Dulcie.'

'Pardon?

Connie coloured. She became as pink as her new cerise blouse.

'I'm sorry, Mairi. I didn't mean..'

'Come on, Connie, out with it! I know about Dulcie. I know who she is..'

'Yes, and.. I told Myra that you're not a child! I *said* she should have told you.. Dulcie's in the same condition as yourself. Her baby's due towards the end of January. She's going to bring it up all on her own, Mairi. Jolly brave. She'll do it, too.'

'*Dulcie's* having a baby..? And the father..?'

Connie shrugging, stretched for the last sandwich. 'Iain Murray.'

'Does he know?'

'Dulcie's written to him several times, but Iain hasn't been in touch. Not since he wrote and told her he was marrying someone from the island.'

'He.. what?'

'We thought that meant you.'

'Och, no. I haven't heard from Iain. Anyway, I'm in love with.. quite another person.'

'But you're having Iain's child..'

'Don't ask me why. I don't understand it myself.'

'Virgin birth?'

'I'm not that good,' said Mairi. 'Not that good.'

Connie looked at Mairi ruefully. Maybe Myra had been right this time. She could see Mairi relapsing into automatic mode before her eyes, assuming that calm, careful mask. It might be protective (Myra said it is) but Connie didn't think it helpful. She whistled under her breath as Mairi stared into her teacup.

'So,' said Connie, when the stretching silence had almost unnerved her, 'what are you going to do?'

'I don't know,' Mairi flexed her fingers. They were puffy, slightly stiff. They weren't like her own hands at all. 'I honestly and truly don't know. Can't decide. But Iain.. loves Dulcie, you know. He told me. *I'm in love with someone else*, he said. He was perfectly clear about it.'

'That's quite a line,' said Connie, 'to get away with.'

'No,' said Mairi. 'I understood. I was in love with someone else too.'

'Then why.. ?'

'Oh, I don't know. I was angry and hurt and cold and lost, but that's no reason,' Mairi sighed. 'It just.. happened. It comes down to lust, old-fashioned lust.'

Connie grinned. 'Nothing wrong with lust.'

'Oh, there is,' said Mairi. 'There has to be more to it, surely. Lust is disappointing.'

'I don't think so,' Connie grinned again. 'I've never thought so. You just need more practice!'

'Once was bad enough! Do I need more of this?'

'No.' Connie hesitated, blinking. She looked at Mairi, at her bursting abdomen. 'Aren't you..'

'What?'

'Aren't you at all frightened, Mairi?'

'What about?'

'*Having* the baby..'

'Giving birth? I try not to think about it. The whole thing is so strange, Connie, as if your body's following someone else's firm instructions. It doesn't feel like *me* at all. Look at my fingers, even.. I can't get my mother's ring on.'

'Well, I think you're incredibly brave. I'd be up the wall by now.'

'That's reassuring, Connie. Just what I want to hear! You could face the front, and shell-fire, but you couldn't face labour. That puts it nicely in perspective for me!'

Mairi had, in point of fact, been lying awake worrying, wondering; now she found herself giggling, unable to stop. Esther, coming into the kitchen a few minutes later found the girls still rolling with uncontrollable laughter.

'What's the joke?'

Mairi tried to explain.

'No joke. That's the joke.'

This started them off again. Esther sighed, removed the tea tray from the table.

'No,' cried Connie. 'I'm not finished!'

The chest at the foot of Mairi's bed is now full to the brim with gowns and caps and mitts; bootees, nappies and shawls. The rocking cot has been looked out, and all its draperies refreshed. Esther is edging blankets for it, has designed a tiny patchwork quilt. One evening John finds her sitting by the fire embroidering a tiny pillow slip in delicate white stitches; he voices a thought that's been in his mind for weeks or months now.

'It seems to me,' he smiles slowly, 'you're more involved in getting things ready for this child than Mairi is.'

'That's understandable,' Esther says, inspecting the rear side of her work. 'Mairi's so young.. and losing Maisie..'

'No, I'm not criticising the lass; what I'm saying is.. this is a little difficult; I don't quite know how to put it..'

John takes his glasses off, cleans them with his tie.

'I wish you wouldn't do that!'

'I've always done it.'

'Yes, I know, and..'

'Don't interrupt, Esther. What I'm trying to get round to saying is.. if Mairi feels the child too great a responsibility.. at this stage of her life.. we could offer to adopt it. I'm sure the thought must have crossed your mind, and I don't think Aeneas would be averse.. not after that ridiculous business at the funeral. It would help the lass enormously. She could move away, find work.. she'd be unencumbered. I don't see, you know, how she can ever go back.. to the island.'

'She could go,' says Esther, 'if she were married.'

'There doesn't seem much chance of that.'

'Not at the moment, no.'

'And you know how long it took her to face even our minister, who's not so heavy handed.'

'Yes,' says Esther, frowning. 'But it's a big question, John. Of course we'd have the baby and we'd love it like one of our own, and our children would love it too.. things would go well, I'm sure.. but Mairi.. Mairi may need the child.'

'I don't see why.'

'She's carried it for nine months. She's its mother. But yes,' Esther looks up at John, 'it's made me want another child.. we should talk about it; there's still time, John.'

'You can still say that after your last labour? We nearly lost you!'

'It's wonderful how you forget,' Esther sighs, returning to her stitches.

That evening Mairi has a run of firm contractions; her womb becomes so stiff and sore she calls for Esther.

'It's all that giggling,' Esther says. 'Don't worry, Mairi. I don't think this is it. Towards the end you'll get more nights like this. Just settle down, be as relaxed as possible.'

'I'm trying.'

'Very trying.'

Mairi's eyes fill with tears. Esther takes her hand, squeezes it. 'What's wrong?'

'Oh, just.. my mother used to say that.'

Esther has been sitting on the side of the bed. She stands up now, pulling the blue chair nearer Mairi, and the light. She brings her embroidery through from the lounge, with her neatly quilted work-basket. She holds the recent work up to the light, examining it carefully. It seems to cause her some concern.

'Did Maisie ever tell you, Mairi,' she asks, 'about your own birth? How she and Aeneas..'

'No. She said it was too painful. Too difficult. She said I should ask you.'

'I don't mean the actual birth.' Esther unpicks a bit of stitching, using sharply pointed scissors. They're silver, shaped like a bird, probably a stork, the long thin blades a fierce convincing beak. The screw that holds these blades together represents the bird's eye, and simple engraving manages to represent four sorts of feather. The stork's ringed legs are particularly realistic. Mairi's fascinated by them. Opening and shutting the scissors gives a definite illusion of flight, though the scissors, like the clipped parrot Myra keeps, have lost, or never had, that power.

Esther's voice is soft now, rough, as if she's trying not to cry. Mairi looks up, she has not been listening, lost in her own thoughts. '..and she and Aeneas had not been been together long when Maisie found she was expecting you. They were very much in love; engaged. They knew, of course, the family wouldn't be delighted, but they didn't expect the degree of anger visited on them. My mother, in particular, was vitriolic, almost washed her hands of Maisie. I didn't see so much of it, being younger; but Helen was so angry at the way our mother treated Maisie that she left home early; that's why she emigrated.'

Mairi shakes her head. 'I didn't know any of this.'

'And Aeneas and Maisie went back to the island married, pretending you were two months early – you were quite a small baby, which helped. The only one who knew was Aeneas's sister, Anna. She has always been a great ally of the pair, as you know, though there's no doubt there's a tongue in her head that could clip clouts! But I think,' says Esther, 'Maisie was very lonely. And remained lonely.'

'She was brave,' Mairi sobs.

'Yes,' says Esther, 'she had you, and Aeneas, and their love was such a strong thing. But love isn't always easy, Mairi.'

Mairi closes her eyes. 'I know. Sometimes it's impossible.'

Esther puts her scissors down now, tightens the hoops, checking the fabric she's removed the stitches from. It seems intact. Mairi is slightly flushed. She doesn't look well. The dull cream of the pillows makes her skin seem sallow. She's staring at the fire Margaret lit for her earlier in the tiny hearth in the corner of the room.

'I like a fire,' she says. 'I never had a fire at home.'

'This room's at the end of the terrace,' says Esther. 'That's why it gets chilly. But I always think it's a waste to have the fire in that corner when the heat could have been shared with another room – bad planning.'

'It looks interesting, though.'

'Yes.. and I quite like the tiles, those little lilies and hummingbirds. I didn't choose them. They were here when we moved in. I built the colour scheme round them. John says they're too fussy.'

'No,' says Mairi, 'I don't think so.'

'Men!'

Esther searches through her basket, choosing a silk thread with care. She cuts it, aims it perfectly at the narrow eye of her embroidery needle.

'I saw you had a letter from home today. Did your father happen to mention his new lodger?'

'No.'

'Well, he's taken on a lodger. Let two rooms in the attic. Isn't that a good idea?'

'Not my room!'

'No. Of course not. The maid's room, he says, and the box room adjoining it. He's made the box room – I can't think which one that is? – into a sitting-room, and put in a table and a couple of armchairs.'

'It was always too good for a box room,' Mairi nods. 'It has the best view in the whole house, right across the bay.' She sighs, wistful now, 'I always wanted that room, but my wardrobe wouldn't go in through the door. It's nice and warm, too. The chimney goes up through it.' She laughs, 'But you know what they'll say, Esther? In the town?'

'No.'

'They'll say he must be getting short of money!'

Esther smiles, goes on with her sewing. Mairi catches her breath as a new contraction swells towards crescendo.

'Breathe normally,' says Esther. 'That's better. They're slowing down.'

'And they're not as strong,' says Mairi, still slightly breathless. 'And they're not lasting so long.' She looks relieved, tries to change the subject. 'Who is this lodger, then? What does he do? Is it someone from the island?'

'A nice boy. I met him at the funeral. I think his name is Calum Morrison.'

'What?' Mairi sits up straight. 'Who did you say?'

'The boy from the *Oran*,' Esther repeats, adding smoothly, 'I might have got the name wrong. Anyway. He fell out with his family and needed a room. It's a good arrangement, don't you think?'

'What do you mean, fell out? What happened?'

'I don't really know.. they've patched it up, Aeneas says, but Calum wants more freedom. Reasonable enough, at that age. Most of his age group are marching home from war, after all.'

'Calum tried to volunteer!' says Mairi. 'He didn't pass the medical.'

'Would you like a cup of tea?'

'I'll go and make it, shall I?'

'No, let me spoil you,' Esther smiles. 'You'll be more tired than you think.'

Esther leaves Mairi in a turmoil. Calum, staying with her father? It is a good thing, yes, for him to have company in the house but.. Calum sleeping two doors from the room she spent her childhood in! He could walk into the room at any time, sit on the bed she slept in. He might find her journal..

No. Calum wouldn't rake through drawers. Would he even go inside the room? Would she mind it if he did?

She imagines him opening the door, entering slowly; hears his footsteps on the bare pine floor. Does he stroke the crocheted bed-cover? Will he stumble on the mats? Does he open her wardrobe, searching for her in discarded clothes? Does he lie on the bed, thinking of her, trying to feel her close to him? Does he find her? Does his body come alive with the thought of her? And is that love, or lust?

Esther has left her embroidery on the bedside table. She's a notable needlewoman; the tiny pillowcase is scattered now with knots and bows and dainty cross-stitched roses, all in white. It's such delicate work, Mairi thinks; the pillowcase will never last, though a small baby, certainly, does not stay small for long, the pillow's necessary life will be no longer than a few short months. Mairi wonders, as a new contraction starts to swell, who will embroider the next, bigger one?

This contraction is more painful than the last few; Mairi,

taken unawares, groans out loud. How will she cope with labour when this is just the practice? How did anyone ever manage? How on earth had Maisie survived those early months on the island, under the cloud of a too-early pregnancy?

The contraction, the pain gradually fade. Mairi breathes more easily, leaning back against the pillows. Her poor, poor mother. It must have been so difficult. She had always known Maisie felt separate, distinct from island life. Other. Mairi had thought it was the Glasgow origins set her apart, but the fear of discovery must have been a difficult, terrifying issue. Look what people said, for heaven's sake, about Kirsty! She can just see her small proud mother standing on the ferry, fighting off nausea, passing it off, blushing, as sea-sickness.

'Sit down, lass.'

'I'm better standing.'

Did Maisie lean across the rail? Probably.

'We'll be fine.'

'I hope so, Aeneas.'

'I love you, Maisie, more than all the world.'

And Maisie looking at the young Aeneas, deciding then to make him all her world.

They needed no one else, the MacDonalds. They were that independent. Folk used to resent it. And Maisie brought Mairi up to be just the same. Independent. Resilient.

The first day she woke up sick, Mairi thought she had eaten something that disagreed with her. The feeling didn't go away. The next two days were equally miserable. She couldn't understand; usually she bounced back. On the fourth day she sat up in bed wondering about her monthly bleed, which hadn't come. It was the end of May. Birds were singing. Maybe, thought Mairi, staring at the cloudless sky, maybe it would go away. It didn't mean anything, that night. One night couldn't mean anything, couldn't lead to.. anything.. surely?

Maisie, ill in bed, knew none of this.

By the end of July, Mairi was tired of the endless nausea.

She'd let out her work skirts; even so, she wouldn't be able to hide the changes any longer. She made a pot of tea and carried it upstairs to ask her mother's advice. Maisie, a little stronger that day, took it very calmly.

Her father was the one who literally staggered.

'That Calum Morrison! Wait till I lay my hands on him! What is he thinking of?'

'It wasn't Calum,' Maisie said. 'It was Iain Murray. Who's off at war, and even if he wasn't, I'd hate to see her marry him.'

'I'd never marry him,' said Mairi. 'He would be impossible.'

'Then *why?*'

'I didn't think. I didn't think this would happen.'

'Poor lass,' said Maisie. 'Come here.' She held Mairi in her arms. 'You've found a child, and lost the world. Never mind. Never mind. A baby brings its own love.'

Within weeks, Mairi found herself in Edinburgh, cloistered, as her body grew. And not a word was there from Calum. She could not expect it.

'That's you settled for the night,' Esther smiles down at her niece. 'I'm off through to bed then. Goodnight, Mairi. Don't worry about a thing. You'll be fine. So will that baby. I don't think it will come for a week or two yet. First babies are more often late than early.'

'Goodnight, Esther,' Mairi turns on to her side. 'And thank you.'

It's lovely to have the fire in her room, a luxury. Esther's left her door slightly ajar. Mairi can hear her aunt and uncle padding round their own room, hear their low voices, working through the various events of the day.

She's very drowsy now. The fire's glow is sweetly soporific.

'Did you ask her,' says John.

'Ask her what?'

'About the baby?'

'No.' Esther's voice drops, becoming virtually inaudible. 'If she decides she can't cope, then we'll offer, of course, but we mustn't pre-empt an issue like this.'

'It would be much better for the child to have a mother and a father, surely?'

'It already has a mother..'

'You know what I mean..'

'John, you're a good man, and a dear soul, but this is Mairi's baby. I don't want to make her feel she shouldn't want it.'

'How will she cope?'

'I don't know. But she will.'

Mairi thinks that's what she heard. Perhaps it was a dream, a nightmare. The voices are very low, so low the fire's occasional spit and crackle make the words uncertain.

'It's my baby,' she thinks. 'Mine.'

She sits up suddenly. With Calum moving in, folk in town are sure to think *he's* the baby's father. Now the child which has been strangely inactive all day, starts kicking, pummelling.

*   *   *

Zoe Wild drove west from Inverness in rain that kept trying to turn to snow. One-forty. She was in good time; the service started at two, and she'd been told the crematorium was easy to find.

She thought this an attractive road, oddly attractive, compared to all the other approaches to the town; it was not a dual carriageway clogged with ugly concrete buildings, there were no supermarkets, no shopping complexes, no industrial estates. Glenurquart Road swerved round the upturned boat of Tomnahurich, passing the green swathe of the Bught and all its parks, then slid over the canal, bisecting Torvean golf course before sweeping uphill towards Dochfour and Loch Ness. The nearer horizon, richly wooded slopes and crofted land extended from Craig Dunain to Craig Phadrig's fir-pocked profile.

The crematorium was clearly signposted. Zoe joined a long slow queue of cars snaking down and now uphill to the large and fairly full car park laid out before an arched and sandstone-harled building. Outside there was a hearse, a limousine, and a low black name-board, slightly out of place, more like one you'd expect to find in a hotel foyer. It bore one name only: John-Angus MacLeod: 2pm.

An undertaker moved forward from the shadows to greet her, shook her hand. He looked a kindly man, grey-haired.

'Have you come far?' he asked.

'Not today,' said Zoe, 'though I live in London.' She was surprised to find herself responding with emotion to what was, after all, professional courtesy.

'A long way,' he nodded. 'Let me show you where to go.'

He turned, pointing out the main door through the sheltering arch and cloister, past a flower-laden coffin. Zoe hesitated.

'There are still one or two seats,' he said, 'at the back.'

She met Finlay by the door. Like an usher at a wedding he was handing out service sheets. He looked young and very solemn.

'Ah, Zoe,' he sighed. 'We'll have to stop meeting like this.'

She stared at him. The offhand tone was very much at odds with the sadness in his eyes. The boy was near to tears. She found she did not quite know how to respond, and thrown off guard, spoke her mind. 'I hadn't realised how much you look like him.'

'Mum said that this morning.'

Zoe nodded. Finlay had his mother's colouring, but the set of the eyes, the expression were very much John-Angus. She blinked, squeezed his arm.

'Catch you later.'

The hall she entered now was large and light, with plate-glass windows opening on a narrow cloister. Wood-lined walls vaulted to an asymmetric roof. Behind the pulpit, Alpha and Omega gates stood to attention and sumptuous velvet drapes softened a recess obviously intended for the coffin. Zoe thought the gates odd, even cabalistic, but the room buzzed with conversation, almost cheery, despite the solemn organ music. The few remaining empty seats were in awkward places.

'There's still a seat available over on the right.' It was the kindly undertaker.

Zoe smiled.'No, honestly, I prefer to stand. That lady needs it more than I do.'

She pointed to an elderly woman hobbling in with a stick. The undertaker rushed smoothly over, ushering the woman gently to the empty place. Zoe was touched. This man really seemed to care. There might be a programme in that.

She glanced at the sheet Finlay had handed her. *A celebration*, it said, *of the remarkable life of John-Angus MacLeod*. On the front there was a photograph of a touchingly young John-Angus, ill at ease with the camera. He stood in Seaforth uniform beside a round-faced girl whose thick brown hair kept escaping from her broad-brimmed hat. She was starting to smile. She had very sparkly eyes. Her bouquet trailed right down past her knees.

On the back were the words of 'Amazing Grace' and a short poem Zoe had no time to scan, for the kind, apparently senior, undertaker now stepped forward.

'I would ask you all to be upstanding for the family.'

He moved to the front of the hall. A side door, neatly hidden in panelling, opened and relatives began to filter in, directed carefully by Zoe's friend, his complete attention on the task in hand. The minister came first, taking his place at the lectern as the four undertakers retired, walked in unison through the hall, black gloves in hand.

'Please remain standing.'

The coffin was wheeled through the silence up the central aisle, positioned at the front. Brakes were unobtrusively applied. The undertakers melted away.

Zoe found herself wondering how many pieces of paper change hands behind the scenes on such an occasion as this.. how many certificates? A precious piece of cargo, a body.

Except in war.

The minister opened his Bible. 'Please be seated. We are gathered here together, to celebrate the remarkable life of our brother John-Angus MacLeod, who was born in Sandwick, Lewis, in 1898.

'In his time John-Angus saw many changes. The croft he was

born in had an earthen floor. He served in France in the First War, where he met his wife, Connie, an ambulance driver. After the war he settled in Inverness, where he started the famous field sports shop MacLeod and Johnson. It has passed out of the family now, but remains world famous.

'John-Angus believed in community. He served on the Town Council from the thirties to the early sixties. He was a supporter of comprehensive education, student grants; and a passionate believer in the Loch Ness Monster, not least for its effect on local tourism.'

He waited for the quiet laughter to settle before going on.

'Late in life John-Angus campaigned for nuclear disarmament: this from a man who won the VC at Arras. He joined Amnesty International, and wrote to political prisoners all over the world. He was a kind man, a thoughtful man, a quiet man, and above all a family man and we give thanks for his life.

'As you will all know, he had little time for organised religion, but he loved "Amazing Grace", which you'll find on the back of your sheets. We'll stand to sing.'

The minister was young, perhaps in his thirties, unassuming. The organist could not be seen, not from where Zoe stood. She'd never liked electric organs, but the congregation's singing soon overwhelmed the plastic chords. Everyone sang loudly, enthusiastically, and Zoe was surprised to find her eyes filming over.

'Amazing grace, how sweet the sound ...'

Zoe did not sing. She had no ear for music, though she liked listening to it well enough. She thought about John-Angus. His smile. His eyes. It was hard to think of him as ninety-seven. He looked twenty years younger, at least. Age was so unpredictable, hardly touching some, while others..

Her own father – admittedly her mother was his second wife – was in his seventies but looked much older. The dementia didn't help. Zoe found it painful to visit him, difficult trying to speak to him. Josh spent his days lolling in a chair – not harnessed in, quite, but not far off it, his head rolling to one side, his fingers rubbing feverishly at sleeves, tray, anything.

'Hello, Dad.'

'Nh.'

'How are you?'

Silence.

'Have you had your lunch? Was it nice?'

He beckoned to her. As she bent forward, he dribbled, saying nothing, mucus dangling from his lower lip.

'What is it, Dad? Do you want something?'

The mouth stayed open, slack. The eyes seemed infinitely old. Confused and lost. He would be better off dead.

She said this to her mother.

'No! How can you say that?'

'He's not there. That's not my father.'

Josh, a mathematician, intensely bright, took his degree after demob from the RAF; taught mathematics in a succession of schools till his chronic forgetfulness became too limiting. Zoe was by then in her second year at Cambridge. She hadn't been home for more than a weekend in eighteen months, didn't realise how things were going. She could still remember the phone call, her shocked voice drifting in the convent-like corridors of Newnham.

'Daddy's what? Tired?' She laughed. 'For a moment there I thought you said *re*-tired..'

The corridor sang back at her. *Re*-tired.. *re*-tired.. *re*-tired..

It was no mistake. Her mother's life contracted overnight, or so it seemed to Zoe, her role in Joshua's life now that of nurse, of keeper. Zoe hated what her charming, erudite father had become.. a blank, uncertain, unresponsive creature. Frustrated too. Violent, at times.

She went home less and less often. Her mother never complained.

Now he was in the home, she seemed at a loose end, visiting her husband every week, sometimes twice a week, kissing that shell as if it still held Joshua. She often phoned Zoe afterwards.

'I once was lost but now I'm found..'

The hymn was coming to an end, the tempo slowing almost

to infinity.

'was blind but now I see..'

The minister raised his hand.

'Let us hear the word of God.

'You are like a light for the whole world. A city built on a hill cannot be hidden.

'No one lights a lamp and puts it under a bowl; instead he puts it on the lampstand, where it gives light for everyone in the house.

'and again

'Your eyes are like a lamp for the body. When your eyes are sound your whole body is full of light

'and again

'There are many rooms in my father's house, and I am going to prepare a place for you. I would not tell you this if it were not so

'and again

'Peace is what I leave with you: it is my own peace that I give you. Do not be worried and upset; do not be afraid.

'If you loved me, you would be glad that I am going to the father; for he is greater than I.

'Let us pray.

'We give you thanks, oh Lord, for the certainty and kindness you bestowed upon us in the form of John-Angus MacLeod. His long and productive life is an icon to all that knew him, a beacon shining to the world at large. He was a generous man whose particular gift was to reach into the hearts of those he knew and loved, to see the world, and clearly. From his youth, when he served in France and won the Victoria Cross for his work with the wounded at Arras, to his long service of hospital visiting, something he did every week in life while he was able, and indeed, into his mid-eighties, John-Angus was concerned to reach out, to help. He was a shining example to us all.

'We pray that you will remember the family in their great loss, Mamie and Ewan, Julia, Finlay and Emma. Age is no barrier to love, and age in John-Angus's case seemed to count for little. We pray that you will help the family and friends – friends old and new for John-Angus was still reaching out – through the next dark weeks and months, lighten their loss. We pray that the certain knowledge of a good life lived to great age, the life that was John-Angus's, will prove some consolation.

'I am going to call on Eilidh Morrison now to say a few words.'

A middle-aged woman dressed in a navy trouser-suit stepped forward. She was slim and small and her white hair bobbed around her wrinkled face. That suit, thought Zoe, cost an arm and a leg. Even from the back of the hall it was obvious that the heavy gold brooch and rings were the real thing.

'Hi.' The accent rested somewhere between Lewis and California. 'I'm proud and sorry to be here. Real sorry. John-Angus has been the biggest thing in my life since he cuddled me when I was maybe two hours old. See, I'd been yelling fit to bust every living minute till then. My mother was sleeping off the effects of a prolonged and painful labour, and my father, exhausted, was at his wits' end, worried about my mother too. When John-Angus picked me up, I stopped crying straight away. I guess I knew even then he was someone you could rely on.

'My father Calum knew John-Angus all his life; they were close friends – they and Mamie's father Alec were pretty much inseparable. After the Great War, when John-Angus came back – Alec being too young, and Calum's bad leg debarring him from the fray, they picked up their friendship and it was a powerful thing – they had such debates, such arguments, political and philosophical and yes, religious too.

'They each lost a son in World War Two. This was a heavy burden, one they helped each other bear. I never knew the boys, but there are so many photographs of them.. Iain, Bob and Ewan.. on holiday in Lewis, in Inverness, in Buckie. The Three Musketeers, John-Angus used to call them. They were so proud of those boys; you can see it in their eyes in every photograph.

'First of the three to die was my brother Iain, in St Valery. John-Angus, his godfather, was devastated.. I still have the letter.. *what it must have been like to see Iain board the* Sheila *when you knew what had happened on the* Iolaire.. *the dark ship of war returning..'* Eilidh's voice broke here. She swallowed, cleared her throat.

'Without the support John-Angus offered, I don't think my parents would have pulled through. But they did, and I was born. My father took up the pen, which he had laid aside for too many years. But he didn't tackle the Second War. He chose instead to focus on the Great War; in particular when he wrote the screenplay for *The Dark Ship*, it was John-Angus he turned to for military detail, though it was a painful for him even after thirty years to relive his days in the trenches.

'My father took a lot of stick for having the John-Andrew character attempt suicide; people from the island who knew their family history, (and who from the island doesn't?) knew John-Angus to have been an out and out hero; but in fact, John-Angus had had first-hand knowledge of the depths of fear that boys could be reduced to in harsh army training; he had himself been badly bullied. Though he never attempted suicide, but somehow found strength to survive and grow, he felt that many a youngster might have succumbed. Throughout his life he was unwilling to discuss his army experiences, mistrusting the bitter strength forged in those terrible days. He wrote this to my father in 1948:

'There is such blackness, such darkness in each of us, Calum, and such light. I am concerned to change the world, what I can of it, in small ways.. to preserve what light I find.

'This from the man who used to say he was probably dyslexic. He was incredibly modest. He was fun too. To visit John-Angus and Connie and stay in the big old house down by the river, with its turrets and its goats.. to get into the back shop, see the taxidermist at work stuffing stags' heads for the gentry, to see John-Angus coping placidly with really difficult customers while Connie was dancing up and down with rage, to hear the endless laughter and the jokes was always my idea of a really good holiday. Indeed it still would be.

'Mr Lively, here, has told you the official things John-Angus did; let me tell you the small ones. He wrote my father every week for nearly fifty years, and after that he wrote to my mother till her death the next year. Since then he has written every week to me. That degree of love and care is typical of the man.

'He came to Inverness after the Great War, realising his city wife would find it difficult to settle on the island. He lavished the same degree of love and attention on his chosen community as on his friends. He was a great believer in community, the strength of neighbourly interest and care.

'There was a television advert in the sixties that went, *Get the strength of the insurance companies around you!* For many people, John-Angus was that strength. His work in the council and in hospital visiting are instances of it; his donations and fundraising work for Inverness charities from Women's Aid to the Highland Hospice are less well known.

'But the biggest secret, the thing no one ever realised, was what a large part John-Angus played in the editing and publishing of Iain Alexander Murray's poems, and co-writing *The Dark Ship*. Not that he actually put pen to paper. He dictated it all to his beloved Connie. Because of that he refused to have his name on the credits but my father has written, and here I quote his journal for 1968, the year before his death, when *The Dark Ship* was re-released:

'*I wrote to John-Angus, suggesting that we tell the world how much he had to do with the ordering and reshaping of narrative for Dark Ship; John-Angus would have none of it. After all this time, he said, it's too late for you to pin the blame on me! I told him that I thought the film would have flopped without his input, without that intensity, that strangely clear view of his, so entirely lacking in romance, so conscious of the good and bad in all of us.*

'*We were both in mourning in the forties, both lost sons in the Second War. Writing that film helped us come to terms with grief. But I couldn't get him to take even a small share of the profits and felt bad about it. I wrote back and said he should name a charity we could send his profits to. What else could I do?*

'The profits, incidentally, went to fund a bursary for Aberdeen University, for students from Lewis or Inverness.

Though John-Angus never went back to the island, he never forgot it; I have heard him say that his island upbringing was the source of anything that was good in him.

'I said I knew John-Angus all my life. I loved him all my life too. I guess we all did. We were so lucky to have him. He was a wonderful husband, father and grandfather, a warm and faithful friend. I don't know where I'm going to go for my insurance now.'

Eilidh left the podium. The minister returned to introduce a young clarsach-player. Zoe had not noticed the clarsach standing on the far right, but a teenage girl carried it forward now, with a small three-legged stool.

'This tune,' she said, 'is "Mr MacLeod of Sandwick", originally for fiddle, composed by Calum Morrison.'

Zoe liked the clarsach, but wondered if the tune might not sound richer with the fiddle's almost human resonance. She must, she thought, try and speak to Eilidh Morrison, who was sitting next to Finlay now, wiping her eyes. Finlay had his arm around her. Julia's head was bent, only Ewan remaining solidly upright.

It was hard to gauge emotion from that stern back view. Did he worry about death? Did doctors worry about dying? It wasn't something she'd ever thought of asking a doctor, though there was no reason why they should worry any less than the rest of us about the actual dying, not when the death was personal, their own. They knew more about the process of illness, yes, more of the pre-death narrative. Afterwards, everyone was in the dark. Or maybe not.

And it was such an odd thing that a body, an amalgam of atoms functioning perfectly well in a certain form, should just stop, lose impetus, as if it had run out of diesel, as if the molecules were folk in a dance who'd forgotten the steps and disintegrated into individual oblivion. When Joshua was himself, he always used to say people died because they were short of breath. And someone told Zoe once that Buddhists had a vaguely similar idea, and that was what was behind the slow breathing, as much as anything. To stretch your life out, carefully. The little Zoe knew about Buddhist ideology made that seem more than a little over-simplistic but you could see the logic in it, if there were a certain preordained number of breaths. If.

None of which would make doctors any more or less frightened about their own death, if imminent. Come to that, how did television journalists feel about it? Zoe wished Josh would slip away, die in his sleep, but his heart, his lungs were strong. For herself, she harboured quiet fears about the process of death and few hopes for existence afterwards, though she always found the religious dimension of funeral services soothing. *In my father's house are many mansions*; not that they called them mansions these days.

'*Our father which art in heaven, hallowed be thy name.*'

They'd moved on to the Lord's prayer.

'I'd like, on behalf of the family, to extend an invitation to you all to visit the MacLeod home after the service. We'll end with Finlay's reading of the poem on your sheet.'

Zoe looked on, intrigued, as Finlay stood up, awkwardly. He did not move to the lectern, but merely turned to face the crowded hall.

'Can you hear me at the back?'

Nods, and a muffled chorus of yes, reassured him. He had a good voice. Zoe waited, expectant.

'My great-grandfather wrote this. He called it *Relativity*.

there is living
and then there is life
the two are not entirely unrelated;

there is loving
and then there is strife
the two are not entirely unrelated;

there is losing
and then there is grief
the two are not entirely unrelated;

there is leaving
and then there is death
the two are not entirely unrelated;

and the greatest of these is love.

Finlay bowed his head and turned back to the front as the four undertakers, gloved, walked forward. They wheeled the coffin into the recess behind the gates. Then, slowly, slowly, two of them began to slide the gates and screening curtain shut. Alpha and Omega came together. The minister called a blessing, and the congregation stood as the family walked first down the centre aisle and through the door.

It's a tricky thing at a cremation; the lack of a coffin leaving. Zoe joined the queue of mourners waiting to approach the family, to shake hands. She noticed the elderly woman immediately in front of her, recognising her as the one who hobbled in and was shown to the last seat. As they worked their way along the line, this woman introduced herself to the family as Dulcie's Elinor; Julia and Eilidh seemed delighted to see her, promising long conversations. 'Did you get to the house all right?' asked Julia. Zoe's ears pricked up.. Dulcie.. the VAD? Was this, then, Iain Murray's daughter? She stared, but could not see much, if any, resemblance to the Iain of *A Private View*.

The male members of the family were the ones most pleased to see Zoe. Ewan squeezed her arm unnecessarily. She was amused to find herself kissing Finlay on the cheek, having avoided Ewan's embrace. She was not displeased when Finlay held her hand all the time she was telling him how much she liked his reading.

'You're coming to the house?'

She moved on to hug Julia.

'The hat,' she said, 'is fabulous. A triumph.'

'Oh, Mamie!' Julia laughed. She hadn't missed the small exchange with Finlay. 'You will come over, won't you?

The MacLeods' house was mobbed. Zoe had to park her car quite a way along the riverside. She hadn't noticed, in the dark, how beautiful it was, the modern house stretching beside the Ness under mature Scots pine and other tall and graceful trees; probably beech, though they'd shed their leaves and she could not be sure. The garden sloped steeply towards the riverbank, and the water's rushing was both loud and peaceful. Mist swirling from the water was clinging to the low shrubs now, beginning to creep across the lawn. She stood for a moment in the drive, moved towards the edge.

'Careful!'

'Emma! I didn't see you.'

'The bank can be treacherous this time of year. Look how high the river is.'

'Does it flood?'

'The garden gets it regularly.'

'It's beautiful.'

Emma stared across the water, did not speak. Zoe waited.

'It isn't my business, Emma, but anyone can see there's something bothering you. Would it help to talk..? I'll be gone tomorrow.'

Emma blushed.

'I'm sorry.' Zoe turned round, shivering.

'I can't stand it here,' said Emma. 'It's too much. Too perfect. And they expect *me* to be perfect too.'

'Not your mother, surely?'

'Oh, not Mum, I suppose. But she never stands up to him!'

'As families go, yours doesn't seem too bad.'

'I hate it,' Emma said. 'You don't know.'

'No.'

'I think I might be..'

Pregnant? Zoe wondered. Gay?

'Happier in a different course,' said Emma. 'I hate

Economics.. want to study History of Art. I want to do Archaeology.'

'So change,' said Zoe.

'He'd never let me.'

'It's not his choice.'

'He pays the fees.'

Zoe shrugged. 'Get a job. Put yourself through college. It's possible. I did that after second year.'

'Why? Were you fighting with your parents?'

'No, not exactly,' Zoe choked. 'My father.. was demented.'

'So's he.'

'No,' said Zoe, 'no.' She found herself in tears. 'I'm sorry, Emma, I'm not usually so feeble.. the funeral, I suppose.. my father developed Alzheimer's when I was just your age, or at least, that's when it was diagnosed. Today he's little more than a vegetable. And, you know,' she wiped her eyes, 'he was quite lovely. Not that we agreed all the time, hardly ever actually, we used to fight.. but he was such.. such a *vibrant* intelligence.'

'I'm sorry.'

Zoe blew her nose, sniffed again.

'When I cry,' she said, 'my eyes go puffy.'

'Come on. Come inside,' said Emma. 'Let me find you a drink.'

'Where have you been?'

Zoe smiled at Ewan. 'Lovely house you and Julia have. A real family home.'

'Thank you. I built it.'

'Mum designed it, ' Emma said. 'She was an architect before I was born. She hasn't worked since then.'

'Hasn't worked?' said Julia.

'I was getting round,' said Emma, 'to the photography.'

'You're a photographer?'

'*Very* expensive.'

'Shut up, Emma,' Julia blushed, 'would you like something to eat, Zoe? There's a buffet in the dining-room.'

'I'd like to meet Eilidh, actually. Or Dulcie's Elinor.'

Julia hesitated. 'Will you still be around tomorrow?'

'Could be.'

'Then come and have lunch here with them. They're holed up in my studio. Both a bit emotional. You can understand it. But the four of us might do quite well tomorrow.'

Zoe nodded. 'I look forward to that. I'd like to see your work.'

'Oh, that,' Julia blushed. 'Well..'

'You'll have to sit for her,' said Emma. 'Another time. Now come and meet Mr Lively. He recognised you in the congregation.'

Julia laughed. 'No peace for the wicked.'

She followed Zoe's progress across the hall. People looked up, registered her passing. She was so striking, her face so familiar. You felt as if you knew her, as if you'd always known her. That was the power of TV for you.. no. More than that. There was something about Zoe, something oddly bright, an energy that touched, made you want to know her better.. a vibrancy that film could only partly communicate. All the same, she'd have liked to try a portrait of the girl, see what might be achieved.

She saw Finlay staring briefly after Zoe too, before he turned back to his conversation with a group of elderly relatives, joining the debate about the angling club with all the enthusiasm he could muster. He did not look round again, though Julia could feel how much he wanted to. The boy was as open as a book. John-Angus, she remembered, had that same eternal patience. It didn't always get you what you wanted.

He was sitting with the same group when Zoe came to take her leave of Julia.

'Where's your car?'

'Oh, just along the road.'

'I bet you're almost at Dores! And the street lights aren't that wonderful.. Finlay, see Zoe to her car, please, love?'

'I don't want to be a bother.'

Julia smiled. 'No bother. We'll see you tomorrow?'

'I look forward to it. Phone me if there's any change of plan. You've got my mobile number..'

'I'm glad you were able to come today.'

'So am I.' Zoe hesitated, adding slowly, 'I've never met anyone like John-Angus. He was a wonderful man.'

'We think so,' says Julia, 'but then we're biased.'

Outside, the sky was almost dark, threatening snow. Zoe and Finlay shivered as they strode along the narrow pavement.

'You're sure you had a car?'

'I'm beginning to wonder.'

'No, I see it now,' said Finlay. 'There.. round the corner.'

The rain had started; heavy, wet drops.

'Finlay, I'm sorry. I wouldn't have asked you to trek all this way.. would you like a lift back to the house?'

'Och, no,' he said. 'I need a bit of fresh air. Zoe..'

She clicked the car doors open. 'Sorry?'

He seemed to find it difficult to meet her eye. 'I wondered.. would you like to have a drink sometime? With me, I mean.'

'Yeah. That would be great.'

He swivelled round to face her, raindrops sliding down his cheeks, sleet whitening his hair.

'What about tonight?' she said. 'Jane, my producer, has gone back to London. I was only going to work.'

'I'll take a taxi. Where? When?'

'My hotel. Eight.'

'Right you are.'

She slammed the door shut, keyed ignition, but Finlay bent down, rapped the window.

'Sorry. Which hotel is that?'

Seven o'clock. The phone rang out in Zoe's room. She heard it from the bath she had filled to overflowing.

'Sorry. No one can take your call at the moment. Please leave your message after the tone.'

There was something wonderfully dampening, she thought, about computerised voice technology. Messages were always short. Hearing a real voice, even in anxious or answerphone mode, people relaxed, ran on for ever.

'Zoe. Ewan MacLeod here. Missed you at the house. Thought

we might meet for a drink? You'll get me at the hospital in outpatients' tomorrow morning. Look forward to hearing from you.'

She cringed, ducking under the water in the deep warm bath, closing her eyes tightly and holding her nose. Not breathing. How long would you last like this? How long did you last under water if you didn't hold your nose, if you let your lungs fill slowly? When would you choke? Would it be quicker or slower with cold, not warm, water? Salt or fresh water, now, that did make a difference.. though you still died of electrolyte disturbances, she'd read that somewhere. And falling into cold water sometimes stopped your heart, vasovagal reflex, so they said.. so you didn't drown, not really. Though sometimes cold water slowed your metabolism letting you live longer.. diving reflex.. fickle things, reflexes.

She started counting.. one two three four five six seven eight.. her lungs were bursting.. nine ten eleven.. it was getting impossible.. twelve thirteen.. she panicked now, couldn't stop it.. fourteen fift..

She sat up coughing. Steam curdled the bathroom tiles, condensing. Zoe, sweating from the too-hot bath, was breathing much too fast, too shallow, starting to feel giddy. The phone rang out again.

'Sorry. No one can take your call at the moment. Please leave your message after the tone.'

'Zoe. Ewan MacLeod again. A sudden thought. We could meet tonight. I think you have my mobile number. Ring me.'

Zoe slid back down into the water. She was not much over five feet; her feet didn't reach the end of the bath. This time she floated, eyes open, ears immersed in bursting bubbles. The noise they made was curious; that tap dripping had resonance of vast proportion, and water swishing down the overflow sounded like a cataract. She could not hear the phone as it rang again.

'Sorry. No one can take your call at the moment. Please leave your message after the tone.'

'Ewan MacLeod. I've been called out to the hospital. Looks

like I'll be in theatre most of the night. Call me tomorrow, Zoe.'

Her fingers were white now, wrinkled. Elephant skin. Zoe examined them closely. When she was a child her mother used point this out to terrify her into leaving the bath.

'The wind will change and your skin will stay like that.'

As it would, it would, all too soon. She looked at her hands, scrying the wrinkles. How much longer had she as a presenter? The TV journalist (female) had a short career. Not that she was old, twenty-nine wasn't old, but it was tough market. She had another six or seven years, then she'd have to decide between production and radio.

Not that she wanted to get into all that tonight. Tonight she would be young. What should she wear? What was left that was presentable? The black shift, or the Chinese trouser suit? The suit looked like pyjamas, felt great on the skin.

The telephone clicked into voice-mail. 'Sorry. No one can take your call at the moment. Please leave your message after the tone.'

'Zoe, Finlay here. I'm so sorry. I can't make it tonight. Dad's been called out to the hospital, and Emma's disappeared, and I can't leave Mum to cope with all the visitors. She was closer to John-Angus than any of us. She's heartbroken. Trying not to show it, of course.. And I'm stuck with a mountain of dishes the caterers didn't finish. Come and help, if you like. Just kidding..'

Zoe climbed out of the bath, pulling on the hotel bathrobe. So. That was it then. Work. There would be no escape.

She shook her head, towelling the short curls dry. No need for makeup. Or fancy clothes. Strangely disappointed, she left her silk suit hanging, shrugging into jeans, her oldest sweater; she curled up on the sofa with a mug of chocolate and *World War One: after the battle.*

Her background notes were more or less complete. She ran through the sheaf of pages, scribbling changes here and there. There wasn't much more to do unless Julia could find the notebook, then they'd focus on the poetry, the film.

She sipped her chocolate, musing.

It really was no wonder Julia was so sad. She'd only met John-Angus for an hour herself, and yet she felt she'd lost a favourite uncle. That talent of listening, of true interest in others was all too rare.

And what a lottery life could be. It might have been John-Angus killed and Ewan surviving.. or even Iain Murray.. so what dictated survival, non-survival? Was it purely chance?

What would Iain Murray have done with fifty extra years of life? Who would he have been at forty, fifty? Would he have looked like Elinor at seventy? What would he have looked like in his twenties? Not like John-Angus. Nor like Finlay. Finlay seemed inordinately gentle, not an ounce of vanity in him. Iain Murray, she was sure, would have been far more conscious of his own worth, not that it mattered. Not at all.

She reached for *A Private View*, flicked through the poems, pausing on the very last page.

Island

I am sailing in the cold
Dark morning of the year
To you, my island.

There can be no other
Destination, no hope for me
Beyond this storm-bound shore

This peat-dark moor. The flood
Shall be my fire, this rock my shelter
From the ocean's wandering.

Was Iain writing here about death? Or love? Or just about living, balancing the pain? The exquisite degrees of love and hate and longing that separate us all from our origins, our human landscape, will always beguile; always pull us back. Iain Murray knew that. Iain Alexander Murray was not a man who looked for peace, for calm.

And what was it, Zoe wondered, about the First World War that was still so resonant here and now at the far end of the twentieth century? The loss of life in the Second War was no less tragic; the huge waste of civilian life, the deaths in concentration camps.. was it the case that poetry as narrative (as critics were beginning now to suggest) hijacked popular opinion, colouring perception, transforming a *necessary* war into a *bad* one? Was it a necessary war? Was there ever such a thing?

Iain never said the war was bad. Or good. He pointed out the cost in pain to soldier and civilian. He survived the war, drank his way through it. Somehow, he found comfort in the moment, though the moment was difficult, sometimes unbearable. He found comfort too in love.. it was in so many of the poems.. *you are the one star in this lack/ of firmament..*

Why did this bring Finlay's face to mind?

She sighed, tidied her papers, folding them neatly in her briefcase. Enough. No more work.

But she opened *A Private View* again, stared at the dedication: *From Barbara to Archie, with love.*

Who was Barbara? Why did she buy the book? It had been read time and time again. By Archie? Or Barbara? What did the poems *do* to them, for them? Did they live to see the film? Did they realise the drowning anti-hero of *The Dark Ship* was their Iain Murray?

Such fragile connections, Zoe mused, ideas. On a futures market, they must be the most unpredictable and yet the most resilient constructions of mankind, arcing across miles, across years. Beyond death. That's what drew her into narrative, into film. Josh would have preferred her to study mathematics. As she could have. She was good enough. An all-rounder. But she knew she needed to communicate more visually, more generally, than mathematics would allow.

She still felt guilty that their last coherent conversation had been an argument.

Not that she said (or thinks) mathematics weren't important; not that she didn't appreciate the importance, the beauty of ideas for their own sake, ideas expressed in number, in colour, in texture. No. Ideas for their own sake were good. Iain Murray must have thought so. He never saw his poems published. None of his friends even knew he wrote. His lyrics came into being, were written for their own sake, for the difference they made simply by existing. Zoe loved the purity in that.

What didn't fit, quite, was the way Calum drew him in the film. Eilidh might be able to tell her why Calum's Iain was so different from the Iain shining in the work.. was there a directorial agenda there? A necessary character arc?

She felt more and more inclined to shape her programme round the men, the Lewis boys, their lives, their deaths; a community of tales as disparate, as strong as each individual telling or retelling. The war had swept them all into mythologies that bind, that had bound and rebounded on mankind throughout the ages. The stories, the poems gave voice to the community's strength, and to its tragic loss. What these men could have been..

She'd need more information, naturally, more contact with the families. That wouldn't be too hard to bear. She'd coped with the likes of Ewan before, and Finlay.. Finlay was definitely interesting. It was hard to predict what he eventually might become, such strength lay sleeping there beneath the gentleness. He reminded her so much of John-Angus, despite the difference in years, despite the Italian genes.

Odd, the things that moved you. Those brown eyes. And to think she hadn't noticed them till the funeral.

The room had grown stuffy now, suffocating. Hotel rooms were like that after a while, no matter how luxurious, how clean. Restless, Zoe pulled her coat on, grabbed a scarf and wandered out into a world where newly-fallen snow was dusting the car park, transforming trees, whitening the streetlights.

There were no stars. The sky was thick with cloud. There would be more snow, and soon. Yes. Soon.

*   *   *

'This is the right platform for the train to Kyle?'

'I certainly hope so. That's the train I'm waiting for myself.'

'You've been in France?'

Iain smiles. 'Since 1916. And you?'

You can always, he thinks, tell a VAD. What is it about them? This one is very thin, looks slightly nervy, and as if she doesn't eat enough.

'No. I worked in London and Brighton. Never made it across the Channel.'

Her hair is brown and wavy, with a strong auburn tinge. The hair under her arms, thinks Iain, will be red; and the hair at the top of her legs too, curly, rich as new moss. On so thin a girl, that crop of hair will be startling, sensual. He glances at her skirt as if expecting to see it now in silhouette. He'd flirt with her if he had more energy.

The train shunts to a halt beside them.

'Can I help you with your bag?'

She smiles, nods at his sling.

'It would be more the thing if I were to help with yours.'

'This is just a sham,' says Iain. 'I'm left-handed, actually.'

'Oh yes?'

'Anything to get off drill.'

'Yes, Corporal..'

She makes for the first class compartment.

'Maybe see you later, then,' Iain shoulders his pack, waves awkwardly. His head is still aching. He's shivering too. He didn't think the hangover would last this long. He hadn't had that much to drink.

'Are you travelling with a party?'

He shakes his head. 'No. I'm in third class.'

'Then come in with me, fool. They never make returning heroes pay the extra.'

'In my experience they do.'

'Would you like to put a small wager on it?'

Iain's smile spreads from his lips to his eyes. For the first time in this encounter, they glow. 'You're on.'

Iain has never travelled first class before, not even when he acted for two or three weeks as batman to a young and rich lieutenant (not a Seaforth) who developed neurasthenia so rapidly he had to be shipped home to Blighty within the month. Still, third class in those days was treat enough. The fighting men travelled in freight cars marked Hommes 40 Chevaux 8. Rookies (Iain remembers doing this himself) always looked dolefully round the trucks jam-packed with human freight, wondering where the horses were going to fit. No, third class was palatial in France.

Now he climbs up into the clean and spacious compartment, with its cushioned upholstery and spotless linen anti-macassars, feeling immediately ill at ease. The face he sees reflected in the mirror below the luggage-rack where he slings his kit bag is hardly recognisable, thinned and aged by two years in the field, a little flushed now, with the sudden heat. At least he's no longer lousy, his uniform free at last of mud and parasites. It is such luxury to feel, to really be, clean. Hospital and the Fort have fixed that.

'You'll be going home for the holiday?' The VAD is sitting by the window, leaning back, watching him reflectively. Iain musters what charm he can.

'That's the general idea, yes. I've been demobbed, actually. I'm out of it. My platoon is in the army of occupation, but I got myself a Blighty in the last show.'

'And where are you from? Lewis?'

'Aye. What about yourself?'

The girl looks oddly furtive as she answers. 'The family.. have a house.. near Kyle. I'm going there for Christmas and the New Year. I'm not sure what I'll do after that; can't see myself going back to the boredom of just being a lady. Sit down, for heaven's sake, man. I don't bite!'

'Actually,' Iain laughs, 'I didn't for one moment suppose you did.' He sinks gratefully into the seat opposite the VAD who leans forward holding out her hand.

'Barbara. Barbara Ransome.'

'Pleased to meet you,' says Iain, taking the offered hand. Her grip is surprisingly strong. 'I'm Iain Murray.'

Barbara sinks back into her own chair now, as the whistle blows, the guard waves his flag and the train moves through a cloud of steam out of the station. They're sliding towards the black bridge over the Ness.

'So what did you do before you went to France, Iain?'

'Nothing exciting. I was the most unruly town hall clerk in Stornoway.'

Barbara smiles. 'And you'll go back to that?'

Iain considers, purses his lips. His head is not right. His limbs are heavy, aching. It's difficult for him to concentrate on such a trivial conversation. He struggles to sound normal as he replies.

'No. I can't see myself fitting into that kind of life, didn't like it that much before.'

'What will you do then?'

'I've been wondering,' says Iain, 'about Canada. They say there are lots of opportunities if you're not afraid of work.'

'It's a long way off, Canada.'

He shrugs. 'Not as far as France, I'm thinking.'

'Come now, it's much further!'

'Only in distance,' says Iain. 'Only in distance.'

He leans back against the head rest, staring out of the window now, at the mud flats of the Beauly Firth, remembering the flat ruined fields of France, the broken villages, the queues of ragged peasants who passed you on the cobbled roads, smelling little better than the troops they smiled at so patiently.

'Tommy! My sister very good jig-a-jig..'

'Tommy, Oofs? Dew Pan? Dew burr?'

'Tommy! Dew van rouge?'

The villagers beyond the line were more mercenary altogether; they intruded gaily with their business offers (though as Iain has noticed in London, and even in Scotland, war has been big business here too).

'My sister very good jig-a-jig..'

Not many of them were.

'Are you in pain?'

'Sorry?'

'You look as if you're in pain.. are you alright?'

'Not quite,' says Iain. 'Not in pain, I've a terrible aching all over. I'm too hot.'

'Open your tunic,' says Barbara.

'In public? That's a crime..'

'I thought you said you were demobbed.'

'I'd hate to have them change their minds.'

Iain leans back, suddenly weak. Barbara is beside him now. She checks his pulse – 100, fluttering, and his – brow – fevered.

'Have you had the influenza?'

'No,' says Iain proudly. 'I'm just about the only one at the Fort to have escaped it.'

He shivers, suddenly so cold his teeth are chattering

'I don't think you've escaped it. Look, lie back there. I've a travel rug in one of my cases..'

Iain shuts his eyes, feels his limbs covered by the softest blanket he has felt in years, perhaps all his life.

'I think I have some aspirin too,' she says.

'Maybe,' says Iain, 'I should move to another carriage.'

'I've had the influenza,' Barbara says, 'don't worry. Try and get some sleep.'

But sleep is difficult, even in the unaccustomed luxury of the first class carriage, even when he stretches out across the whole seat, with another of Barbara's blankets pillowed beneath him.

The inspector shakes his head over him.

'Poor lad doesn't look good.'

He doesn't come too close. Barbara asks him for a pillow to replace the second blanket. Even so, by the time they get to Kyle, Iain can hardly stand.

'You'll have to stay here for a few days, Iain,' Barbara says. 'Is anyone expecting you?'

'No,' says Iain. 'No one.'

'Then we'll send them a message when you're better.'

She half-carries him to a waiting cart and the furious gaze of its bearded middle-aged driver.

'Hamish,' she calls, 'come and help! We must make this poor boy comfortable in the back.'

Iain is eventually, and with not a little difficulty, settled in the cart on a bed of rugs and bags. Barbara sits up front with Hamish as they drive the three miles or so east from Kyle to Eilean Mor. It's starting to snow. Barbara shivers slightly.

'We'll put him in Teddy's room.'

'What will your mother say to that?'

'She's not here, Hamish.. she's not to know. If we'd put this poor chap on the *Sheila* he'd never make it to Stornoway. You can see how ill he is.'

Hamish looks back, sighs. Iain is flushed and sweating, delirious. From time to time he cowers as if ducking shell or shrapnel. He's mumbling away in Gaelic, the words unrecognisable to Barbara who has none. Hamish, following most of it, frowns.

'This boy's fought everywhere from Vimy to Passchendaele,' says Barbara. 'He can't be more than twenty.'

Hamish shrugs.

'Wild animals are always vicious.'

'These wild animals have been suffering hardship you would never dream of, Hamish. Don't be so judgmental. Think of Teddy! These poor boys have gone through hell, and they're going to have it hard enough without your criticism in this fine new world we've all made.'

'Hmmph. Fine words,' says Hamish.

'If you don't be quiet this minute, I'll dispense with your services, Hamish MacLaren, and you can walk back to Eilean Mor.'

'Hmmph.'

'I warned you.'

This time there's no reply. They travel on in silence, apart from Iain's groaning.

'What's he saying?'

'I couldn't possibly translate it, Miss Barbara.'

'Yes, you could.'

'He's talking about soft red hair.'

'What's wrong with that?'

'It's not for me to say, Miss Barbara. It seems he's an expert on moss-like hair. Whoever heard of red moss?'

Barbara giggles.

'What's he saying now?'

'That there is no one in France with eyes like Dulcie's but no one in Edinburgh with a.. ahem.. chest like Bernadette's.'

'And now?'

'That there is a coal-box coming over and we must run for it.'

'And now?'

'It's not repeatable. Miss Barbara, not even were you a man.'

Hamish starts to intone a loud Gaelic psalm, as if to drown out Iain's mumbling. He seems to hear it all the same, thinks Barbara, watching his expression.

Iain remembers very little of the next three days. When he comes to himself it's the day after Christmas. He opens his eyes in a high-ceilinged room filled with books and cricket bats. The bed he's sleeping in has a light wooden bed-board at head and foot, and the blankets are light and soft. There's a fire in the hearth on the wall opposite the bed, and in a chair beside the fire sleeps a tall thin girl with hair that wisps sweetly round her face. She looks a little familiar, no more than that.

Iain doesn't know this girl, or this room. He tries to sit up and falls weakly back against the cushions. The bed squeaks noisily. The girl stretches, opens her eyes, turns them immediately on Iain.

'You're awake at last,' she says. 'How are you feeling Iain?'

'Like the dog had me for breakfast.'

'He very nearly did. Do you remember me?'

Iain looks blank. He doesn't remember the face or the unusually low, rich voice.

'We met,' she goes on, 'on the train to Kyle. I'm Barbara

Ransome, and this is Eilean Mor, my parents' house near Kyle. You became ill on the train – influenza. We couldn't just shunt you on board the *Sheila*. That's why you're here. I've written to your family to say where you are; took the liberty of reading the address on the envelope of the letter in your pocket.'

Iain still looks mystified.

'I'll go and ask Morag for some chicken soup for you. You must try to eat, Iain, though you may not feel like it. It'll help you get your strength back.'

Barbara rises to her full five-feet seven.

Iain remembers now; the VAD on the platform. He feels as weak as a new-born calf. He tries again to sit up, coughs.

'Let me help you.'

Barbara lifts him, deftly arranging extra pillows behind his head.

'That's better, eh? I'll go and get that broth.'

She moves swiftly from the room, her footsteps muffled by the grey-green carpet. Iain stares around his new environment. It's very strange. To suddenly find himself awake, and in a place like this tall and narrow green room, with its scrubbed oak furniture.. there are pictures on the walls of cricket teams. Beside the bed is a large photograph of what Iain thinks must be a whole school – boys and masters standing dourly outside a castellated building. This is how the other half spent their childhood, Iain thinks.

There's a bookshelf at the foot of the bed, with dictionaries and encyclopaedias, a complete set of Dickens, and Palgrave's *Golden Treasury*. Most of the shelves are empty except for the cricket bats laid neatly on them.

'Not a reader,' Iain says aloud.

'I beg your pardon?'

Barbara has just swept back into the room with a steaming bowl of broth on a light wooden tray; a glass of milk too.

'Sorry,' Iain blushes, 'I was thinking aloud. I was thinking your brother isn't much of a reader.'

'Wasn't,' Barbara says. 'He preferred cricket.'

'Ah. Where did he?'

'Gallipoli. They sent some of his things back, a letter, the usual thing you know, *it's a jolly good show, I'm doing fine..* they sent this too.'

She leaves the tray on a table by the bed and moves to the mantelpiece, bringing Iain something small and dark.. a smooth flat stone, rounded.

'It bothers me,' says Barbara, 'that they sent this back. Why send a stone?'

'It was in his pocket?'

'Yes.'

'I wasn't in Gallipoli,' says Iain, 'but I know that when it's hot like that, and it's difficult to get supplies and water is scarce too – the men choose a stone and suck it. This must be your brother's stone – see, it's like a pandrop?'

Iain runs his fingers respectfully around the stone's smooth edges.

'What was his name?'

'Edward – Teddy. He went straight from school. Died on the hospital ship two days before Liverpool.'

'I'm sorry.'

Iain hands the stone back. 'I'd hold on to that,' he says.

'Thank you.' Barbara takes it, lays it on the mantelpiece. 'Your soup,' she says brightly, 'will be getting cold.'

'I should get up, sit in a chair to eat.'

'Tomorrow,' says Barbara *'Petit à petit l'oiseau fait son nid..'*

'Sorry? I don't understand?'

'Well, that makes up for all the Gaelic ravings of yours I couldn't follow.'

'Probably just as well,' Iain blushes.

'So Hamish said.. all the way back from Kyle. I've never seen him so red about the jowls.. how's the soup?'

'It's very good. Just right.'

Barbara manoeuvres the last of the broth on to the spoon.

'I'll leave the milk beside you. I'm going to get some fresh air now. Stay in bed. If you need anything, ring this bell,' here she indicates a small hand-bell on the table, 'and Morag will come.

She's lovely, much less disapproving than Hamish. Morag and I have been looking after you the last few days.'

'Days?' says Iain, dismayed.

'Yes it's the twenty-sixth today – you've really been through it. Still, as I said, we wrote to your parents. They know where you are. They know you've had the influenza.'

'I don't know why,' says Iain. 'But I wanted to be home for the New Year.'

'That's understandable. The first year of the peace. We'll see how you get on, Iain. You might make it yet. It is only the twenty-sixth. But you mustn't overdo it. You're not over that arm wound yet, and the earlier wound to your chest must have taken it out of you. Did you lose a lot of blood?'

'They kept draining it from my lung,' says Iain. 'But that's almost a year ago..'

'Your body's had a hard time,' Barbara nods. 'You'll have to give it space to heal.'

'You're very bossy for a VAD!'

'I'm not a VAD. I'm a surgeon. Was. Finding work in peacetime won't be quite so easy – not that I regret the peace,' Barbara smiles, slowly. 'Don't think that. I wish the war had never started.'

She picks up the stone again, rubbing it gently, before she places it beside the picture of young subaltern; then she turns back to Iain.

'Right. I'm off. I'll see you later.'

'Where are you going?'

'Nowhere. I like to take the dogs through the woods. Get my head clear.'

'Barbara..'

'Yes?'

She's almost at the door.

'Thank you. You've been very kind to me.'

'How would you know? You've been on a different planet for the last three days.'

'I've been on a different planet for the last two and half years! But I mean it. Thank you.'

'Try and get some sleep, Iain. We'll talk later.'

Iain sinks back into the pillows, content to let things drift. He's still conscious of a general ache throughout his body, and though his headache's nearly gone there is still a shadow of the pain flickering behind his eyes. He has no idea where he is, but weakness is the all-pervading state he finds himself in. He can do nothing about it. His usual review of a new situation, be it billet or trench, is no longer applicable – he can do nothing about food, water, possible danger, communication, protection against weather, provision of fuel and light – but sanitation, now.. perhaps he needs to do something about that. He stretches for the bell, rings it.

It's not Morag, but Hamish that comes to answer.

'You must be Hamish,' says Iain feebly. 'I'm sorry if I was swearing in the fever, Hamish.'

'You were swearing and more than that,' says Hamish, stiffly, 'but there's no doubt you had the fever right enough.'

'I need to relieve myself,' says Iain. 'But I don't know where to go.'

'I'll bring you a pot,' says Hamish.

'No, I'd rather go..' says Iain, lifting the covers back. Even that small movement takes an effort. He tries to stand, topples over.

'I'll bring a pot,' says Hamish.

Barbara Ransome walks through the Caledonian pine that stretch behind Eilean Mor back up to the road. It's a daft name for the house, Eilean Mor, particularly daft so near the blue hills of Skye, for all that it was built on a tidal island. Lochalsh is beautiful though. There's no denying that, even at this time of year when the mist hangs heavy and the light sinks back into night shortly after three. Such a difference there from London. She doesn't want to go back, doesn't want to marry Archie, spend her life raising a clan for him. Yes, he's lively. Yes, he's interesting. Yes, he makes her laugh. Yes, there are times he makes her heart beat faster, but no more than that poor boy in Teddy's room does. Seeing him on the platform in Inverness, with his neat light hair, and proud profile and something about the way he held his body, for all the illness, all the hard times written in his bearing.. something about Iain Murray touched her. If he was well, what a figure of a man he'd be.

'Cuchullin! Dileas!' She calls the dogs to heel, having reached the bridge, the highest point on her walk. 'Here, Cuchullin! Come!'

The dogs run yapping towards her and she pats their golden heads.

'Good boy, good girl.'

She always carries a biscuit in her pocket for them.

No, there is no doubt, if she were being absolutely truthful, that if Iain Murray were well (which luckily, perhaps, he isn't) she would feel quite different towards him. His influenza puts him beyond lust; he's a patient to her now, and she has only ten more days in which to decide whether or not to accept Archie's offer. Her mother is desperately anxious that she should. (How old-fashioned of Archie to have approached her father over the matter, as if they hadn't already, as he put it, hit the hay.)

'But Barbara, you can't go away at Christmas! It's only the second Christmas since..'

'I know it's hard, but I've got to try and clear my mind. I'll go up to Eilean Mor. Do some walking.'

'You're a selfish madam,' her father said.

'I know,' Barbara conceded. 'I have always modelled myself on you.'

And here she is, trying to choose between a life with Archie and a life spent wearing spectacles, looking suitably serious, blue-stocking, yet not shocking people, being earnest, strong.. concealing this behind a veil of appropriately feminine apparent indecision and incapability.. which would be more tedious? She had, it must be said, already purchased spectacles. And yet.

'Come Dileas! Cuchullin! Heel!'

Even Hamish refuses to take her seriously. In war you were eventually taken seriously. Her talents had been exercised almost as much in the troop hospitals in England as they might have been in France. Not much chance of that now.

She wanders back through the gathering mist and into the scullery where she sheds her outdoor coat and boots. Cuchullin and Dileas drink water energetically from their individual dishes – each one, as usual, drinking from the other's – before slinking to their baskets.

The kitchen is warm and light; Morag lights the lamps at the first sign of dusk. She's busy now, preparing dinner, kneading away at the puff pastry.

'Where's himself?'

Morag smiles, a tight and narrow smile. She raises her grey eyebrows, almost to the white cap she insists on wearing at all times.

'In with the boy. He's been there all afternoon, newsing away in the Gaelic. Just like you said he would. And ringing that bell, ordering tea and cakes as if he thinks I've nothing better to do, or am I running a teashop!'

'I'll get my own cup.'

'You'll do nothing of the sort. You'll sit there and wait till I finish this wee bit of work. Seems a nice enough lad,' pechs Morag, 'even if he is a Lewisach.'

'You must let me listen to that chest of yours,' says Barbara. 'The breathlessness is sounding worse.'

'Oh, it's nothing,' says Morag, 'time won't cure.'

She puts the pastry aside in its cool ceramic bowl, and slams the kettle on the hob.

'Nice walk?'

'It was lovely. I saw Jimmy the Post, Morag. Anything for me?'

'Yes, one or two things actually. They're in the hall. Let me get them for you.'

'No, you get the tea. I'll slip through.'

Barbara moves into the shadow of the hall, finds the tray on the sideboard by feel rather than sight. She scoops up all three letters and goes back into the kitchen, tossing them on the table.

'I've not cleaned that yet!'

Barbara retrieves the letters, flicking through them.

One from her mother. Oh dear, not again. One from Archie.. and yes, one from Edinburgh. She opens this last.. *Dear Dr Ransome, It is with regret..* she stuffs the page of copperplate back in the heavy vellum envelope. It had been a long shot. She hadn't really expected that they would consider her application seriously.

'Great tea, Morag. No one in the world makes tea like you.'

'It's the water, I'm thinking,' Morag nods. 'It's that pure.'

As she brushes her hair that night, Barbara sighs. She is no nearer reaching a decision. She can see Archie, almost see him, as she reads his letter, his cheerful handsome face, his kind concern for others. Though he'd been in France, he'd never got beyond Harfleur, where he lectured to the troops on keeping happy in the trenches when he wasn't acting as liaison officer. His excellent French kept him well behind the lines, on staff duties. Not that he liked it. He was wangling himself an urgent ticket even now, desperate to rid himself of military stringency that irked in war and made conscripts mutinous in peacetime. He wanted to stand for Parliament. If she marries Archie there will be no medicine, but the way things are going, there will be no medicine anyway. What will she do? What can she do?

Barbara stands up, ties her dressing gown tight about her, and moves through the cooling house to the kitchen for a glass of milk. She knows the house so well, she does not take a candle. There is a moon too, and its silver-blue light is casting shadows in the hall. When she was a child and they came here for Christmas and New Year to visit the grand-parents, Barbara used to take delight in wandering round the house after dark. She had never, unlike Teddy, been frightened of ghosts, or darkness, odd noises in the night. Who was there to harm them? She used to try to reason with him. It never worked. Often she would find him curled up in a panic in the corner of the landing, afraid to go upstairs. Poor Teddy. What had he known of life? She's been thinking of him more and more since the armistice. Having Iain in his room will have something to do with it too – a boy of roughly the same age, a boy who's been in the shadow and somehow, lived through it. It's odd, thinks Barbara, how the shadow on the half-landing takes on Teddy's shape. She moves towards it, hears it whimpering.

'Teddy..?'

Barbara is not one of those who puts their faith in spiritualism, but the shape grows more and more like the solid image of her brother. Teddy?

She stretches her hand out slowly to the shaking shadow. Teddy? The shadow is warm, is living, breathing flesh.. Teddy?

A torrent of Gaelic reaches her unbelieving ears. She bends down, shaking.

'Iain, what are you doing out of bed? Hamish!' she calls out. 'Hamish!'

When Morag and Hamish come running down the stairs, they find Iain still shouting in Gaelic, and Barbara trying to soothe him.

'What's he saying?'

'He says he doesn't want to die in the trenches,' says Hamish. 'He's asking us to pull him from the mud.'

'Poor boy,' says Morag. 'I'll put the kettle on.'

'We can carry him between us,' says Barbara. 'Tell him he'll soon be out of here, to put his arms around us.'

Hamish translates this for Iain and, though he is so weak that their progress is slow, they eventually reach Teddy's ground-floor room. Iain seems to fall asleep the moment his head touches the pillow.

'I'll sleep in here tonight, I think,' says Hamish. 'The poor lad may take to wandering again.'

'It's not unlikely,' Barbara says. 'That's very good, Hamish. You go and get the camp bed. I'll sit with him meanwhile.'

A few moments later Iain opens his eyes. He looks at Barbara with such an expression of joy that she is almost overwhelmed by it.

'Dulcie.. I..' he stammers. 'You do see? I've got to find Mairi.. make things right. But it's you I love, Dulcie.. tell me you'll be alright. Tell me you'll be alright. Tell me Dulcie!'

His voice is is rising, louder and louder and the grip on her wrist is iron-tight.

'I'm fine, Iain. I'm fine. I miss you, but I'm fine.'

'I knew,' says Iain, 'you had strength. You and me, Dulcie what a pair we would have been.'

He lies exhausted on his pillows. His fingers unloose themselves. Barbara rubs her wrists. What was it Hamish said? Vicious? This boy, weakened as he is, would fight his corner. She wonders who Dulcie is, and Mairi. Poor soul. Poor Mairi. And poor Dulcie. Barbara guesses Iain will not have been in touch with either. It's a not uncommon pattern.

'Miss Barbara, your tea is in the kitchen.'

Hamish has come back with a folding bed and blankets.

'Thank you, Hamish. Good night. I hope you have a peaceful one.'

'We'll be fine,' says Hamish. 'Never you worry. I'll look after the lad.'

'He couldn't be in better hands.'

Next day Iain wakens to the sight and sound of Hamish snoring on the creaking camp bed. It's still very dark, no more than six. The window on the wall opposite his bed, uncurtained, looks south across the Kyle, not that it's visible yet. He has to get on his feet, must be home for the New Year. He owes it to his mother to be there this year. Afterwards, who knows? Canada seems more and more an exciting prospect, and it seems he's still a free agent; something that excites and worries him.

He needs to find out if Mairi's had the child yet. He's had no reply from Calum – regrettable but hardly surprising – and as little response from Aeneas, to whom he had written after Maisie's death. The man is, of course, beside himself with grief, the whole island knows that, just as the whole island seems to know Mairi's baby is Calum's, but she won't have him, and no wonder, they say, he's that moody after all – but a strange move that, Calum lodging with Aeneas. And they say, no longer going to the church, though the owner of the *Oran* is threatening to give him notice.

Then of course there's Dulcie. Iain is tired of women, their over-reaching fecundity. Why can't they just do it for the pleasure in a simple way, like men?

Not that it's been all that simple recently. Since the armistice, since this last wound, he's found it harder and harder to feel at all excited, to function. Last week in Inverness with that girl in Falcon Square, he'd found he couldn't do it.. couldn't get it up at all. She laughed, thought he was shy. He went along with her conclusion. It saved him loss of face. The money, of course, was irretrievable. He bought her a drink in the hotel opposite the station.

'Slainte!' she said.

'Slainte mhor!' he prayed.

When he first went to France he'd had this thing about Mairi, used to see her face before him when he visited the Red Lamps. Then, gradually, he'd forgotten her living face: the only photo he had was a bit severe, virginal, with Calum in the background too. Then he used to think of Bernadette, this girl (he calls her girl, but she was in her thirties certainly), this girl from an estaminet known for her kindness. Kindness to soldiers meant only one thing in France, and it wasn't the type of care he was receiving here, no sir. He used to think of Bernadette latterly, but not her face, no not her face; her full heavy breasts were what he saw, what he touched, on even the oldest, scrawniest of Red Lamp women.

He got crab-lice from Bernadette, thought it was the clap, thought he'd be clapped in irons, but no, the MO laughed at him and quoted the *three seconds with Venus three years with Mercury* adage at him. Threw him some Blue ointment and told him to invest in prophylactics.

'You mean like they say in the "How to keep happy in the trenches" lectures, Sir?'

'Watch it, Murray. I'll have you on a charge.'

But the MO was feeling good that day. Iain got off with it. Come to think of it, that was the time the poems fell out of his pocket, and the MO saw and demanded to see what Iain was hiding so furtively.

'These are yours?' he asked in disbelief.

'Why shouldn't they be?'

'Because you're the biggest cynic in the Battalion! These are.. *good*!' The MO choked.

Iain blushed.

'If I could have them back please, Sir?'

'Come back for them tomorrow.'

'Sir, it's kind of private, you know? I wouldn't want..'

'You wouldn't want your shit-hard image cracked?'

'Not with the ranks, Sir.'

Iain had been happy enough for the officers to know he was an intellectual. A *private* intellectual. The best sort.

The poems had become an addiction with him; the need to scribble in quiet moments. You didn't have to hide the activity. Most folk thought you were writing home. If Eddie Shields had known, though, that Iain was a poet.. that would have been a different matter. He wished he had paper and a pencil now. The bell-like sound of Hamish's snoring in the early grey of morning would have been a start, the light slowly settling on the dead boy's cricket bats, his only reading.. the few books on the shelves obviously unread, like his life – unread but not, Iain thinks, unused. The lieutenants understood that sort of thing. They respected other men, tough men, who understood it too. The Ewans and John-Angus's of the platoon were not exactly cannon-fodder to these young lieutenants, but less important than a man who knew about metre and rhyme. And did not boast about it.

It had won Iain many's the shared bottle of whisky in the foulest dug-outs of the day. And the writing itself had often helped to still him, centre him. There was no point in looking far beyond the orgasm of line, of verse.

What is he doing here? He should be home. If only his head were not so fucking light.

*　　　*　　　*

On Christmas day, Aeneas comes downstairs to find that Calum has already made breakfast for him – it's on the kitchen table, porridge and kippers, tea and toast. Beside his plate is a parcel neatly wrapped in shiny brown paper.

'What's this?'

He looks across the kitchen table to Calum. They've got into the habit of eating breakfast here, where it's warmer. Chrissie doesn't come in till after eight. She cleans the house and bakes for them and cooks the midday meal, which they eat, for form's sake, in the dining-room. Tea and breakfast are more comfortable in the kitchen, at the old pine table. It's warmer too. Sometimes they sit long into the night over a glass of beer, a dram, putting the world to rights. Aeneas finds these nights oddly soothing. The nights Calum is writing, he tiptoes round the house as if it were the Sabbath.. till half-past ten when he insists on taking Calum up a wee dram. Just to settle the mind, as he says.

Now he stands beside his chair, staring at the parcel; after a moment or two he reaches down, picks it up.

'What's this?' he asks again.

Calum blushes, twisting round to reach the brown metal teapot on the warming plate. The handle is too hot. He burns his fingers, shakes them, grips the teapot handle with a dishtowel.

'Nothing really, just a very small Christmas present. Tea?'

Aeneas's expression drifts from curiosity to pleased surprise.

'Why, thank you, Calum. I haven't had a Christmas present since I was a boy. Well, well.. a Christmas present.'

Calum smiles, pours the tea. Aeneas still stands at the table, holding the parcel, playing with the string.

'Open it, go on..'

'I haven't got a present for you.'

'I wasn't expecting one.'

Aeneas still hesitates. His thin face, so wrinkled, aged, since Maisie's death, looks curiously young.

'I'm reminded,' he says at last, 'of the birthday presents my mother used to give me when I was a child. I must have been six, the first time, I think, six or maybe seven.. and I could see the huge box standing by the table – couldn't wait to open it.. I was that excited, wondering what would be inside. A drum? A ball? A wooden ship? When I opened the box, I found a pair of stout leather boots, brown boots for school.. and my mother standing there, so proud and pleased, telling me I need no longer go barefoot – so sure I would be happy that I had to pretend I was. But I spent the rest of the day wishing I had left the parcel wrapped. And every birthday afterwards, there would be a large box for me, waiting by the table, a replacement pair. My mother said she always knew exactly what to get me; I was always so delighted with a good pair of boots.'

'It's not a pair of boots,' says Calum. 'I'll tell you that much. It's something I made myself. I'm good, but not that handy. I couldn't make a pair of boots.. though I could tell you where to buy one, right enough.'

Aeneas unties the string and slips the smooth brown paper from a navy leather-bound album, filled from cover to cover with handwritten text about the island, and all of Calum's own arranging: legends, history, even the geology and current land-use; and illustrations, hand-coloured sketches he has made over the years. The first page bears the title, beautifully illuminated: *Legends of the Storm.*

'But it's beautiful,' Aeneas says. 'Why have you not published this?'

'I made it for you.' Calum blushes now, looks down at his plate.

'I'm aware of that.. but I think this is quite commercial, Calum. Think of all the folk from Lewis in Canada alone. Think of all of the Canadian Lewis boys cooped up across Scotland in camps, waiting for their ticket home.. think how many of them you and I know between us! Wouldn't this be the perfect gift for them to take back with them? We could do well publishing this, boy.. but not, of course, unless you're agreeable to the idea.'

'It's a great idea,' says Calum. 'I'm glad you feel like that Aeneas. I didn't want to tell you, not till after the holiday, but I've been given notice from the *Oran*. No one in Stornoway will buy the paper while I'm editing it, or so the directors say. So I'm for the mainland, I think. Who'd give me work on this island?'

Aeneas thumps the table. 'That damned Bethune!'

'Och, he won't change, Aeneas; and really, it doesn't worry me. It's a fundamental disagreement I have with the God-fearing folk of the island. And it's little enough they have. I appreciate their position. They don't, can't, see mine. Eat your breakfast now, before it gets cold.'

'But,' Aeneas says, 'eccentricity frowned on in an editor can be perfectly acceptable in a writer! Or a publisher. And with your printing and organisational skills, we could set up right away.. Morrison and MacDonald, printers and publishers. Sounds good, eh?'

'I think you'd be taking a big risk.'

'Not at all.' Aeneas looks through the book again. 'This is good stuff. What's more, Calum, in a year or two we could look at those war stories of yours. They would really sell, and not just on the island.'

'I don't think,' says Calum, 'I could use my own name for them.'

'No need,' says Aeneas. 'They're universal, boy. They're about the island at war, yes, but they're also about any boy from any small community, and even in cities they have small communities, as many have found to their cost these last few years. I'd do the advertising. I'd enjoy that. A new challenge. Peggy and Colin have the shop so well in hand I'm hardly needed there.'

Calum sits, astonished, shaking his head. Aeneas seems perplexed at that.

'You don't think it's a good idea?'

'It's a marvellous idea. Wonderful. We'll start tomorrow, if you're sure. Today, if you like.'

'Yes, and we must be on the lookout for other island talent.'

'We certainly must.'

Throughout the morning, they sit in the kitchen, working on the idea, making plans, writing lists, thinking of suitable premises, necessary equipment. Aeneas keeps modifying his plan. It gets grander all the time.

'And of course,' he twinkles, 'you'll need to grow your hair a bit, Calum.'

'Why?'

'All famous writers have long hair and bootlace ties. Or plaids.'

'Not in Lewis they don't!'

They carefully do not mention Mairi, though Calum is very much aware that the baby must be imminent. A sense of honour keeps him from reading Mairi's letters to her father, though Aeneas leaves these scattered through the house, a house that is, it must be said, much less tidy than it was when Maisie was alive, for all Chrissie's efforts, Calum's too.

Calum lives in dread that the birth will go horribly wrong, and Mairi die. So many young girls die in childbirth. The odds may be better in Edinburgh, perhaps; he doesn't know. Fear is stalking him these nights, keeping him awake, fear for Mairi and the child. He lies unsleeping, worrying, his throat dry, heart racing, head in turmoil. In the first few weeks he lived here, he sometimes used to slip through to her room at night, just to sit where she had lived so long. Somehow it stilled the loneliness, brought her closer. It doesn't work now. The room feels empty, but for the furniture, the clothes, the books. Mairi's not there. She is gone. He knows the gossip in the town about the baby's parentage; it doesn't bother him if people think he is the father, quite the reverse. If only Mairi were here, and he could touch her, talk to her.

Aeneas, seeing his struggle, says nothing, having nothing to offer that will be of any comfort. Before Christmas, he wrote to Mairi, specifically mentioning Calum; saying what a pleasant boy, what a helpful lodger he has turned out to be. She has not replied and Aeneas is afraid she may be suffering, though Esther's letters seem as encouraging as ever. At this stage in pregnancy, Maisie had found life well-nigh impossible; she'd been breathless, cross, unusually emotional. It had been such a relief to them both once the ordeal of labour was got through.. and an ordeal it had been. Maisie never quite recovered from it. The puerperal fever didn't help. It seems so long ago. Nineteen years, not so long; his poor Maisie.. but he mustn't go down that road, not today.

He looks up from his list, opens his mouth, closes it. Opens it again.

'I.. I forgot to say I was speaking to Catriona Murray yesterday, Calum. She tells me Iain is stuck in Kyle now, with a bout of influenza.'

'There are so many down with that!'

'Aye, and it so virulent. Let's hope we escape it, you and I. Still, it looks as if we'll be seeing Iain back on the island for a short time at least. There's something about that boy you can't completely dislike..'

There is no response from Calum. Returning to his list, Aeneas finds himself humming a few bars of 'The Dark Ship'. When Calum first came to the house, he used to play and sing that tune all the time.

'But you haven't played your fiddle for weeks now, Calum, lad. Go and get it out. Play to me. You know how I love it. Will Alec be round later?'

'I think so, after work.'

'Have you told your parents about the paper?'

'No.'

'Tell them I offered you a job in publishing,' Aeneas suggests. 'Tell them that first.'

Calum shrugs.

'It really doesn't make a difference. It's a matter of principle'.

'Sometimes,' Aeneas says, 'principles get firmly in the way of life. Go and see your parents, a' bhalach. Don't break with them completely. They love you.'

'They don't understand.'

'No reason why they should.. just as there's no need for you to alter your convictions on their behalf. You're your own man, and big enough to see their corner too.'

Calum raises his eyebrows.

'Where were you brought up, Aeneas?'

'Here, as you well know. In a cottage very like your father's. But I had the good fortune to meet and marry Maisie. A rigorous intellect she had.'

'You were very much in love,' says Calum.

'Always.'

Aeneas can say no more. His eyes are brimming with tears, the love, naked grief and loss almost palpable. Calum fills the kettle, slams it on the stove.

IOLAIRE

(Eagle)

Barbara Ransome wakes early on Hogmanay; not that she's slept well, not at all. She knows Iain is determined to cross the Minch today, though he's by no means fit, still very weak and breathless on exertion. There's little to be gained in arguing with him, but through the night she had an idea, a good idea. She has seen, in the drapers in Kyle, thick woollen vests; they would at least keep him warm. She'll get Hamish to drive into town for a pair of them; he could get Iain's ticket too, check the time of the *Sheila's* sailing. And he could wire Iain's parents, ask them to meet him at the other end.

They have all enjoyed his stay, for all that he was so ill at the start of it. He's an able boy, likes to write, which surprised her. He hadn't seemed the type.. but then, she thinks, what is? Iain is intelligent, curious. He has a ruthless sense of humour. He's excellent company. He hasn't spoken any more about the Dulcie he'd mistaken her for in his fever, hasn't mentioned a Mairi either; Barbara is wondering now if either girl exists.

His pulse was very uneven yesterday, and listening to his chest she'd heard a murmur, a loud one. When she told him he laughed and said he felt fine, perfect, actually, but he'd get Doctor Smith to check him over after the holiday. Barbara advised rest, a delay in travelling of a week, maybe two.. though she'll be away herself, Hamish and Morag live at Eilean Mor the year round. They'd look after him. Iain wouldn't hear of it.

'No, Barbara,' he laughed. 'You've done far too much already. I need to get home.'

There was no more she could say.

It's still dark when she rises, the morning wet and rainy. Early as she is, she finds Morag in the kitchen, the stove already busy, ovens and table full.

'What on earth are you up to?'

'Och,' says Morag, 'I thought I'd make the boy a scone for the journey. And cake for his mother too. It's Hogmanay after all.'

'That's lovely, Morag.' Barbara curls into the big pine chair between the stove and the table.

'The tea's hot. Would you like a cup?'

'Certainly would,' Barbara yawns. 'Oh, Morag.. that boy needs another two weeks in his bed, at least'

'He'll not listen to any of us, Miss Barbara. And we've all three told him to stay put. Even Hamish! He's offered to take him to fish his own special pool! But all Iain said was he'd come back in the season for it.'

'The special pool..' Barbara raises her eyebrows.

'It's like having young Teddy back.'

'Yes,' says Barbara. 'Yes it is, a little.'

Morag's shaping and cutting the scone mixture, laying each frilled pebble on the greased baking tray. Her fingers work neatly and swiftly. Barbara never tires of watching the nimble handiwork.

'How do you do it so fast?'

Morag smiles, 'Practice. Years of it. So..' she cuts another line of scone, 'have you decided, then?'

'Decided what, Morag?'

'Whatever it is you're going to do.. I doubt but there's a young man at the other end of all these letters.'

'Morag, you see too much.'

'Practice. Years of it.'

Barbara sighs. 'I don't know what to do. I do like Archie, but he wants to go into politics. He's fun, though, Morag. Fun but not light-weight.'

'That's quite a mixture. Does he have a big nose like the man in the French story you and Teddy were always acting?'

'What do you mean, big nose?'

'There must be something putting you off.'

'No, he's good-looking. Not like Cyrano. Oh Morag.. remember the fun Teddy used to get out of constructing those amazing noses.. wooden, paper..'

'The one I liked,' said Morag, 'was the papier mâché effort he tried to model on himself!'

'Oh yes! And it must have been so difficult for him to lie still for how long was it – two hours?'

'And he was that heartbroken when it hadn't set!' says Morag, laughing so hard now her sides are starting to ache. 'That boy!'

'What boy?' says Hamish, sweeping into the kitchen. 'Good morning Miss Barbara. What's this about a boy?

'We were just talking about Teddy making all those false noses.. remember, Hamish, when we used to do that play about the Frenchman with the long nose..'

'As if I would ever be able to forget? Wasn't it always me had to wear them? Is there any tea, Morag?'

'In the pot. You'd better pour some for Miss Barbara too, she's been waiting patiently for the last hour.'

'No, I haven't! But I would like tea. Hamish,' says Barbara, 'I wondered if you'd go up to Kyle and find out when the *Sheila's* going to sail. I think we should book Iain on to it. I'm sure it will be busy, and we don't want him standing around for hours in the cold. Oh, and Hamish, I thought you might buy a couple of those thick woollen vests from Chisholm's. We'll give them to him. Even if he wore them both at once, it wouldn't be a bad idea.'

'It's a grand idea,' says Hamish.

'And if you give them to him, he'd probably wear them,' says Barbara. 'You know what he's like.'

'I do indeed,' says Hamish. 'That's good thinking Miss Barbara. I'll get off right away.'

'What about your breakfast?'

'I'll just take one or two of these,' says Hamish, scooping up some of Morag's pancakes.

She slaps his hand. 'They're for Iain!'

'There's plenty more!'

Hamish fairly runs out of the kitchen with his contraband, almost knocking Iain over in the hall.

'Good morning, lad. And how are you feeling this morning?'

Iain holds himself straighter.

'Fine,' he says, 'ready for the road. Where are you off to so early?'

'I'm away to get your ticket,' says Hamish. 'There were twenty-two ratings sleeping on the quay last night in Kyle. We want to make sure that doesn't happen to you.'

'No indeed, that would be awful,' Iain says.

'And I'm going to buy you a fishing quality vest and make you put it on to keep the sea air out.'

'Sounds good,' says Iain.

After breakfast, Barbara calls the dogs to heel. Every morning at this time she walks them through the wood.

'Where are you off to?'

'Just round the grounds. Do you want to come?'

'I'd like that fine,' Iain nods. 'I'll get my coat. They're good these overcoats,' he says. 'I'm going to hold on to mine.'

They emerge into the morning's drizzle. Dileas and Cuchullin race on ahead of them, yelping with pleasure. Barbara begins briskly, is forced to modify her stride to Iain's lack of fitness. The ground is soggy underfoot. As they walk there is only the sound of the soft rain falling, and twigs and cones snapping underfoot; the soft fresh smell of the Scots pine they are walking through fills the damp grey morning. Iain thinks he has never known anywhere quite as beautiful as Eilean Mor. He turns to his silent companion.

'It's not like you to be so quiet. Is there something bothering you?'

'Nothing new,' says Barbara. 'I don't think you're fit for travelling, but you already know that, just as you already know you're not.'

'I'm better than I was.'

'Granted.'

'And it's Hogmanay.'

'Yes.'

'And I want to see my family.'

'I can understand all of that. But look how breathless you get even on the slightest hill.'

'It's been like that since the chest wound,' says Iain. 'That's partly why I ended up with the second Blighty.'

'Why were you ever sent back?'

'I told them I was fit.'

'Why did you do that?'

'Don't know. They were sending everyone anyway.'

Iain trudges on in silence. Barbara doesn't break it.

'Yes,' he says eventually, 'I do know. Going back was easier for me, less complicated than staying in Scotland would have been. Personal matters.'

Barbara waits. Iain says no more.

'And have you resolved these.. personal matters?'

'No. Don't know. It's one of the reasons I need to go back.'

He stops, sits on a rock at the edge of the path, out of breath, ostensibly watching Dileas and Cuchullin chase a rabbit in the undergrowth. He coughs, gently at first, then deeper, faster. When the paroxysm ends it leaves him red-faced, weak. It takes him an age to catch his breath.

'You've been so kind, Barbara. A good friend. I've never had a woman friend. They're usually.. well.. let's just say it's been a pleasure getting to know you without lust intervening.'

'Is that a compliment, I wonder?'

'Oh yes,' Iain looks right into Barbara's eyes, and there's not a hint of flirtation there, no coyness. 'Up till now I've haven't talked to a single woman in my life except my mother and wee sisters without assessing the possibilities.. like some soldiers assess risk.. one in fifty, one in ten and so on. You're a lovely girl, Barbara, but I think because you've been my doctor, there's been a useful distance.. you've been a colleague and helper, not an object.. nor in any way a rival, as some men are. You've been a real friend.

'I think,' he says reflectively, 'you may have felt the same. You're a strong character. The girl I love, she's quite like you.'

'She's on the island?'

'No. She's in Edinburgh. If she's still there. There's another girl, not so independent, not so strong: she was on the island. I don't know where she is now. I have to try to find her.'

He coughs again, struggles to suppress it.

'You know, my mother spoke to me the night before I went off to the Seaforths. She told me people judge us by our deeds, not our words, not our aspirations. Our deeds speak for us as sharp and succinctly as the Beasts of Holm breach the sea at Holm Point. Everyone can see them. She's right too. You're like my mother, in some ways. She's quiet. Sees everything. That's one side of the story,' says Iain, standing up, stamping his feet. He rubs his hands, stares through the wood, embarrassed now, unable to face Barbara after so much honesty. He pretends to look for the dogs, but Dileas and Cuchullin are nowhere to be seen.

'The other half of me,' he says as if to himself, 'wants to slip away to Canada and start over again, making all the same mistakes.'

'You wouldn't do that,' says Barbara. 'You're too intelligent.'

'Wouldn't I?' says Iain. 'You don't know me! Not like my mother does.'

Barbara shivers, 'We should be getting back.'

'Yes. I'm not really fit for the climb, not that it's much of one..'

'These things take time. I told you. You mustn't overdo it. Your heart's been badly weakened, Iain.'

'That must be why it's fluttering these days like a bird inside a cage.'

'Yes.'

'Dulcie, the girl I love,' says Iain. 'She has these two birds – budgerigars, they're called. One green, one blue. She got them from a friend who'd been afraid to let them fly. They'd been in their cage – and it was tiny, mind – for two years. Dulcie wasn't having any of that; her birds, and they were now her birds, you understand, were never going to lose the power of flight. So she spent hours with them with the cage doors open, and they wouldn't come out, Barbara. There was no way they were coming out. She couldn't even starve them out and offer food. It simply didn't work. She perseveres – or did – trying every morning to give those birds their freedom. They never take it. But when the door shuts, Jude, that's the bigger of them – claws his way to a corner of the cage, the furthest from the door; and he pecks at those bars, and he tries to bend them in his beak, and he sticks his wings between the bars trying to slip through them. But go through the open door? Too scary. Is that what my heart's doing, Barbara?'

'No,' she says. 'Not your heart.'

They amble on in silence for a few moments. Even at the slow pace, Iain's breaking sweat.

'Have you ever been to Lewis?'

'I'm afraid not.'

'You'd miss the trees,' says Iain. 'These are Scots pine, aren't they? Generous trees.'

'I think so.'

'This is the most beautiful wood I've ever seen. When I think what passed for wood in France – splintered stumps and corpses – it's criminal what we do to our world, to ourselves, Barbara. Listen.. what's that?'

Barbara listens. 'Just a thrush.'

'It's music. There are so many musics, if we only listen.'

'Do you ever listen to yourself?'

Iain stops. 'What do you mean?'

'You talk such good sense. Do you ever listen to it?'

He shrugs, shakes his head. 'When I'm able.'

Hamish rolls back mid-morning with the news that the *Sheila* is likely to be inundated with naval ratings, two train-loads of them, coming home on New Year leave.

'But never worry,' he says, 'the Admiralty are sending the *Iolaire* over from *Stornoway*, and I've booked you on the *Sheila*. You'll get on, all right. They said to bring you along at three. That's just before the train's expected. We should be able to get you a good seat inside.'

'Thank you, Hamish,' smiles Iain. 'You're a good man.'

'We'll need to get you packed, then.'

'That won't take long. '

'Have you seen the amount of baking Morag's been doing for you?'

'I'll never be able to carry it!'

'I'll take it on board for you, and likely you'll have friends at the other end. I wired your father to say you'd be on the boat and need transport.'

'What a sergeant you'd have made'

'Aye, if I was twenty years younger. Come on, lad. Let's get organised.'

Hamish whisks Iain off to his room and leaves him sitting in a chair while all his belongings are carefully packed into the one bag.

'What a neat job!'

'Practice. Years of it. Now you'll not forget, Iain, that fishing date? It's not everybody gets the offer.'

'I'll be over like a shot!'

'We'll do some shooting later in the year. You'll be feeling better then. I know it's rough; must have been awful over there.'

'Yes, it was, Hamish. But there's a great spirit too, in the lads; a reliance on each other. I've never seen the like. It changes all the rules, but then the rules are all to hell anyway.'

'You're home now. Nearly home.'

'Aye. As good as.'

'Put your feet up, Iain. I'll call you for dinner.'

Iain leans back on the chair, closes his eyes. He's asleep by the time Hamish has left the room.

*   *   *

Catriona Murray is alone in the croft when she sees old Nessie walking slowly over the road, past the township. There is only one house she'll be coming to. Catriona shivers, suddenly cold.

It's not just the weather. She dreamt last night that an eagle roosting in her cottage dropped an iron ring on the hearth, breaking the stone, scattering the fire. This is a bad omen, Catriona is sure; the roosting bird, the ring that binds, the iron that will break her heart. Worst of all the scattered fire. She will not rest till Iain is safe home. The telegram, meantime, is coming nearer. Nearer.

But old Nessie is smiling.

'Good news, good news, Catriona,' she calls. 'Your boy will be on the *Sheila* tonight. He'll be home for the New Year! He's not that well, but much better.'

'Thank God!' Catriona cries.

Nessie hugs her, stays long enough for a warming cup of tea and sets off on the long road home. By the time she leaves, she has told Catriona all the main news of the day: the boys coming home, of course, so many of them, so many island homes busy today preparing for the future; then there's the new publishing firm Aeneas and Calum are setting up.. most folk think Aeneas is sliding off the rails, but well, he's had a terrible year, poor man; and last but not least, she says, there's his poor wee girl. Mairi is in labour, and not doing all that well. So the telegram said.

Catriona thinks of the lass, her pleasant untroubled face, when last seen. Such a shame. The word is that it's Calum's child which somehow doesn't fit. She waves Nessie along the coast road, but does not immediately enter the house. The tiny grave on the cliff top seems to beckon her. She has no flowers for it, but there's a stick of dried honesty growing just beside the door. She plucks that, walks the short distance up to the grave, the plain white stone she'd chosen and carried up herself from the shore. She sticks the honesty as firmly in the turf as it will go, the blond dried leaves rustling in the gale, its quiet tune drowning in the greater blast.

The sea is grey today, angry beyond the rocks, the surge between rocks and shore forcing spume and spray high in the air. It screams towards her, clawing at her face, her skin. It's a foul day right enough. As to the other.. maybe her anxiety is founded on nothing more than wind and driving rain.

She pulls her shawl tighter round her shoulders, hurries inside to start the New Year baking.

Calum is at home alone when the telegram arrives. MAIRI POORLY STOP WILL WIRE AGAIN THIS AFTERNOON STOP.

He panics, runs to find Aeneas; racing through the town, through all that wind and rain, without his jacket. He has no success. No one has seen the man.

He is not in the shop. He's not in County Hotel. He's not in the ironmonger's. Calum drifts into the tearoom to ask Seonaid's opinion; there he finds Aeneas drinking tea, and Seonaid sitting, patting his hand. He'd had the news already, delivered orally. Seonaid is saying the telegram is probably just a code way of saying going into labour, not bad news at all. Aeneas had not thought of that. He is looking at her with astonishment and gratitude.

Calum has to admit Seonaid is doing good work, and says as much to Alec later on.

'And you know, I think Aeneas really likes her, Alec.'

'Och man, ye're well off track! I've nivver seen a man sae lost in grief.'

'Folk need companionship,' says Calum.

'He's got companionship. You lodge with him.'

'Not that kind of companionship! I mean a woman round the house. It doesn't in any way demean the first love, or the second. He's still a young man, Alec.. and Seonaid's no spring chicken.. and she's very kind.'

'Ye're lettin' your imagination run awa' wi ye!'

'It's better,' says Calum, 'than dwelling on other possibilities.'

Alec sighs.

'Dinna worry. It'll a' come richt. When wis I ever wrang?'

'You said the *Oran* wouldn't sack me.'

'I wis lyin' through ma teeth,' says Alec, 'hopin' against hope. But why are ye runnin' roon the toon, ma loon, wi'oot yer jacket? Cultivatin' the crazed writer image, eh? Ye'll be growin' yer hair next, an' wearin' bootlick ties..'

'Bootlace,' says Calum. 'Actually I'm going to affect the plaid.'

'Awa' hame wi' ye. I'll ca' roon' efter work.'

Alec watches Calum out of the bank before he lets his face show any of his all too real anxiety. Poor Mairi. It must be bad when Esther and John send a telegram like that. Certainly, Seonaid's interpretation is possible.. and the most optimistic possible. He hopes Aeneas and Calum will both hold on to that hope for the next few hours at least. What will they do if it all goes wrong? He'll have to get a message to Effie and Anna, let them know.

'Alec..'

'Oh, fit like, Alec Mor?'

'My, the Gaelic's coming on!'

'Nae before time. Fit can I be daein' for ye?'

'Actually, I've been looking for Calum. They tell me he isn't at the *Oran* any more.'

'Ken, he's workin' wi' Aeneas.'

Alec Murray hesitates. 'It's just, Iain's been very ill, had the Spanish Influenza, and he'll be off the boat tonight, needing transport home. The boat is likely to be very late. I wondered if Calum..'

'I dinna ken. Ye'll hae tae ask himsel'. They werena' speaking last winter.'

'Aye. I know.'

'He'll be at Aeneas's house. Awa' an ask. Ye've naethin' tae lose.'

'Thank you, Alec Beag.'

'Alec Og,' says Alec. '**Alec Og**.'

'Gle mhath,' says Alec Mor. 'The Gaelic definitely is coming on.'

*   *   *

Mairi wakes on Hogmanay to find that her waters have broken overnight; her bed is soaked in birth fluid; liquor, Myra called it, warning Mairi of the possibility of its happening.

So it's the day. At last. After today she'll have her body back, if not her life. She can see how much energy and time children take. She's not afraid of that. She'll have energy and time once she can breathe again, once she can walk without the nagging pain in her lower back and in her hip.. Esther's doctor said the baby was lying on a nerve. He said everything was fine, would be fine, though she was, of course, very small, had small feet too.

'First labours,' he warned her, 'can take a little longer.'

Once she's changed into a dry gown, Mairi pulls the sheets
and blankets from her bed. This leaves her panting for breath,
and her womb begins to harden, not the usual firming up in
response to movement that has happened for a week or two now,
but a strong, more painful, gripping. She holds the bed-head
tightly till the muscles soften.

Afterwards she sinks into her chair, trying to compose
herself. Her body has come to this, after nine long months of
working to its own rhythms, none of her choosing. There is no
escaping it, no choice, only pain, only feeling. Mairi is terrified.

She looks at the little clock on the mantelpiece. It is not
half-past three. Too early to wake Esther. She rises, sweeps the
soiled sheets aside and a new contraction surges across her
swollen belly.

Between contractions, Mairi fetches cleans sheets from the
linen cupboard and gradually remakes her bed. It's a long process,
but she doesn't have to turn the mattress; they've had a rubber
sheet over it for some weeks now, since her first night of
contractions. Not that any of them were as strong as these.. as
painful. Somehow it's easier moving about. Mairi tries to be as
quiet as she possibly can, doesn't want to completely ruin the
holiday for the family. John is taking the day off, and tomorrow too.

'The first New Year of peace,' he said, 'should be a time of
celebration, don't you think?'

Carrying the dirty sheets down to the scullery, Mairi is
overtaken midstairs, has to stop, sit down on the stairs till the
discomfort passes. She rests in the kitchen lying her head back
against the firm high headboard of Esther's rocking chair, closes
her eyes, wishing life were easier, less complicated. Wishing her
mother were here.

If things were different, Mairi wonders, would this be a day
of joy, of eager hope for her? She is not sure.. feels lost in an
interminably ancient dance, her body freewheeling, intent on the
continuation of the species, with a total disregard for her, the
personality inhabiting that body.

Any intervention from her seems as hopeless, as unlikely a possibility, as the production of a battle plan by privates sent over the top by distant generals. She grins at that. How daft. Comparing her body to the infantry. Ridiculous. Yet her life is at risk; if she is one of those who birth well, she'll be fine. If not, there's a long struggle ahead and there's not a thing that she can do about it. It's as difficult, she thinks, to control your body's life as it is to change the course of a river.

Why is she here? Not for love. Not for romance. Why did she lie with Iain?

Mairi sits through two contractions considering the matter. All these months she's been avoiding this. Her father's Christmas letter praising Calum, saying how kind, how lovely, he's proving as a lodger, disturbed her. He stopped short of saying Calum would have been a lovely son.

He would have been.

A sensual lover too.

When she turned to Iain Murray, Mairi was not looking for these things. It was not anger either, not revenge on Calum she was seeking. Nor was it lust; Iain's looks and person affect her less than Calum's ever did.

What Calum sensed, what Mairi had refused till now to contemplate, was her ruthless, quite impersonal physical need for Iain's energy, the confidence that is his main attraction. It's what everybody seeks in him.

She can rationalise her behaviour. She tried, but weakly, to avoid their coming together. She had not in any way engineered it. Had it not happened last March, had she and Calum married, Mairi thinks Iain would have been a factor somehow, an affair, a lifelong grudge. It would have happened, when the physical explosion between her and Calum waned, or Calum's low self-esteem overcame his love again, as it had that spring night.

Maybe, though, that sensual flare between them might have lasted?

No.

When is there ever a physical joy that lasts? The body

dampens down responses, be it to sound, to smell, to touch.. It would have happened. What you tell yourself and what you do, thinks Mairi, never coincide.

*   *   *

Alec Murray went to school with Aeneas and Murdo, but he has worn less well than either of them. He's in his early forties and has trouble with arthritis; it's getting hard to manage the croft, even with Catriona's help, and young Allan and Hamish seeing to the animals at the weekend. Catriona's spinning ekes out their rather meagre income, and the large chunk Iain sent home of his army pay helped too. The lad did very well, all things considered.

It will be grand to see him home.

He'd been difficult, aye, the last time. But heavens, that was in the middle of the war, when there seemed no possible end to it, and the Germans advancing at such a pace. Iain knew the risks, the enormity of them. He also knew he'd have to go back to the trenches. How would anyone relax, given that? And couldn't they be excused a little over-indulgence? Alec marshals his arguments as he opens Aeneas's gate and walks up to the door. He opens it, walks in.

'Calum? Calum?'

There's no reply. Chrissie is not in today, it being Hogmanay. There's no Calum, no Aeneas. Alec goes through to the kitchen. It's empty too. A nuisance that. What can he do? He finds paper and pencil and sits down at the kitchen table to leave a message.

Calum –
Iain will be arriving on the Sheila tonight. He's been ill, needs transport. Can you meet him, bring him out to the croft? My hip is bad again. I know he'd like to see you.

Catriona and I are very grateful for your help.

Alec.

That will have to do. He leaves the note on the table, and exits the way he entered, through the front door, being superstitious about the matter.

Calum, meanwhile, is shivering beside his mother's fire.

'What were you thinking of,' she says, 'running through the town and not a stitch on you?'

'That's hardly accurate, Mother,' he says. 'I just forgot my jacket. I hadn't time to go back for it.'

'Here,' she says, 'you'd better drink this.'

'What is it?'

'Never you mind. It'll do you good.'

'I'm wondering,' says Calum, as he sips the rather pleasant mixture, 'if we might do a book about the old island remedies. What would you think of that?'

'It would be a good thing,' Flora says. 'Though some of the plants are disappearing, right enough. Still, it would be a help to people, to know the old herbs. Now, tell me what's it all about?'

'I'm sorry,' says Calum. 'What do you mean?

'You must have had a reason for launching yourself virtually naked into the storm. What was it?'

'This,' says Calum, handing her the telegram.

Flora takes it, holds it in both hands to read it.

'I see.'

Calum closes his eyes.

'I'm so afraid she'll die,' he says, 'before I have a chance to make things right between us.'

'You should have gone to see her.'

'How could I do that? She's sent no word.'

'I would have gone, in your shoes.'

Calum sighs, 'Too late now.'

'Aye,' says Flora, still holding the telegram. 'She's in the shadow. The outcome is not clear, Calum. There will be a birth, a death. But whose..?

'Keep hoping. Keep your love bright. It's all you can do.'

Calum is sobbing openly. Flora takes him in her arms.

'Life, boy, is never easy. But it's all we have.'

*   *   *

Margaret, the maid, gets quite a fright when she trips over Mairi in the kitchen. It's six-thirty. Margaret has risen to light the stove, doesn't see Mairi sitting in the dark.

'How long have you been like this?'

She looks anxiously at Mairi's dripping brow. The contractions are more frequent now, and very painful.

'I'll be fine,' says Mairi, 'when it settles.'

'Let me get the mistress.'

'No,' says Mairi. 'She'll be up soon enough. Don't wake her, Margaret. I don't want to be a nuisance.'

Margaret goes on with the stove, sets the kettle to boil. By the time she's made the tea, she's decided on a course of action. She leaves a cup with Mairi and slips upstairs, knocking on Esther's door.

'Is it that time already?' John replies.

'I need the mistress,' says Margaret. 'For Mairi.'

Esther pulls on her dressing gown, flies to the door.

'I thought I heard someone about,' she says. 'But it was so early! It got mixed up with my dream..'

'No, Madam,' says Margaret as Esther turns towards Mairi's door. 'She's in the kitchen.'

'What on earth?'

'Don't ask me why,' says Margaret. 'That's where she was when I found her.'

Esther fairly flies downstairs, then up again to the bedroom.

'John,' she whispers, shaking him, 'you'll have to go for the midwife.'

'Yes,' says John, turning over.

'John,' says Esther, 'get up!'

'In a minute, in a minute.'

'John, Mairi's been in labour half the night. If you don't go for the midwife now you'll have to act as midwife. It's too late to take her to the nursing home.'

'What?' John sits up, awake at last.

Between them, Esther and Margaret help Mairi back upstairs.

'Didn't you sleep in your bed at all last night?' asks Esther.

'The waters broke,' says Mairi. 'I changed the sheets, went downstairs with the linen.'

'Mairi, why are you so stubborn? No, don't answer that. I know. You couldn't be like a sibber frien'.'

'I've heard that one before,' says Mairi.

'I wonder where?'

'I wonder.'

'Have you had anything to drink this morning?'

'No,' says Mairi. 'Didn't fancy tea.'

'I'll make some lemonade,' says Esther. 'Stay with her Margaret. I'll not be long, dear.' She's back upstairs shortly with freshly squeezed lemonade, and water to sponge Mairi down. The contractions have stabilised at five-minute intervals. Mairi is suffering constant back pain too. Esther helps her change her sweat-drenched night-gown.

'The baby's the wrong way round,' the midwife says, when John finally gets back with her. 'How long has she been like this?'

'Half the night,' Esther frowns. 'What do you mean, the wrong way round? Do you mean breech?'

'No. Back to front. It'll have to turn before it can slide down the birth canal. We're in for a long labour,' says the nurse. 'And the poor wee lass looks exhausted already.'

By twelve o'clock Mairi seems so weak they decide to wire Aeneas, give him warning. At two o'clock, the nurse shakes her head.

'It's not advancing. We'd better call the doctor in.'

John is dispatched to the Doctor's surgery.

He comes back at four, alone. The women look at him mutely.

'He's at another delivery,' says John. 'His wife says she'll send a message.'

'Well,' the midwife says, 'let's look on the bright side. She's difficult, not desperate, not yet.'

'You'd better wire Aeneas before the post office shuts..'

'What can I say?'

Esther hesitates.

'Say.. making little progress.'

'Right,' says John.

'And John,' says Esther. 'Go and ask Connie if she'll come. She always cheers Mairi up.'

'Good idea.'

John sets off again into Edinburgh's dark streets, where the lamps are only now being lit. Across the city he sees people making ready for the New Year celebration; windows bright, houses shining.

He sends the telegram, the clerk in the post office wishing him a Happy New Year when it comes. John thanks him, trades the warmth and brightness of the shop for the city's gathering night. There's an air of expectation John is too anxious to share. He remembers all too clearly how near a thing it was with Esther last time.. giving birth.. it's such a dangerous time. Women seem so frail, and yet they cope with that?

What if Mairi dies? He hails a cab, asking it to wait in the New Town while he knocks on Myra's door. It's Connie who comes to answer. She's been baking, has flour on her nose. She takes one look at John.

'Mairi? Is she..'

'She's exhausted,' John says. 'Esther thought, if you came..'

'I'll get my coat. Myra! Myra!'

All the way back to Leith, Connie and Myra and John sit in anxious silence. Outside, every street seems full of busy, happy people, folk rejoicing at the end of 1918, as if there could be no more grief in the world.

*   *   *

By three o'clock, when Hamish and Iain reach the pier at Kyle, the small town is already crammed with soldiers and sailors. The morning's drizzle has passed, and the clearing skies still boast fading blues and greens. The wind is brisk.

'Are you warm enough, lad?'

'What? With two vests on? I'm fit to boil!'

'Maybe you'll need them before the night is through.'

'You're a pessimist, Hamish, I'll say that for you!'

'Nothing like the truth,' says Hamish.

When they reach the *Sheila*, the word is that hundreds of naval ratings must be accommodated, and the train from Inverness is already late, will not arrive till after six.

'We cannot promise passage,' says the MacBrayne representative.

'That's not what you said this morning.'

'I didn't know then how many men we were expecting! I suggest you wait in the Red Cross Rest. If you don't get on today you'll get on on Thursday.'

'But we have a ticket,' Hamish protests.

'I'm sorry, Sir. We'll have to see how many turn up. We'll try to do the best we can. We're expecting the *Iolaire* over from Stornoway at any moment. We should know within the next few hours how many men can be accommodated.'

'Come on, Hamish,' says Iain. 'Let's go for drink. We'll sort it out one way or another.'

'Let me take that bag then,' says Hamish. 'It looks as if you're in for a long night, Iain. Even if you sail at the earliest, say seven, you'll not be home before the New Year.'

'Ah but as soon after it as would make no living difference,' Iain laughs. 'No, come on, we'll make our battle plans.'

The bars in Kyle are full of Lewis men. Iain nods to two or three in each. Soldiers and sailors are spilling on to the streets, there are mountains of luggage, luggage stacked with dolls and balls and drums, homecoming presents for children who have not seen their fathers or brothers in the last four years.

'Come on, Hamish,' says Iain. 'This is no use. We'll never get served at this rate. I've a better idea.'

He walks back to the pier, finds a sheltered corner where crates of freight are stacked high on three sides.

'We'll use the bag as a seat. Come on, Hamish, it's an army trick. No one will judge you by it.'

Hamish says, 'Why should they? Who's going to see?'

'Exactly.'

Iain sits down, fishes in his pocket for a whisky flask.

'A dram?'

'Don't mind if I do.'

'What time is it?'

'Och, nearly four. It's taken us an age to get round all those places.'

'Never worry. We'll be here for hours. Did they tell you when the *Iolaire* is expected?'

'Between four and five.'

'Well,' says Iain, 'I think we should look at that boat. Chances are I'll know more of the folk on the *Iolaire*. They'll be from the Depot. It'll be easier to get them to turn a blind eye.'

'Iain..'

'Relax, this is how things are done in wartime.'

'It's not wartime any more.'

'It's relaxed military time, Hamish. Rules are made to be bent, if not broken.'

'This is how it was in France?'

'Only when the officers weren't looking.'

Ten minutes later, Iain and Hamish, happily drinking, are startled by a loud reverberation on the pier, an unearthly squeaking, wrenching sound that builds to fierce crescendo. Hamish jumps to his feet, while Iain throws himself flat on the wooden timbers, only looking up when the noise has settled.

'Christ! What on earth..?'

'You wouldn't last long under shell-fire,' says Iain. 'You jumped the wrong way.'

'It wasn't a shell,' says Hamish.

'Lucky for you.'

Hamish shoulders Iain's bag, and they emerge from their temporary shelter.

'It's the yacht,' says Hamish. 'Bumped the pier. Are you sure you want to go on it?'

'Not if there's a hole in it. There must be quite a big one after all that.'

'It looks okay,' says Hamish. 'I can't see any damage at all.'

'And the quay? That was quite a dunt.'

'Harder to see that. She's a fine looking ship, though, Iain.'

'Isn't she just.. I think this is the ship for me, Hamish – much smoother altogether than the *Sheila*. Look at the lines of her.. let's hang around a while, see if I know any of the crew. Think how lovely it will be to sail home to Stornoway in a class-outfit like that.'

'Beauty,' Hamish says, 'is skin deep.'

'So is style,' nods Iain. 'Look at her.'

Hamish has to agree, even in the midwinter dusk, the *Iolaire*'s lines are hard to fault.

'And look,' says Iain. 'See that man over there on deck? Angus MacVicar. Stornoway. That's my ticket, Hamish, boy. We'll wait till he comes off, then I'll catch him.'

*   *   *

Mairi has almost forgotten what it's like to be without pain. It's as if she's on fire, pulsing, burning. Nothing seems to stop it. No change of posture helps. She's exhausted, but the pain won't let her sleep; hungry, but the pain won't let her eat. She's thirsty too, but even when she drinks, she feels sick, retches constantly. Her body cannot seem to expel its nine-month guest – not unwilling but unable to complete the cycle.

The midwife shakes her head.

'I wish the doctor would hurry. Mrs Maitland, would it be possible for you to ask your husband to go back again? The message may have gone astray somehow.'

'I'll ask him to go right away,' says Esther.

She slips out of the room, meeting Margaret on the stairs.

'How is she, Madam?'

Esther shakes her head, 'Exhausted. Where's the Master, Margaret?'

'In the parlour,' says Margaret. 'He's just fallen asleep.'

'Oh dear.' She slips into the room where John is lying in an armchair, eyes closed, arms folded across his chest.

She walks across, touches his arm.

'I'm sorry, dear, can you wake up?'

John opens his eyes.

'I wasn't asleep, not really. Resting my eyes.'

'The midwife is wondering if you would mind going back again to Doctor Sievewright's house, in case the message has been lost.'

'A good idea,' says John. 'How many hours is that now?'

'Well, it's after nine o'clock.'

'I'll take a cab.'

'I hope you'll be able to find one. Do be careful, John.'

John stands up, yawns and stretches, kisses her forehead. Passing Mairi's room, he hears her moaning. The poor girl sounds exhausted, too tired to even make a noise. Connie and Myra speak to her constantly, their voices soft, encouraging; even they sound tired now. And Esther is beginning to give up hope. He can see it in her face.

When the door shuts after him, Esther goes through to the children. John is fast asleep, but Hannah lies awake, her small face white and anxious.

'Is Mairi going to die?' she asks.

'Who said that?'

'I heard the nurse tell Myra on the stairs.'

'I don't think she'll die,' says Esther. 'I think she'll be just fine. She's in a lot of pain, that's all. She'll be better when the baby comes. I think you should go to sleep, and in the morning you can come and see the baby. The quicker you get to sleep, the quicker the baby will come. And do you know what? When you wake up tomorrow, it will be next year! This is the night the years change. Won't that be exciting? A new year and a new baby..'

Hannah smiles.

'Can I have a hug?'

'Of course, my darling.'

Holding her child, Esther feels tears rising, cannot stop them.

'Good night, my love.' She fairly rushes from the room, scrubbing her cheeks with her handkerchief.

'Tea,' she thinks, 'is what we all need.'

*   *   *

The second telegram is not delivered that day. Aeneas and Calum sit all afternoon, waiting for the message that does not come.

'No news,' Aeneas says, 'can be good news, Calum.'

'Aye.'

'I'm glad you went to see your mother. No point in letting the New Year begin with a quarrel.'

'I didn't actually go to see her,' says Calum. 'I tripped over her in the street and got an earful for not wearing my coat.'

'Quite right too. I would have given you a row myself if I thought it would make any difference.'

'I asked her,' says Calum, 'if we could publish some of her traditional remedies.'

'Good idea!'

'She seemed quite keen, actually.'

'What,' says Aeneas, indicating Alec Murray's note, 'are you going to do about this?'

'Och,' says Calum, 'I'll have to borrow a cart, I suppose. It sounds as if Iain's been well and truly ill. Maybe Alec will come with me.'

'Is he coming round tonight?'

'He said he'd pop in after work.'

'That'll be good,' says Aeneas. 'Try not to worry too much,

Calum. We won't get any news now till Thursday.'

'I hate waiting,' says Calum. 'I'm not good at it.'

'Who is? Who could ever be?'

'I think you're better than most,' says Calum.

'My father used to say *Everything comes to him who waits.* I'm not sure if that's true, but I do know this; most things I've worried about have never happened. That was another saying of his, in fact. *Sufficient unto the day is the evil thereof.*'

'In other words,' says Calum, 'eat, drink and be merry for tomorrow we die!'

'Maybe we should try the eat bit,' says Aeneas. 'What do you say? Are you hungry?'

*   *   *

Iain emerges from the shelter of the crates just as Angus MacVicar's foot touches the quay.

'Iain!' he calls. 'If it's not Iain Murray from Holm! Is it you, cove?'

'Last time I looked in the mirror it was!'

'You've got terrible thin, a' bhalach.'

'Well, I've had the influenza. This is Hamish, Angus, Hamish Munro. He caretakes at Eilean Mor, the house I've been recuperating in.'

'Right good to meet you, Hamish,' Angus smiles, shakes hands. 'Angus MacVicar. Stornoway.'

'I'm sorry, Angus,' says Iain. 'I'd already told him that!'

Angus laughs. 'So what's the craic, Iain? What are you up to?'

'Trying to get back to the island,' Iain says, 'for the New Year. I've been demobbed. This is a right fine ship you've got here.'

'Oh, aye. Not so fast as the first *Iolaire*, though. We've come over today to help out with these ratings they're expecting. Word is they'll not be in Kyle till after six, now, the train's so late. Are you on the *Sheila*, Iain?'

'I'm not sure I'm on anything,' says Iain, 'with the flood of men they're expecting.' He looks despondent. 'And,' he says, 'I'd wired my parents too. They'll be waiting for me.'

'Well, why not come with us? It's going to be a New Year and a half!' says Angus. 'You could slip aboard right now. Everyone's in good form. No one will complain. I'll show you to the saloon and you can rest up there. You look as if you need to take the weight off your feet.'

Iain smiles now, a charming smile. Hamish is fascinated. He hasn't seen Iain in this mode before.

'He'll need help with his luggage,' he says. 'He's gey weak, still: only pretending to be well.'

'I can see that,' Angus nods. 'These Holm boys. Gluttons for punishment, all of them.'

Angus shoulders Iain's pack as Iain turns to the older man.

'Hamish, you've got my address. I expect to hear from you about the fishing.'

'First week,' Hamish says.

'If not, there'll be trouble.' Iain shakes Hamish's hand. 'Now be sure to thank Morag and Dr Barbara again for me.'

'I will,' says Hamish, 'safe journey, Iain lad. God-speed.'

Iain stands and waves as Hamish disappears along the quay into the growing dusk. The quay is already so full of kilted soldiers, munition workers and ratings that Iain can't imagine where the two or three hundred more that are expected will be able to find standing room.

'Come on, then,' says Angus. 'What's in all these boxes?'

'Food,' says Iain. 'Baking. Take some for the crew. They were so kind, those folk.'

'Funny name, though,' Angus smiles.

'What name?'

'Dr Barbara. I never heard of Barbara as a surname.'

'It isn't a surname,' says Iain. 'She's a female doctor.'

'Female doctor?' says Angus. 'Some folk have all the luck! Mind I've heard about you before!'

No one challenges Iain's presence on the ship. Angus shows him to the large, well-fitted saloon, settles him in a corner. Iain presses two or three boxes of Morag's baking on him.

'I only need the cake for my mother.'

'This'll be very welcome,' Angus says. 'I'll tell the boys it came from you.'

'Well, this is some ship,' Iain says again. 'I'm very grateful to be on her. Look at the wood on her!'

'She belonged,' says Angus, 'to a rich Clyde shipowner. She was built in Leith in 1881.'

'Leith, eh?'

'She's been everywhere, owned by millionaires in America, London. The Navy had her down in Yarmouth before we got her up here.'

'Well, they haven't managed to ruin her yet. Not even the guns spoil the line of her.'

'No,' says Angus. 'Look, I'd better be getting on. You lie down, get some sleep while you can. Word is the train will not be here before six or seven. We'll not be off before eight, so I'm thinking we'll be seeing the New Year in on the Minch. It won't be so quiet then!'

'At least we'll be nearly home.'

'Indeed we will. Now you'll excuse me, Iain. I'll mention you to Sub-Lieutenant Rankin; ask for him if there's a problem.'

'Thank you, Angus,' says Iain. 'I'll not forget this favour.'

It's dark outside. In the saloon, two small lamps are burning. Angus trims one before he shuts the door, leaving Iain in shadow. He lies back closing his eyes. He can relax now. He's on his way as so many boys should have been. He thinks of Ewan MacLeod, Dan Macrae, both shot by snipers. Of Eddie Shields. Eddie got it in no-man's land, near Albert. Iain was crawling through the mud on patrol when he heard Eddie's moaning.

'Murray, Murray, ye fuckin bastard, come an' help me.'

Iain wriggled over to him. Eddie's tunic was ripped apart, intestine spilling out into the mud.. Iain's hand inadvertently invaginated in it – the slimy, warm, jellied sausage, coils and coils of it.

'Does it look bad?' spluttered Eddie.

'Och, no,' Iain lied. 'Are you in much pain?'

'I'd morphine,' Eddie said, 'I took it a' .'

'Good,' said Iain. 'Are you thirsty, man?'

'Aye.'

'Have a wee dram. It might help.'

Iain held his water-bottle to Eddie's lips.

'Fuck's sake, Murray,' sobbed Eddie. 'Are ye tryin' to kill me?'

It was then Iain noticed the ragged hole in Eddie's jaw, the left half of his face blown to smithereens, the whisky trickling over raw flesh. His voice had sounded odd but not that odd..

'It'll wash the tablets down,' he said. 'I'll come back for you, Eddie. I promise. Just hold tight.'

As Iain squirmed away, Eddie's wails crescendoed, attracting the machine-gun fire that silenced them at last.

They're all gathered round him now, even Eddie. Iain feels their presence; all those boys who wanted to be home, who fell in mud, writhed in it, waited in slow agonies for death, in frost and snow, or ruthless sun. They are always with him these days, waiting to be laid to rest back on the island.

*   *   *

Doctor Sievewright's wife is apologetic.

'He's been home and gone out again,' she says. 'An emergency.'

John is nearly frantic, struggles to contains his anger; knows it will not help.

'The midwife says she's at death's door, the lassie.'

'I'll send a message to him,' she promises. 'Which midwife is it again?'

'The one he recommended. Jeannie MacMahon.'

'Just you go on home, Mr Maitland. I'll send out a boy after the doctor. I'm sure he'll be with you within the hour.'

'An hour,' says John in desperation, 'may well be too late.'

He turns on his heel and runs back to the waiting cab.

The town is so busy tonight, so happy. There are boys on every corner, bright-eyed. In some darker corners, street women, barely more than girls, make eyes at passing men. John wants to shout at them, be careful! Youth is no protection! He doesn't, of course; he sits restless in the cab till it reaches his own door.

'Well?' Esther asks.

'He's out on an emergency. The wife said she'd send a boy after him.'

Jeannie MacMahon shakes her head.

In the Sievewright residence, the doctor's wife returns to the dinner table and her guests.

'What was it, dear?'

'That Maitland man again.' She picks her fork up, takes a dainty mouthful.

'And?'

She finishes chewing, wipes her mouth with an embroidered napkin.

'The girl. I told you this morning, remember? She's in labour. The midwife seems to think it's not going well.'

'Which midwife?'

'That MacMahon woman.'

'And,' Dr Sievewright stops with his fork in mid-air, 'what exactly was the message?'

Mrs Sievewright glowers, whispering furiously.

'You promised you'd be here for dinner tonight, of all nights. You promised faithfully!'

'The girl's in danger?'

'That woman always exaggerates!'

Dr Sievewright stands up.

'She's the only one that never does. When did they send for me, Isla? When?'

'You were at the Cartwrights'..'

'God, woman! What were you thinking of?'

'You promised!'

Dr Sievewright smiles urbanely at his in-laws.

'Emergency,' he says. 'I'm sorry.'

'The girl is as good as a common whore!' his wife shouts. 'What's the hurry?'

'Isla,' his voice is very quiet, very quiet indeed. 'We'll talk about this later. If that girl or her baby dies it will be your responsibility.'

She follows him into the hall, still spitting with anger.

'Don't think I don't know about you and that woman. Don't treat me like a fool, Michael. I know what I know.'

'You're a mealymouthed, low-minded idiot!' he says. 'I repeat; if that girl dies it will be all your doing. We'll have to leave Edinburgh, Isla. Concentrate on that!'

Sievewright's car pulls up outside the Maitland's house not ten minutes after John has stepped despondently back over the threshold. The doctor is shown quickly upstairs and is not much cheered by Mairi's obvious exhaustion and dehydration.

'We'll have to get some fluid into her,' he says. 'I am sorry I was so delayed.'

'You're here now,' Jeannie nods.

He shakes his head. 'I only hope it's not too late.'

Mairi is dimly aware of a new presence in the room, a deeper voice. She stares unseeing at him.

'Calum?'

'It's Dr Sievewright, Mairi. Don't worry. You'll be fine.'

'Calum?'

'I'll need to make an examination, Mairi. To see how you're doing. Your aunt will stay with you. Don't be frightened.'

'Calum?' Mairi whimpers again. 'Calum!'

Afterwards, Dr Sievewright shakes his head. 'Not much more than two inches. She's got some way to go.'

'What about the hospital?'

'She's too weak to move. We'll have to sit it out till she dilates, try the forceps..'

'Pituitary extract?'

'It's not the contractions that are at fault,' he says. 'Her pelvis is a little on the narrow side. That's why the head's the wrong way round. It may turn yet. We've seen it do that, Jeannie, many's the time.'

Jeannie looks less confident, but nods.

'Try and get her to drink. Sweet drinks. Let's give her some sustenance.'

'She keeps being sick.'

'That's the risk. The baby's heart sounds good so far.'

'Her own pulse is not so regular.'

'She's exhausted. So are you. Go and have some tea. I'll watch her. Go on. Off you go.'

'Come on,' Esther says, 'he's right. We're both exhausted, Jeannie. We'll feel better for the break.'

'I'll be here too,' says Myra. 'I'll come and get you if you're needed. What do you think the chances are, doctor?' she asks as the door swings shut.

'Shh..'

He takes a damp cloth, and gently wipes Mairi's forehead; then moves on to similarly soothe her hands, her lower arms.

'Mairi,' he says as he works, 'I know you can hear me. I know you're in great pain, but you can do this, Mairi. You can. You're a strong, fit girl, and your baby needs all your strength, all your effort. Listen to me Mairi. You'll be fine. We'll get there. It's nearly midnight, Mairi. Nearly the New Year. Just keep strong, be strong for Calum and the baby.. You can do it.'

Mairi's eyes flicker towards him.

'Calum?'

'That's right. You'll be fine. You can do it, Mairi..'

The doctor keeps washing her forehead, her neck, keeps talking, encouraging.

Myra, listening, begins to feel a little more confident.

*　　*　　*

Angus MacVicar, passing the saloon at seven-thirty finds Iain awake, looking rested, much less pale than earlier.

'We'll be off soon, I'm thinking,' he says. 'The boys are here, all lined up now. Shame you're not stronger, Iain, we could do with help. We're short-handed, what with the holiday. That's why I'm here. They're wet behind the ears. All fresh from Yarmouth.

And,' he adds indignantly, 'they treat us as islanders, as if we're worse than monkeys, useless.'

'Well, I *would* be useless,' Iain laughs. 'I'm the world's worst sailor, always have been.'

'Och, it's going to be flat calm,' says Angus. 'You'll be fine. We'll be crowded, though; they've sent twice as many men as they said were coming.'

'So what's new?'

'Aye, well. Are you hungry, man?'

'No. Haven't got my appetite back,' says Iain. 'It'll come in time. Did you enjoy the scones?

'What? They were just like my mother's!'

'Good. I'm glad. See you later on.'

A seaman bursts through the door signalling to Angus that he's wanted for'ard. 'No rest for the wicked, eh? You see and enjoy yourself. It's going to be a lively night.'

Angus's prediction begins to fulfil itself even as he speaks. The first of the ratings is already on the gangway. In less than twenty minutes the saloon is chock-full of men and kitbags. The smell is utterly distinctive, sweat, cigarettes and exhaled alcohol. The quiet fragrance Iain had assumed was due to wood polish is gone, banished completely. Iain is reminded of the hours he's spent in overcrowded trains, in Channel steamers, though the mood is quite, quite different tonight. Six hours steaming, Angus said, now separates them from the lights of Stornoway. Six hours. Iain wonders how many men, how much fevered anticipation one two-hundred-ton steam yacht can hold.

And the sigh of happiness, and the cheering as the *Iolaire* slides out of Kyle around eight o'clock! Iain, the only soldier in sight, has to put up with a fair amount of ribbing about that.

'The way I heard it,' says one, 'skirt-wearing dervishes and Harrismen were ordered on to the *Sheila!*'

'Well, at least I'm a Lewisman,' Iain laughs. 'Did you think it was only sailors could travel in such style?'

It's a good-humoured company. Stories fly fast and furious. Rough seas, rougher rum. Easy women. Lost loves, absent friends.

Iain, for the most part, sits and listens, thinking how much they will all have to conceal. No one else seems to realise what they're going back to.. a world they have not walked for years, a world that has not shared the violence, the destruction that has become their daily bread. These boys have dreamed of home but will find it strange, as it will find them strange. Poor lads. He gazes round them, crushed round benches and tables, drinking, smoking quietly. A pall of smoke has gathered in the room, and in the haze his comrades look unreal, feel distant.

The smoke is not so good for his chest. The irritating cough, the phlegm gathering in his throat, are not to be denied. Recovering from yet another weakening bout of coughing, Iain's chest is heavy, weighed down, the dull and angry aching at odds with the fluttering of his heart. He's breathless, weak as a kitten. Perhaps that's the whisky. Barbara warned him when she gave him the flask not to overdo it.

'It'll bring on the palpitations if you're not careful,' she said.

'Yes, fairy godmother,' said Iain. 'I'll be good.'

The goodbye kiss he'd meant to be a peck on the cheek had turned into something infinitely more passionate. Perhaps it was as well they'd heard Hamish's footsteps in the hall. Neither of them blushed as they moved apart. Barbara sighed almost imperceptibly.

'Good luck, Iain,' she said. 'Safe journey.'

'Barbara,' he smiled at her, shaking his head. 'Barbara.. you're.. indecent.'

'It takes one,' she said, 'to know one.'

Even Dulcie never showed such bare-faced hunger. Iain wishes he had not been ill on meeting Barbara. Still it proves, he thinks, his spirits rising, that the episode in Falcon Square was merely caused by the influenza he was incubating. It's a great relief to him.

'Iain?'

'Ewan?' Iain looks up, cannot believe his ears. It can't be Ewan, surely? Ewan MacLeod? But it's Ewan's voice, and Ewan's frame moreover, his red hair and his goodnatured, tired face. He's standing above Iain, towering, actually, his broad chest throwing Iain into shadow. He still has on his khaki kilt, mud-stained, Iain notices, feeling glad that he had kept his own tartan kilt, or at least, found one the quarter-master didn't miss, in readiness for this homecoming. The girls all like the kilt.

'Move over, Iain,' says Ewan. 'Make a bit of room for an old friend!'

Iain swings his legs down from the bench he's been lying on. His chest feels a little easier. It's odd. Just seeing Ewan makes him feel much stronger.

'Ewan, man.. it's that good to see you!'

Ewan's half–smile is just as Iain remembers it in so many attacks, so many tight corners. Ewan hesitates, searching for words.

'I hear,' he says, 'that Mairi is in labour..'

'Ewan,' Iain grips his arm, his voice taut with emotion, 'that child is mine. Mairi's baby. I'm going to marry Mairi.'

'Good,' says Ewan. 'Iain, let's drink to that. To Mairi!' He stretches down to lift a rum pig from the floor, raises it to his lips.

'Mairi!' Iain sighs, watching Ewan drain the bottle, wondering at how long he's managing to swallow, wondering if he'll ever stop. It is unlike Ewan, drinking to excess. Odd. It's also odd that he, Iain, did not see the rum pig before Ewan picked it up. It must have been at his feet, for God's sake. 'Mairi,' Iain sighs again.

'What?' the rating standing next to Iain bends down now. 'What did you say? You're getting married?'

Iain smiles. 'Aye, I'm going to be a father!'

'Then we'll drink to that,' the boy says. 'To fatherhood!'

'Shh,' Iain pats the boy's arm. 'They'll all think you're a Fritz.. *they* call it the fatherland, and all that.. all that's over, in the past.'

'Iain, I think you've had too much fire-water.'

'Shh,' Iain says, gripping the boy's arm. 'Shh. Don't tell. Don't mention it.'

'I won't,' the boy says, smiling, 'you can count on me. I've had a dram myself.'

Iain turns back to Ewan who is sitting back contentedly, leaning against the saloon's panelled wall. He looks that well. No sign of his head-wound even. Iain scrutinises the left temple, the one he had seen shot away. Amazing, he thinks, what time will heal. Amazing, right enough. His heart is fluttering again. Iain shivers, takes another good slurp of whisky.

'Isn't it grand,' he says, 'to be going back to the island?'

Ewan doesn't seem to hear. He hugs the rum pig, his attention focused on a young lad a few tables off who has taken out a mouth organ and is playing a medley of island tunes. So many of the boys are sitting back now, listening, singing along when they have the words, humming if it's just the tune they know.

'Listen to that,' says Ewan.

'Och, isn't that Calum's tune?' Iain finds himself humming, many of the boys do. They all seem to know it.

'Doesn't it take you back?'

And Iain remembers that evening at the dance, how he prowled the floor, searching for Mairi, how he found her too. He can see Calum on stage, looking down on them both, trusting, loving both of them, equally, it seems to Iain, from this distance. And now he sees himself, angry, scheming.. Mairi running to Calum at the end of the tune, taking his arm.. Iain knows it all again, all as fresh and bitter as that first time; the impotence of thwarted need. For need it was, not love, not lust, not quite.

'Doesn't it take you back?'

He sees Dulcie moving down the ward that first day, sees her tiny waist. Those hips.. sees Dulcie clinging to him the day he left again for France. She's in her chinese robe, the long silk dragon-embroidered robe she always wears on rising. He puts his pack down, kisses her, her warmth and softness sweet, so sweet.. they come together there and then, on the hall's cold patterned tiling. How Dulcie laughs when the morning post showers all around them.

Thinks of Barbara. That kiss.. Maybe, before Canada, he

should spend some time at Eilean Mor.

'Doesn't it take you back?' says Ewan.

'What's the name of that tune, Iain?' The boy next to him bends down, 'I never heard it before. It's beautiful.'

'"The Dark Ship",' Iain says. 'It's one of Calum Morrison's..'

'That explains it,' says the lad. 'His stuff was always good..'

'And this,' says Iain, 'This new tune is "Mairi's Waltz".'

But Mairi's waltz falters. In the far corner of the saloon, they're counting out the war years, counting down the seconds to the future and peace. All the boys join in, chanting

'Deich

naodh

ochd

seachd

se

coig

ceithir

tri

da

aon

.. Bliadhna Mhath Ur! Happy New Year!'

*　　　*　　　*

Aeneas and Calum toast the New Year quietly.

'It will be a better one,' says Calum. 'Bound to be.'

Aeneas quickly downs his dram.

'Let's go and see your folk, Calum,' he says. 'When did you say the boat was due?'

'I don't know,' says Calum, 'which boat. The *Sheila* and the *Iolaire* have both left Kyle, but with the storm there's no saying when they might arrive. There's plenty of time, Aeneas.'

Calum's dreading the boat's arrival. What can he say to Iain? How can they bury the past?

'Come on, then,' he says, reaching for his jacket. 'There's no point in sitting worrying.'

'Before we go,' Aeneas says, refilling their glasses, 'a toast.. to Mairi.'

'Mairi.'

Calum's hand is shaking as the glasses meet.

'I love her so much, Aeneas.'

'I know that, lad. I know. Come on. Run and fetch your fiddle. You'll have need of it before the night is out, I'm sure.'

*   *   *

In Leith, the New Year is rung in with great rejoicing, folk dancing in the streets, ex-soldiers and sailors renewing with their families all their hopes and wishes for a greater peace. The Maitland home is quieter. The blinds are down, the curtains pulled to discourage revellers. John and Esther toast 1919 on the landing with Myra, Connie, Jeannie and Dr Sievewright, Margaret too; sherry and whisky are handed quietly round. Connie asks for a second dram. Myra shakes her head. The group disperses, Jeannie and Esther to the labour room, the rest to the parlour where they sit, trying to feel happier than they do.

Esther stays with Mairi, wishing now there would be an end of it one way or the other, an end to Mairi's pain.

'Happy New Year, love,' she whispers, bending down to kiss her forehead.

'Mother,' Mairi whispers, 'Mother.. you've come!'

'No,' says Esther, horrified. 'No, Mairi. It's me, Esther.'

'I knew,' said Mairi, 'you wouldn't let me down. I've always liked that perfume.'

'Mairi, it's me,' says Esther.

Jeannie puts her arm round Esther's shoulder, whispers. 'Esther, it'll do no harm if she thinks you're her mother.' She looks at Esther's anxious face. 'You're exhausted. Go and lie down. I'll come for you if there's anything.'

Esther shakes her head. 'I'd rather stay. I'll be alright, I promise.'

Mairi takes her hand, grips it.

'I knew you'd come,' she says.

In the parlour, there is no taste for light conversation.

'How much longer do you think, Doctor?' asks Myra.

He shakes his head. 'Impossible to say. I do think,' he adds, 'she's rallied a little. Whether it's enough.. the baby's heart is strong, too. I wouldn't entirely give up hope.'

Connie walks over to Myra, kneels beside her, takes her hands.

'She'll be fine,' she says. 'I know Mairi. A little bit of pain won't defeat that girl.'

'A little bit no, but..'

'She'll come through, mark my words.'

Myra looks at the doctor. He shrugs, 'There's still a chance.'

*　　　†　　　*

Iain is dozing now, light-headed. It's the whisky, he thinks, not the fluttering in his chest. The sea has reverted from calm to a heavy swell, the saloon's windows spattered with squalling rain and angry waves as the boat lurches from one peak to the next.

'A bit of weather, eh?' the boy next to Iain laughs. Iain tries to smile, tries not to feel sick. When Ewan takes his arm the nausea passes.

They pass the Milaid light half an hour into the New Year, the sea growing more restless the nearer they come to the island. Now the Arnish lights are twinkling in the distance. Soon they'll be able to see the lights of Stornoway itself. Most of the boys are restless, thinking of home, the homes they have not seen in months or years of war. They're beginning to gather all their belongings neatly together, ready for disembarking. It's an odd thing, Iain thinks, how folk will do that, always much too early. It just takes one to start, then there's a fever to it; like sheep startling themselves into stampede down a hill. Some of the boys have their greatcoats on already.

The seaman next to Iain is staring through the window.

'What?' he says. 'Look at that. Look at that, will you? It's not right. This is an odd kind of course.. what are they thinking of?'

The mouth organ player is watching the shore-lights too.

'Imagine them taking us so close to land! Some sailing, eh? Some newfangled military approach they've worked out, probably.'

Iain's companion stands up. He is white with fear.

'It's madness. We'll never make the harbour of it.'

He walks across the saloon, heading for the bridge. That's the last Iain sees of him. With a sudden tearing crash the *Iolaire* pitches forward, topples starboard, listing heavily.

The previously orderly if over-crowded saloon is now a seething knot of desperate men, vehement in sudden darkness. As their eyes become accustomed to the lack of light there is concerted movement towards the doors, a forced acceleration of arms and legs and torsos, pushing, pushing.

Some have fallen, been injured. Iain tastes blood, finds he's bitten his tongue. The sweet thick taste, the pain, confuse him.

The saloon doors are jammed with sailors struggling to scramble out on to the deck. One or two, like Iain, sit back, almost dazed, wondering, watching, hands in pockets. More than one is trampled, injured.

Others break what doors or windows they can. Iain sees one boy shatter a starboard window, jumping through it overboard, only to struggle back in, soaked. For himself, Iain has no idea what to do. If this was a battlefield he'd know, his instincts more attuned to the dangers on dry land. Not that there was ever dry land, the thought comes unbidden.. it was always mud.

Feeble as it is, the joke rouses him from stupor. Iain smiles, picks himself up, clinging to a table to prevent himself slithering down the saloon. The ship's engines have stopped now. His ears, his head are filled with the shouting of frightened men. Iain cannot seem to hear them clearly. No one has given orders, no one seems in charge. There is no sign of officers, no one from the bridge. There is no one offering lifeboats, lifebelts.

He tries to think logically, tries to formulate a plan of

appropriate action. What would he do in battle? But this is not battle. This is sea, not land. It can't, he thinks, be all that different, surely? He should make an effort to reach the port deck.. yes.. but his arms and legs are suddenly so heavy, so weak.

'Come on,' says Ewan, dragging him, 'this way, Iain.'

The crush around the doors has thinned. Iain stumbles in the wake of his taller, surer-footed friend through the ripped off port-side door, not an easy climb. He can't see what he's climbing on. Sometimes he has the uncomfortable sensation that his feet are sinking over, into, human flesh.

'This way,' says Ewan climbing up into the rigging. 'Come on, Iain, it's easier to hold this. Come on. Hurry!'

Iain doesn't find it easy to follow. He is almost over-whelmed by the bitter wind whipping all the warmth and light out of him. He has not had time to slip his greatcoat on, and his uncovered legs and head are raw with cold and rain.

'Hurry!' repeats Ewan. 'Here, take my hand.'

Iain feels warmer for the contact, starts to climb.

And the angry waves smash against the ship, mountains high. They're caught between the darkness and the water's anger. Wind and towering waves make movement almost impossible. Time and again the decks are lashed by churning foam. Everything that's not tied down is washed overboard as the waves keep pounding deck and men. Most of the boys climb to the upper deck where it's easier to stand.

Two whalers are lowered, but are ground against the sides of the ship, splintered, useless, all the seamen drowned. From the rigging, Iain has an uninterrupted view. In the light of the distress beacons fired from the bridge, it's possible to see the land – very close – not more than twenty yards away, but the sea between the ship and shore is now so wild that any man attempting to swim ashore – and fifty or sixty do jump overboard – risks being dashed against the rocks and drowned. Iain recognises the rocks now, in the light of the distress flares.. the Biastan Holm.

And in the flares' harsh light Ewan's wound is clearly

visible, a dark, malignant festering.

'Ewan,' Iain whispers, 'Ewan..?'

'Yes?'

Ewan turns to face him, his skull, his skin intact. Iain cannot understand it, stretches a hand forward as if, like Doubting Thomas, to test what he cannot believe.

'What is it?' Ewan takes his arm, and Iain feels stronger, more in command.

'Those poor boys,' he says. 'They must be..'

'Aye,' Ewan nods. Iain knows. It's as if they both know, as if both Iain and Ewan are actually with the boys flung from the boats, cast in the sea, dragged and raked at the mercy of the scouring tide, now thrashed against rock, now pelted against the metal slopes of the stricken ship.. and some have been sucked down, down beneath the waves. They hold their breath till they can hold no longer, till the body's desperation for air, for oxygen, over-rules the knowledge that one breath of seawater, even one swallow, will mean the end.

Iain had heard somewhere that drowning is a soft death, like drifting in a green and pleasant cloud. He knows now this is not true, or not true of here. The waters by the Biastan Holm are sharp and cold, vicious.. so icy, so violent, the wind-pipe freezes in reflex spasm, the pain as shocking and immediate as if a shell had pierced the chest.. and the spasm precludes breath, is asphyxiation as sure and unremitting as if a ligature were tightened around the neck. These boys do not drown, but suffocate in agony. This is a pain that will outlast the body's knowledge of it.

Another boy is down here, rolling in the darkness, quietly gulping black sea, his hands wafting before him, helpless, uncontrollable; his mind running on former days.. but I'm going home, he thinks, I can't be drowning here, not here, not fifteen miles from home. This is not happening. The dull grief in his chest is failing, and the last thing he will see is the breached hull of the *Iolaire*, grey above him.

Yet another is screaming, hanging from the port rail, his

wrist jammed between two supports. Iain feels the pain, feels the shoulder muscles tearing slowly apart, the joint dislocating. The boy stops yelling, hangs his head.

Another, when the ship strikes, pulls out his own lifebelt, and casts himself into the waves, drifting almost dead to a tiny rocky outcrop where he lies exhausted, vomiting, waiting for the rising tide he knows will finish him. Hiding his head in his oilskin, he stretches out, falls into an exhausted sleep.

Iain, for his own part, knows his strength is ebbing. The storm is far too strong for him. He's near the end. He can hardly move one foot after the other. Only yards from home, he might as well have been in no-man's land, strung on the wire.

His hands are white and useless. He can barely hold the rigging. His legs keep giving way, will no longer hold him up. He feels dizzy, sick. His heart thumps as erratically as coffin nails driven into awkward wood.

'Ewan!' he cries. 'Help me! Ewan, please.'

'Come on,' says Ewan. 'Iain, see.. those men have a rope. There's a man over there making for the shore..'

Iain forces himself to concentrate, watches distantly as one brave fellow launches himself from the rocks below the gunwhale into the boiling sea and is carried, on the first attempt, away from land.

He does not give up. Spitting water, retching, he struggles back, still with the rope in hand; he seems to hang fire, counting.. Iain counts with him, for him. This must be a local fellow surely, to know about the fath, the claith.. the seven smaller waves and the following three giants..

The swimmer waits, surfs ashore on the third, high wave, gaining the slope. What a man! What a feat! A few inches lower and he would have failed, been dashed against the steep cliff face, but he makes it, he makes it, and crawls a few yards up, winds the rope around his back and uses his body, his own weight, as ballast. The strain of the first two men coming over from the ship drags him right back to the cliff, and almost over the edge of it.

Then a heavier rope is found and a loop wound round a jutting rock, and rescued men take turns to stabilise the line. Thirty, nearly forty men pass that way to safety.

'Come on, Iain. That's for you.'

Iain looks at Ewan, smiles.

'I don't think I can make it.'

'Don't give up. Here, take my hand.' Ewan stretches towards Iain, one arm extended. The gash on his temple is clearer now, yawning, gaping, dark blood dripping slowly down the neck and shoulder. It doesn't seem to hold him back. 'Hurry, Iain! There's not much time..'

Iain tries to follow Ewan, but his arms and legs are useless. He can barely grasp the rigging as he struggles to climb down.

There's no strength in his grip.

His hands are numb.

His chest is aching.

He cannot breathe.

He cannot move.

'Come on, Iain. Hurry!'

'I'm coming. Coming..'

He has not left the rigging when the yacht lists heavily to port, and disappears into the boiling sea, all but the masts; a column of flame shooting up, then quenched in darkness.

'Iain!'

Iain is pitched forward into air and water.

*   *   *

'Iain! Iain!'

Mairi is panting, desperate. Dr Sievewright restrains her.

'Don't push,' says Jeannie. 'Don't push any more, keep panting, let me check the cord is not around the baby's neck.. that's fine.. Good, Mairi. Good girl.. Here he comes.. a fine son, Mairi.. a fine boy! Iain, did you say? Iain? That's a good name for this lusty fellow!'

The baby's high-pitched fury echoes through the house. In the parlour, John hugs Connie, Myra too.

Mairi falls back against the pillows, drenched with sweat.

'Look, Mairi, he's lovely,' says Esther.

'It's five to two,' says Dr Sievewright. 'Someone write that down. Now, let's get finished. Just the afterbirth, Mairi, lass. Not too much more work. After this young soldier, it'll be a dawdle. You did so well! Not even a tear on you! And you managed it without the forceps, clever lass.'

Esther wipes her brow, wipes her tears away.

'They'll have to tell Dulcie,' Mairi says. 'Iain's dead.'

'Shh, now,' Esther soothes her. 'Shh. The baby's fine, Mairi. Fine.'

*   *   *

Calum, waiting in Stornoway for the boats from Kyle, knows early on there's something far, far wrong. Those flares.

'Fit a pairty thon must be!'

'No Alec.. I don't think so. The pilot boat went out too long ago.'

When the *Spider*, a small fishing boat, docks, Calum finds the engineer in a panic.

'There's a ship on the Beasts of Holm!'

'Calm down James. Have a drink of this.. here.. that's better. Now, tell us exactly what happened.'

'It passed us on the starboard side as we were sailing past the mouth of Loch Grimshader. I thought it was the *Sheila*.. we were going in its wake, saw the course was wrong. It was obvious that it would hit those rocks if it didn't turn. And we couldn't do anything to help, Calum.. nothing, in those seas.. We'll have to tell the Admiralty!'

'They'll know,' says Alec. '*The Budding Rose* went out to get her.'

James is shivering.

'We couldn't do anything to help,' he says again. 'Nothing. And all those poor men shouting..

'But the seas are too rough, Calum; and the wee engine we've got on this boat.. we'd have been ground to smithereens ourselves.'

'Have another drink,' says Calum. 'Get yourself warm.'

'Those poor men, shouting.'

Calum turns to Alec.

'Come on, Alec, lad. Let's go to Holm, see if we can help.'

*   *   *

Catriona and Alec Murray have not gone to sleep, waiting for Iain. Braving the storm to fetch more peat, Catriona sees the first of the distress flares. She sends Alec and Allan down to the shore, builds the fire up and picks her way carefully down the cliff to find the first few men have now struggled ashore.

'Sailors,' Alec tells her. 'Not soldiers, Catriona. She's the *Iolaire*. She was full of naval ratings. Away home, lass, get the kettle boiling. These boys are going to need a hot drink. I'll send them up.'

Catriona, reassured, clambers slowly back up the cliff, followed by one or two of the fitter survivors. All the way up she laughs at herself for being such a fool. Didn't the wire say the *Sheila*? Iain was coming on the *Sheila*. And the way things are, so many boys travelling, his journey may even be delayed again. He may not be home till Thursday.

She's nearly at the croft when Alec and Calum appear.

'Oh, boys, boys,' she cries, 'what a terrible thing. And New Year too.'

'What's that noise?'

'She's gone,' Alec says.

364

Sure enough, the sharp explosion is from the *Iolaire*. She slips into the dark waves, belching fire. The rope is lost. There will be no more saved that way. Catriona turns away from the rocks.

'Come and help me now, boys, there's men needing to rest.'

Allan comes running towards them, out of the darkness.

'There are people on the mast,' he says. 'Stuck there, at the top. And nothing we can do for them between the storm and the sea.'

They crowd into the croft house, drinking strong black tea.

'Thank goodness Iain wis comin' on the *Sheila*,' says Alec.

'Iain?' asks a young rating, sitting dazed beside the fire. His forehead is cut and bruised. His hands are shaking, rope-burned. 'What Iain do you mean?'

'Iain Murray. Catriona's son '

'He was with us,' the boy says, 'in the saloon. He was the only soldier on the yacht, the only one I saw anyway. I didn't see him after we struck.'

Calum looks at Catriona. She's heard. All too clearly. The light in her eyes is dying.

'He'll be alright,' Calum says. 'Come on, Mrs Murray. You know your Iain.. more lives than ten cats any day.'

'Aye,' says Alec. 'Whit aboot a cup o' tea?'

They sweep Catriona into her chair by the fire. She's still sitting there, frozen, when her husband stumbles back in, cold and sore. He's heard the news already. Unlike his wife, he has not given up all hope.

'What can we be doing?' asks Calum.

'They'll be needing carts,' says Alec Mor. 'The navy are combing the beaches. They've not found much yet. It's too early.'

'And the boys on the mast?'

He shivers. 'No one can get near them, poor souls. Not a chance of it till daylight. And it so cold.. it's a wonder they're still there. How many boys are here, Calum? '

'Oh, ten or so,' says Calum. 'More at Stoneyfield. They've had to put one or two of the most exhausted boys to bed. I tried to get Catriona to go to bed herself..'

Catriona speaks now for the first time.

'I'll not rest, Calum, not till we get Iain back. Once he's in the house..'

'Come on, mother,' says Alec.

'No,' she says. 'I'll sit on here. He'll be coming.'

'What time is it, Calum?'

Calum looks at his watch.

'Nearly six.'

'It'll be dawn in an hour or two.. try and get a little rest, Catriona. We'll go out at daylight.'

It must have been like this in France, thinks Calum, waiting for men to come back. Waiting to look for the bodies. The storm outside is still raging fierce, furious. Inside, the mood is no less fierce. What will the day bring?

What's happening with Mairi?

He looks round the darkened croft. Catriona sits dry-eyed, spinning her empty wheel. Alec Murray, leaning back in the rocking-chair, has closed his eyes. Alec Stenhouse has closed his eyes too, is probably asleep, from the sudden awkward twitching of his head.

Catriona stands up suddenly.

'Calum, come with me.'

He follows her out of the cottage, down to the beach. They take the easier road, avoiding the cliff. The cloud has thinned a little, the wind dropped but slightly. A grey light is filtering through torn cloud in the eastern sky, the light firming slowly as they walk on, past the boathouse. The wreck is now clearly visible between the Rocks of Holm and the shore, with one small figure still outlined on the mast, marooned at the top, clinging for dear life. The two who had been with him have lost the battle, fallen into churning waters where they drowned.

The light is brighter now, brighter every moment. A grey dawn, comfortless. Here and there on the sand they see a cap, a bag. Some dolls, the odd book. There are bodies too, washed up with the kelp.

Catriona picks her way along the bottom of the cliff to where a crumpled form boasts not naval uniform but kilt. Calum follows. Iain looks as if he's sleeping peacefully, though the skin is very white, slightly wrinkled. Very cold. In his hands tightly clasped, a scrap of writing paper bears just four words.. *with all my love.* It is not Mairi's writing.

Calum holds Catriona's arm as she sways, eases her to the sand.

'Sit down, Mrs Murray, please. I'll go and get the naval men to help.'

Along the shore are men with stretchers ferrying the tide's forlorn cargo up to Holm Farm. They come with Calum, lift the stiff curled form on to a stretcher; Iain is slowly borne to the family croft, his blonde hair thick with sand, his lips smiling gently.

Calum follows, taking Catriona's arm. She is not weeping. His own tears spill unashamed. He does not try to hide them.

'Oh God,' says Alec. 'Oh, man..'

* * *

Five days later Calum arrives in Waverley, stepping stiffly off the train into the station's bustle. So many cars, so many people, he is dazed, confused. Inverness was bad enough, that Station Hotel palatial certainly, but so noisy.. but Edinburgh! Even coming into it, it seems a universe of brick and stone. He finds a porter, asks him where taxicabs are to be found. The porter does not seem to understand plain English. Calum tries Scots.

'Fit like? Foo d'ye fin' a taxi, man?'

The answer confuses him.

'Sorry,' says Calum. 'Come again?'

'An' I thocht ye were frae Aiberdeen,' the porter sighs. 'But ye're no!'

'I'm from Stornoway,' says Calum.

'Follow me,' says the man. 'Fit like yersel'?'

'Chavin' awa',' Calum grins, 'or so my friend would say. My friend Alec from the Bank. He's speaks the Doric.'

'A guid job fur an Aiberdonian, the bankin'. We're a' mean, just natural, like.'

Calum takes the hint, gives a generous tip when they arrive at the taxi rank.

There is only the one taxi. Calum climbs in gladly, but just as the cab is about to drive away, he shouts, 'Stop. Stop!'

'Is there a problem?' the driver asks.

'No,' says Calum. 'I've just seen a friend. How do you get this window open, a' bhalach?'

'Open the door,' sighs the man, thinking foreigners! Why do I always get them?

'John-Angus,' yells Calum, 'John-Angus, man! John-Angus MacLeod!' He stands up on the taxi's running board, waving, shouting.

John-Angus hears the voice, sprints across the station square. 'Calum! It's right good to see you!' He looks at Calum closely. 'Are you expected?'

'No,' Calum shakes his head. 'What about you? Where are you off to?'

'Back up north on the next train. I've been down at yet another board. I couldn't get leave to go back to the island.. for the funerals. How is everything?'

Calum sighs, shakes his head. Finds no words.

'It'll take time,' John-Angus says. 'A long time.'

Calum thinks of the lorries heaped with dead, the bodies laid out in the Battery, the beaches littered with toys and caps and boots. He thinks of the silent town of Stornoway, deep in grief. 'A long time,' he echoes.

The cab-driver has grown impatient. His time is valuable. 'Are we going or what?'

'I've to get my train,' John-Angus says. 'I'll have to run. I'll miss it. Come and see me on your way back through Inverness. Come and tell me how things are.'

He hesitates, then smiles. 'She loves you, Calum. She always has.'

Calum nods. 'I know.'

***

Edinburgh seems profligate, over-excited, with the castle so prominent and the crowded brown streets that go on and on, it seems to Calum, for ever. There are so many of them! So many schools and houses and shops. How can the cab-driver possibly remember them all?

'How long have you lived here?' Calum asks.

'I don't live here,' the man replies, 'I've lived in Leith all my life. Where are you from yourself?'

'Stornoway.'

'Oh,' says the man, 'That's where they've had that shipwreck, isn't it? The what d'you call her?'

'The *Iolaire*,' says Calum. 'Yes, that's where she foundered. Actually, that ship was built in Leith.'

'You're not serious? Good heavens. How awful. It's a tragedy,' the man says, shaking his head. 'What a thing to happen.' He brightens as he turns off Princes Street.

'And are you down on business? Or pleasure?'

'Both,' says Calum. 'I've come to ask the girl I love to marry me.'

'Good luck, then,' says the driver. 'Good luck to you, Stornoway.'

Calum finds the Maitlands' drive a little daunting, the house so heavy-looking, so completely city, so tidy, even at this time of year. Net curtains everywhere, making it impossible to see within. No sky either. Roofs and trees have gobbled that, eaten it completely.

What if Mairi has decided she needs to stay in the city? Would he cope? How will they manage if they go back to the island? Calum stands on Esther's front step, paralysed. When, finally, he rings the bell it's Margaret who answers, in her black maid's uniform and best white apron. She frowns at the strange young man standing on the step below, clutching a ragged carpet bag.

'Yes? I warn you, Madam doesn't buy from travelling salesman.'

Calum shrinks from her disapproval, his confidence daunted.

'I..'

'Who is it?'

He can hear a voice.. Esther's?.. behind the maid, and the reedy wail of a young baby's crying.

'Who is it, Margaret?'

It's not Esther, no. It's Mairi.

Calum takes a deep breath, starts again.

*   *   *

STORNOWAY 1939

The nearer home he gets, the slower Calum walks, as if some heavy sorrow waited there. He can hear the side gate banging, its forced irregularity a foil to the wind's insistence. The gusting wind cannot whip that gate from rusted hinges, try as it may, try as it does. Inside the thick-walled cottage, Mairi and Iain, immersed in conversation, miss the battle of the elements. But Calum, limping down the road from the shadowy lane that cuts behind the cottages, is all too aware of it.

It annoys him, that ceaseless banging. He'd meant to change the catch last spring. In summer, wind dies down, that's the trouble. He could have fixed the gate in the long bright nights but they're gone now. He'll do it one day soon; Saturday, maybe.

Reaching the house, he lingers at the shivering gate, stands uneasy, has to take several deep breaths before he walks into the yard. He shuts the gate firmly, easing the renegade catch into position, securing it. It holds. The sky is black tonight, darker than usual – and no street lights and not a house light, either, to guide him – but Calum knows his way, could walk it blindfold. He knows the uneven nature of the paving, knows where puddles gather, can avoid them. As he reaches the house, an angry gust of wind rattles the fence, shaking the gate, wrenching the weak catch open. The gate resumes its wooden litany.

Calum swears under his breath, enters the cottage, slamming the door, pulling off his jacket which he hangs on a peg in the cramped lobby. He carries his felt hat into the kitchen, throws it on the table.

Mairi and Iain are sitting in firelight, a single candle burning. Calum's conscious of their eyes on him. It's like a wake. Calum feels irritated by this; illogical anger simmering within him. He knows the whisky hasn't helped. He is a little unsteady, more than a little, actually. He should have come straight home.

But they should be more respectful. They should be glad he's home at all. Sitting in the County he'd had more than half a mind to stay there, miss the difficult business altogether. How dare Mairi glower at him like that? And Iain be so reproachful? And them sitting in the dark. Bloody morbid.

'Why don't you put the bally lights on?' Calum staggers towards the switch.

'No,' says Mairi. 'We've no proper blackout curtain here, you know that!'

Iain stands up, lifts his bag. His tone is soft, mollifying, the way you'd talk to an invalid, or a spoilt child. 'We'll need to be going, Dad. You should have left your jacket on.'

Calum doesn't know why, but his anger is subsiding. 'No, lad. This is a night for the best coat a man can offer.'

'Maybe you should have gone to the Communion after all,' snipes Mairi.

'I'd tomorrow's editorial to write.' Calum's defensive, almost whining.

'And the County Hotel to visit.'

The voice is sharp, a poisoned knife. Calum swings round, looks at Mairi. She drops her eyes. He'd be happier, a different man, if he wrote more, drank less. Not the journalism, no, his own writing.. the stories that riddled his head, his heart. But where was the money in that? He tried it long enough. You can't eat words. No, nor drink them, Mairi always retorted. For now, she held her tongue.

'You'll need to hurry, Dad,' says Iain. 'We've less than half-an-hour.'

'Aye,' says Calum. 'Aye. I know that fine.'

He stomps through the room, takes the candle Mairi holds out to him silently, and mounts the wooden stair. It's very steep, that stair, narrow. Even the treads are tiny. Calum's never found it easy, so between the drink and his limp, he has a difficult time reaching the top. Iain watches silently.

'Stop fretting, Iain. We've plenty of time.' Mairi stretches her shaking hands towards the fire that is now the only light in the room. Upstairs, Calum's charging round the bedroom. They hear

him rattling hangers, opening drawers, these unpredicted sounds somehow soothing above the fire's hiss and crackle.

'Mairi! Where's my coat?'

Mairi rubs her fingers, suddenly cold.

'Mairi! I said, where's that damned coat?'

'Behind the bedroom door,' she shouts. 'Where you left it after Lachie's funeral.'

Iain giggles. Mairi smiles, in spite of herself, stands up, scans the kitchen, blankly.

'Where's my hat, Iain?'

'You're as bad as he is. Look, you left it on the dresser.'

'Och, so I did.'

Mairi picks the hat up, stretches to see her flickering reflection in the oval mirror above the fire. Her face is anxious, set. Iain takes her arm. 'You mustn't worry, Mam. They're saying it'll be over by Christmas.'

Mairi shakes her head, tries to smile. They said that last time. She remembers all too well. 'Calum,' she calls. 'We're off. We're late already! Put the candle out when you come downstairs.'

'Mam..'

Iain nods upstairs. The last thing he wants is to leave without his father. Mairi knows it. 'Take your bag out, Iain. We'll wait at the gate. Calum!' she shouts, 'hurry up!'

She follows Iain outside, to the open gate, finds him standing, slightly daunted, one hand on each pillar, rucksack at his feet. The street is full, suddenly full, a sober, worried crowd stretching all the way to the pier, to the dark ship they have all been hoping might somehow evaporate, never sail. Mairi and Iain stare into heaving darkness. The silence is the hardest thing. Calum, joining them, trips on the rucksack, sprawls headlong through the gate. Iain catches him, steadies him.

'Take your time, Dad.'

Calum tries to make a joke of it. 'What a crowd,' he whispers. 'Doesn't this remind you of the old days.. those dances they used to have at the Town Hall, Mairi?'

'Oh?' she says. 'The ones you drank too much at?'

'Mam.'

Mairi shrugs. 'I didn't mean it, Calum, love. It's just..'

'Mam, they're starting, look.'

And there is movement right enough, the first uneasy trickle of heads and bags and shoulders up the gangway. No bands play. Even the young men, off to their life's first great adventure, feel the sadness of the moment. Their friends and families watch in silent anguish, all too conscious of other leavings, sad returnings.

For a moment, Mairi thinks she sees Iain Murray.. is that not him, leaning there against the rail, smiling..

'Mam, I'll have to go.'

'I know. I'll be thinking of you, Iain. We both will.'

She wants to fold her son in her arms, hold him close. She knows she'd never let him go, so instead she takes Calum's arm, tries to smile.

'I hope the crossing won't be too bad.'

'Mam.. I'll write first thing. Every week.'

'Iain, son..' Calum , lost for words, presses Mairi's arm tightly, grips her hand as if it were the only lifeline in violent seas. 'I'll write,' he says at length.

'I'll be off then.'

They see his fair head bobbing through the crowd. That might be Iain slipping up the gangway now, but in this lack of light it's difficult to know, to be certain. The waiting crowd – surely the whole of Stornoway – stands breathless, hushed, as the ship prepares to cast off, quiet farewells over.

The night could not be blacker. But as the Sheila slides into open sea, a single ray of moonlight splits the clouds, silvering the dark ship, the boys still fixed on home, their young taut faces. On the shore a lone voice intones the psalm 'God is our refuge and our strength'. The weeping town, the whole ship's company follow, voices rising, falling over waves as dark, as deep as life itself, as war. As love.

GAELIC GLOSSARY

balach/ a bhalach:	boy (nominative and vocative)
beag:	short, little
beannachd leat:	farewell, adieu
cailleach	old woman
ceol:	music, melody
ciamar a ha uth?:	how are you?
Di-h-aoine:	Friday
dileas:	faithful
Di-domhnaich:	Sunday
Di-sathuirne:	Saturday
eilean:	island
gle mhath:	very good
og:	young
machair:	an extensive beach, links
mor (mhor):	big
reiteach:	an espousal, celebrated by a banquet
sgoth:	boat
slainte:	good health, cheers
strùbag	a mouthful, a drink
tha mi sgith:	I'm tired
urlar:	the main tune, or ground of a piobaireachd: a floor: a layer, or vein as in a mine.

A PRIVATE VIEW

POEMS BY
IAIN ALEXANDER MURRAY

N.H. WILSON Lᵀᴰ, PUBLISHERS; GLASGOW.
MCMXIX

Iain Alexander Murray was a son of Lewis. He was full of life. I knew him all my life, but till I read his poems, I think I did not know him. I, his oldest friend, did not know he wrote.

It is not a surprise, should not have been. The Murray family have long been tradition-bearers – that Iain should had inherited a lyric voice along with his innate intelligence is natural. I was suprised. I am ashamed to say it.

These poems are full of life, of the too acute understanding of its frailty forced on all the young men who fought in the War. They are full of humour too, and love.

When Iain died on 1st January 1919, I thought we'd lost him for ever. In these poems he will live beyond us.

CALUM MORRISON

November, 1919. Stornoway.

THE CLOTH OF MORNING

I will carry in my heart
The cloth of morning;
My father's shore, my mother's
Quiet step; the stove door clanging
Water bubbling on the blackened hearth;

The cuckoo and the rising lark.

GEIS

Cuchullin left his name here:
Knife-toothed, angry-mouthed
Black peaks spit at Torridon, Kintail-

Cuchullin learned to fight-
we too must don the helmet
master the Gae Bolg, the battle fury!

FORM FOURS!

Feet are marching through my head, eight-booted-
Each stride a seven-leaguer, each footfall
Complete with pack and rifle; the sergeant's voice
A litany.

                    I wish he hadn't lit
On me!

BEGINNING

This is the beginning: journey's end
Unpredictable, our path
Prescribed, not chosen.

There is truth in this,
And freedom; limits
Fed by bayonet, rifle-butt;

There may be life—
there may be death.

FALL-OUT

There's never a good march-
Plod, plod, plod-
The rain and the wind
The straps cutting into you..
Stick to it, lad.
Easy for them
        On their horses
To offer advice!
Ten minutes an hour
We fall out, release
The belt, use the pack as a pillow;
Dreaming of home,
Of cold beer,
Of the nearest estaminet-
Short minutes,
Over too soon-
Feet bruised and bleeding
Slide back on the cobbles.
There's never a good march
And some worse than others.

THE WARNING

After pay parade we form up in a square.
Our Colonel tells us we are for the trenches.
Military Law - the strictest - will apply
To these crimes following: mutiny, desertion,
Leaving the trenches without permission,
Cowardice, sleeping while on sentry duty.
Conviction by Courts Martial will mean execution.

The adjutant reads a list of recently convicted-
Eighteen, twenty men – name, rank, unit, crime-
The date they were shot, the time.
We stand to attention, blinking
Oddly shrivelled sun.

LYING IN THE SUN

Lying in the sun in France
Is not so different:
The sun's rays are the same
The skin is just the same-
Sunburn is the same
The lack of shade
Is not so different
From working at the peat-
The sun is cruel, just the same,
On the peatbank, in the trenches.

LETTERS

i
My mother wrote today of two lambs
Half-way down a cliff: though Allan
Pulled them back, the ewe
Would not accept them. Those lambs
Rest in our byre, bottle-fed.

Pet-lambs. The sort that don't forget
Rub your legs for years, hard to eat;
Grow old and scraggy, hard to eat
Flesh withering on bone. Their wool
Easier to harvest, better spun
Than spurned on moor, or machair.

ii
Mairi's ink was full of flowers
Speedwell, primula,
Campanula, armeria-
If I had the book,
I might know what they look like.

[cont.]

iii
Calum praised the spring, so well advanced;
He'd had the toothache, written a new tune.
Cuckoos sang, and corncrakes, louder every day.
Two lambs had fallen down a cliff –

iv
My father's arthritis
Was not keeping him from fishing,
For which the Good Lord must be praised.
Amen!

THE WHEEL

I have seen my mother spin
The sands of time-
An empty wheel, the bobbin soaring
Ghostly on the parapet
Fates distilled in morning light-

I have heard my mother sing
The sky awake
Notes strumming living ears
The corn, the men
                    Both rising
In indifferent warmth, unfettered rhythm

I have heard my mother weep
Her sons cry out.

[viii]

ZIGZAG

'Anglais soldats beaucoup zigzag tous les jours!'
criticism from a French girl March 1918

Aye, Mamselle, I'm at the old zigzag
And can you blame me?
You *know* where I've been –
To hell and back!

Vin rouge helps a little;
Your beer too watered-down
To slake anything but thirst.
I can't afford Old Orkney. No,

The private view is not blessed
By the spirit of the bothan, though
That would help. Rum helps too,
At stand-to
        (If you get it.)
Ask the officers.
        They know!

You shake your head, Mamselle,
Flounce away, *Zigzag*!
Turn your nose up-
Mamselle, you should know

[ix]

[cont.]

I'd rather be in Lewis at the town-hall dance,
Flirting with the island beauties.
Understand - I *chose*
To come to France to die in mud-
My blood, your soil,
                    Collude.

Damn your *Zigzag*!

WAITING WOUNDED

Our artillery has been at work
three days; and tonight's yellow moon
Brighter, I think, than usual-

In no-man's land, the corpses are
Crawling, piecemeal, home;
A thoughtful gesture.

When our blithe bombardment ends,
Space will be necessary;
New-blossoming flesh will flit

Through shell-holes, sweep the open meadow
Like waves beating the shore,
Flotsam, decaying kelp

Four hours to go—

TO THE BLACK FIELDS

I did not come to the black fields of war
To find your green eyes shining

White breasts echoing the slender moon,
Forests spreading eagerly, now brown, now bare:

I did not seek, yet I have known you, known
The shocked embrace of dreaming love; my warring joy

Undreamt, incalculable.
                    My love
As we have sown, so shall we reap.

BACON

The smell of bacon is what damns
The suckling pig, as in Chinese legend;

Even here, with mud and death and lime,
The smell of bacon cheers

Even Fritz's bacon!

FRENCH PEASANTS

Work as hard as we do back at home:
Plough and sow, harvest
What the shells allow

Their beasts are husbanded
Like ours when cooler days
Dictate, necessitate;

(The rural life of France, of Lewis
Not so untranslatable.)
There's more soil here,
More fertile. They enjoy

More sun, more snow, less wind:
Their roughly-cobbled roads
are ill to march on;

Their pauvre as poor
Their faim as starving.
Et la morte? As dead.

A MAN FROM HOME

The stretcher-bearers picked up
What they could of him.
We put the rest in sandbags
(Bone and brain, still warm,

And bright blood flamed on revetting.)
We drenched it clean
With water, chloride of lime.
We could hear the screaming.

Sniper-shot. Finishing sentry duty
He stood on the fire-step
To let a stretcher pass. Ewan
Was tall. He'd taken off his helmet.

What was left
Took several hours to die.

ISLANDERS

Islanders – an odd word –
Is-land-ers as if
The *is*-land dreams, a drowsing beauty,
Guarding thorns of war:

If I go back.
If I escape the thorns
And know the *magic* word
Wield the magic *sword*
Will *is*-land be?
Will *is* remain?

What changes will endure?
The magic sword – will I use it
To encompass change?
Or wish for war, thorn-trained?

Will I be the same?
Will I be sane?
Tha mi sgith.

BATTLE-FURY

The battle-song is not so different:
Meeting you, I knew we'd come to grips
Hand to hand, our sweat would mingle-

If I seem too gentle, it is that we met before
Another place, another time; and out of battle
Saw each other clearly-

Your gae bolg has filled me, killed me,
Pain in every fibre, each extremity
Will soon begin - as yet I feel but battle fury

Shivering. You are my geis.
I could not have avoided you, nor would have;
You are light and spring, my death,

My love come quickly, come,
Or let me live-

BOMBARDMENT

It was like nothing I have known:
Worse than the winter waves on Holm cliffs, worse
Than the fiercest North Atlantic wind, the storm
Of shells that flew, did not abate, for three taut days.

All around us, lyddite flew. Earth sobbed, torn apart,
And men sobbed, torn apart; and heaven was black,
Metal rain shuddering the dug-out walls.
We prayed for anonymity, even those who own no Gods,

Not even Caesar. Shared the water out, tightening
Our belts. Thought about breaking into iron rations.
On the fourth day, silence intervened. We crawled
Up the steps. The parapet was gone. My periscope

Gained two holes, quickly. We sat in silence,
Wondering when the wave would come.

CHATTING

The best thing about Blighty is..
Yes? I hear you ask.
Guess, I say. You sit
Beside my bed, thoughtful.

That you're out of battle?
No. *The food?*
The food is good, but no.
You sigh, *The beer?*

French beer is terrible
All waste and water,
All the same.. *The girls then,*
Red Lamp creatures?

They're not often girls..
The quiet? Disconcerting.
I sleep better in billets,
in the trenches, than here.

[cont.]

The weather? No.
The lack of mud? No.
Seeing your family?
They've nothing to say to me

Nothing I can understand.
Give up? I'll give
You one last chance.
Clean sheets?

That's warmer, yes. True
Cleanliness. The lack of lice.
No need to *chat*,
Squash and kill them..

Itchy beggars.
I've lost blood to them
Time out of time. Now I
Kill first, talk later.

SUCH A SIMPLE THING

And love, like fighting, a matter of the moment;
The past irrelevant; the future unforeseen,
Irrelevant; the moment overwhelming-

And yes, you *will* lie with me
Soft against my wounds, a living bandage:
Ease my pain, your breast

My moon, my living light, the moment
Unforeseen, irrelevant; your living heart
Sensibly astray-

Matter of the moment;
Simple flesh-

THE FERRY

Leaving the island, I am more completed
Less complete. My past lies there and there,
My future on the lilting wave, as yet
Unfurled, a bright coin in my teeth
                              Held lightly.
How to endure increasing distances
A question of delight; endure
The seconds, minutes, hours;
                              Sparse infinity
Levering the safe, known shores
The glare of love, of touch

I pay the ferryman, drift east

AN ODD THING

An odd thing, after
Such cold, such hunger:

Sky seemed to hang and fall
The air hummed loud, furious bees

Grew frantic, blinding red,
Shock waves singing in the bones, the blood

[cont.]

The balance gone, all gone;
One sharp thump between the shoulder blades-

An odd thing pain, after
Such cold, such hunger-

DAFFODILS

There were no daffodils on the island
But Edinburgh, profligate
Dances, prays for Spring:
The grass outside my window
Rotten with yellow trumpets
Strange, stiff flowers
That bend and break
The gallows wind

So many graves with daffodils
Blowing over them, or cut,
Tossed on first-year soil;
So many graves
And not a human flower from one
Not even poppies.

THE ARTIST

Was a quiet man: I didn't mind,
Sat peaceful in the trench as he photographed and drew
Whatever angle seemed appropriate;

Actually I thought of you
Digging this trench clean the night the shrapnel flew
Deafening us all. The sun shone

On the artist's pencil. Where he sat
Was where young John MacPhie
Disappeared; poor John-

I had a drink or two that night.
Never saw the photographs. The sketches
Looked O.K. but not like me.

DULCE AT DECORUM

I would show more decorum
If you weren't so sweet-

See? I learned Latin too-

THE DARK SHIP

Sometimes
Even in the trenches
They'll take out a harmonica
Someone will –
    And the tune they'll play,
            The tune I hear,
Is always the same-
      That *Dark Ship*

Not the sgoth of boyhood
    Not the oar-fed twenty-footer
        Skimming the Shiants,
    Robbing the herring nets
Not the sgoth of summer,
But the low black steamship gorged
With fighting men
    Tired of battle.

        Oh, we sailed at first
With hope of glory, floated pale
Becalmed in blood, deserted by our fear,
(Our automatic bravery
    Enforced by rifle-shot
        By gunwheel)

[cont.]

Over the parapet
We taunted death. It came-
Or did not come- in waves of steel,
In pain as red as breath,
Red as rueful Sabbath cheeks;

And death called those it sought,
The Dark Ship ferrying our youth
To different music-

A song as sweet as cherry blossom
And as unexpected

CHILDREN

If I sit here long enough, that child
Will turn and smile at me,
Hiding in her mother's skirts.

She looks half-starved;
They wear black bands; no shoes
No overcoat, the bulky shawl

[cont.]

Wound three times round. No wonder
The child can hardly move
Feet blue with cold!

No child of mine
deserves a shell-torn house.
No child deserves

The scar on that girl's cheek,
Shrapnel; the mother said
It killed her son-

The girl will never marry now.
I stretch my hand to livid skin.
It will improve-

The child evades my touch
Turns away.
How many children?

AFTER THE SHOW

They talk about the things they'll do
After the show, back in Blighty.
What about you, Iain?
I'll drink, I think.

They laugh and chafe me.
No, really. What will you do?
University? You're a clever bugger!
Well.. I think I'll drink.

But they're right, of course. I can't go back
To old days, old ways.
I'll have to find a stout line
To lever me from the mud. A source
Of pride. An open door, a place
to sit and breathe and sing—
and drink, I think.

SLEEP THOUGHTS FROM ABROAD

Don't laugh! But-
When I lay me down to sleep,
Forty angels watch do keep,
All of them snoring heavily!

It's not like Fettes Row
Crystal candle-holders blessing us
With winged light- this hammocked barn
Couldn't be less illuminating;

Your lace and linen are not represented here.
White breasts live but in memory,
And spilling hair does not
Cascade across my willing face.

I lie, stave off sleep,
Dreaming of them.

CHICKENS

The oddest dreams are those
you cannot quite discount.
Last night I dreamed of chickens,
Brown chickens in a warm barn,
Pecking each other fiercely:
The farmer's answer?
To take his knife
Shave off their beaks, every one!
So much blood.. so many chickens
Tongueless.

I find it hard to drink, to eat today.

BLACK NIGHT

The black nights are the ones
That follow days without your face–
Days I cannot make my mind
Retrace your features,
Or my fingers search your likeness;

You are the one star in this lack
Of firmament.

ISLAND

I am sailing in the cold
Dark morning of the year
To you, my island.

There can be no other
Destination, no hope for me
Beyond this storm-bound shore

This peat-dark moor. The flood
Shall be my fire, this rock my shelter
From the ocean's wandering.

AFTERWORD

Those of us who fought in the recent conflict will have no trouble seeing ourselves in the poems of Iain Alexander Murray; indeed the picture may be too close, too acute for comfort. It may not be possible to read certain of these short poems without reliving terrible events we can never leave behind.

We can laugh at some; *yes, I was there, I was that drunk soldier! I was that boy with the sore feet too!* We all knew the stringencies of military discipline in the trenches, on the parade ground, but did not complain. There was nothing to be gained by that. What we did instead was turn discomfort into laughter whenever and wherever possible.

There has been a movement towards the real in recently published war poetry; Siegfried Sassoon's volumes *The Old Huntsman* and *Counter-attack* were not well received, *1914 and Other Poems*, Rupert Brooke's posthumous collection, being often preferred. But those of us who were there know what it was like, and know, too, the difficulty of communicating even the smallest part of that experience. Unlike Alan Breck in the roundhouse of the *Covenant*, we did not immediately translate our efforts into verse, into glorifying song. The trenches did not lend themselves to the tradition of praise poetry.

Still, the sense of place (however difficult) of community (however stressed) was strong; and for those of us from the island, the *particular* island, it was perhaps even stronger. Iain's poems, poems we did not know he was writing even as he wrote them, describe both accurately: elevate the mud and toil. Even the fear. We were there. We endured. Some of us survived. Relatively unscathed, but not unmarked.

The world has moved on. We are no longer embroiled in what at one time seemed like endless war. The matter of the moment is regeneration, rebuilding of families, and of nations. Had Iain lived, his sheer exuberance, the energy that made him such a brave and effective soldier – for he spent the last three years of his life on active service at the Western Front – would have taken him into the forefront of any profession he chose. His growing wisdom, his great compassion, the maturity emerging in these poems (written, as far as we know, in the given sequence) render his loss all the more tangible. Our island lost many men in the Great War. Iain, in speaking for himself, gives all a voice.

J.A.M.

Stornoway, November, 1919.

Between 28th September and 25th October 1918, the 7th Seaforth, as part of the 9th Division, took part in the series of attacks that carried the line twenty miles from Frezenberge Ridge outside Ypres to Harlebecke. The final operation was carried out at a cost of 331 casualties. Corporal Iain Alexander Murray was one of these. Instead of finishing the war in the army of occupation, Iain crossed the Channel in a hospital ship, his arm and thigh wounds responding eventually to the excellent care he received in Reading No 4 War Hospital, where he celebrated the Armistice. From there he entrained to the Depot at Fort George, near Inverness. He obtained his discharge papers in December and was travelling home to Lewis when he was lost at sea on 1st January 1919.

The Dark Ship
Anne MacLeod
This vast literary saga celebrates love, music and poetry in a finely woven story that reflects the complex past of a community on a Scottish island.
1-903238-27-7
£9.99

Dead Letter House
Drew Campbell
Suspend your disbelief for a bizarre trip into the surreal. On a twenty mile walk home a young man explores time and space and discovers his own heaven and hell.
1-903238-29-3
£7.99

The Gravy Star
Hamish MacDonald
One man's hike from post-industrial urban sprawl to lost love and a burnt-out rural idyll.
'A moving and often funny portrait ... of the profound relationship between Glasgow and the wild land to its north.' James Robertson, author of *The Fanatic*.
1-903238-26-9
£9.99

Strange Faith
Graeme Williamson
This haunting novel tells the story of a young man torn between past allegiances and the promise of a new life.
'Calmly compelling, strangely engaging.' Dilys Rose
1-903238-28-5
£9.99

About 11:9

Supported by the Scottish Arts Council National Lottery Fund and partnership funding, 11:9 publish the work of writers both unknown and established, living and working in Scotland or from a Scottish background.

11:9's brief is to publish contemporary literary novels, and is actively searching for new talent. If you wish to submit work send an introductory letter, a brief synopsis of your novel, a biographical note about yourself and two typed sample chapters to: Editorial Administrator, 11:9, Neil Wilson Publishing Ltd, Suite 303a, The Pentagon Centre, 36 Washington Street, Glasgow, G3 8AZ. Details are also available from our website at **www.11-9.co.uk.**

If you would like to be added to a mailing list about future publications, either register on our website or send your name and address to 11:9, Neil Wilson Publishing Ltd, Suite 303a, The Pentagon Centre, 36 Washington Street, Glasgow, G3 8AZ.

11:9 refers to 11 September 1997 when the Scottish people voted to re-establish their parliament in Edinburgh.

'They [the first six 11:9 titles] are my unreserved recommendation for this or any other year.'
Carl MacDougall, *The Herald*

Hi Bonnybrig 1-903238-16-1
Shug Hanlan
'Imagine Kurt Vonnegut after one too many vodka and Irn Brus and you're halfway there.'
Sunday Herald

Rousseau Moon 1-903238-15-3
David Cameron
'The most interesting and promising debut for many years. [The prose has] a quality of verbal alchemy by which it transmutes the base matter of common experience into something like gold.'
Robert Nye, *The Scotsman*

The Tin Man 1-903238-11-0
Martin Shannon
'Funny and heartfelt, Shannon's is an uncommonly authentic voice that suggests an engaging new talent.'
The Guardian and *Guardian Unlimited*

Life Drawing 1-903238-13-7
Linda Cracknell
'*Life Drawing* brilliantly illuminates the contradictions of its narrator's self image ... Linda Cracknell brings female experience hauntingly to life.'
The Scotsman

Occasional Demons 1-903238-12-9
Raymond Soltysek
'a bruising collection ... Potent, seductive, darkly amusing tales that leave you exhausted by their very intensity.'
Sunday Herald

The Wolfclaw Chronicles 1-903238-10-2
Tom Bryan
'Tom Bryan's pedigree as a poet and all round littérateur shines through in *The Wolfclaw Chronicles* – while reading this his first novel you constantly sense a steady hand on the tiller ... a playful and empassioned novel.'
The Scotsman

Already available from bookshops and the 11:9 website: www.11:9.co.uk